CIRCLES

A Novel by
Ruby Standing Deer

SECOND EDITION SOFTCOVER
ISBN: 1622539567
ISBN-13: 978-1-62253-956-7

Edited by Lane Diamond

Printed in the U.S.A.

www.EvolvedPub.com
Evolved Publishing LLC
Cartersville, Georgia

Printed in Book Antiqua font.

DEDICATION:

For my loving and understanding husband,
who let me write while he did everything else.

Introduction

Because this book is steeped in the American Indian culture, and because many readers will need a little help with the names, allow me a moment to introduce you to some of the main characters (you can also use this as a reference, in case you need to look back).

The significance of the characters' names will be evident in the story. As you will see, Native Americans choose names based on a kind of relevancy, on what is happening at that special moment when a child enters the world. Names may also change when something new and relevant happens. Even a name can have magic.

I've used many words that would have been unknown in the mid- to late-1500's. I had to use them to clarify some things. Words such as cousin, aunt and uncle, grandmother and grandfather, it, thing, winter and years (I used "moons" to reference aging so it would be easier to understand) did not exist in the language of those Peoples. However, to keep things simple, I used words today's readers would better understand. I've tried my best to be careful with word choices, so as not to offend anyone.

Sometimes I capitalize animal names, and sometimes I do not. When I capitalize them, their name stands alone in reverence, out of respect. Other times, I use them much like any word, in a more generic sense, and I do not capitalize them. You will see some words always capitalized; this is because they are Sacred. All life is Sacred, of course, but some things are very special. These methods are in keeping with the American Indian traditions.

Horses had several names: big dogs, elk dogs and more. The first true mustangs looked very different than today's. They had few colors, boxy faces and stripes on their legs. A small herd still lives in a protected valley in a western state. I added the word mus-tang myself later in the book.

My own bloodlines are mixed, but my heart and Soul belong to the First Peoples of Turtle Island (North America).

***

Feather Floating In Water – Feather is my main character, a gifted young boy who, as a Dreamer, must face his adult responsibilities early in life. He is the son of Makes Baskets, and grandson of Hawk Soaring and Bright Sun Flower. Although he is only eight years old at the outset, he would be on a par with a thirteen-year-old today. Indeed, 500 years ago, "children" of thirteen to fourteen often had a child of their own. Different times.

Bright Sun Flower – She is Feather's grandmother, a woman with great spiritual insights. She is Makes Baskets' mother, and Hawk Soaring's companion.

Hawk Soaring – He is grandfather to Feather Floating In Water, and companion to Bright Sun Flower.

Chases Butterflies – She is Feather's cousin, a young girl who becomes more to her cousin than even she thought possible.

Running River – She is Makes Baskets' cousin, and mother to Chases Butterflies.

Sees Like Eagle –He is Running River's companion.

Bear Tracks – He is the Holy Man of the Band of Fish Peoples, and future companion of Makes Baskets and father to Feather Floating In Water.

Blue Night Sky – She is a Holy Woman whose Power helps guide Feather Floating In Water, making his destiny possible.

Morning Star –She is the second companion to Sees Like Eagle, granddaughter of Blue Night Sky, and mother of Rising Moon.

Rising Moon – She is the daughter of Morning Star, with a special future link to Feather Floating In Water.

White Paws – He is a Sacred Wolf, who comes to guide Feather Floating In Water.

Moon Face – She is the mate of White Paws.

Chapter 1

The beginning of change....

Feather Floating In Water woke shivering in the warm lodge. Dreams like this haunted him more as he became older, but this one—so real—made him jump up from the sleeping robe he shared with his grandmother. Screams and shouts of people running from burnt lodges still tortured his mind. Their confused expressions! And the fires, so real, had warmed his face.

How is it that dream flames can burn my face?

He sat up in the dim light and peered toward the top of the lodge, where Father Sun peeked through the flap that allowed smoke to escape. *Sunrise. I am home and I am safe.*

Bright Sun Flower stirred beside him. She must have heard him, probably felt his every movement. "Grandmother," he whispered, "I hear mother and grandfather sleeping. I need a walk, by myself. I will not go far, just to my favorite ridge."

"What troubles you, little one?" She too whispered, as she broke small sticks and tossed them into the low burning embers of the lodge's fire pit.

Flames from the freshly fueled fire brightened the lodge. Bright Sun Flower reached for her thick robe, dense with the hair of the humpbacked animal that thundered across the lands. She wrapped it around the dress she had managed to slip on before the lodge's fire came to life.

"I... I need to be alone."

"You are but eight winters old. Let me go with you, so your mother will not worry when she wakes."

Most nights, after his grandfather had rolled over to sleep, Feather made his way from his mother's robes to his grandmother's. His mother's rhythmic, soft snores never changed. She seldom stirred, sleeping the peaceful nights of one not plagued by dreams.

Like him, his grandmother had dream visions, maybe the same ones. After one such bad dream, Bright Sun Flower had taken him out to wander the canyons to help him clear his mind. She had told him her dreams showed that he had a destiny, an important one. They had talked and walked until he relaxed enough to laugh and dance around her again.

She had also told him she once held great Power, but gave it up to have a family. Now that her moon times were no more, her Power had returned. Feather, like all of the children, was part of everything that went on in the band. No one kept secrets from the next generation, and he understood moon times... as much as any male could.

What did all this mean — this destiny? Feather leaned up on his knees and watched her add a few more sticks to the hungry fire. Sweat beaded on his forehead and he caught her staring his way when he wiped it with the back of his hand. He wrapped his own robe around himself and crawled past his mother toward the lodge's flap.

"Too young for so many worry lines, Grandson. We should go talk about what bothers you."

Feather Floating In Water knew his grandmother wanted to help, but first he needed to understand what *he* needed help with. "Not now, please? I need to think."

Too much confusion muddled his mind to want to speak about it. She watched, and he knew she would soon follow no matter his protests.

Nine lodges held the twenty-two members of the Fish People, most now sleeping. Only their sister bands knew of their secluded location nestled amidst the red-orange boulders of the canyon. The large river north of the camp provided abundant fish, and two days' walk away, the plains rumbled with the big humped beasts during this time of budding leaves. The People enjoyed peace and plenty.

The troublesome dream played out again in his mind while he walked the winding path, to the high perch where he could watch Father Sun greet the land. He sat on the ledge watching the soft oranges and yellows slide across the valley below.

Home. I am home. He wrapped his robe tighter. *Was this dream a... vision?*

He remembered the elder woman from his vision, with long, loose hair flying behind her. She had motioned to several others to follow her into the dense shrubs. They hid themselves within the branches and huddled together. A baby cried, sparking shouts in the strange guttural tongue of those they fled. The People jumped up and ran. The mother tried in desperation to silence her baby, and ran another direction, away from the small group. The elder woman yelled at her to come back, but she ran anyway. The elder grabbed a younger woman, who clung to a girl, and ran into the thick grass while the other woman's scream drew the attackers toward her, and away from the rest of her people.

Her sacrifice saved her people, but what happened to her? These strange creatures must be bad Spirits. They looked like two creatures, but acted as one. Only bad Spirits could be this horrible. Why do they come into my dreams?

Above him, Eagle called, and another came to fly beside the first. They dove into the valley and faded into the canyon's deep purple shadows. Feather smiled and inhaled the cool morning air. The red-orange land burst into life, as dark dots across the valley turned deep green, and the air filled with birdcalls.

The dream faded, as they always did, leaving him to wonder if his mind had again, as his mother often claimed, made things up.

Father Sun warmed his body and he tossed the robe. Comfortable in just his breechclout, he raised his arms to pray.

"Great One, Creator of all, I thank you for this day and for everything I will learn. I am grateful for all you have given me and my people." He lowered his head, but only a moment passed before he raised it again. "Creator, I am scared. Forgive my weakness, but I am only a boy. What are these dreams that come to me? What can I do? Do I have Power, or does my mind make up things as Mother says?"

He dropped his arms at the sound of footfalls approaching from behind — shuffling with a slight limp.

Bright Sun Flower stopped at the top and breathed hard. "I see you tossed your robe. We elder ones do not warm so fast."

Feather smiled and ran past her, down the path to the bottom of the canyon. He splashed in the newly formed stream made by the nearby river, which sent its overflow down the dry washes. He dove down and pretended to catch a fish in his make-believe talons, and fell on his backside in the water. Unhurt by the fall on the rocky pebbles, he jumped up and stomped his way down the stream, back to his grandmother. She quickened her pace to catch up to his open arms.

"You caught me, Grandmother. I was flying so high, I thought maybe you would not be able to reach me! You are taller than I thought."

"You silly one! You are like a bear cub who races without thought to where he is going." Her laughter echoed down the winding canyon.

She put him down and reached for his hand. They walked beside each other, enjoying the fresh scent brought on by the early season rain that had danced a gentle patter on their lodge all night.

"Grandmother, why are there so many smells, and why does the rain make them smell better? I bet it is because the rain has special medicine."

She smiled and rubbed his wet hair. "Yes, every being has special medicine. Even you have special medicine."

"Why can I taste the plants in the air after a rain? Why do birds only make nests after the snow comes no more? What about the cold season? They need a home then too, right?"

"The birds make nests to raise their young in, where they are safe. When they teach them to fly, they no longer need the nest —"

Feather raced down to the stream again, arms spread wide. He sped back his grandmother's direction, but twisted his body and dashed past her.

"Little one, come back to me," she called out. "I have something important to show you. I have much to teach you this day, things that you will remember the rest of your life. Things you will pass onto your children someday." She sat on a boulder next to the canyon wall.

He reluctantly turned from his playing and ran to her.

"Walking is not your way, is it?"

He dove onto her lap in response.

"Ugh, little one, not so hard. I am made of flesh, not stone." She pointed to a small group of plants growing out of a crack in the jagged wall next to them. Tiny white flowers forced their way from the buds that imprisoned them, ready to burst forth. "See how the buds try to bloom? New buds struggle to be born so they can become the flowers they were meant to be."

Feather held up his left hand to shield his eyes from Father Sun's intensity, and held a flower bud in his other. He offered it to her and grinned. "This is for you. Soon it will bloom like the smiles on your face." He smiled as she accepted the flower. "Tell me the story about my name."

She stretched her knees under his weight. He tried to stand, but she pulled him back onto her lap and brushed his damp, shoulder-length hair out of his eyes.

"I know your knees hurt. You are old now and I must learn to be careful that I do not break you." He tightened his lips and stared once more into her eyes.

"Little one, I am not so old that you will break me." She chuckled and went on with the story. "Your name came from your grandfather's father. He gave you his name long before you were born. He said you would carry on with the journey he could not."

"And then what? Tell me about the bird." He squirmed on her lap.

He had listened to the story of Hawk Soaring's father too many times to count, but still he begged to hear it whenever he could.

She held him in place with her eyes. "Your grandfathers' father looked up as a big blue-grey bird flew across the river and dropped a wing feather in the water's current. He understood right away that he must lead the people to a safer place.

"He heard the call of his Spirit Guide, and went on a Vision Quest to pray for answers. On the fifth morning, he returned to camp and told us to prepare for a long journey along the little river we children played in. We would go toward the place Father Sun sleeps."

She leaned in closer and whispered. "Visions are not normally spoken of, but he felt the need to tell us. His Spirit Guide warned him that our people faced a danger, and that we would suffer if we did not move and follow the river.

"For many days, we walked. Days turned into moons, and the late season of falling leaves came upon us. We had to stop."

Feather sat tall, shoulders back. "He led us to this land, right? The big waters where we never hunger? So we named ourselves the Fish People."

She pulled him closer and hugged him. "The cold was long and hard, and he knew he would not be able to lead us when the snow melted." She paused and sighed. "He told your grandfather of a boy that would be born to our daughter, and that, in time, this boy would know what to do. He asked us to give the child his name."

He pulled his shoulders back further, took a deep breath to push out his chest, and tugged at the fringe on her sleeve. "I am that boy, right? But how will I know what to do? I will know, right?"

"Do not worry, little one, the Spirits will guide you. Besides, it is many seasons away."

Worry etched crisscrossing lines on her face, and he caressed her cheek as she had touched his so many times.

"It is okay, I will make you proud." He wrapped his arms around her, hugged her tight, and then pulled back to gaze into her eyes. "How do we know things? Like dreams? Why do I sometimes have dreams that make me think I am awake?"

"Dreams are often that way, carrying messages we must try to understand. Sometimes we should tell someone we know about them." She reached for his chin and held it in her hand so he had to look into her eyes. "Someone like a caring grandmother, maybe?"

Feather continued talking even with her holding his chin. "How do we know when to wake and when to sing blessing songs? Grandfather says Creator gave animals life first, and they taught us to survive. He told me we are all related. What does this mean?"

"Feather, do not speak so many words at once. Speak slow so your mind will not get confused. Do you want to talk about your dreams? I will tell you mine."

He bowed his head and would not look into her eyes.

With a heavy sigh, she put a hand on either side of his face and stared into his eyes. "I will answer your most important question now. All things are joined, meaning one cannot exist without the other. Everything that exists is part of everything else, making it a single thing. It all connects in some way to us, to the canyon, to the sky, the stars, the animals, even things we cannot see. It is only possible to understand something if we understand how it is connected to everything else."

She placed soil in his hand and put a seed, which had fallen from a nearby plant, on top. "The seed needs the soil, which needs the rain that comes from the sky. The animals eat the plant and leave the remains on the ground, and it goes back into our Mother, her body. It is a Sacred Circle. Everything needs something else in order to live. We need the animals, and they need food, but what makes plants grow?"

"Water, like the word in my name! I understand. Everything needs something else."

He jumped up and ran over to the water, and stooped down to wave his hands through it.

Before long, he stood with arms spread wide and splashed down the stream again, laughing and racing out of sight around a curve.

***

Bright Sun Flower leaned and stretched her tight back against the canyon wall.

Red and yellow quillwork zigzagged around the edge of her dress. She caressed the colorful artwork with withered hands, wondering how her daughter, Makes Baskets, had created such picturesque detail. Her daughter's ability to weave the bright colors so well, using Porcupine's quills, impressed her—the quills' sharp tips could stab fingers, if not dampened first to soften them.

A yellow- and green-quilled turtle climbed her right hip. She followed his path with her fingers. His colors shone vibrantly, as those of the turtle in her dream had many winters before. That new hatchling had turned away from the big salty water, rather than enter it, until she gently guided him back.

She had also had a vision that Feather Floating In Water would be born backwards. She had spent much time away from everyone, to pray for his safe arrival. Four days later, he had been born the right way, and with the birthmark of a yellow and green turtle on his back. The dream had shown her that Feather would need guidance, or he might turn away from his destiny.

She searched for the familiar pair of Eagles who always followed her, but instead heard the cry of Wolf. Though it echoed far away, it still made her shudder. *Wolves have started to howl in my dreams. They are protectors, but who needs protection? Feather? So soon?*

She needed to allow her mind to focus on other things. She admired the beauty of the canyon's red, orange and off-white colors—the way they swirled and mixed, forming designs on the canyon walls. The smell of the damp soil and the freshness of the damp plants comforted her.

This is our home. Many seasons will pass before anything happens.

She looked away, but a tug on her silver-shot braid turned her mind back to Feather, who stood grinning in front of her.

He said, "Are you going to finish your story?"

"I would like to, yes. Sit on my lap, little one."

"Grandmother, your smile is as warm as Father Sun."

Bright Sun Flower hugged him to her breast. "Ready to listen?"

Feather nodded and leaned back when she let go of him.

She pointed to the flower missing a bud. "This is an important story, one you will carry in your heart all of your life. Look again at the flowers and describe their shape."

Feather knelt onto his bare knees to get a better look. "As you said before, round. Even the plant's leaves are growing in a circle on the ground where the plant came out." He looked closer still. "Even the tiny yellow centers inside the flowers are all round!"

He jumped up and gazed at his grandmother's face. "Your face is round too, and your eyes are round." He touched his eyes. "Are mine round too?"

He reached out and touched her face before she could answer him. "Your face has lines of secrets and wisdom. Grandfather told me that is why he has them. I asked him why I did not have any, and he just patted me on the shoulder and told me that someday I would have them too. He says you have many more lines than he does. Does that mean you are wiser?"

Well, you old— "Why yes, that is exactly why I am wiser than your grandfather. He knows he will never have as much wisdom as me." She shook her head. "Poor man."

I will stretch out your wrinkles, old man!

She smiled at her grandson while planning ways to get back at her man, Hawk Soaring. Before Feather could ask what she was thinking, she stood up.

Her knees crackled as she leaned forward. "Let us take a walk and see what else we can find that is round."

Bright Sun Flower smiled at the little boy who stood taller, proud of his discoveries. As they wandered the canyon, he pointed out many more plants, round tree trunks and stones, and a spider's web glistening under Father Sun's angled light.

"Look, Grandmother, it has the colors of the rainbow, and it is round. Spider could have made her web any shape, but she chose to make it round." He looked up. "And Father Sun is round too. I want to see more!"

"Little one, some Peoples call Sky, Father Sky and Sun—" *Falls on empty ears....*

Farther down the canyon trail, the boy's energy finally wore on her. An oval-shaped boulder nestled into the canyon wall provided a place for her to sit and rest. She used her hands to stretch her tired back, praised him and held his little body close to hers. She enjoyed the fragrant scents of all the wild plants he had been kneeling in that morning.

"So, what did you learn today?" She held him at arm's length and looked into his expressive eyes.

He scratched his head and squinted in thought. "Well, I learned everything is round in its own way, even our own bodies. Father Sun is round, so our Mother we walk upon must also be round. This roundness connects us, like the dirt and seeds and rain and the animals. All are parts of the Circle."

He tilted his head and grinned at her. "I also learned you are much wiser than Grandfather."

He had learned about connectedness, an important lesson for one so young.

How did Feather understand our Mother is round? I was much older when I understood. Much older.

"You, my little one, are my Shining Light."

Eagles above called to each other, and in their sound, she heard the future. She thought of her vision—a future she did not understand.

Strange people cast dark shadows and overwhelm the land. Animals flee with nowhere to run. The people take and take more, until they crack the Circle of Life. The Mother's body turns grey and plants crisp from lack of water.

She had seen all life end, and wondered if the Circle could survive and put itself back together. No sense telling others her vision—not yet anyway. They would just think her addled.

The Mother was forever. Yet even Bright Sun Flower saw the landscape change when boulders became loose after a hard rain. Nothing stayed the same. Nothing.

She looked at her hair, once black as a moonless night, now silvered as the starlit sky. *Everything changes.*

Chapter 2

The small group of women sat near the edge of camp, under a stand of leafed-out trees, preparing the pemmican for the fast approaching cold season. Soon ice would hide fish from them, and snow would make it difficult to hunt. The pemmican would keep the people fed.

Tiny flying bugs tormented Bright Sun Flower's face and whined past her ears. She brushed away several loose strands of hair, and the mixture of meat and fat, mixed with small amounts of berries, clung to her hands and now in her hair. This attracted even more of the flying creatures.

Argh, I cannot stand this! Where has the warm season gone? It was only a few sunrises ago in my mind that Feather and I walked the canyons and looked at new life. Now we must prepare for the cold. She sighed. *Age does make seasons race past and leave me to wonder where they go.*

Feather raised his arms and soared around them, screeching with talons ready to strike as an imaginary hawk determined to catch prey.

After a third bug found its way up her nose, Bright Sun Flower snorted her irritation, but grinned at her grandson. "Feather, you need a walk, one that will slow you down. Come with me. I need to wash up. Then we will go."

She headed toward the river and let her grandson catch up. She bent down, splashed cool water on her face, leaned back and enjoyed the sensation of cool drops running down the inside of her dress. A familiar chuckle came from behind her, as Hawk Soaring cleared his throat. He opened his mouth to spew his clever words, but—

"Go away from me, old man!" She shooed him without looking back. "Go tell more stories of how you saved us from winter starvation when we were young and all the hunters were sick. This left only you, a mere boy, to feed the entire band of twenty-six people by risking your life in the freezing water, chasing fish with your bare hands."

She paused to inhale and thought of Feather. *We are much alike, that boy and I.*

Her man winced at the growl in her normally sweet voice, and scurried toward another path, a different part of camp.

No ornery man would ever get the best of her. She grinned, stood, and smacked right into her snickering grandson.

Feather put his hands on his hips, as if trying to look bigger. "You scared off Grandfather! I sure hope my woman will not scare me so much that I turn and go another way."

He faced her, squinting and squeezing his lips tight, but he could not contain his giggling. Both grandmother and grandson broke into laughter, and quickened their pace toward the canyon. They looked back only briefly at the five women, who still mixed pemmican while they swatted the small, winged annoyances.

She wanted to climb high, where the breeze would cool them. "I have my own favorite place I like to go and look out over the valley. Would you like to see it?"

"Hurry, I want to see this place! Why have you not told me of it before? Does anyone else know of it?" Feather pulled her hand and trotted backwards.

"You are the one leading us, so you tell me."

"Oh, I cannot take us somewhere when I do not know where it is. Show me. Please show me!" He let go of her hand. "Why are you laughing? Are you laughing at me?"

"We walked past it and must now turn around. May I lead?"

"I thought you were in a hurry to leave too. I helped you go faster."

"Yes, you did, but we went too fast!"

The narrow path led upward along a winding trail that echoed with the memory of footprints, both human and creature. Many had come before the pair, and many more would wander these same trails far into the future.

Bright Sun Flower's body chilled as an ominous sound touched her mind... and vanished. *It must have been the howl of Sister Wind as she found her way through the canyon.*

Eagle's call high overhead calmed her. Eagle would warn her, as she always had, if danger lurked nearby.

She reached for small indentations in the stone wall as they climbed the narrow path. "Look at the carved handholds. Feel how smooth they are. They are as echoes of the past carved in stone, whispering secrets of those who put them here."

He ran his hand inside the carved-out holes. "Why are they so smooth? I can see where someone used something to paint a carving above this one." He squinted to see the details. "What kind of animal is this? It is round and has two tails, one in the front and the back."

She too had pondered this strange creature many times. "I have no idea."

She reached out and felt the smooth, cool, reddish stone. "Many hands touched them long before us, and their hands made them smooth. They offer us a hint of what the Peoples saw in their time. They chose to honor these creatures here, as they too made their way up this very path. Now, even though the Peoples who carved these are long gone, we know they lived and had families. Maybe they lived right where we do now."

She ran her hand over her grandson's shoulder-length hair, and bent down to look into his eyes. "Never take humans or other beings for granted. I need your grandfather, and he needs me just as much. Being alone would be a terrible thing."

Inside, she scolded herself, not Feather. The words were for her—for having growled at her man beside the waters. She would make much time for him this night.

At the top of the path, she sat on a flat, shady spot where the cool air caressed her. She leaned back against a boulder, stretched her legs, and smiled as Feather played a game of "Diving Eagle."

Her grandson's imagination took him toward the ledge, where he spread his arms and pretended to float out on the currents.

"Do not get too close to the edge, little one."

The warm day cast the horizon in a shimmering, hypnotic wave. She focused on the distant red hills, tinted purple where they melted into the turquoise sky. Late mid-season colors dominated the land, with dots of green here and there in the light red soil. Far below them, the azure river wound along the canyons and faded beyond sight.

Trees followed the river's course, forever chasing the water they needed to survive. Three deer grazed lazily along the bank, while two others rested in the shade of Cedar trees. Occasional clouds floated by and hid Father Sun's face, offering temporary relief from the heat.

She whispered to herself, "Beautiful. So peaceful and calm."

Her aunt had told her that her own mother came up here to speak to the Spirits, to ask questions she would not share with others. Her mother, when she tried to rescue four-winters-old Bright Sun Flower from a fast-moving current, had drowned in the early season run-off. Now an elder woman, Bright Sun Flower had her own questions, perhaps the very same ones her mother had asked.

Yet the answers did not always come.

She thought back to the day of her first vision in this place. *Was I eleven winters old? It is nearly always the same—an invasion of strange beings, animals running in terror before them as the land dies.*

She shook it from her mind and reminded herself that today was not that day. This day belonged to her and Feather.

She stood up to adjust her dress, worried that the rough stone would harm her quillwork—too much labor and too many sore fingers had gone into working the hollow, sharp-pointed quills into the smoked leather. A deep breath brought fresh, cool air into her lungs, which made the long walk to the top worth the pain in her knees.

Feather still played with his arms spread in pretend flight, calling out as Eagle would. All children his age played, content to be in their own world, but Feather, as usual, poured forth a flood of questions.

"Why do flowers not bloom in the cold season? Why are there hills and valleys?" He stopped long enough to hand her a stone. "What makes some stones different in color from others?"

Off with arms raised, he again danced along the canyon's ledge before she could answer.

She raised her voice. "I wonder about some of these things myself, and must be honest—I do not have all the answers. I know plants need warmth to grow. Like us, plants do not like standing out in the cold."

"It is all right." He ran to her and wrapped his arms around her middle. "Only Creator knows all the answers."

Surprised by his answer, she squeezed him back until he gasped for air. *I am happy his mother came back to live with us.*

Hawk Soaring and Bright Sun Flower had welcomed Makes Baskets back into their lodge six winters ago, after the boy's father lost his life fighting in a battle. Strangers had come in search of easy food, and the attacking band had lost many lives, but the band of Fish People had lost some too.

Makes Baskets had refused another man even after her grieving time had ended. Many had offered, but her heart could not bear another loss. The baby boy brought enough joy into her life. Bright Sun Flower took care of the little one while his mother did extra work for the four of them. Her daughter worked hides, fished, and made her exquisite baskets and quilled clothing for trade. The child filled the old lodge with laughter and gave his grandparents much joy.

Bright Sun Flower sighed, happy with her memories. She turned to see her grandson inspecting a big black bug on the ground. He pushed at it and giggled. When he shoved it toward the end of the cliff, she rushed forward to stop him.

Feather jerked back in surprise. "Why, Grandmother? This is just a bug."

She stood over him with hands on hips, her voice stern. "Why, then, were you going to push him over the side?"

He looked down at the bug, crinkled his nose, and looked back up at her. "I wanted to see if he could fly like Eagle. Did I do something wrong?" He stared at the ground, not looking up at his grandmother.

She eased to her knees and hugged him. "Do not be sad. Everything is all right. You need to remember how special the creatures are that we share our Mother with everyday."

He gazed into her eyes. "I remember now. Grandfather told me if not for them, we would not have lived very long when Creator put us humans here. The creatures have taught us much."

Her knees ached, so she sat on a grassy spot, stretched out her legs, and pulled her grandson onto her lap.

He reached for her necklace, the bug momentarily forgotten. "What are these stones you have around your neck? They have so many different shapes."

He turned each one in his fingers. "I do not remember seeing this color before in the canyons. Why are they blue like the sky? Why is the sky blue? And the water too? Why is the water not blue when we swim in it? Why—"

"One question at a time! Too much spills from your mouth all at once." She laughed and stared into his dark, bright eyes. *The eyes of wonder stare into mine.*

She pointed to the strand around her neck. "These are sky beads. Your grandfather brought them back from his trip down into the land where it gets very hot. The Peoples there dug them from big rocks and caves."

She took off the necklace so he could hold it. "Our ancestors said that when Creator made the sky, some pieces fell and landed in the hills while they were still soft—a very, very long time ago. The hills hardened and caught the sky pieces inside. When I was young, the storyteller of our band told of how the sky had no color and was sad, so Creator asked the big waters to share her color with Sky. It was then some of the pieces fell. The color made the sky feel heavy. Soon, Sky adjusted to the weight and thanked the big waters for the color. That is why the stones around my neck are called sky beads."

"Chases Butterflies told me Turtle made the ground." His eyes squinted as he cocked his head. "Is this true? If it is true, how did Turtle do this? Chases Butterflies said Eagle asked Turtle to do it, but my cousin didn't explain the rest. Why did Eagle ask Turtle and not us? Were we too busy? What were we doing?"

"Yes, Turtle was a great help to Creator, and I will tell you this story when the time is right. Every story must be told in its own time—"

"What time is it now? How do you know when it is time? Does someone tell you? Who tells you—?"

She put a finger to his lips. "Let me speak. Someday you might run out of words because you used them all up. It is time for you to listen to my words now."

"Because it is time? Time for the story you are going to tell me now?" His voice raised in tone. "Tell me, Grandmother! You better hurry, or there may not be enough time."

She gently shook him by his waist. "Oh, how do all your words even fit into your mind? Do not answer. Such a silly one you are." She snuggled her nose against his, then leaned back. "Close your mouth and give your mind a rest. I must tell you a story about our Spirits. Listen well to me."

She gathered her thoughts with a deep breath, gazed up to watch Eagle play on the air currents, and then set her breath free. *Eagle, give me the words I need.* Her Spirit Guide never left her sight, so long as she felt Eagle in her heart and offered thanks everyday for the great winged one's guidance.

She turned toward the boy's attentive face. "Everything on our Mother is alive and has a Spirit. That bug you were going to push over the edge would not have flown. Did you think he would just vanish and be no more?"

She wrapped her arms around him, and leaned backwards so she could stare into his bright eyes.

"I do not know. I have never thought about such a thing before. Would he just vanish?"

"No. That bug has a Spirit—just like you. You would have shortened his life, and Creator would have had to come get him. He would not have lived long enough to fulfill his life's purpose. We all have a reason for being here, for living. Some find out early on what they are to do, while others wonder for a long time. It could be many little things, or it may be one big thing."

"A big thing? How do we know?" He glanced up. "Look at that cloud. Do you see—"

She put her hand over his open mouth, tried to look serious and not laugh at his raised eyebrows and widened nostrils. "The Creator's Spirit exists in everything, and this is how we are joined. Like Spider's web, one strand must depend on another, to keep it safe from coming apart. That bug is connected to you through Creator."

She made a circle in the dirt, took his finger, and put it along the edge in one spot. She then put her finger in another spot.

"Watch what happens when I move my finger." She put a line across the circle. "Now you do the same."

He did, and then looked to where his finger made his own line. His face widened with a smile. "The circle has two breaks in it. One is me, and one is the bug! I understand." He drew the circle whole again.

She pointed to a little Cedar that struggled to grow through a crack in a large boulder. "Where there is life, there is Energy. Where there is Energy, there is Creator. Energy is what makes everything grow — even little boys."

Feather Floating In Water curled up in her lap and relaxed. "I love you. I am glad Creator made you my grandmother."

They sat on the hill and watched as the sun lowered in the sky in a burst of soft peaches and pinks. Feather's chin dropped to his chest, and he fell asleep leaning against Bright Sun Flower's side. She gently brushed away his hair to look at his closed eyes. He smiled and his little nose twitched.

He was still just a little boy, but soon the season would pass and he would gain another span of time — nine winters. She still saw the baby in his face, but she felt much more.

From above the ledge behind her, Sister Wind's fingers gripped her dress with icy claws and wrapped themselves around her, unusually cold for this time of season. She shivered, laid her head back, and allowed her mind to find the silence. Sister Wind brought with her voices. Bright Sun Flower made out one to be her own mother's soft cooing; the same cooing she had heard when she was a child.

My little Flower, my sweet child, listen to your mother. Do not dismiss your dreams or those of the boy, my daughter. They are not just thoughts passing through. They are the future. Your future, your grandson's future, the future of all your Peoples. All the People who listen will be safe, but those who do not will have a very different future.

She wrapped her arms tighter around the boy. A different future could only mean one thing: the end of *their* comfortable lives as another pushed forward, trampling into grey dust everything the Fish People knew.

Did the People even have a chance?

Chapter 3

Hawk Soaring walked with his grandson, Feather Floating In Water, on this cool day of changing leaves. The landscape embraced them with richly colored leaves of bold yellow, shimmering gold, deep maroon and bright orange. Birds chattered, invisible in the thickets. The blue-green river teemed with hungry fish, which jumped from the water to catch hapless bugs flying too close to the surface. Eagles with outstretched wings disappeared and reappeared in effortless grace through the clouds.

He breathed in the changes—strong smells of seeding Sage, musty leaves crunched underneath their feet. He walked straight while his young companion bent over to gather rocks to toss in the slow river.

Today would be a good day to teach him about why we have a cold season, that everything in nature needs a resting time.

He watched as Feather tossed flat stones in the hopes they would skip across the river.

The boy stopped and turned to him. "Grandmother said she had too much to do this day to play with me, but that you had lots of time, and that I should take you out for a walk. She did not want you getting stiff. What does stiff mean?"

"Ah, stiff means bent over from too much work. I work so hard, she worries that I might get sore. Such a caring grandmother you have."

Feather's wide eyes and big smile stopped Hawk Soaring from telling his grandson he was not about to get stiff. He couldn't help but grin. He had spent so many winters with his woman that he couldn't remember them all.

She remains as beautiful as ever. Perhaps just a bit more opinionated. I could love no one else.

Feather grinned back. "Why are you smiling so much? Better be careful— you could lose some more teeth. They could fall out!"

Hawk Soaring bent over with laughter. His grandson had long been amused by his nearly toothless bottom jaw. "Little one, if I lose any more teeth, you will have to feed me, because it will be your fault!"

He stood up, reached out to Feather for support, and wiped happy tears from his eyes. "There, now none will fall out, because I am standing up. You are such a joy. You should walk me more. I would like that."

"Really? Grandmother says you sit around with your old friends because, at your age, you cannot do as much as you used to do, and she says you need lots of rest. I would not want to tire you out."

He maintained his serious tone, tightened his lips, and squared his chin. "Will I wear you out? Because if I did, Grandmother would have no one to help her when she gets as old as you. I would have worn you all out and used you up."

"You will not wear me out. I am just as young as your grandmother." *I will get that old woman. We shall see who needs more rest in the morning!*

"Grandmother says you are really old, past sixty winters now, and that you're long hair is filled with stardust."

"Stardust! My *long* hair does not have stardust in it." His eyes squinted as he knelt beside his misinformed grandson. "My hair is sprinkled with wisdom." He leaned forward, allowed his hair to fall over his knees and shook it. "See my wisdom now? Many women of our band say I am good to look at. That my body is strong and I have the face every woman wishes her own man had."

His grey-white hair fell below the middle of his chest, over the elegantly quilled yellow and green arrows that started at the top of his tunic and shot down in pairs to the bottom edge. Bright Sun Flower had quilled the middle of his leggings with the same design, and had nicely fringed the sides.

"Perhaps it is your grandmother's fault. She makes me such nice things to wear." He stood up and mumbled to himself before taking his grandson's hand. "Boy, soon it will be time again to sit around the fire, while the cold and snow take over the land. The band will get together in the Counsel Lodge to tell stories from years past." He turned and made sure Feather listened. "This way, no one will forget where we came from, or why. Without the stories, we would have no past to link us to the future. Those who had already gone to the stars — their memories — are as important as those who live today. Those people were the ground — the rock — upon which the band now builds their lives."

"What rock? Where is this rock? I would like to see it."

Hawk Soaring tried to make himself appear serious. "The rock I speak of only means — "

Feather let his hand go, ran ahead and started picking up stones to skip in the river again. "Perhaps I will find it by the water!"

Hawk Soaring sighed and grinned. He wanted to use this time to teach his grandson important things, while he was still able to do so. The boy was growing fast, and he had many personal stories to share with his only grandchild. He had taught him to fish and hunt small game, as an uncle would have traditionally done. Sadly, Makes Baskets had been their only gift from Creator. A son would have been nice, but for reasons only Creator knew, they had not brought one into the world.

The river trickled peacefully, interrupted by the occasional plop, skip, skip of a stone. Purple and yellow wildflowers blended with the silvery Sacred Sage. The elder inhaled deeply and thanked Creator for the gift of all living.

He picked out a nice thick splay of grass upon which to sit, and called to his grandson, whose many stones spilled over his tunic. "Let the stones go free and come sit beside this old man. I have a story to tell you."

The stones fell from Feather's tunic as he turned and ran to Hawk Soaring.

"Dust off your breechclout and sit." Before Hawk Soaring could add, "away from my face," sparkling dust sprinkled his cheeks and eyes — and his mouth tasted of dirt. With his grandson now sitting, he stood to brush himself off.

The young boy looked puzzled by his dirty tunic. "How did you get so dirty, Grandfather? I do not remember *you* throwing stones."

"Oh, I think it was maybe some boy who tossed dirt on me." He laughed as Feather turned looking for that boy.

"I did not see him. He must have been very fast!"

"Yes, he was very fast. Too fast to see." He sat down again. "Fast, all right."

"Why do birds have wings and we just have arms? That boy was maybe a bird, but he was too fast to see for sure. If we all had wings, would the sky get too crowded? I bet then birds would have to walk. But then—"

"Feather! Too many words spill out of your mouth all at once." He grabbed his middle and laughed. "You will make this old man's belly come apart if you do not slow down."

The boy's eyes widened with disbelief. "How could your belly come apart? Everything would fall out, and then I would have to run and get Grandmother and Mother to sew you back up before you turned into nothing but skin!"

Hawk Soaring fell and rolled onto his side, until he choked and had to stop to catch his breath. Tears streamed down his cheeks and chin. "Oh! Oooohhh, you are a precious little one. I hope you never grow up!"

He rolled back over, sat up, pulled his hand through the soft hair on the boy's head, and yanked on it. "Soon, your hair will be as long as mine. You will grow up to be a proud hunter with a woman and children. Maybe even more than one woman."

No sooner had he said it, than he wished he could stuff the words back into his big mouth.

Feather Floating In Water's jaw dropped. He cocked his head and stared at him. "Why do I have only Grandmother? I bet she would love it if you got another woman. She would have somebody else to help her and my mother, and they could all be friends. I would have two grandmothers, and they could take turns cooking and helping each other with all the hides after a hunt. And when it was time to move our people deeper into the canyons during the colder winters, we would have more help, and.... Why do you look like you are holding your breath? Are you choking on something? Why is your face a strange color?"

"I... I just took too much air in all at once. I think a drink from the river will help me feel better." *Learning not to let words spill from my mouth before my mind has a chance to think would also help!*

He leaned forward and used his hands to pull himself up. He laughed and shook his head as they walked to the river.

The boy mimicked his actions by kneeling beside him at the water. The drink soothed Hawk Soaring's throat and gave him a chance to catch his breath.

The boy also sipped the cool water from the bank's edge. "What if we sucked up a fish? Would he just go down with the water? I bet that would tickle. Have you ever sucked up a fish?"

Hawk Soaring choked and spit out his water, and choked some more through his laughter. He would definitely have to let the boy walk him more.

He had forgotten how much fun a child could be, especially one as amusing as Feather.

Man, then boy, stood and turned around... and remained still.

An unexpected guest stared at them from just a few steps away.

Hawk Soaring reached in vain for the bow and arrows he had forgotten to bring. He could not help but stare into the amber eyes that stared back.

He whispered, "Do not move. Just be very still. We must honor his presence, thank him, and move away."

Looking directly into the wolf's eyes could spark aggression from the great creature, but this one remained calm. *A grey-colored wolf? I have heard of them, but the wolves here are red-brown. Where did this one come from?*

"Do not worry, he is just hurt." Feather pointed to the wolf's swollen front left paw. "He needs our help."

Before Hawk Soaring could grab him, his grandson was in front of the wolf. Feather bent down, held the wolf's swollen paw, and pulled out several deeply lodged porcupine quills.

Hawk Soaring stood behind the boy, his breath barely moving his chest. This wolf was different—he could feel it in his Soul—but instinct readied him to do what he must to protect his grandson.

Feather acted as if he and the four-legged had always known each other. He gently squeezed the wolf's swollen paw and talked to him as he would another person. "There you go, no more quills, no more pain!"

The boy ran his hands over the wolf's front legs and nearly white paws. "I have never touched a wolf before. I am sorry it hurts. It is okay to cry. I cry when I'm hurt too. How did you get so many quills in your paw? It is so swollen, they all came right out."

Feather relaxed, perfectly at ease. "I only had to squeeze them, like Grandmother did for me when I was silly enough to sit on some. I did not tell her what happened. I tried to keep it a secret, but they hurt so much after a few days, I had to tell her. By then, bad Spirits had found their way in."

He turned the white paw sideways, as if to make sure he had gotten out all the quills. "After she warmed them with a soaked piece of scrap hide, she squeezed them and they popped out, and the bad Spirits came out too, just like yours did. Good thing you found us. Now you will not get sick."

Feather and the wolf locked eyes. "Your eyes are like golden drops from Father Sun."

He reached up, rubbed the wolf's ears and scratched behind them. The wolf lowered his head, and the boy sniffed the thick grey fur, inhaling his scent. He then turned around, the wolf's paw still in his hand. "Look, Grandfather, he has nearly all white paws. And he smells of Sage. Can he stay with us? Can he?"

Hawk Soaring remained motionless. Never had he seen what now played out before him—Wolf and human boy acting like the best of friends. "That wild animal is not meant to be with us humans. Somewhere he has a mate, maybe pups." He looked around for movement.

The grey wolf licked the boy's face, turned and trotted off with his nose to the ground, and disappeared into the shrubs along the river. Feather sat in silence and watched where Wolf had gone, and shivered as if goosebumps raced up and down his arms.

"Well, this is a Sacred Happening. Wolf just claimed you as part of his pack." Hawk Soaring shook his head. "And for the first time, you are silent."

The boy may have touched Wolf's fur, but Wolf had clearly touched the boy's heart.

Feather spoke with a wisdom that belonged to an elder of the Band, not a boy. "I have looked into Wolf's eyes and seen his Soul. He and I are now one." He walked to the river and picked up stones to throw into the water, but turned. "I'm hungry. Can we go home and eat?"

The elder looked with new eyes at his growing grandson. *So much more than a child.* He couldn't put his feelings into words.

Here I came out to teach my grandson a lesson, and the boy teaches me something about life I do not yet understand. Does he understand it himself?

The two of them walked side-by-side back to the camp. Hawk Soaring remained immersed in deep thought, absorbed by the strange incident. Feather wandered close to the river and looked back several times.

He too must be trying to understand it. What Power is at work here? I must tell the band what has happened. My grandson is, as my woman said, special.

Chapter 4

The crunch of pine needles mingled with animal chatter in the chill of the late season air, a busy time for humans and animals alike. Makes Baskets, with the help of her son, Feather Floating In Water, gathered the last bits of useful needles the canyon trees offered.

He held a handful up to his nose and breathed in the last hint of their aroma. "Mother, how do you make baskets? I see you doing it, but you go so fast my eyes get dizzy watching. Every trader comes to our lodge first to look at your baskets. Are you the best?"

Heat rushed to her face, and she tried to hide her embarrassment. "I have never thought of being the best, little one. It would be wrong to boast, because that can hurt the feelings of others—if you do that, they might decide not even to try. So watch your thoughts when they come out of your mouth. Never say you are better than anyone else."

She took his hand and swung it as they continued their walk. When they reached a big pile of needles, they leaned over to pick them up.

"So you want to know how we weave?"

"I did ask, Mother. Why would I ask if I did not want to know?" He bunched up his eyebrows and imitated his grandmother's withered fruit-face expression.

She turned her face away so he could not see her laughing. *So now, he imitates his grandmother.*

She cleared her throat and turned back toward him. "The needles can be either fresh, or late-season, like the ones we pick now. We bunch up the needles in our hand and wrap them with sinew, bend them into the shape of a circle for the base, and continue the circle until the basket is the shape and height we want it."

She showed him with her expressive hand movements. "I weave in quills to make my designs. We work an unopened pine cone into the top of the lid—"

"Oh, you sure know a lot. I hope I am as smart when I get old like you. Grandfather says he is very smart, so I bet you are too."

"I am not old!" She looked down at him to speak more about her age, but he was already well ahead, scouting out more supplies of needles—when he wasn't distracted by the entire world around him.

She brushed stray black hairs from her face and tucked them behind her ear, and called him back before he vanished down another path. He loved to follow his senses wherever they would lead him.

Her hair flew loose in the gentle breeze. The long, shining mass fell to where a quilled, dark green vine of leaves wound around her waist. The bright yellow and orange design on her fringed dress-top imitated Father Sun rising over the canyons.

Her father had told her she was a beauty that many men wanted, and her skills at basket weaving and quilling added to her desirability. She remembered one man had told him she was as beautiful as the first flower breaking through snow. Yet whenever men approached, she would tighten her strong, square chin, and raise her proud head. If a man had eyes for her and came to her parents' lodge to offer gifts, all she had to do was adopt this posture and look at her father.

Hawk Soaring would know her answer. She had her man, her little son.

Feather grumbled and stood with his hands on his hips. "We need to find better needles and fill our baskets faster, so we can eat the fish you cooked and brought along with us. I sure am hungry! Are you hungry, Mother?"

He returned to his search before she could answer. A pang of joy shot through her chest when she watched her babbling boy, who often chased off others of the band with all his wonder.

This one will learn a lot, if his ears are as open as his mouth! She tried not to laugh out loud, but her mind wouldn't let go of the thought.

"You sound like you are trying to sneeze. Are you all right?" Her son looked up at her with one eyebrow raised. "Did your tongue get in the way? Mine does that sometimes too. It's like tripping over a strand of leather dangling from my summer footwear... only in my mouth."

He reached into his mouth to tug on his tongue, and gagged for his effort.

The canyon echoed her laughter. She would have to tell her mother this one.

Makes Baskets turned at the outbreak of chattering birds, and gaped at what she saw. Another path, buried by thick shrubs that stubbornly held on to their last leaves, hid many raspberries growing low before them — more than usual.

"What a great find, Feather! We need to put the needles in one basket, so we can save the other three. They have a cone shape that is perfect for berries — the ones on the bottom will not get crushed." She paused and gazed to the sky. "We must offer our thanks."

Mother and son raised their hands to thank Creator, sang a prayer for the Spirits of the plants and the great bounty they offered, and thanked the berries for their life-giving sustenance.

They took only part of what they saw, for the greed of one would upset the balance for all.

They stuffed as many needles as they could in one basket, left it on the path, and dumped the rest on the ground for retrieval later. Makes Baskets looked at the fading late-day sun but decided not to rush their gathering. They could always return with more women from the camp to pick the rest tomorrow.

Feather slowed down and put his basket of raspberries on the ground. "Mother, will they keep growing in the baskets? If they do, we can just pick half a basket and wait a few days until they grow some more and fill the basket. That way, they will not be so heavy to carry back."

Shame overtook her for not considering her little one properly. "We should sit and rest on the boulder under that tree. We will relax, eat, and then return home. Our baskets are full enough, and I can pick up the pine needles on the way back."

She reached into her food pack, pulled out a small basket of fish wrapped in moist leaves, and handed it to Feather. "Remember to give thanks to Brother Fish for giving his life so you could have a meal."

He took the fish, said a small prayer, and asked Creator to guide him safely to the big lake, where all his relations waited to reunite with him. He then put the fish down and stared at the fruiting shrubs.

"I had another dream vision last night," he said. "I saw deer dancing, but they had shiny things on their backs. I think maybe they were not dancing, but maybe they fought to be free of these things. I wanted to tell you before, but we were so busy." He paused to take a bite of the fish. "Mother, why do you never speak of dreams? Am I strange? One boy said I was as strange as seeing a fox playing with a bear's cub. Not natural."

Her son took another bite and leaned back against the canyon wall, picking at something invisible on his thumb. His brows crinkled and his mouth drooped.

"You are not strange. Who tells you this?" She held him close and caressed his hair. "I do not have the gift you and your grandmother have. Your dreams are from Creator, and someday you will understand what you see. Son, look into my eyes."

Feather looked up at his mother, and a small tear lay next to his right eye, lingering, waiting for more to push it down his cheek.

"You are very special. You are a Dreamer. It is time you tell your grandmother of this. She knows of your dreaming, but waits for you to come to her. This much she spoke of to me."

She hugged him and ran her hands up and down his shoulders. "I wish I knew more. I will talk to my Spirit Guide." She looked around, then back to him, and whispered, "Never, never tell anyone, but I speak to Spider. That is why I have the gift of making baskets. She showed me in a vision, when I was not much older than you are, how to weave them. Spider also taught me to be a good mother. Speak of this to no one, Son. It is our secret." She put her finger to her lips.

She pointed to the discarded food. "Finish your fish so he knows he was not taken from the river for nothing, and we will head home. We will bring others to help pick the berries after we have all had our morning meal."

Feather picked up his fish and held it to his nose. "They smell like the plants you sprinkled on them. Will you teach me about the plants, please?"

She could see his thoughts had eased. She felt at a loss when it came to his dreams, and had asked Spider once, but the answer — *'he helps to weave the web of life'* — had only confused her more.

Her son continued his endless questioning. "I see you and Grandmother pick and dry the plants, but I do not know which one is for what. Which ones are on the fish? Are they the same ones you gave Grandfather this spring when he had to leave the lodge all night long? He sure was funny! He acted as if he was practicing for the runs the men do when the warm days come, to prove who is the fastest. Was that what he was doing in the middle of the night? Was he trying to be sneaky about it, and surprise everyone?"

The boy laughed so hard, he nearly dropped his fish off the boulder he sat on. His laughter continued as he stuffed fish into his mouth with one hand, and berries with the other.

Makes Baskets leaned forward and smiled. His berry-smeared face proved he had eaten as many as remained in his basket. Wonder and innocence shone within his eyes. She saw in them not a warrior or great hunter, as all the other mothers said they saw in their sons, but rather a gentle, kind, forgiving Soul. And a hidden mystery.

She reached out and squeezed him to the basket of raspberries that sat across the front of her dress. "What a lucky mother I am to have such a son, so smart and so good to look at. Girls will fight over you like a dog fights over a bone."

"Um... Mother?"

She drifted into thoughts of how special her son would be to another woman someday. *Another woman? How could my son ever leave me? She would have to be a very special woman to take my son! I would not allow just any woman to take his hand and lead him away from me. She would first need to prove herself worthy of such a fine man. Never —*

"*Mother?* Mother, please listen to me!"

She shook her head to clear her mind, and focused on Feather. "What is it, my son?"

She gazed into his laughing eyes. Puzzled, she pushed him back, and gasped at her wet, sticky arms, red with tiny seeds stuck all over them — and her dress! The berries had oozed through the basket when she had squeezed him to her bosom.

"Hoohaaa-haaa! The only place you do not have berries on you is red too!" He pointed to her ever-warming face, laughed, and fell backwards off the boulder.

Good one — another story for the long winter. This will be real fun, walking back to camp with an empty basket and a red-seeded dress top. "Son, stop laughing and look at me!"

He obeyed and looked at her — for a split second — then roared with laughter and held his belly. He kicked up red dust that painted him the same color.

She could not escape this one; they would tell such stories about her! At least she could wash some of it off in the stream before going home. She picked up her red-dusted son by the arm, and led the giggling boy down the path to scoop up the needles before they went to the river.

She reached for the basket, and a menacing growl echoed behind them.

She pulled Feather behind her, knocked both of them to the ground, and scooted her son back away from the basket of needles until the canyon wall stopped her from going any farther. The cautious grey wolf stepped toward it. Makes Baskets sat on the ground between the wolf and her son, fearful but determined. Her heart beat in her chest like Hummingbird's wings.

Her voice trembled. "Why, Wolf, would you want to claim us? Have we passed into your land? We have walked these paths since I was a child. Please, Brother Wolf, let us pass unharmed, and I will leave an offering of food for you."

She gazed down, her head lowered so he knew she meant no threat, but her hand gripped the sheathed knife at her side.

The little boy peeked around her and pleaded with his wolf friend. "White Paws, what is wrong?" Before she could stop him, he darted between her and the wolf. "White Paws?"

A hiss came from the basket, and the wolf snarled, frightening the boy back against his confused mother.

The wolf bared his teeth, grabbed the basket, and shook it to shreds. A large rattlesnake rolled out, coiled up, ready to strike. The wolf grabbed the snake with his teeth and violently shook the serpent, stopping only after the bloodied creature was still. He then dropped the defeated foe, walked over to Makes Baskets and her frightened son.

He licked both their faces.

Makes Baskets wiggled away from his muzzle and sat dazed. "Thi—this is the wolf who had quills in his paw?"

Her son was busy scratching behind both of the wolf's ears. Feather hugged him tight to his body. "Now I understand, White Paws, but you must tell me next time, before you scare us so much, silly wolf." He laughed and scratched him some more.

Makes Baskets scooted closer, but kept an eye on the dead snake... just in case the creature had any movement left. "Thank you, great Wolf Brother. I shall sing a prayer to Creator for letting you come to us. You will always be welcomed in our lodge. You have saved my child. I know of no better story to tell winter after winter."

She sensed his unusual gentleness within her Soul, just as her father had said he had experienced during his first encounter with the wolf. She hoped that, in time, she would be able to pet White Paws as her son did, but for now, she sat uncertain.

The People will not forget this day—ever! I will see to that.

Chapter 5

The wolf sat at the edge of the village with a rabbit between his front paws. Onlookers hurried by with quick glances. One man approached with a club, swung it, yelled, and tried to scare him away.

The wolf stepped back, but returned to his spot. No one would harm Wolf. Wolves were Sacred beings, and several people in the band carried Wolf as part of their name.

But to have one come into camp? What did this mean?

People stopped what they were doing, and waited to see which brave person would approach Wolf. Women held onto their children while the men whispered among themselves.

***

White Paws watched as Feather hurried from the bathing pond and ran for his lodge. He yipped and wagged his tail to get the boy's attention.

When Feather saw him, the boy squealed and ran to where he danced in place. White Paws lowered his body, wagged his tail low, and brushed the ground clean of the light dusting of snow and loose dirt. His body language signaled a gentle greeting. The excitement in the little human's squirming body was all he needed. He stood, wriggled in anticipation, then scooped the rabbit in his mouth, leaned toward the boy, and dropped the prize a few inches from the young human's feet.

The boy giggled. "White Paws!"

He moved closer so the boy could touch him. He felt Feather reach deep into his fur, and pushed closer when arms went around the thick grey mass of his neck. He watched the boy reach for the rabbit, and cocked his head as Feather spoke.

"What is this? Have you brought your meal with you?" A white cloud formed from the boy's breath. "Where have you been? Two moons have passed since you saved us from the snake."

White Paws wagged his tail and backed away a few steps to give the boy room. He sat down with his tail slightly tucked—a passive posture—and waited. He was too large to be a pup, but displayed the mannerisms of a young one. Perhaps he had wandered too far and simply kept going. He panted, his tongue bobbing to one side.

He stood and wriggled even more as the boy took the offered gift. Now they were pack members.

With great excitement, he licked his new Human Brother's face and knocked him down. Feather squealed again as his near-naked body hit the frosty ground.

***

Feather spun around at a loud shout from Bright Sun Flower. She dropped her basket of edible tubers she had spent the morning gathering, and ran straight for him and White Paws.

She reached out for him. "What are you doing? Come to me now!" She grabbed his arm.

He freed himself and stood stubbornly between his grandmother and the wolf. He reached back and dug his hand deep into White Paws' fur without taking his eyes off her.

"Grandmother, this is White Paws! Remember me telling you about him? I pulled quills from his paw, and then he was happy. Grandfather said he was special, that we had a Sacred something, and then we looked up and he was gone. But he was there again with Mother and me when that rattlesnake was hiding in the basket and —"

He paused to inhale. His face felt like a lodge fire at night.

His mother had run barefooted from her lodge, dropping the set of footwear she had been mending on the ground behind her. She now stood in front of him and White Paws, her arms held out and palms forward. "He saved us from being harmed by the snake. Remember *me* telling you?"

Makes Baskets pleaded with her mother and the rest of the band to understand. Everyone who had not already stopped what they were doing now gathered close together a few steps away.

Bright Sun Flower stepped toward her daughter and chuckled. "What I remember most, is a grown woman who came home with her clothes full of red berries. You looked like the biggest raspberry I had ever seen."

Others joined in the laughter.

Feather's grandmother knelt beside him, and looked at him sideways while watching the wolf. "How has it come to be that a boy and Wolf are now beside each other?"

He smiled and held the rabbit out to her. "Grandmother, is this his way of wanting to be friends? He *did* save our lives." He pointed to her knees and giggled. "Your knees sound like you walk in snow when you bend down. Crrrunch... crrrunch...."

"Enough, silly one who befriends wild beasts! This one could have eaten you. What is Wolf doing here?"

He shrugged and mumbled, "I do not know."

White Paws leaned forward and sniffed his grandmother. Bright Sun Flower held out her hand, and his new friend offered a quick lick before stepping back behind him and his mother.

His grandmother nodded in understanding. "He has asked for my acceptance. I am honored, Wolf."

She spoke to him with soft words. "Brother Wolf, you have walked in my dreams many times. I know you protected me as I sought to go deeper within, in search of answers. I just never thought to touch you outside my dreams. I accept you, as you have accepted me."

White Paws stepped forward again, sat in front of her, and stared into her eyes.

Feather watched as they shared this connection, and his heart warmed at.... He jerked his head up and swallowed hard.

The band's Holy Man came forward.

Bear Tracks, dressed in a long, deep brown elk-skin tunic and leggings decorated with sky beads and elk teeth, walked past the people and stood staring down at boy and Wolf. "So, this is the boy who never stops to listen to his own voice."

The Holy Man had not sounded sharp. He smiled at Feather, rubbed his head, and looked down at White Paws, who stared into this stranger's eyes without fear.

Holy Man and Wolf accepted each other instantly.

Bear Tracks wore a long scar across the left side of his face, a reminder of the attack many seasons ago that had left Feather Floating In Water without a father. His eyes expressed the strength of his mind. He stood tall and raised his chin, in preparation to speak.

No one would cross words with him.

"This is a Sacred Happening." He pointed to Feather, who remained silent holding the rabbit in his hand. "This young one some of you call strange. He *is* different, but not in the way some of you think. I, Bear Tracks, your Holy Man, say this boy will one day become much more than any of you can at this time understand or believe. Know that a young Eagle will not fly until the time is right for him to do so."

He paused to allow everyone to consider his words. "I will speak no more of it until the time comes. Know this: my dreams and the boy's have mingled. A new way will soon find us."

Bear Tracks looked down at Bright Sun Flower, and then knelt beside her, his voice low but not as quiet as it could've been. "Woman, your daughter should come to my lodge, so that I may teach this young one and make him my son. But I will not place the burden of decision upon you or your daughter. Time will take care of things, as it always has."

Feather took a couple tentative steps toward their lodge, hunger rippling through his stomach at the thought of the rabbit he carried. White Paws trailed behind him.

Hawk Soaring walked past the people, appearing taller and prouder than he had been in many seasons, grinning as he passed Bright Sun Flower. "I do not know about you, my woman, but I am hungry, and the newest hunter in our lodge has brought home a meal I wish to share."

"Just leave your woman on her old knees," she mumbled while struggling to stand.

His mother hurried to help his grandmother, but her eyes remained on Bear Tracks. He was not so old, and perhaps not so bad for a woman to look at, but Makes Baskets had always said she could control her own future, one that need not include a man.

His grandmother grunted as his mother, with her eyes—and apparently her thoughts—still focused on Bear Tracks, pulled her up from the ground with an untended jerk.

He watched the unfolding scene with great interest.

His mother let go of his grandmother's arm, walked past them all, and away from the Holy Man. She yanked open the lodge flap, ducked under, and disappeared.

His grandmother struggled to keep up behind her.

"Grandfather, I never knew Grandmother could move so fast! She was like the little yellow and black winged one moving to a new flower before another could get to it. What made her do that? And Mother too! She acted as if Grandmother was going to scold her. Is that it? What did Mother do? Maybe I better go see if I—"

Hawk Soaring grabbed the back of his breechclout and pulled him back. "Here, boy, wrap up in this hide and put on your footwear so you will not get cold, and we will go for a walk. Let the women be alone for now. They need to talk. Women need to be alone sometimes, and it is a better idea to walk away than ask questions."

"Talk? Why do they need to be alone to talk? Did we do something? Did I do something? Oh... *Bear Tracks*! He said something to Grandmother that made Mother's face turn red. What did he say, Grandfather? Is he mad about White Paws? I will not allow Bear Tracks to harm him! White Paws saved my life and Mother's too. Wolf is my brother, as Hawk is yours. Grandfather, I will be proud to die, if I must, to protect him. You see a boy who is eight winters old now, but I am more."

He stood as tall as his small frame would allow, and put his hands on his hips. He stared at the few remaining people milling nearby, puffed out his chest, and projected fierceness into his voice.

"I, Feather Floating In Water, have this to say: if I have to, I will go to live in the canyons with White Paws. He will protect me and we can hunt for our own food. White Paws and Feather Floating In Water are now human and animal Brothers. I have spoken!"

He took the unyielding stance of a man, and the people looked everywhere but at him.

His grandfather tightened his lips as they spread, as though he were in severe pain. He wrapped Feather in the hide robe, picked up Feather's footwear, and scooted him away from the camp.

White Paws scooped the rabbit up in his mouth.

Bursts of laughter followed Feather, his grandfather... and the wild Wolf that fell in behind—his new Brother in the small band of the Fish People.

Chapter 6

Boy and Wolf sat side-by-side as Father Sun sunk into the cloudy, peach-colored sky. Snow blanketed the top of the mesa, enough to hide the red-orange boulders. Shrubs, now brown, sparkled with untouched flakes of fading rainbows on their leafless branches. Plants slept and the land appeared quiet and still. Life was peaceful, calm.

A newborn's mind yet to worry about life, as Grandmother would say.

The lodges below, active with people at cooking fires, sent the smell of food up to Feather's nose. He wondered at the passing of time as Father Sun lowered in the sky. Small pink shadows lengthened the lumps of snow where rocks hid. He stared down at the fires and listened to his belly speak of its hunger. Next time he would bring more than dried fish.

Wisps of frozen air came from Feather's mouth as he spoke. "The cold season deepens, White Paws. The land goes to sleep, but this passing of knowledge never stops, not even for the elders who tell stories and share memories. Families sit together and teach us young ones how to make things, while we listen to stories we will pass on to our own young ones. Many good things happen, but I feel something is wrong, out of balance, as Grandmother would say. Why do I feel this?"

He shrugged his shoulders. "I am confused about so much."

He found comfort in the wolf's amber eyes, and put his left arm around the thick grey fur of his animal Brother. "I know you understand me. Others in camp think I am silly when I say you and I talk."

He squeezed himself tighter to the wolf. The frigid air could not reach his arms, warm within the gift that Rabbit's fur offered his winter wear, but he shivered just the same.

He spoke in a low voice to his companion. "I am not so cold, but I have a chill. Those strange beings come into my dreams more often. They ride a creature like deer, but these animals have long hair hanging from their necks and tails. They are not all the same color as deer, but about the same size. And... these beings have shiny heads and chests."

He snuggled tighter to White Paws. With misty eyes, he gazed deep into the wolf's own attentive ones. "What am I to understand? I feel these creatures go through me in my dreams. Right through me—as if *I* am the Spirit, not them."

"You do not remember the last trader who spoke of the heavy, shiny thing he found. You were not with us yet. He hid it because it was too heavy to carry with all his other things, and everyone just laughed at him when he spoke of how it fit on his chest. I was only four winters old, but I remember the story."

He let out a deep sigh and stared down into the darkening valley. "I see these same things attached to the beings. What do you think? Could we go to find this thing? I wonder where to start."

***

"Such talk for a little boy!" Bright Sun Flower climbed up behind Feather, reaching for handholds as she went. Her breath came in short gasps. She knew he could sense what she herself had earlier, when the warm season was waning.

I wish I could see things more clearly to help him. He starts to make words like an adult, and sounds like he is many winters older than he is. How is this possible? He is a little boy!

She pushed the thoughts from her mind. "I see you and your Wolf are enjoying the view, but the cold takes the night. Come back down with me to the warm lodge. You have been in your head all day up here. Your mind must be full now."

She reached for his reluctant hand.

He furrowed his brow, as if puzzled over her appearance. "How did you know I was up here all day? I left early and the snow had just started to fall, so I left no tracks. You could not have seen me. It was dark and White Paws and I were careful to wake no one. How did you know where to look?"

She grinned. "Grandmothers know everything about their sneaky grandchildren, especially when they step on feet that belong to others. Yes, do not look so surprised! That lump you thought nothing about was my feet. Your little toes became tiny bird claws when you stepped on my bare feet."

She pointed to her thick-furred boots. The leather above the fur, decorated in bright yellow quills shaped like small versions of Father Sun, circled all the way around the top. "Besides, did you not wonder why the whole band was not out searching the canyons for a lost boy?"

She motioned with her head at the women below, busy readying the night meal and chasing after small children. The men sat in groups making new snowshoes for the coming cold season.

"Little one, please, never leave again without telling us where you are going. Your mother was frantic when she sat up and saw your robes were empty. She called out and woke us up. I calmed her down and told her where you were, but you are too young yet to wander off whenever you feel the urge. Take my hand and we will go back to the camp."

The boy took her offered hand, stood and motioned for White Paws to follow. "I am sorry, but I needed to clear my head of a dream vision. I see you do the same thing when a dream confuses you. Your eyes have a faraway look in them after you have a dream vision, and you see things no one else does. You do not answer when someone speaks to you. And something else—your eyes take on a soft blue glow."

She paused and looked down at him in amazement. The thought of her little one carrying such a burden made her heart break. "You are so young to have dreams that confuse you, let alone to know when I have such a dream. Do you want to talk about it before we go to the camp?"

She inhaled a deep breath of cold air and waited to hear of his dream. Already she saw in her mind the racing creatures that would come their way.

"I think I already know we see the same things now, Grandmother. The look in your eyes speaks what your mouth does not. I will tell you now." He stared over the darkening valley. "These creatures leave behind such destruction. I worried that I was the only one who saw these things, and feared what I did not understand. They do not care about things in their way, and...."

His body became rigid. "We are in the way."

Bright Sun Flower was grateful for their deep bond. She reached out and hugged him to her body.

"They consider us worthless. Are they human? Have I not been taught all things have worth and usefulness? These beings intend to kill us. I see it. I feel it. I know it. I sat here and heard a drum, and looked down at the camp, but no one was drumming. White Paws nudged me, sat back down, and used his nose to point toward the flat top of the mesa.

"We both—and I know White Paws saw them because he watched just like I did—we saw very old Spirits dressed in long-furred animal hides that went to the ground, not skins like we wear. They had no decorations, but necklaces of Bear's claws and Elk's teeth. Their faces were painted black."

He bowed his head. "They scared me, but White Paws nudged me again when I tried to look away, so I held him and kept watching. They locked arms as they danced, and they sang in strange words. I think these were Spirits of people who lived long, long ago."

Feather let her hand go and leaned against a boulder. He picked up a small stick, broke it into tiny pieces, and stared into nothingness. His body again grew rigid as he continued to speak.

"They wore animal heads over their own and danced around a fire, but I could not feel the heat from it. First, they danced in a circle, but then swayed toward me, past me, in the direction our people came from long ago. Then, they turned across the canyon's ridge and danced some more. Grandmother, they danced off the ridge, and each one pointed to where the land gets cold and... and each one had a shining light around them. I heard them in my mind. They said we needed to leave our home and go toward where the cold winds come from."

Feather stared blankly ahead, as if still seeing the old ones dance in his mind. "Gourds rattled to the beat of their chants. The only words I could really understand, they spoke out loud—'Soon, leave soon.' One carried a turtle rattle. Turtle was yellow, with green dividing the circles on his body. The Spirit shook it at me. Could this be the faded turtle on my back? I feel so much older. Too old for—"

"—for one so young," she finished his words. "I see my little grandson before me, a little boy, my... baby." *Yet I feel the mind of a man staring out of that boy's face. My grandson becomes a seeding flower, full of potential if the seeds drop right.*

She leaned on the boulder alongside him, and took a turn playing with a stick, breaking it into tiny pieces. She spoke to him as she would a man. "I think these very dream visions may have bothered your grandfather's father. Perhaps he thought we were safe here in the canyons. One night, I heard him whisper to your grandfather that the time would come when we would have to leave, but I thought he meant because our band would outgrow this place."

Bright Sun Flower stared off as if she herself might dance across the ridge. "I too have seen this vision, but a few winters ago." She inhaled the cold air and watched it fade. "You are not alone in your worries, little one. You and I can wander the canyons and speak of our dreams whenever you need. I can see the Spirits working through you, aging your mind while you are still a boy. Your mind will continue to grow beyond your body. Soon—sooner than most—you will be a leader in your own right."

She paused and gazed about them. "Now, darkness takes the path away from us. We must leave while my old eyes can still see."

She knelt down, held him at arm's length, and took a deep breath. "I had hoped you would be a man before this happened. You are a true Dreamer, a powerful one. More Power follows you than I knew. Soon it will be time for you to go to the Holy Man and speak to him. Do not fear him. He knows already that you dream. A Holy Person knows things, even when no one tells them."

She tried to chase away her sadness before Feather could see it on her face. "We are safe for now. You were born with the first snowfall, so you are now nine winters old, as you said when you defended White Paws." She smiled, as much for him as for her. "Come with me. Your mother has made a special meal just for you."

She stood and took the boy's hand, and they made their way down the narrow path in silence. The darkening sky worried Bright Sun Flower, and she picked up the pace.

My mind is just being silly. We are safe.

She hurried just the same.

By the time they reached the bottom of the trail, Feather Floating In Water's mood had lightened. "I hear crunching, and I know it is not coming from the small amount of snow we walk on."

He giggled as they made their way down into a nearly dark camp. She hoped the smell of food would make his mind see cooking fires, instead of ancient elders dancing around their Spirit fire.

"So, my grandson still has humor with which to tease his old grandmother. You see, sharing what bothers us eases our dark worries." She swung his hand within hers. "My knees have a voice of their own."

She exhaled softly. At least he was still her little Feather Floating In Water... and could still smile. She squeezed his hand hoping he understood he would never be alone. "I love you. Know that even when you are a man, this old one will always see you as her little one."

She would be with him even after she was finished with her body. *His* life was one his people would remember long after he was gone to the stars.

Feather squeezed her hand back, but looked forward.

White Paws walked behind the boy as they entered the camp. Seldom did anyone give a thought to the boy's constant shadow, anymore. Children ran up to him and offered him bits of food. The wolf twitched his ears, and stared back to where he and Feather had come from. Another wolf howled in the distance.

As they approached their lodge, two people awaited them in silence. "Grandmother, am I in trouble?"

Before Bright Sun Flower could speak, Makes Baskets ran to her son and pulled him close. She then held him at arm's length and smiled.

Her dark eyes brightened as Feather looked into her tender, soft face. Instead of anger and worry, they displayed relief and love... so much love.

"I did not mean to make anyone worry. I just wanted to be alone to think." He pulled away from her arms and sucked in air, trying to look taller. "I am not a little boy anymore, Mother. I am now nine winters old—almost a man, you know. I can hunt—well, almost anyway—and I am not afraid of the dark or strange noises as I used to be. I can make fire and skin any food Grandfather catches. I am a great fish catcher too. Grandfather says so, and Grandmother says old men like him have no reason to lie anymore, just brag. Mother, I am...."

Bright Sun Flower turned and saw the single eyebrow raised on Hawk Soaring's forehead. "Well, you do brag, old man. You told the wildest story late last winter, about single-handedly bringing down a humpback bull with nothing but a skinning knife—while riding on top of him! Tell me you really did that."

She walked closer to her not-so-sure man, holding a knife. When she realized why he gave her a strange look, she grinned. "Silly, I was just about to gut the fish you caught. Maybe you *should* be scared. I am not sure you caught enough to feed the new man in our lodge."

She pointed to Feather Floating In Water, who still stood puffed up, with the same tight chin his mother used when she scowled.

The two elders shared a secret smile and gazed at each other. She whispered, "I love you more than there are campfires in the sky to look at, old man."

They had shared their robes for so many winters that they had lost count. Like her once black hair, their time together had slipped into the grey passage of time.

Feather interrupted their trance. "Grandfather, my belly is not so big as yours. I do not need as much food. Grandmother, I will take only two fish tonight, one to share with White Paws. He can hunt if he wants more."

The boy knelt down and said to the wolf, "I am not a man. Grandmother is just teasing Grandfather. I must go on a Vision Quest to be a man. There are ceremonies too, and things I do not understand."

A flash flew overhead, and the boy looked up in surprise at the brilliant blue color. He looked to Bright Sun Flower with wide eyes, but they needed to speak no words; both knew they had just seen a passing Spirit.

Food forgotten, Feather stood up. "Grandmother, I must go see Bear Tracks."

She saw no fear in his eyes. This little one had already seen too many things to show fear.

"White Paws needs to be fed. He has had only some dried fish this day." He turned and rushed toward Bear Tracks' lodge, where the Spirit's light had come from. Bear Tracks' grandmother, on the other edge of camp, had been sick since the cold season moved in.

***

As people watched him pass, most understood that her Spirit had just passed to the stars, but only his cousin, Chases Butterflies, spoke. "Mother, Feather is special. Someday soon, my cousin will carry much on his shoulders. I will walk with him."

Feather turned to talk to her, but paused when his cousin's mother glared at him.

Running River pulled on her daughter's shoulders, pressing her close. "Somehow, Daughter, I hope you are wrong." She turned to go into her lodge, pushing Chases Butterflies before her, and closed the flap behind them.

White Paws brushed his cold nose into Feather's hand. He looked down at his Wolf Brother. The two had become inseparable. Where Feather went, White Paws followed. "I knew you would follow. I could see that elder's Spirit, White Paws!"

He picked up speed. "I now understand why I saw the flashes of yellow when Grandfather had taken the pair of geese from the sky. It was their Spirits."

Even though Hawk Soaring had not seen what he had, he had understood and explained to Feather never to leave a lone goose to grieve. Some animals mated for life, and he must always try to take the mate too. His grandfather had felt, rather than seen, their Spirits follow each other into the afterlife place.

Without invitation, Feather walked into the Holy Man's lodge. White Paws stayed outside at the entrance.

Bear Tracks was already busy. "I do my part to prepare my grandmother's body for her journey. I do not want her to search for family who no longer walk on our Mother." He didn't even look up. "Hand me those plants, boy — the silver-grey one, and the braided grass. Now take the bowl of Cedar chips and sprinkle them on the hot rocks — Sweet Grass first, then Sage, and finally the Cedar."

Feather did as instructed.

"My grandmother was the last of my family, and asked that her name be taken with her, and not passed to another until it came as a dream."

Bear Tracks shook Turtle's shell rattle filled with tiny round sandstones. The handle, made from elk antler, wrapped in the middle with ermine fur and tied in place with the sinew from a deer, also held feathers in place.

The lodge's herb smoke filled Feather's nostrils, and he felt it cleanse his body.

Bear Tracks sang his grandmother to the stars, and the boy sang with him. White Paws sang his own song, howling outside.

"The women will come in the morning. We leave now." The Holy Man stood up and motioned to the boy to leave, but called him back. "Wait, boy."

He handed him the still burning Sage. "Use your hand as I did, and use Eagle's feather. Allow the smoke to flow over you, to cleanse your body and Spirit again before you leave. What you have done here for my grandmother is honorable, and I shall not forget it. Now go, leave me with her for a moment, before I too must leave until Father Sun's rising."

Bear Tracks rubbed his forehead with black ash and pushed the boy from the lodge. "Tell White Paws I said thank you."

He watched the Holy Man gather his Sacred Items and wrap them in a bundle, then take a heavy robe and depart for the canyons to be alone. The Spirit of a woman whose feet did not touch the ground followed at his side.

Chapter 7

With the rising of Father Sun, the women came to clean the elder's body and purify her with more song and prayers. Bright Sun Flower sang a song of blessing with the others, and thanked the elder for the time she had shared with the band, and the knowledge she had left behind to help the band grow. They dressed Bear Tracks' grandmother in her best clothes and ornaments.

The sounds of singing and cries of sorrow left Feather with mixed emotions. He sat in silence and listened to his mother, who tried to comfort him.

"She lived seventy-four winters, little one. Some band elder's walk away to be alone when they start their journey, but Bear Tracks took great care of her and made her feel needed, so she stayed. I heard him once tell her not to walk away, that he needed her as a child needed his mother. I watched her smile as she turned and went back to their lodge."

His mother snuggled close to him. "You do understand why we stayed here?"

Feather nodded without looking up.

"This is a very Sacred ceremony and only Bear Tracks is to speak. Look around and you will see other mothers who also stayed home with their children. Understand it is the way, nothing you did wrong."

The two of them watched the people from across the camp. Once Bear Tracks blessed his grandmother again, the women put the elder on a litter. Several men carried her, resting the litter on their shoulders. A line of people followed behind Bear Tracks, who walked behind his grandmother. They sang songs about the good life that awaited her in the stars.

The final ceremony would take place in a secluded area of many trees, where others who had gone before her rested in wrapped robes, their litters placed in trees, their faces left unwrapped so they could see when a loved one came down for them.

Feather knew this because his mother had taken him there once, to the edge, so he could see where Hawk Soaring had laid his father's body. The people would remain on the edge, only venturing further when the Holy Man led the ceremony.

Feather wrapped himself tighter in their robe and sat closer to his mother. "He loved his grandmother. He looks sad under his painted face. I can feel his grieving. He is alone now. Bear Tracks never took a woman and he has no children."

He really *did* feel Bear Tracks' Energy. When someone walked past him, he sensed that person's mood—almost shared it.

He leaned closer to his mother, fearful that someday she would suffer such loss.

"Feather, my little son, you speak as a grown person who knows the way of a Holy Person. How do you know what he is feeling?" Her eyes serious, she stared at him. "Never mind, Son."

***

Makes Baskets hugged her budding son to her breast. *He grows too fast in his mind. His body is that of a little boy, but his mind.... Who is he becoming? He learns so fast, with a Power that surrounds him – and his Wolf. His Power comes from my mother and father, not me.*

She never remembered her dreams, or felt the Energy he and his grandmother did, but she could sense his carefree childhood was nearing an end.

Should I go to Bear Tracks? The Holy Man stirred feelings inside her, which had distracted her since he had spoken to her mother. *He is nice to look at. I see other women look his way. He stirs feelings in me I have not known since Feather's father. What if he takes another? I would stand up to her. He is mine!* She squeezed her son tighter. *Mine? Why does life have so many confusing choices? I am a rabbit trapped in a corner by a fox who plays with his prey.*

"Mother, I can feel your thoughts, your confusion. Did you love Turtle Dove too?"

Makes Baskets jerked his arm in panic. "You cannot say her name! She took it with her, and only a Dreamer—"

"Mother!" He pulled away. "Turtle Dove told me I could say her name and that I should name my first daughter after her. She told me in my dream last night, said it would be good for Bear Tracks to hear her name again, but that will not be for some seasons. My woman will come from another band of Peoples we do not know. Turtle Dove said she would tell Bear Tracks who she was even before I knew. Besides, you said I was a Dreamer, remember?"

In the place of burial, the people sang the song of Turtle Dove's life.

"And Mother, she had a message for you too." He leaned down and ran his fingers through Wolf's dense fur.

White Paws leaned toward him and wagged his tail in response, but got up to follow the people who had walked to the burial place.

"I wonder why he follows." Her son watched him go, then looked up at her. "No, somehow I know. I feel the answer in my Soul."

"What? Tell me what Tur—I mean, what Bear Tracks' grandmother—told you." She could not contain herself. "Please, Son, answer me!" She shook inside their robe as she wondered at the message.

"I am sorry, Mother. My mind followed White Paws. He goes to show his respect for Turtle Dove, who does not want anyone to be sad. She is with her man now, and their son and his woman. In my dream, she said she would make the first rain from her tears. I am to tell Bear Tracks' new woman that."

Feather grinned and looked straight ahead. He wrapped his arms around his crossed legs. The smell of his rabbit's fur wafted to her, soft and gentle, just like Rabbit's Soul.

"His woman? What is this you say?" She was more than a little jealous, and suddenly she wanted Bear Tracks. *No other woman had better lay claim!* She would stand up to such a woman. He was hers—he had said so—and she *knew* he would not take another woman.

Her son giggled like the little boy he was. "You silly, you will be his woman in the spring. When Turtle Dove makes the rain, he will come for you."

"Come for me? Just like that, huh? Like he thinks *I* will have *him*?" Her chin tightened up as she stood. She turned away from her son and crossed her arms, sending the long fringe on her cold season parka flying everywhere. "*I* will decide if I will be his woman, not *him*!"

She stood and stomped off, her son chuckling as she bolted toward the canyons.

In the distance, humans and Wolf raised their voices to Spirit and sang Turtle Dove home.

Chapter 8

Feather saw him first and ran down the canyon's ravine. He shouted, "Here he comes! The trader is here with his helpers."

His voice carried to everyone in camp. He ran to his own lodge with muddied feet from the late season's melting snow, through back the flap, and yelled again.

"Feather, you do not need to shout in here. And do not come in with those muddy feet!" His grandmother's face widened with a smile. "I do hope he brought some more colorful quills and sea shells with him."

Women started the cooking fires throughout their secluded camp. Soon the people would dance, and their songs would echo off the canyon's walls.

Bright Sun Flower said, "It has been nearly two cycles since he came this way."

Feather turned and dashed from the lodge again. He ran after the trader to see how many drags he had. "White Paws, he has dogs. Maybe we should stay back. Those poor things look so tired, and I bet they are hungry too! We need to go look for scraps to give them instead." He need not trouble the trader; he remembered the drags from other times. "The man does not like me. He told Mother I am too noisy."

***

Inside the lodge, Makes Baskets stopped the quilling on her basket and shuddered. "Mother, I wish to remain in the lodge. I do not want him to see me. Too many times, he has smiled my way." She was certain he wanted to take her as his mate.

"Daughter," Hawk Soaring stopped wrapping his new arrowhead to the shaft, "I will not allow him to bother you. Stay close to us and you will be fine."

They only saw Walking Stick, who came from a band many moons away, every early season or two. He always brought the Fish Peoples items of great interest.

"He carries goods the people asked for long ago," her father said, "so he will be too busy to look your way."

Her father only tried to reassure her, even if he was not so sure himself. She dropped her basket and left the lodge in time to see Walking Stick passing out straw dolls to the children.

He only does that so parents think he likes children. I know better. Children are of no use to him until they are old enough to carry packs!

She spun and ducked back into the lodge before he could see her, but peeked out to watch him. He craned his neck looking around.

He hopes I was running around like the other women excited by his arrival.

He tossed the rest of the dolls in the air and made his way to the Counsel Lodge.

Ha! He looks for me. She bit her lip and closed the lodge flap.

***

Feather watched as Walking Stick had one of his helpers unload his burden. The trader ordered him to help the other seven young men carrying heavy packs. The two eldest, around sixteen or seventeen winters old, carried the heaviest packs, which held the promise of items from faraway places.

"White Paws, I wonder what could be in all those packs."

They unloaded the packs on the dogs and promptly tied the exhausted animals up.

"Poor dogs! We will feed them with every scrap we can find. If he were not such an important man, I would yell at him for the way he treats his dogs. He even looks mean, with his white hair tied on top his head in a knot and, look, his long nose reaches his lips when he squishes them up. His big belly tells me where the scraps go!" Feather turned around and started his quest for scraps.

Several people of the band scurried to make the Counsel Lodge ready to receive Walking Stick and his helpers. Two young women of the Fish People eyed two of the new helpers, obviously brothers. They had the exact same face shape, round eyes and long straight noses. They whispered to each other while looking the women's way.

Feather hid his treasure of scraps behind a lodge and went up to a trader boy. "I remember you. Walks Far, right? And who are you?" He pointed to a slightly bent over boy who was busy smiling at the two pretty girls.

"Bends Stooped Over." Without a look Feather's way, he went back to flirting.

Bright Sun Flower reached for Feather just as he was about to ask why the boy had such a name. "Some children should have been born with drawstrings on the sides of their mouths." Her low mumble did not escape nearby ears. "Come with me, Grandson."

"Grandmother, how come you are everywhere all at once? I never can be alone without you knowing right where I am!"

She grinned and put her hands on her hips.

He tilted his head and glared up at her. "Please let me feed the scraps of food to the trader's dogs first." He ran, grabbed the scraps, and fed grateful dogs while White Paws stayed at a distance.

The dogs gulped down the food and licked his hands. "Maybe White Paws will let you stay. I know it is wrong to take another's belongings, but you are not belongings! Walking Stick should treat you better, and should have to carry more than he does. Perhaps he will be missing a couple of you thinner ones when he leaves!" He looked around to see if anyone heard. "Grandmother has taught me that we are all Sacred beings, and should be treated as such."

He noted some of the dogs had sores on the upper parts of their hips where a strap had held the packs in place, and made a promise to himself to help them.

His grandmother pulled on his arm. "Feather, come help gather some extra robes to put down on the Counsel Lodge's floor." She raised her voice and sounded excited. "It would be a great honor to help get the Lodge ready!"

She pushed him in that direction, and behind them sharp words commanded the girls to get robes into the Lodge. He looked just as the girls fell backwards into the Lodge, each watching the young men instead of where they placed their feet.

Laughter echoed throughout the camp. Today would be a day for dancing, eating, and hearing new stories from other lands — some maybe not so true, but entertaining just the same.

***

Running River stood with Makes Baskets and watched the unloading. "You know, cousin, traders are well thought of and get much of what they want." She glanced sideways at her cousin. "Some fathers offer their daughters as mates, because the trader would become a relative and much would come from this relationship."

She meant it as a joke, but Makes Baskets mumbled not-so-nice words, turned around, and went in her parent's lodge and tied the flap shut.

***

So many people squeezed into the Counsel Lodge that children had to wait outside until the adults completed their business. They crowded as close to the wide open flaps as possible. Feather Floating In Water had slipped under the fold on the side of the Lodge.

He plopped into Hawk Soaring's lap, and White Paws poked his head through next to Bright Sun Flower and a grumbling Makes Baskets, whose mother had dragged her along by her arm to the Counsel Lodge. She scooted closer to her mother to make room for the wolf.

Chases Butterflies had undoubtedly seen Feather's act and mimicked him. Others did the same. Now the Lodge filled with the chatter and laughter of children who sat where they knew they should not. The adults, occupied by their own excitement, paid them no mind.

Bright Sun Flower fidgeted while she sat and waited for her turn. She wanted to ask about her sister, Song Bird, and her two new grandchildren, part of the Beaver People along the river nearly two days' walk away. Too many people in one place might damage the land, so Song Bird's band had gone toward the place Father Sun slept. The land was more open there. The Beaver People would watch for the great humped beasts, and then send runners to the Fish People, and they would have a good hunt together.

Her sister had stayed in the band of their birth, but Bright Sun Flower had followed Hawk Soaring when the bands split up.

For there being only twenty-two people in the band, the talk is taking too long! She shifted her knees, which hurt from the cramped quarters. *Ah, my turn to... no, not yet. Patience, I need patience.*

The young woman sitting next to her wanted to know what furs the trader brought, what new foods, what new plant dyes. Bright Sun Flower coughed to let the younger one know she talked about matters that concerned only her at this time, and she would find out when he opened his packs.

Amazing how many words a cough conveys.

The younger woman became silent while her mouth was still full of words. She sat with her hands in her lap, looked down a bit embarrassed, and played with the fringe on her boots.

"Why, Bright Sun Flower, how are you this fine day?" Walking Stick looked at her but for a moment, then stared at Makes Baskets.

This was not lost on the many people in the Lodge.

She ignored the stares. Small talk was not what she wanted, but it was expected. "I do well, Walking Stick. Thank you for asking. I would be honored if you came to our lodge for the evening meal."

She really did not care for him, but as an elder, everyone expected her to make the first invitation. She knew he had a woman in every camp he graced with his presence, and his eyes this day were on her only daughter, who managed to scoot behind her, out of his view.

"Yes, of course I would be honored to spend my first evening at your fireside. I am sure my helpers will find others who will welcome them as you have welcomed me." His crooked nose made his smile more of a jeer. "What have you to ask of me?"

He surely knew already but wanted her to ask, as the others also must ask, out of courtesy.

A chill rose on her arms as her daughter cleared her throat a bit too loud, sank deeper into her shadow, and lifted the lodge's flap. "Ah, I want to know how my sister, Song Bird, and her grandchildren fare. Her son in the joining, as I remember, said he was going to stay with my sister's band."

Makes Baskets made matters worse for her mother's knees by pressing from behind and scooting out under the hide to escape the trader's gaze.

Walking Stick noted her attempt, but answered Bright Sun Flower. "Your kind sister asked after you and yours this summer last, while I stayed with her and her man in their lodge."

"Your sister does well and loves caring for the new baby—a boy, I think. She thought she would never hold a grandson after two girls." He smiled and looked Running River's way.

She had two daughters already and a new roundness in her belly. If he knew of her true feelings, and how she had often teased Makes Baskets of his desire for her, he might not be so kind toward Running River.

He returned to the conversation. "Your sister sent you a small gift of green quills, and even some rare blue ones she traded for from me when I saw her last. She asks after your daughter, wanting to know if she had taken another man yet. I briefly saw her next to you, alone. I take that to mean no?"

Bright Sun Flower gritted her teeth, but sweetly smiled and looked Bear Tracks' way, who sat next to the trader. "Well, not yet, but I expect soon."

The look on Walking Stick's face told her she had gotten one up on him.

"I have no more questions, and must leave now to prepare a good meal for you."

Hawk Soaring stood with her, explaining that he must go hunting if they were to have enough food for everyone, since his woman had also invited Bear Tracks for tonight. Grandmother, grandfather and grandson all lifted up the bottom of the Lodge instead of making their way around everyone.

Hawk Soaring shook his head as they exited. "The sooner the better! Poor Bear Tracks is stuck where he is, since the Holy Man is the last to leave important gatherings."

***

Bear Tracks looked up in surprise at the trio's quick getaway, but regained his Holy Man composure.

He would be at their evening meal to give Makes Baskets her bone choker with the bright blue sky beads, for which he had asked Walking Stick's son, Walks Far, over two summers ago. Now, he was sure the trader knew why he had asked for the pair of chokers. No one else knew but his grandmother, now sitting next to her man at a campfire in the sky.

He felt a bit brazen after the last conversation, and by right could do as he pleased, so he got up to leave... but had to turn around and stare at the trader.

Walking Stick's mouth dropped open, but he began telling one of his traveling stories to the others, about his encounter with a mother grizzly and her three young ones—how he saved his helpers by acting as bait.

Satisfied, Bear Tracks turned and left, but he could not help but choke on his smothered laughter when the flap to the entrance dropped.

He looked for Makes Baskets and noticed the flap to their lodge tied shut. He would wait for her parents to head to their lodge, and follow them before the trader could.

The air smelled of Sister Wind's promise of a late cold season, which drifted by him in tiny flakes. He wondered if it would be enough to make the trader settle in.

I must act fast.

Chapter 9

After his hasty departure from the Counsel Lodge, Bear Tracks searched for Walks Far. Annoyed that the young man had not been at the Counsel Lodge to help his father unload, he stomped around the camp calling his name.

From behind a large boulder that the women used to lay fresh hides on, soft laughter stopped him from embarrassing himself and the hidden couple.

"This is Bear Tracks and I seek Walks Far."

Walks Far and his female companion became silent. Bear Tracks heard the woman wrap herself in a hide, and watched her drag her clothes behind her in a hasty retreat into the canyon.

A cherry-faced young man cleared his throat. His head rose above the boulder. "I... I am Walks Far, Holy Man. I... we were just getting to know each other before we asked... um... before I *told* my father that I had taken a mate."

Bear Tracks stood with his fists on his hips.

He tried to act bold and spoke in a strong voice. "My father took the chokers when he found out they were for you. I made them to match, as you asked. I spent much time on each choker—most of the winter, as time allowed me. They are the best chokers I have made, meant for a great man." He realized his boasting was shameful and lowered his head. "I hope they please you as they pleased me to create. Had I found more time, they would have been even more suited for a Holy Man."

"Look at me, young man who now has a mate." Bear Tracks waited for him to look up. "Walks Far, you do not need to brag to make me feel you have done your best. I picked you knowing your skill. Humble yourself, and your life will be a good one. Boast and you will be too busy trying to live up to your boasts to find real joy. Now go find your mate and bring her to camp. We will have a joining."

Walks Far turned and raced into the canyon as fast as Sister Wind could push loose, dry snow from the ground.

Bear Tracks thought of his own desire for a joining, how sweet the night would be and.... Behind him, Walking Stick's high pitched, nasal voice resounded, and he spun around at the annoyance.

"I have the chokers, Holy Man."

He cringed at the leer that exposed the aging man's cracked and yellowed teeth. Walking Stick's narrowed eyes stared at Makes Baskets' lodge, and Bear Tracks frowned. He knew the trader's mind, had followed his eyes earlier as they had traced over Makes Baskets' slender build. He knew that even if the trader's eyes could not see her now, his mind did.

Walking Stick handed the chokers to Bear Tracks without bargaining, showing his weakness. Traders had to keep a straight face to get the best of people, but this one lusted for women, and it affected his judgment. If Bear Tracks wanted, he needed only to speak up and Makes Baskets would be his, but he wanted her to desire him. The Holy Man had Power, which he would use to prevent Walking Stick from taking Makes Baskets, but he needed to make his move first.

He left the trader behind and headed directly to Makes Baskets' lodge, and scratched at the flap.

"Who disturbs my sleep?"

"Woman, it is me, Bear Tracks. I have something I wish to give you. Please let me in." He had not intended to sound so desperate.

She opened the ties and poked her head out. "What do you want of me?"

He held up the beautiful choker.

She gasped. "For me? Why would you give me such a wonderful gift?"

She reached out and touched the choker, and he let go of it. She had to tighten her grip before it fell to the ground. She inhaled the chilly air, looked into his eyes, and smiled.

Bear Tracks grinned back. "I... I um."

Stupid, say something! My hands tremble. She is looking at them. What must she think?

"I had this made for you, and... I have one too, made to match. I hope you will accept this gift from me. I wanted so much to please you."

Now, why did I say that?

"Bear Tracks, never have I seen such detail. Each bead matches, and the bone beads between them are exact so everything lines up." She climbed out of the lodge and stood straight and tall. Her chin relaxed as she giggled. "Please put this on me?"

His fingers fumbled as he tied the leather strap around her neck. Never before had his hands touched her. "Makes Baskets, I want to ask—"

"Oh, here comes my mother. I must give her these robes for the Counsel Lodge."

Her smile made him tremble, and his tongue tripped over his words. "Um, yes, help you must her. I must get go ready—must go get ready to...."

Bright Sun Flower grinned at him and turned to Makes Baskets. "Why, Daughter, what is this fine gift I see around your neck?"

"The gift is from Bear Tracks. I have no idea why he would do this." Her face blushed and she lowered her head.

"I need to go." Bear Tracks spun around and darted off before either woman could say anything else.

He picked up his pace and walked past the trader with purpose, and without even a glance his way.

Chapter 10

The small fire crackled just outside the center of the lodge. Stones edged the pit, dug one foot deep and one foot across, to radiate warmth. This also helped direct the smoke up and out through the open flaps at the top of the lodge. Hides hung on the inside for extra warmth and thinner hides, sewn together and stuffed with grasses, padded the hard ground.

Bear Tracks sat next to Hawk Soaring and watched as the women and Feather Floating In Water sorted the quills. He had no desire to help. The last time he did, he was a boy and he poked himself more often than he wanted to remember. He could not take his eyes off Makes Baskets' fire-lit face.

So soft looking, so touchable.

He clenched his hands and rested them on his lap. Sorting quills was boring work, but he acted interested anyway. The women and Feather sat on a tightly woven matte covered in a thin hide, which caught any rogue quills.

White Paws stretched out behind them, away from the heat of the fire and the sting of sharp quills. He normally slept outside in front of the lodge, but this day he took his place inside, as any pack member would when company was present. He showed his distaste for the quills by moaning when the women laid them too close to his paws.

Hawk Soaring turned to Bear Tracks and said, "The chokers you traded your points for are beautiful, Holy Man. Anyone would see it as an honor to have even one of your points, and yet you traded Walks Far ten for the chokers. My daughter's looks perfect for her slender neck."

Hawk Soaring now looked toward the trader. "The sky beads are just like the ones I brought back for Bright Sun Flower years ago, after a hunting trip down in the hot lands."

Feather looked up and smiled at his grandfather. "Grandmother told me the story of how the sky beads were once part of the sky, and they fell when Creator made that part of the land into the still hot rocks, and were caught as the rocks cooled. She told me the Peoples down there dig them out of the rock and shape them and then make them into beads."

The boy sat taller and looked at Walking Stick. "My grandmother loves hers. She told me she was proud to wear them. Grandfather must love her very much to give her such a fine gift, and now Bear Tracks and my mother both wear the same beads." He turned to his mother and smiled. "Mother, does Bear Tracks love you?"

Makes Baskets choked on her son's words and seemed particularly occupied sorting the larger quills out of the pile. She absently reached up and touched her choker. The sky beads, carefully shaped to match one another, alternated with the bone beads, each the size of a child's small finger, to create four layers. A leather strip, with holes to guide the beads through, connected the layers. Elk's teeth hung around the four lower-middle bones. Some warriors wore these not just as decoration, but also as protection from arrows that might pierce their necks.

Over two cycles of seasons ago, Bear Tracks had seen one of the trader's helpers wearing the sky beads, and had offered to trade some obsidian arrow points for a pair.

He had seen their exactness; many hours had gone into making them. He had insisted the trader's helper match them perfectly, or he would not trade his arrow points, which the trader's helper dearly wanted. They would give the helper status in his "leader's" eyes because obsidian was difficult to come by, as none existed in the canyons, and they had to trade for it several moons from here. It was well worth it, for while the available flint made fine arrows, they were not as sharp as the obsidian ones.

"Such great skill went into these chokers." Bear Tracks admired the choker that graced Makes Baskets' neck in the glowing firelight, waiting for her to look up.

Instead, she continued sorting quills.

Walking Stick cleared his throat and spoke too loudly. "Several men of other bands had mentioned your daughter would be a fine catch, especially since I bragged on not only her talent, but also her beauty."

Hawk Soaring glared at the trader.

Bear Tracks did not appreciate it much himself. Each of the "helpers" looked too much like the trader, and the Holy Man knew none of them had the same mother — he had shamelessly asked them.

This man knows nothing but greed. His anger showed only to Walking Stick.

Bear Tracks watched the women and Feather separate the quills as if nothing could be of more interest. He and Feather had brought extra fish for Bright Sun Flower to sprinkle with herbs. She had wrapped them in the wide slender leaves of the swamp plant to keep the juices in while they roasted over the coals. He wrinkled his nose as the food outside began to burn, but no one else cared to notice.

He cared nothing for the food he smelled. *Let it burn.*

He longed to hold Makes Baskets in his arms. He wanted so much to smell her hair and touch her skin. He worried she might look a certain man's way, and now he worried the trader might want to walk with her in the canyon later. He needed to escape his anxious mind and make talk.

Hard as he tried, Bear Tracks could not get Makes Baskets, absorbed in her task as if nothing else mattered, to look his way. She pricked her finger, shook it, and whispered angry words. She caught him eyeing her and whispered something shyly to her mother, who let out a small laugh behind her hand.

Heat rushed to his face. *What else does she want? I feel like a small boy who has affection for the first love of his life. She makes me feel shy. Me! The Holy Man of the band should never have to ask for a woman's attention, yet here I am acting as if I have no say. I do not have to ask, nor offer anything, yet I would give all I had....*

He took in a deep frustrated breath, and his heart's desire gave him another quick glance as she shifted her legs.

Many Holy People choose to live alone, but I desire this woman, and have for too long.

He looked down at his calloused hands, wishing they were softer for when their hands would first touch — if they did touch. He dared another glance her way.

What is on her mind? Me? Surely not that... that... Walking Stick! He is old and cruel to his sons. Even Feather noticed how he cared for his dogs. He cannot be in the Spirit's favor.

He fumed as Walking Stick shamelessly stared right at her.

She placed Feather above all else, but had also looked out for her parents, putting them above any new joining.

He would care for them as he had his grandmother. He had loved her, and had stayed home many times instead of going on walks to hunt days away, as he should have.

He grinned at a memory of many seasons ago. Hawk Soaring had saved a frightened boy of ten winters from an angry humpback mother whose bawling calf ran to her side, when a not-so-brave boy held a wobbly spear and screamed his lungs out. The elder man had never told anyone their future Holy Man made water down the front his breechclout while both his legs shook.

He showed me respect when I could have ended up the joke of the band. I care for both Hawk Soaring and Bright Sun Flower, who took time to teach me the plants. My own mother and aunt crossed over before they could teach me, as did my father. They show me they care by allowing me so near their daughter.

Their daughter....

This time, Bear Tracks tried to smile directly into Makes Baskets' eyes, instead of looking down as custom dictated. "Maybe the trader will come this way again with more sky beads to honor a new couple. Perhaps enough beads to make a choker for their son... if they have one."

Bear Tracks looked at an unusually quiet Feather, who leaned back and scratched White Paws' ears. He shared a quick glance with the boy's grandmother, then stared back at the boy and his wolf.

Frustrated at Makes Baskets' silence, he could think of nothing to say that would define his respect for her. He wanted to scream out his love for her, for all to hear. In his mind, he did just that, but she did not look up. He watched her every movement while she continued to sort the quills. He had no interest in the quills, but in the slender woman who sorted them.

He needed to hear words. Normally, when Walking Stick arrived there was never silence. "Maybe the trader will tell all of us about his trading in strange lands, and people he met along the way. I hear of other Peoples' unusual way of dress, and of the stories they pass along to people who come their way. I am sure we are all interested, as we only see the trader every couple cycles of seasons."

Walking Stick raised his upper lip until it touched the tip of his long nose, giving him the look of a hungry vulture. His hair, still tied into a tight bun on top of his head, did not help his appearance.

The trader briefly closed his eyes, then smiled and looked at him. "Ah yes, so many stories of places some think my mind only makes up. Big waters with huge fish, so large they could toss a fishing boat with their tail. Strange creatures with hard shells that cover their entire bodies — even their legs — and with cupped-like clawed hands."

Walking Stick showed what he meant with his own fingers pulled together, and licked his lips. "So good to eat."

Feather's eyes widened. "I would like to see a fish that big. He would feed the whole band all winter! Maybe you will take me and show me? I would catch one and bring it home. Everyone would be so happy and we would have a celebration in my honor, and I would have great respect among the People, and the girls would smile at me! I am past nine winters old now and could be of great help. I could go with you on your next trip." His last words were more of a question to his mother than a remark to the trader.

Makes Baskets never looked up from her task. "When you have lived one hundred winters, then I will allow you to go." Her firm voice ended discussion of the would-be little fisherman leaving for any such faraway place. "Besides, you turned nine winters only a few moons ago."

Bear Tracks looked down and grinned. The boy was suddenly interested in sorting quill sizes for his mother and grandmother again. Both women looked over the boy's head with silent smiles.

Bright Sun Flower leaned over and added another small branch to the fire, and opened up the flap for better lighting. "Not one complaint about it being cold. That is why I added more wood. We busy ones in here need more light."

She looked up with furrowed brows, waiting for any complaint, and turned to Walking Stick. "It will take most of the cold season to work these quills in perfectly. I need to get the water boiling for the dried plants we picked for dying the quills."

She shifted her weight as if to stand. "I need to check on the food. I am sure it is fine. I only smell the swamp plant leaves burning."

"Mother, no need to stress your knees. I will go to the river to get water." Makes Baskets was out the flap before her mother could even get a hand under herself to offer help.

Bear Tracks stretched his arms above his head and yawned. "Perhaps I shall wake myself up with a walk. It is not so cold today."

He grabbed his robe and mittens, pulled back the flap, and headed in the same direction Makes Baskets had walked.

***

Bright Sun Flower smiled, but then looked at the trader again.
Walking Stick sat with his mouth agape. He cleared his throat and sat

tall. "Hawk Soaring. I wish to ask you about your beautiful daughter. Since she is alone and getting older, I would be happy to take her as my woman and—"

She no longer cared about being courteous to the vulture in her lodge. "Never in all my life have I heard such terrible talk about my young daughter. She is not some old dog who now sits in the shade doing nothing! She works hard. She cares for us by doing extra work, making baskets everyone wants, fishing, hunting for tubers, making our parkas and boots every winter. She is too good for you!"

Bright Sun Flower's face burned with the fire in her heart, and her voice, she knew, carried farther than their lodge. She no longer cared. He spoke of their daughter as if she were a piece of worn leather. "Everyone knows your helpers are your sons, and not one of them has the same mother. Do you ever see your women more than but a few times?"

Hawk Soaring laughed. He looked around, perhaps thinking to take back his outburst, and laughed even harder.

Walking Stick, clearly embarrassed by a mere woman's words, and the laughter he knew to be an insult, stomped out of the lodge, knocking over the cooking fish on the way. "I have the right!" He stopped in the middle of camp and stared at anyone who dared look his way. "If I want a woman, she should be mine. Perhaps no one in this... this disrespectful band wishes to hear news of relatives, or to trade for things they would not get if I chose to go around this horrid place. I only want the woman. The child is not my concern. He may stay with his mouthy grandmother."

He walked toward the water where Makes Baskets had gone, but glanced back at the sound of grunting. Three heads tried to poke out the open flap at the same time. White Paws pushed his way through them, and humans and Wolf all spilled out at once. Bright Sun Flower tried not to laugh, but could not hold back.

Bear Tracks looked back at all the commotion. His face's scar reddened and his eyes narrowed. Even Walking Stick could see the change from where he stood. Bear Tracks took a step in the direction of the trader.

"Break his—"

Bright Sun Flower clasped a hand over Feather's mouth before he could finish yelling.

***

Bear Tracks smiled inwardly at Feather's stifled command.

Walking Stick shuffled backwards after hearing the boy shout to the Holy Man, and tripped over a log used for sitting. He landed on his back in a pile of discarded quills destined for a fire pit.

The scream that turned everyone's heads was not Walking Stick's, but Makes Baskets'. He turned to see that she had lost her footing on the water's icy edge when she leaned forward to fill the water bladder.

He darted for the water and zipped past Running River, who had just bent over to grab for her cousin. He reached out first to the struggling Makes Baskets.

He smiled. *The trader knows he has lost any chance to woo Makes Baskets.* Now I can.... "Woman, let me help you. Do not struggle so."

He tried to look stern but could not help but grin. He grabbed her so only her boots suffered the wet and cold, held her up to his face, and looked into her defiant eyes.

She held her tight chin high and looked above the man's face.

She shakes, but is it from the cold?

"Can you not see with the eyes of your heart that I want you?" He squeezed her shoulders and held her so she could not look away. "Am I so bad to look at? Do I have warts on my nose? Are my teeth crooked and yellow, as another's we both know? Did I ever do anything to anger you? Why... why do you not relax in my arms?"

He lost himself in her face — so pleasing, round, willful — with bright eyes that captured his. A small nose enhanced her well-formed lips and stubborn square jaw. Half her face hid beneath long hair. Her mind belonged to her, but her heart would be his.

***

Makes Baskets, unable — maybe unwilling — to get away, softened in his arms and, for the first time, stared into his bold, dark eyes. She found gentleness in them. His outer shell was for show, so the people would think him fearless and powerful, perhaps someone to fear.

She smiled. He *was* good to look at. The soft lines on his face told secrets only a mate would understand. Like stardust on a still night, tiny hints of white sparkled in his loose hair. Her hands disobeyed her mind and her fingers gently ran through his soft hair. Her finger traced his jagged scar from his cheek down to his lips. The stone center of her heart crumbled. She exchanged a searching gaze, felt the pull of two rivers colliding and becoming one strong current. She closed her eyes and felt a warm mix of compassion and wonder — long-forgotten emotions.

Taken out of the trance, she pulled back. "But, Bear Tracks, what of my parents? I cannot leave them. They have no one who will care for them as they age — "

A warm mitten brushed across her mouth, and the Holy Man lowered her to the ground. He turned partway from her, but held her gently within his grasp, and spoke for all to hear.

"I, Bear Tracks, take this woman and her son to be my family. And I take her parents to live in our lodge if they choose, now and forever." He added with a cocky grin, "And that wolf."

Makes Baskets needed to hear no more words to convince her, and she surrendered her body into his arms. *Strange, I feel raindrops on my face.*

She remembered the promise made to her son about the first rain, but this was just the beginning season of newborn animals, and snow still fell.

Behind Bear Tracks floated a white and grey mist. A young woman stepped out of it and smiled. Her hair, dark as chokecherries, hung down to her knees.

The woman's soft voice whispered through Makes Baskets' mind. *"Tell your son, sometimes love cannot wait for the first rain of spring. And tell him he is the one. He will understand. Your life and that of your new man's will be long and fruitful."* Turtle Dove smiled and faded with her final whisper, "Children...."

Bear Tracks stared into his new woman's eyes. "Feather Floating In Water has gifts from both women in his life. Yes, my woman, I heard my mother's Spirit whisper to you. She also told me you have gifts you have not discovered. We are all born with them, but it is our choice to use them."

She relaxed her jaw.

"I will teach you, if you will allow me. Soon your parents will hear the laughter of another child."

He picked her up and she wrapped her arms around her man.

He made his way toward the surprised trader, who tried in vein to reach his painful quill-embedded back with clawed fingers.

The soft laughter of an unseen Spirit woman helped him to find new speed, and the trader disappeared into the canyon.

Everyone in the band looked down for wood, which did not exist so close to the camp, and picked up tiny twigs that offered little use in campfires—anything to divert their eyes. Ordinarily, no one showed that kind of affection out in the open, but who was going to say anything to the Holy Man?

***

Two small girls made their way to Bear Tracks' lodge, where they poked their heads through the flap. A panicked Running River ran to scoop them up as a growl and laughter echoed from within. She grabbed her two squealing girls and ran for her own lodge. Inside, her man bent over from laughter and fell onto his side.

She dropped one girl on either side of him, onto the thick bundles of furs. "You wanted girls, now you have them. I am going to visit my uncle, who will groan when I tell him I carry another one of your children in my belly, if he has not seen it yet!"

Running River turned, leaving a very surprised man trying to hold down two little daughters who wanted to follow.

Sees Like Eagle gulped air. "A child in your belly? I thought you only put on.... So you did not use the herbs to prevent another?"

Running River smiled as she stomped off. She could have taken birth control herbs, but she had chosen not to because she wanted her man, who had no blood relations, to have children of his own blood—so long as they could care for them.

Chapter 11

Bright Sun Flower made the joining between her daughter and Bear Tracks. She smiled with a feeling of serenity. Father Sun decided to offer warmth to the day. "Listen well, band of Fish Peoples. Today we make prayers and song for two who make this day special with their joining."

She waited for Feather to hand her a quilled leather tie, and admired her daughter's joining dress, which she had secretly made. She had decorated the nearly white dress with tied elk teeth from the shoulders down to the breasts, where she had added bright blue quills made to look like the sky. A belt of white leather and dangling teeth draped the waist. She had created a carpet of grass around the bottom of the dress with green quills, and used bright yellow quills for flowers, which danced in the grass and reached toward the warmth of Father Sun through a pair of orange- and red-quilled hands, crossed over each other to signify the joining.

The barefooted Makes Baskets' ankles tinkled softly with a string of small bird bones, which Bright Sun Flower had gathered over three cycles of seasons.

Tiny grey and white feathers, made into matching headbands, graced the couple's heads. Bear Tracks' chest was naked save for the bear claws around his neck. His grandmother had created his leggings in hopeful anticipation years before. She had skillfully quilled a bright yellow sun above wavy water signs, signifying the band's chosen name, and bright green quills shooting upward with tiny yellow flowers.

The fine detail impressed Bright Sun Flower. *Her choices and mine look a lot like the others. I am glad we both had the same ideas. I do wonder how she knew. Odd, but rain falls softly now, not snow.*

Feather Floating In Water nudged her. She took the tie from his hands, and as she did, a white, cloudy mist appeared behind the couple. *Ah, my old friend... you have been here waiting. Wait no longer. Your grandson and my daughter are about to be united in life.*

"I, Bright Sun Flower, take over this day for Bear Tracks as a Holy Woman of the Fish People. I offer this tie and wrap it around these two people, who will be forever united in life. I cannot tell them what to do after this life is over, but in this life, may you bring forth children to strengthen this band, and to create great harmony for not just the band, but for your lives as well."

As she spoke, a wolf pressed his way through the crowd. He carried a live rabbit in his mouth, and sat the startled creature in front of the couple.

Bear Tracks picked up the half-grown rabbit and held him closely. "Thank you, White Paws, for such a gift. A live rabbit, as we all know, means fertility." He laughed. "That you know this shows me we are kin."

The band nodded in agreement. Still holding the gift and still tied together, Bear Tracks and Makes Baskets entered their lodge.

The band sang and danced until Father Sun set, and beyond. The newly joined pair did not join in the festivities. Rabbit sat at the entrance of their lodge, unafraid of the wolf that followed a dancing boy.

Chapter 12

Feather Floating In Water and White Paws wandered the canyons farther from the camp. Now past ten winters, Feather had more freedom to explore. It gave him time to himself, time with his wolf, and time to walk off the dreams that would not go away.

A cycle of seasons has passed since Mother's joining, and I still see the old ones in my head. I am still a boy! What do they want me to do? What can I do? I hear their drums beating the same rhythm as my heart, and at night I hear them chanting... but what? The one word I understand is 'fear.'

He shook his head, trying to get the sound to go away.

The thawing snow left most of the red and orange stone of the canyons exposed. Birds chirped in hopes of locating a mate. Evergreen plants glistened with sparkling ice crystals that shimmered rainbow colors, and showed off tiny leaf buds trying to break free to greet Father Sun. The small frozen stream made walking a bit slippery, so Feather grabbed hold of stones that jutted out of the canyon wall. The still, blue sky remained cloudless for another day, and in the distance, the call of one Eagle echoed the call of another.

Boy and Wolf reached the end of the narrow ravine, and were about to turn back when Feather saw an odd-looking stone jutting out of the snow. The mixture of browns and off-whites were not the normal colors found in the stone. He tried to brush off what he thought was snow, but the white covering was part of the stone.

"White Paws, come and see what I have found!"

He swept the snow off the narrow wall around the stone to get a better look, and tried to pull the wedged-in stone free. Not to be beaten by a mere stone, he pulled and pulled until he landed on his backside with the stone in hand.

White Paws jumped on top of him, whined and cocked his head, as if wondering why the silly boy was lying in the snow. Feather could not hold his laughter at the wolf's odd behavior, or at the happy tongue that made his face wet.

"I am all right, silly! I just fell backwards, and I still have my breath." He rolled over and tried to grab one of the wolf's paws.

White Paws jumped up and raced off, expecting a good chase.

Feather granted his wish and dashed after him with the strange stone in his right hand. He giggled until he had to stop.

"I am out of air! White Paws, slow down." He bent over and grabbed his knees.

The wolf curved back around him, ran straight for the stone, ripped it from his hand, and took off with it down another canyon path that led to the camp.

"Wait, I only have two legs! You have four! No fair." Feather ran after the playful wolf, who tore through the camp and ran directly into his grandparents' lodge.

***

Hawk Soaring hollered, "Hey, you Wolf! What have you brought into this lodge? I finally get to nestle deep in my robes, happy for the quiet! Bright Sun Flower took her chatter to our daughter's new home. Why do I tell you this, White Paws? You cannot understand."

He sat up, yawned, and tossed some small pieces of wood in the fire pit for warmth and light. He had just enough time to protect himself with his robe before an excited boy's voice grew closer.

An out-of-breath Feather crash-landed on top of a now wide-awake old man.

"Grandfather, good, I was worried I would wake you. I see Grandmother is still gone. Did you get enough sleep? White Paws took a strange looking stone from me that I found, and he ran away with it, so I chased him to get it back, but he tricked me and ran in here and—"

"Feather, slow down! Your tongue will fall out of your mouth and then you will not be able to taste food." Hawk Soaring rubbed his eyes and wished they were still closed, with him blissfully asleep.

Feather reached into his mouth to touch his tongue. "I am not so young anymore. I know better now. You tease!"

Hawk Soaring sat up and coughed. His belly ached from laughing. He tugged at the exposed hair sticking out of his grandson's furred hood. "You grow too fast. Soon I will not be able to tease you. Show me this stone I was nearly knocked in the head with. It must be special for White Paws to take it from you and bring it here. He must have known its worth. How that wolf knows things amazes me."

To the bewilderment of both humans, White Paws dropped the stone in front of Hawk Soaring, and went outside to lie on his robe. He stretched out and yawned as if nothing important had happened this day.

"He seems to teach you things I cannot. Let me add some more wood pieces to the fire so I can see better this interesting stone that has stolen my sleep."

He held the stone up to the firelight, and could see it was not a stone.

"Oh my, this is a find! Feather, this is no stone. It is an ancient bone, much older than even our own people who have wandered this land for longer than I can remember."

He leaned closer to the light of the fire so his grandson could see it better.

"Look closely. See the shape of this? You have found part of a jaw that still has two teeth. They do not look like teeth but they are." He paused to think back many winters. "When I was a boy, I too found such a bone. My father made me put it back, saying it was not right to take it. Like our ancestors, we do not disturb their bones. It would upset them. But for today, this bone will be with us."

He rubbed it with some Sage he always kept by the fire. "This will help the bone to understand I have purified it in a respectful manner. Run outside and tell your new father to make ready the Counsel Lodge. We must share this story with everyone."

No more sleep would find him this day.

***

They kept the Counsel Lodge ready for ceremonies, advisers, and visitors when the gatherings came to their camp. In winter, the band's elders would bring the children together to tell stories, and unless it was too cold, they would sit outside the entrance.

Inside, the small band gathered: sixteen adults, eight children, and one wolf. Running River sat next to Makes Baskets, and Hawk Soaring heard her say something about wishing her cousin many more children, one for every finger she had. He watched as his niece rocked her new daughter.

He stood up and asked for silence. All eyes went to him; not even a whisper to disrespect him. From a very early age, adults taught children to be still when an elder stood to gain attention.

"I have a story to tell that everyone will want to hear, one that will be repeated to small children some day."

Hawk Soaring cleared his throat, held up the bone, and turned around in a circle so everyone could see it. The center fire cast light upon it, though no one had any idea what it was.

"A long time ago, when I was a small boy, younger than Feather Floating In Water, I found what I thought was an odd stone, long as a child's arm with a knob on each end. I took it to my father, whose eyes grew big at my find. He made me show him where I found it. Because of the look on his face, I feared big trouble, but he laughed and said someday I might pass on his story.

"This is what I do today." He held the partial jaw higher.

"This odd-colored stone is not a stone, but a bone of a creature from very long ago—just as the one I found. My father said mine was part of a tail from some large creature."

Low whispers and quiet laughter filled the lodge. Bear Tracks started to stand, but Hawk Soaring motioned to him to sit. He would handle the disbelief himself.

"I speak only the truth. What would I have to gain by a joke?"

Hawk Soaring continued. "I will pass this around so all can judge for themselves. You will see two teeth still in the back part of the jaw. As everyone looks at it, I will continue to speak. You can see how old it is. My father told me the one I found was older than even the first human. He could not say why they no longer walked on our Mother but, as for me, I am glad they do not. They must have had a very big appetite, and I would bet, as we like the taste of rabbit, they would have liked the taste of us."

Everyone laughed this time.

"We must honor this creature as we do our own in their time of passing, and put the bone back. No Spirit likes to have his or her body moved from their resting place, whether by nature or a loved one. It would be wrong to keep this. I say this so you will not forget if you someday come upon a body of any kind. Always pass with honor in your heart, and never take anything, not even a necklace. It belongs to that grandfather or grandmother. Even in the Spirit world, they wear their decorations. We may see them, but the Spirits of those things are on the other side."

He smiled. "I cannot, for all I am worth, understand why anyone would dig up a body and take it away for any reason."

Others joined in his laughter and shook their heads in the wonderment.

"Who would do such a thing? Dig up a human or creature just to look at it? Those bones were there from a time so long ago, only Creator knows who they were, as it should be.

"Think about our grandparents' grandparents. We may have forgotten their names, but their blood still flows in all of us, and we must treat them as we would want to be treated. This is a good lesson to teach our children, so they can teach it to theirs.

"This is why I asked that all of you come to hear my story. I ask everyone old enough to remember what I have told here this day to pass on my words.

"When Father Sun wakes in the morning, we will all go to where the rest of this creature rests, and sing him back to Creator, so he will know he is respected. This is all I have to say."

He turned to Feather Floating In Water. "When everyone has had a chance to see the jaw, give it to Bear Tracks so he can cleanse it with herbs, to prepare the bone for the journey back."

He walked outside the lodge and looked up into the beautiful clear sky. "Thank you, Father, for what you taught me." He smiled and headed back to his own lodge.

Bright Sun Flower followed close behind him. "My man has the wisdom of Creator. This is a good thing that you did, sharing Feather's find with the whole band. Now this story will be passed to Feather's children and beyond."

His woman stopped before their lodge and stared at him with misted eyes. "I have always loved you, old man, even when we were children. I told my aunt I would belong with you someday. Of course, she laughed, but I knew then you were special. I could feel it in my heart. You have much wisdom."

They climbed inside and sealed the flap, signaling they did not wish to be disturbed. Age could not take away her beauty. Her eyes still shone with vibrant life and her lips were still firm, with very few lines flowing up to her full, high cheekbones.

She smiled again, and he could no longer contain himself. He reached out and pulled her to his own body. Theirs was a love time could never steal. Even when they crossed into the next life, they would still hold each other close.

They stretched out on their robes and embraced each other. For them, this day had ended, and not until Father Sun rose again would anyone see them.

Chapter 13

Bright Sun Flower pulled her robe tighter. The wind picked up and cold rain bounced off it. Her silver-black hair flew into her face, and with a withered hand, she brushed it away.

The cold season nears its end, but Sister Wind has forgotten. Plants already grown must survive this unusual mid-season blast. How is it that my daughter's joining day was warm and now flowers bend in the cold wind?

As she approached the Counsel Lodge, noise of excited children's laughter competed with Wind's own howling. She opened the flap, instantly embraced by the warmth of the fire's heat, and smiled. She scooted toward to her spot just off-center in the back, to keep everyone in sight as she spoke her stories. Fur-lined, booted feet moved away to make sure their storyteller did not trip.

She laughed along with the giggling children and looked for her family. Feather poked Chases Butterflies in the ribs, and Makes Baskets and Running River tried to separate the pair. Her grandson obviously loved making his cousin squeal and squirm; no matter how many times he was told to settle down, he had to do it just one more time. White Paws lay next to Feather with a dejected expression, as if waiting for some attention from the leaping boy.

Now, when another wolf howls, he slips out at night. While pretending to sleep, I have watched Feather follow. I do wonder where they go — White Paws to his mate, and Feather? After their wanderings, he comes home alone in the low light, with misty faraway eyes. I heard him cry out in his sleep for the first time in moons. I had hoped it had ended until he was older. Yet now, he acts like any other ten-winters-old boy.

She longed to ask him, but knew he would not share himself until he was ready.

Antics within the Lodge gave people a chance to work off their restlessness. Today was no different. Hawk Soaring's nearly toothless grin gave away his thoughts of the wrestling pair. He got Feather's attention by reaching over and gently twisting his grandson's nose. The boy turned around and twisted his in return.

Bear Tracks tried to look stoic, failing miserably. He laughed at Running River's attempt to drag Chases Butterflies across her belly, to get her away from the rib-poking Feather Floating In Water. Too sorry, too late, Running River threw a glance the Holy Man's way that would make Bear himself turn tail.

Sees Like Eagle grabbed the little girl and snuggled her in his arms. All could tell he loved being a father, and even the testy Running River smiled at her man.

Bright Sun Flower grinned at all the silly behavior and deeply inhaled all the smells within the lodge: smoked leather, the sweet smell of burning Sage mixed with the scent of Rosemary, left by a trader for them to enjoy as a medicinal gift, and cooked food brought to still small children.

All fell quiet when the storyteller took off her robe and let it fall behind her. This day she wore a beautiful garden of quilled yellow, white and orange flowers on the top of her dress, and their green leaves made their way down past her waist.

"This special dress made by my daughter," Bright Sun Flower said, "is to celebrate the beginning of my fifty-seventh winter. I am so honored that I wanted all to see her handiwork is not just in making baskets." She stared Bear Tracks' way and made sure she made him blush.

Always, she acknowledged everyone in some sort of way. "Sees Like Eagle, you are such a wonderful father. Your daughters, I can see, love you very much, and Running River, you give this band reason to smile. You have the patience of Mother Fox when her young ones discover the world. Fox gets little time to herself, but she does not mind, knowing that she is raising the next generation of her kind. Such a beautiful name for your baby—Waterfall. Bear Tracks dreamed her name the very night she decided to join our band as the youngest."

Running River sat taller, prouder, and pulled her shoulders back, her daughter asleep in her arms now that Hawk Soaring had calmed Feather.

"I see many of our men and women have returned from a very successful hunt." She shook her head. "I will never understand why some bands do not include women in the hunt, as we do. I know it took three long, cold days to find the humpbacks' wandering herd, and many days to come back and get the younger people to help with all the work. I must thank all of you who helped. The grandfathers and grandmothers who stayed behind to watch over small children were just as important.

"The little ones brought much joy to the camp while their fathers and mothers were busy making this season a better one. Not a single person will go to bed with an empty belly! We owe this to everyone, for every single person made this possible. You were willing to do your part, share your skills, and assure all our families would benefit."

Everyone looked around the Counsel Lodge and acknowledged each other with nods and smiles.

"And these words are for Feather."

Feather stopped his nose games with his grandfather and raised his eyebrows at his grandmother.

"I know many of you see him leave with his wolf, and sometimes not return to camp until the cooking fires bring his nose back." She smiled at her grandson. "This boy is claiming his manhood faster than most. He dreams as his father does, as I do. Soon, he will pass us by in his Power. A time is coming when we will gather in this Lodge and hear his words, which will affect us all."

She stopped and gave her words a chance to open closed ears.

Many looked at each other and whispered, and some pointed his way, while the elders remained silent.

"I say this now so no one will be surprised when that time comes. When the weather warms and many of you go to see your relations in other camps, tell them my words. Tell them they are not just for the Fish Peoples, but for all, and we all must gather to hear him."

Feather blushed, pulled his legs up to his chest, and picked at the fur on the tops of his boots. He glanced down, reached for White Paws and buried his face in the wolf's fur.

His grandmother noted he was still unsure of himself. He would need to find his courage soon, and to say what his dreams have told him for over two cycles of seasons.

"I have a story to tell now. I remember it best as the cold season with little food. I was but a girl then, maybe nine or ten winters old. There was such promise of a good hunt that year.

"All the adults agreed to meet in the tall grasslands after hunters spotted countless humpbacks, with their now grown calves enjoying the rich offering of grass. As with every gathering, many came to see friends and relatives, and to trade. The hunt, a bonus, would feed many for the entire season. People came pulling empty drags, made of wood and grasses woven into ropes, to carry the anticipated bounty back home.

"Children scattered everywhere, and all the adults, even ones of other bands, made sure they were looked after and fed. Elders who had a hard time walking came on their own special traveling mats, covered on the bottom with thick leather, which people happily took turns pulling. Entire camps just pulled up and moved, knowing no one would disturb their chosen snow camps."

Bright Sun Flower breathed deep with the memory of being young, and looked around the Counsel Lodge to see if anyone might be uninterested in her story. All eyes were on her, waiting for her to continue. She cherished moments like these. All was well in their little band. No one was sick, every belly full, and all were warm and safe.

With a contented sigh, she continued. "A new band never before seen came with all their finery. Beautiful necklaces adorned every person, even the children. Some wore so many that no one could see them all, unless they walked up close. They wore fine tanned clothing of many colors of brown. Their quillwork, even from a distance, competed with Nature's own colors. Heavy packs on the men's backs meant they had much to trade — or so we thought."

All but her grandson watched her. She felt his mind and White Paws' join with each other as they wandered elsewhere. He took Bear Tracks' hand, and she knew they shared much emotion.

Is it a gift or curse to feel so much?

"We did not know these new people, but we welcomed them and gave them food. Their hair, adorned with many shells, hung loose over their backs. They wore footwear so decorated it seemed a shame to walk in them for as long as they did. Not a single person looked like they were in traveling clothes, but dressed as if for a special occasion. Our bands always traveled simple, saving their good clothes until the gathering.

"Our elders noticed one thing that bothered them greatly. There was not a single elder among those people. An elder woman from our band walked up to a woman with a child, and asked why the grandmother was not caring for her child. The woman's reply was not a kind one.

"'Why would she be doing that? She is too old to travel this far. It is a six-day walk. She is in our camp, where all the elders belong who cannot walk this far.'"

"Our elder replied, 'Ahh, then some of your band stayed behind to care for them. Too bad, all would have had a good time.'

"The young woman said, 'We left no one behind who could not care for themselves. They would have made the walk take longer. One of our runners came into camp and told of this great gathering he saw from afar, so we came to see. The elders can hunt—at least some of them can—until we come back.'

"Her words were sharp to our elder, who stood and watched as the younger woman dragged her child by the hand. The little girl had to run to keep up.

"The elder woman did not know what to do. Never had anyone spoken such harsh words to her. She started to walk after the woman, but her daughter gently guided her back and told her to let it go, that they were not of their band. The daughter comforted her mother and told her that maybe they were just tired. They would be friendlier after a night's rest.

"The next day was devoted to the hunt, and many men and women gathered their weapons and formed into groups. Each one had a special thing to do, and everyone waited for the men of the new band to join. None came. Not one person looked their way. Even after several of our own motioned them to join, they did not come. Instead, the new band, quickly gaining the name People With No Respect, sat in the shade eating food they did not bring. Our hunters left without them.

"After a successful hunt, all our bands joined in making meat, tanning hides, and carrying many loads to the place of the gathering. The People With No Respect offered no help.

"Their selfish manner, by the fifth sunrise, caused us concern. Many tried to trade for their beautiful necklaces, and offered their own, as well as much meat. The People With No Respect took everything offered to them, but gave nothing back. Some of them even spoke about wanting more meat to take back with them, saying we should give it to them just because they came so far.

"Many of our gathered bands did not want them around our children. After they took their playthings to share, the People With No Respect's children took and kept them. Their parents started to brag about all the land they said belonged to them, and everyone knows no one can own the land any more than they can own the air Wind brings.

"They showed off by changing their clothes every day, so everyone could see they had much in vanity, but nothing in humility. The heavy burdens they brought with them were not to trade with, but to prove how special they thought they were."

Bright Sun Flower paused when her grandson cleared his throat to gain attention.

His mind is back. I wish I knew where his thoughts took him. As hard as she tried, the part of the Circle he had wandered into remained closed to her. *I doubt even he knows how deep within he had been.*

Feather Floating In Water stood up to be seen. "Grandmother, why would such a People be so mean? How could they even survive if they did not care for their elders and children? How could they have so much, but have so little? They were rich in things, but they were poor as a People. Without sharing and being respectful and... and being so lazy! Where did they get so much when they gave nothing? Grandmother, I do not understand how this could be so."

White Paws jumped up and licked Feather's face, whining and wagging his tail.

The boy hugged the wolf and smiled at his constant shadow. "I am so happy to have such a caring family, and a caring band. How sad those children must have been."

He sat down and with one arm hugged White Paws, and with the other his grandfather. Hawk Soaring leaned over and hugged him back.

Everyone sat silent. Several children crawled into a parent's lap.

She watched as everyone hugged their children. "We are gifted to have had elders who taught us, Grandson."

Adults sat closer to each other and squeezed hands, an unusual display in front of others.

She started the story again. "Our own people began to argue about how to make them leave. This was not our way, but we had to do something soon. The elders decided, and told the strangers to carry as much meat as they could, instead of our just chasing them off.

"We did not want to do this. Many felt it was more than a bribe, but rewarding them for being disrespectful. Some said to give them the meat anyway, to get them to leave us. Seeing no other way, we gave them the meat and told them the gathering was over. Without a word, they gathered all they came with, plus all the meat. They had no way to haul everything, so our elders gave up their traveling mats to them.

"After they were gone, everyone packed up in silence. The gathering ended long before it was meant to, because everyone had to go home quickly in order to hunt for enough meat to get them through the harsh cold season.

"The elder woman, who still stung from the sharp words spit at her, walked to the river to fill her water container, and heard a baby crying. She dropped the water and went to find the baby. Somehow, a mother from the People With No Respect had left her baby behind."

Whispers among the band filled the lodge, and Bright Sun Flower watched as Sees Like Eagle bowed his head, refusing to look up.

Running River reached for her man's hand. "Sweet, loving man of mine, had she not found your father, you would not be here among us. Your father and mother, who raised you as one of the Fish People, would have been proud to see you and your children, had they lived past the attack on our camp those long seasons ago. I do know they look down from the stars and smile, as all our elders do who have gone to the stars and watch over us. And you *are* of our people."

Sees Like Eagle looked into his woman's tear-filled face, and tears of his own fell. "You are my heart, woman."

Bright Sun Flower watched the pair, and knew she did not need to finish the story. Their trade with the People With No Respect, accidental or not, could not have been a better one. They had traded meat and, in return, one baby did not have to grow up poor.

Somewhere during the story, Sister Wind ceased her blowing. The rain no longer beat against the Counsel Lodge, and birds called to each other.

We will have a nice day after all.

She cleared her throat and spoke with slow words. "We are all family here, even if some of us do not share the same blood. Being family means always being there for someone in need, and never looking away. In our band, unlike some others, we look each other in the eye and acknowledge everyone. Even my daughter's man looks at me and speaks to me. I have heard in some bands this is not so. That is their way, but not ours."

She turned to see Bear Tracks staring at her. He nodded.

"We have those in our band who have special ways, speaking to the other side, sensing dangerous weather, feeling and dreaming changes, and one who talks to a wolf."

Feather looked up and grinned. He gently dug his fingers into White Paws' deep fur and massaged him until White Paws sighed in enjoyment.

"Our people never waste anything. We find a way to use even scraps of leather. Creator gave us everything we need without ever wanting for anything else. But the most special thing Creator gave us is our families. We all need each other. Even my sister who lives two days' walk from here comes to see me, and I visit her several times throughout the good weather. We miss our parents, but know they are with us still. Our aunt took us in after the humpback took our father's life... and our mother gave hers for me."

She stood tall, no tears. "Grandfathers, grandmothers, all the way down to the unborn, are important. We need each other to be happy. Of course, we do not always agree on things, but we still find a way around our problems and move beyond them. Never remain angry, never hold a grudge, and never walk away from a disagreement until it is resolved."

She stopped briefly and watched Running River and Sees Like Eagle take each other in with their eyes. Tears still flowed down their faces. Showing emotions like this was not shameful.

"Keep in contact, even if you must walk many days to do so. Never miss out a chance to hug someone, to hold them, to tell them how you feel. Some day they will not be there, and then what? They may reach out to you from the Spirit world, but never will you wrap your arms around them but in a dream.

"Think about these words and remember the story, so you will not be like the People With No Respect. Think instead of what you have and of what others need, and always share what you have. Your family always comes first, and your family is whoever you make them to be. This is forever, not just for the good times in life.

My story is finished."

Her knees pained her while she stood, but she never complained. She had a good life among a good people. Who could ask for more?

She walked out into the warming day and raised her arms toward the sky, and thanked Creator for all she had. The flap opened and Hawk Soaring stood beside her. He stared at her with joy in his eyes, and also raised his arms and thanked Creator.

A young boy and a large wolf came to stand beside them. The boy raised his arms and thanked Creator. The wolf pointed his nose upward and howled. When his mate responded, he lowered his head and trotted off into the canyon.

Father Sun smiled down upon the Fish Peoples.

Chapter 14

"Son, wake up," Bear Tracks whispered. "Your dreams are in your mind again. The stars are still awake, but we need to go for a walk."

The boy crawled next to his mother and mumbled in his sleep.

He would dress and go out to clear his mind. He himself feared what his dreams showed him, but he did not know what to do about it.

Feather speaks words in his sleep that echo my own dreams. My new son has a special way with White Paws, and the Energy that passes between them when that Wolf sleeps – or pretends to sleep – passes through me. I sense fear.

The time fast approached when he would go off alone to pray for help and ask his Spirit Guide for answers.

Strange. As I think of Bear, wings weigh on my shoulders. Is my Spirit Guide about to change?

He understood that when one Guide had given all he or she could, another stepped in to offer more.

He stepped out into the warm night air, his heart beating to the distant drums that had awakened him. He had heard Feather speak strange words.

He whispered, 'The way is forward. Follow the river.' These are not the words of a boy, but of a Spirit who speaks through him.

Bear Tracks turned at a dark image, a tall shadow moving against the white. His heart pounded two quick beats in his chest before he recognized Bright Sun Flower.

If not for her clearing her throat, I would have thought her a Spirit!

The light of the moon shone on the two, casting large shadows against the Holy Man's lodge. In them, he thought he saw ancient dancers with arms wrapped around each other as they moved to the sound his heartbeat.

"Holy Man, why are you awake so early?"

Bright Sun Flower brought him back to the present, even though he still heard soft drums beating in the night air. She stood only a few feet from his lodge.

She said, "I knew Feather was dreaming. We may no longer sleep in the same lodge, but I will remain connected to that boy no matter where he lays his head. Let him go back to sleep for now, and we will talk." She held her gaze steady, and the gleam in her eyes filled him with Energy.

The Energy gave him courage to speak up. "I do understand part of what he is going through." He shrugged his shoulders. "What I don't know are his deepest thoughts. He is old enough to understand that he has the gift of dreams, which foretell a possible future. Feather shares them with White Paws, and I absorb the emotions between them, but what I see in my mind is as a mist over the land. All I know for sure is that the future of our Peoples is changing."

He had heard the chanting in his dreams too. They were in old words he could not understand. Bear Tracks played with an invisible thing in his hand, trying not to look up.

"My daughter's man," Bright Sun Flower said, "I remind you, our people say you can look at me when we speak. There is no taboo against it among the Fish People."

Bear Tracks raised his head and slowly brought his eyes to meet hers. He saw her concern.

She loosened her robe to the warming air. "I remember you were but nine winters old when you lost your caretaker, your grandfather, who fell in the canyon. He was very old. Nearly ninety winters had passed by him. You turned away from your dreams for a long time after that." She stepped closer to see his face better. "I know you were dreaming as a young boy, just as Feather does now. You must teach Feather the ways. I am giving my grandson to you. His childhood vanishes so quickly. Guide him well."

She paused as if waiting for him to respond, and said, "It is time for you to go into the silence and find yourself again. Fast, sweat, and await a vision."

He watched her eyes sparkle in the moonlight. She was right. His own emotions — or perhaps it was the Spirit's whispers — had reminded him of the need since he had become part of a family again.

"Tell my daughter when she wakes," she continued, "that you will be gone for a few days. Explain why, as best as Spirit allows you, and tell her to come to our lodge for a while, Bear Tracks Who Dreams."

She turned near, so he could not help but look into her eyes. "Yes, I remember the name you received. I was the one who guided you back out. You got so deep, you froze, and I went in and brought you back." This time she looked away. "I see wings around you. Do not put this off. The time approaches and your new son will need your guidance, but you first must find your own way back."

"I... I must prepare myself first and wait until Spirit guides me to do so." In the distance, two ravens called to each other in the darkness — an unusual thing to hear at night. He wanted to take the subject away from himself.

To leave so soon after joining with Baskets? "Why did you not continue as the Holy Woman? You had Power." He turned his head up to see the stars, and picked out one to focus on. Raven called in the distance, and he listened for the second one to respond.

***

"When I joined with Hawk Soaring," she said, "I lost part of that Power. When I gave birth, I lost more. Only now that I am past my youth does my Power return. You are twenty-five winters younger, and have more time to go within the silence. I had a child to nurse and raise. You did not, nor do you now. My daughter will care for any new child."

It was hard for her to admit she was one of the oldest women in the band. She had been past thirty winters old when she had her daughter, their only child. The birth had been hard and she had feared having another, a secret she kept to herself. The birth had weakened her mentally, and prevented her from connecting to Spirit as she had before the birth.

"I was surprised you took my daughter and her son at the risk of losing your own Power. I knew a long time ago you wanted Makes Baskets, but she had eyes only for Feather's father." She turned away and stared up at the stars. She knew Bear Tracks watched the one he thought might be his grandmother's star. Soon, she too would need to seek the silence. It had been far too long.

She turned back to him, and softened her voice. "Bear Tracks, your Power grew until you became afraid of it. This, I understand, but your Power is still alive. Take your full, gifted name back, or the new one I feel is possible, and use it. The Spirits do not give names to have them tossed aside. Like you, I can only see so far, but with that boy's help, and with your guidance and perhaps a little of mine, we will see what our dreams have only teased at. Feather can take both of us out of the shadows, but we must first show him the light. He is so young to carry such a burden.

"We will wait a while longer, but I feel something will change soon. His mind grows much faster than his body. I no longer hear the voice of a child, but of a young man. Somewhere, someone comes to teach him what we cannot. Not long after your joining with my daughter, I sensed this person's presence. Much Power comes with her."

Bear Tracks nodded. "I too have felt this person. I know I have a young man, not a boy." His smile showed in the moonlight. "I care for the boy more than I thought possible. I had no idea he would take my heart as he has. I never thought I could feel so much after losing my parents."

"You were young when you lost your father and mother, a hard thing for anyone to face. But your grandparents raised you well. Now you must teach Feather the ways."

"My Power grows stronger. My joining with your daughter has enhanced them, not weakened them. She has her own Power too, but Feather is the one who has the strength. I feel that the Spirits planned the joining."

He smiled at her, perhaps understanding that she would be a powerful ally. "I thank you for this talk. It was good for us both." He turned to leave.

She needed to know, and for the first time she looked down. "I... uh... was wondering when my daughter was going to tell me of her unborn child?"

Bear Tracks shot her a look of surprise. "You know, then? Women always seem to know what a man can only guess. She told me only a moon ago."

"She must be nearly five moons past. Why does she still hide it? And from her own mother?" Her voice lifted a bit. "Within another moon, all will know."

Bear Tracks lowered his head, but Bright Sun Flower reached out and pulled his chin up. "Do not look down when I speak."

"She hides it. She thinks Feather will have a difficult time adjusting to not being the only one, that he will have hurt feelings. My silly woman thought to pretend she found the baby. I told her that she carried my child also, and I would have no more of her crazy words."

Bright Sun Flower gulped air and choked on it. "I will speak to Feather, and he will not be hurt with the way I explain it. Go, rest now. Send me my grandson when he wakes. We will go see where White Paws hides his mate. We both followed White Paws one night, or we think we followed him — maybe he led us to her. She looks different from him, with a nearly all white face and her back mottled in browns, but her two front legs are pure white, as is most of her tail.

"Feather calls her Moon Face. They have yet to see each other up close. I knew she carried pups, and to my disbelief, so did Feather." She hesitated, trying to find the right words. "You know, her new child will help her to let Feather go when he must stand on his own." This time she looked down. "When we all must let him go to his future — for the safety of many people we have yet to meet."

***

With that, Bright Sun Flower returned to her lodge, hunched over more than usual.

Bear Tracks understood her worries.

He would announce the taking back of his name, or the taking of a new one, after he had gone on his Vision Quest. He needed a little time to prepare his mind.

He climbed in through the flap to the sound of soft snoring. He would take the boy out afterward, and teach Feather the cleansing of his Spirit and mind. The boy seemed too young, but Bear Tracks remembered his grandfather teaching him when he was just a bit older than his new son was now.

Besides, age was of little consequence when Spirit called.

Chapter 15

Feather Floating In Water woke with boundless energy, gobbled down his meal and ran outside. "Mother, I feel as if I slept for a whole moon! Here comes White Paws!"

The boy and wolf ran toward one another, collided on purpose, and rolled on the ground.

"I wonder which is more Wolf these days." Makes Baskets stood and reached for the basket that had their morning meal in it, and turned to Bear Tracks. "Your son will grow two more legs very soon."

He and his woman laughed and watched the antics of boy and wolf.

Even though the cool air still claimed the nights, the warm days had returned. Most of the camp was a flurry of activity.

Bear Tracks watched as Bright Sun Flower made her way through the flap of her own lodge. Her knees clearly pained her. He would give her the salve he had made a moon ago. She never told him when she was out, but instead tried to hide her pain, or to make herself believe it did not exist—as her age did not exist.

"Your mother comes to take Feather out for an important walk. She knows, woman. She has known for some time, and says she will talk to Feather."

Makes Baskets stood to stop her mother. "I cannot let her do this. Feather will not understand."

He pulled at her dress. "Sit down, Baskets, come under the robe with me. Your mother knows what she does. Besides, I need to talk to you today. Our plans for the gathering in the time of ripe berries may change."

He picked up a stick to stir the fire before looking at her again. "Be proud of your unborn daughter. She will bring much joy to our lives."

She grabbed his hand and squeezed it. "Daughter? How do you know such a thing? I actually had a dream I was going to have a daughter, but I seldom dream anything. I thought it wishful thinking."

"Your wish was heard by the Spirits, my sweet one. I also wished for a daughter."

Everything else forgotten, the pair stood up and went back into their lodge, and tied the flap shut. The talk could wait.

***

Bright Sun Flower watched the pair disappear and chuckled to herself.

Good thing that once a baby is made, another cannot start to grow, or those two would have a lodge full, come next winter! I do wonder why some Peoples will not sleep next to each other after the woman carries a child. I think it makes the baby stronger, but what does an old woman know?

"Grandmother!" Feather Floating In Water ran to her and smiled, his arms spread wide, his clothes muddied from play. "Can we go see if we can find White Moon's puppies? Please?"

The boy jumped up and down as any boy his age would. Bright Sun Flower inhaled her relief. He was still her little grandson, ten winters old and acting like it. She wondered how he lived in two worlds, the dreaming and the waking one, without mixing them.

She looked up at the canyon wall that protected the camp from most of winter's onslaught. The red-orange and off whites of the canyon mixed with the green of pine trees in mystical wonder. Why had she never seen it as she did today?

Eagle called to Eagle. *They must be teaching their young ones to hunt. They do not soar but dive as if hunting.* She linked briefly with the mother Eagle, and saw the trio of new ones in the nest. *Ha! I can still do it, and even stronger now than before.*

She embraced the bind of Power and felt stronger. Soon, it would be time for her to walk alone into the canyons, but today belonged to a bouncing little boy.

"Look above you, my muddy grandson, at the pair of beautiful Eagles who have come to bless our camp. Today, good things will happen." She was so relieved to know last night's dreams had left him.

The two trader's sons, who had stayed and joined with the young women of the band, came into camp after an early morning of fishing, quite pleased with their catch. Walks Far grinned as he and Bends Stooped Over strutted past her, each carrying full baskets of fish.

Walks Far reached into his and handed Bright Sun Flower four fish. "For the most beautiful woman in the band, the brightest flower in the land." He did not wait for a response; he hurried to his own waiting woman, whose belly rounded with their child.

Feather's eyes grew wide, and he laughed and pointed as Bends Stooped Over started to go his way. "Grandmother, his nose is bigger than Eagle's beak. Look!"

Her face flushed with heat as she apologized for the boy's remark. "He is too full of words not thought about, and should swallow some of them before speaking. Please do not take offense."

Bends Stooped Over, not sure what to say, smiled weakly and walked toward his lodge, mumbling something about it being time to seek out a new name to enhance his looks.

"Feather, do not speak such words! They are disrespectful and mean. Words like that can hurt people. You must never do that again."

She took the fish to her lodge, then grabbed Feather by his hand. "Come, let us walk." She needed to make him understand and apologize, without breaking his Spirit.

***

Feather Floating In Water looked at the ground as they left the camp. He was not sure what he had done wrong, but knew another lesson would come his way this day. He waited for his grandmother to speak, but she remained silent.

The home of White Paws' mate was in a different direction than they walked. White Paws did not seem to mind, and ran off ahead, sniffing his way as he ran.

"Somehow he knows when I am in for a talking to," he said.

"Smart wolf. I myself wonder how he knows so much. He must have had a good grandmother to teach him." Bright Sun Flower smiled, then squeezed his hand and let it go. "Such a beautiful day for a walk."

They walked on in silence, Feather waiting for his grandmother to talk about what happened in camp. White Paws decided to dig near a leafless bush. Feather watched as the wolf stuck his head in a hole and gulped down a grey form.

"What a shame Running River had another daughter. And the baby looks like she has a crooked head. With those looks, I wonder how she will ever find a man when she grows up." His grandmother looked ahead, speaking as if talking to herself. "You know, the gathering is coming soon. I sure hope that woman of Beaver Swimming does not come this time. She cannot quill as well as me, and I think she should just stop wearing clothes she thinks look good when they do not. And that daughter of hers—"

"Grandmother!" Feather scolded. "Why must you go on about things that do not matter? You never talk in such a way. What difference does it make what that baby looks like? Who cares if Beaver Swimming's wife does not have the skill you have? At least she tries. At least Running River's baby is alive and... and.... She does not have a crooked head! I cannot believe these things matter to you. Why should they matter? It is not right to judge a person for the way they are."

He stopped walking and let go his grandmother's hand. "You are a clever one, Grandmother." He looked up at the face of the woman who had tricked him into learning this new lesson. "I wonder what I will teach myself next."

"I just happen to have the answer to that very question."

"Somehow, I knew you did."

"Then you are the clever one, Little Boy Whose Mouth Grows Bigger By The Moment. Perhaps that shall be your new name." She looked down at him and broke into laughter. "You will make my belly burst, and then you will have to run and get your mother to sew it back up."

"Oh funny! I know who told you about that one. I am not the same little boy as I was then." He puffed out his chest. "I happen to be a winter older now. No one will catch me saying silly things again!"

***

He took off on a fast walk, leaving his grandmother behind to find her breath after her belly-busting laugh. "Grandson, wait, I have a surprise for you."

The boy who would never be caught doing anything silly again ran back, reached out and grabbed both her hands, looked in them, then ran around her to see what she had hid. "Where? Where do you have it? I do not see it!" He jumped up and down and begged for his surprise. "Can I see it now? Please?"

"This is a special surprise that you must wait for." She tried very hard to look serious and not smile.

He put his hands on his hips and eyed her carefully. "How long must I wait?"

"About four, maybe five moons. You will like this surprise. It is so special that I am not sure I should tell you right now."

She looked away from him and stared at the bouncing Wolf, who had just caught another mouse. He reminded her of a little boy she knew, and she smiled to herself.

"Five moons!" he said. "What could be so special that I cannot have it now? How could anything be *that* special? It cannot be that special. Nothing is! Please stop teasing me and tell me what it is. Please? Grandmother, do not be so mean to me."

He reached for her hand and moved it to look inside her robe. His face turned sour, and his pouting lip brought another smile to her face.

"Oh, all right," she said. "But I wish you would wait."

The boy's wide eyes made her break into tears of laughter. She knelt down and waited for the usual remark about her crunching knees, but he must have been too excited to think about knees.

She wore an excited smile and grabbed him on both sides of his tiny waist. "Your mother is going to have a baby! Now you will be the eldest child. You will have a sister to teach everything you know! I am so jealous. I did not get to be the eldest child. I was born second and my sister had already taken a mate by the time I was your age. This is a great honor. You must always look after her and keep her safe. Can you do that?"

Feather grinned with joy, as she had hoped he would.

The pups would have to wait until another day, as boy and wolf sprinted toward the camp, boy yelling with excitement, Wolf dancing in circles around him.

Chapter 16

Makes Baskets sat outside her parents' lodge and enjoyed the warmth of Father Sun on her body. Berries were ripe, and this should have been the gathering time for relatives and old friends. Instead, runners sent to the other bands told them to wait until their Holy Man returned from his Vision Quest. She sighed as her mind followed where her eyes could not. She knew he was safe; her father watched over him, though from a distance, so as not to interfere.

Bear Tracks took only a robe, water and Sage with him. Vision Quests were a solitary decision. She did not like being away from him so soon after their joining, but understood that as the Holy man he had to pray and fast for the good of the people. He sought guidance for not just himself, but for everyone. She had accepted this when she became his woman.

She sighed. *Still, the nights are empty without his embrace.* She smiled thinking how silly she had been to avoid him for so long. *I had no idea he was so gentle and loving. He cares for Feather as he would his own blood son. My son and I are blessed to have him... and now I carry our child.*

She sat while artistically weaving quills into Spirals — the cycle of life — into her basket. She grunted as she bent over to reach quills on the robe in front of her. Her belly, now grown large at eight moons, made even that simple act difficult.

The great care she took with the quills brought the basket to life. She used the natural colors, white and black, to make the zigzag design stand out. She soaked them in her mouth, careful to keep the tips forward outside of her lips, to soften them so she could flatten them with her fingernails. This way the tips tucked under as she wove them in. The pattern's design was even, except for the one tiny mistake everyone made in his or her work to show that only Creator was perfect. She held her basket out in front of her, turned it all the way around to make sure the design took on the look she wanted. Zigzagged lightning strikes followed each other in unison.

Her baby moved. "Your kicks are strong. I wonder if you will want out sooner than Feather did."

My mother was right. Feather is excited about his unborn sister. How silly of me to think otherwise. Every night he lays his head on my belly, 'listens' to his sister, and whispers secrets to her. He even sings to her as I do.

Makes Baskets watched her twenty-nine-winters-old cousin sitting in the sun in front of her own lodge, with her face raised to the morning warmth. Her cousin's third daughter, First Star, made her content.

Makes Baskets understood Running River's need for more — to give her man the family he craved. Even if her cousin acted the part of a grouch, she was a very loving mother.

She jumped when her baby kicked again. *Little one, I love you, and will forever. In time, you might have a younger one to play with. Only Creator knows for sure, but I would welcome another baby someday.*

"Where is my daughter? Inside her belly talking to her baby?"

Makes Baskets looked up and smiled, not realizing her mother had come to sit beside her on the log placed in front of the lodge. "How did you know where my mind was?"

"Just an old mother's guess. I am glad you are happy, Daughter. I wanted to spend some time with you — mother-daughter things, nothing important. I just needed a woman's company."

Her mother, who often said she had special medicine when it came to her artwork, leaned over to watch her weaving. "I could never master that skill of yours with baskets. I could never keep the tension right, and you do it so fast you hardly look down."

The elder woman leaned back and arched her back until Makes Basket heard it pop.

"Mother, *your* skill is in quilling. You are the master here. I could never make the quills come to life on our clothing as you do. Many say you are the best in all the bands."

While the two women filled each other's heads with compliments, Feather Floating In Water ran toward them with White Paws racing after him. They almost landed on Makes Baskets' soon-to-be-finished pine and quill creation. Weeks had gone into making this one, and no boy or wolf was going to smash it for her. She raised it over her head and laughed at the energy of the bright-eyed boy. She could never be angry with him. No child, no matter his age, deserved a parent's anger.

"Easy, my little one, you may find out why White Paws does not like quills. Be careful, they are all over the robe in front of me! Catch your breath before it gets away from you, and sit with us for a moment." She knew her son had other thoughts, and sitting still was never one of them. "Slow. Breathe slow, Son."

"See wha— Wha—" He took in a long breath and slowed down, gasping for more air. "Did you see me with Chases Butterflies, Running River's daughter?"

"Silly boy, we know who the mother of Chases Butterflies is! What did you do with her that excites you so? Oh no. You did not promise to take her as your woman, did you? She is your cousin from your grandfather's side. You do know that, right?"

The boy looked so confused he became silent, an odd behavior indeed for him. He stood and scratched his face, trying to absorb what he had heard.

At last, his eyes shot open wide. "Mother!"

Both women nearly fell backwards in amusement. Makes Baskets had to grab her belly to stop it from jiggling.

"Mother, stop, or you will wake my sister! She must be sleeping. I bet your silliness shook her all up. You never know, she could come out screaming at you."

Again, both women could not control themselves. Tears ran down cheerful faces. White Paws howled at the high-pitched noise, causing many who were close enough to hear all the teasing to join in with their own glee. Little went unshared in the small band. Two elder women, nearby under the shade of cottonwoods, had to stop scrapping their hide and chuckle.

Makes Baskets tried to stop laughing as eight-winters-old Chases Butterflies came to the aid of the flustered boy. She shook her finger at the pair of women. Her round eyes squinted and her long thin nose wrinkled above her pressed in lips "You should not be so mean to such a smart boy! He just showed me a bunch of things that grow in circles, and showed me that birds make their nests in circles, and that Father Sun is round, just like our faces. Why, he was brave enough to touch Grandmother Spider's web to show me the circles and the rainbow in it, and he showed me lots of other things too, and I bet you don't even know anything about it!"

She stood with defiant fiery eyes. Her arms squeezed across her tiny waist, she glared at the two women.

"I bet Feather is way smarter than both of you." Her lecture finished, she turned and stomped off, loose hair flying behind her.

Bright Sun Flower whispered behind her hand, "Just like Feather, a mouth so full of words they all spill out at once!"

Makes Baskets reached out for the painfully self-conscious boy. His mouth was full of words so mixed up they could not find their way out. He gratefully reached for her embrace. "What you did, teaching Chases Butterflies, is a wonderful thing, Son. This shows your grandmother and me just how grown up you are. I am so proud of you! You taught her a lesson she will now pass on to another. Look." She pointed. "See her trying to teach her younger sister, Dances In Wind?"

She held him against her belly, and pointed to the girl who stood proud as she showed her sister a clump of white flowers. "She will never forget your words."

She squeezed him, patted his back, and pushed him back at arm's length, where she could see his now beaming face. "And to think I have you for a son. I will never worry about your sister not learning about life that goes on around her. I am so proud of you. I know she will be safe with her older brother because you listen to what you are taught."

She hugged him a little too tight and he squirmed to get away.

"What is it, little one? You have a question on your face."

He stood tall with his hands on his hips. "I am ten winters old and hugs are for small children."

Both women stopped teasing him, allowing him his grown-up moment.

"I was hoping Grandmother would go with me to look at White Moon's puppies. I know the way. I... um... well, I followed White Paws and Moon Face and saw her three pups. Moon Face would not come to me until I turned my back and sat still. She then came and sniffed me and walked away. She likes me and knows I will not harm her or her babies!"

Makes Baskets dropped the basket, her wide mouth silent. She swallowed and stared into her son's eyes. "So my son knows where the wild mother Wolf has her den? You are lucky she did not feed you to her pups!"

"Oops." The boy looked at his feet. "Maybe I will just go for a walk now and—"

Makes Baskets grabbed his arm. "Wait, Son, I need a break. Since you want to go so badly, I will go with you, but we must keep an eye on the light so as not to get caught too far away."

"Hey!" Bright Sun Flower struggled to get up. "I will not be left behind to talk to myself. I am coming too. Just let me get a robe for us to sit on if we get tired."

***

Bright Sun Flower, always thinking ahead, returned to her lodge to get the robe. She wanted it not for herself, but for her daughter who tired out more easily these days.

So many little flying creatures in here today. Cold weather on the way at this time of season?

She thought this odd, and decided to grab some dried fish and water along with the robe. Earlier, she had noticed blackbirds, usually cawing to each other, sitting high and silent in the trees.

Caught up in wanting to see the pups, she dismissed the omens.

The robe was more awkward than heavy, so she tied it in a bundle and slung it over her shoulders, since her daughter could not carry it.

She stepped outside the lodge and said, "Feather, go back inside and grab the water and strips of dried fish, and put them in the carry-all bag. I want to tell Running River where we are going, since Hawk Soaring is watching over your father. Walk slow and I will catch up to you."

She looked for the Eagle pair, as she did everyday, but they were not flying today.

Odd. I always see them. Perhaps they teach their young to hunt. Too many things are strange this day. I sense warnings from the creatures around us, but I myself sense nothing out of order....

She pushed it away from her mind. *I am simply being overprotective of my daughter.*

Chapter 17

The trio of humans, accompanied by White Paws, set out around the outside of the canyon, heading down along the fork leading away from the big waters. The shoots of different grasses grew tall, up to their calves, and small white flowers dominated the landscape. The small yellow and orange ones that normally hovered over the flowers were absent.

White Paws raced ahead of Feather Floating In Water who started to run after him, but his mother caught his tunic and pulled him back. "Son, you know where you are going, but we do not. You must wait for us. I cannot run with your sister in my belly, remember? She is sleeping." Makes Baskets put both hands on her belly so her son would understand.

Bright Sun Flower looked at her beaming daughter. "You are a good mother. You show great patience and understanding." The grandmother remembered when she too carried a baby.

"You showed me the same when I was his age, Mother. I learned from you and Father how precious children are. As you once told me, they are the future of the entire band, and beyond." She watched her self-proclaimed "Wolf Boy" growl and wrestle with White Paws. "Who would have thought such an alliance possible?"

"Come on!" Feather motioned with an excited hand to the two women. "We go in here, inside this small canyon. It is not far. White Paws and Moon Face dug into a big cave that was already there. They made it bigger, and it has a big ledge for the puppies to play on!"

Makes Baskets turned to her mother with brows raised. "I wonder how he knew they dug it out." She sighed. "Ever since Moon Face howled her loneliness in early winter, Feather has spent more time with White Paws than his human family. Several nights I stood watch in front of our lodge while Feather sat at the edge of the camp hugging White Paws, talking to him before the wolf left.

"I cannot help but think that he and those wolves will change our lives. We could be known as the Wolf People before long, instead of the Fish People." She took in a deep breath and gasped. The wolf danced around Feather, making the boy trip so he would jump up and chase White Paws. "Look at that pair! Maybe Feather will come back from his own Vision Quest carrying the name of Wolf. I know that is some time off, but look at they way they act, as if they are blood related."

Her boy trotted ahead, trying not to run too fast and lose sight of them. He kept turning back and waiting for them to catch up, as they plodded along talking to each other.

She turned to her mother. "He is so excited. Now, I wish I had taken him sooner. He is about to jump out of his clothes!" She let out a laugh that made birds hidden in the thickets take flight.

At the entrance to the canyon, Feather waited and bounced up and down with excitement. "Here, here!"

***

Bright Sun Flower thought Eagle screeched a warning, but she looked up and saw nothing

They turned toward the small canyon, climbed down the rocky side, and wound around a small trail. The wolves' den opened high above them in the rocky cliff face.

White Paws ran up the side and greeted Moon Face, licking her muzzle. She stared past him at the humans, and stiffened, her nose testing the air for their smell. Three pups came to stand at her side, less worried over the strange, two-legged creatures. One of the pups made his way toward the boy.

Feather reached out as one pup climbed down, jumped into his arms, and licked his face. "Hi, little one."

He sat on a boulder along the well-worn path the wolves had made, and squeezed the pup, which was mostly grey with mottled browns and a small, crooked white blaze shooting down his face. A white dusting on his ears ran down around his neck, where a large splash of white covered his chest. His feet were a darker brown and his toes showed spots of white.

"White Blaze." The boy wrestled with him as his mother and grandmother both stared in astonishment.

Bright Sun Flower started to reach out to Feather, but Makes Baskets prevented her from possibly spooking the mother wolf. "Mother, relax. Allow Moon Face to see we are not a threat. She does not know us, and we are close to her pups."

The other two pups came down and pushed their way past the first pup to greet the boy. "Wood Ash, do not knock your sister down into the canyon!" He raised her up as the other pup landed in his lap. A nearly pure grey wolf pup, with one white paw, wriggled his excited body for attention.

Moon Face slowly wagged her white and brown tail, and then sat down and watched with nervous caution as her pups played. White Paws sat next to her, tongue dangling to one side. He looked past everyone as if seeing something that made him uneasy.

"Do you want to explain this to your mother and your confused grandmother? How did you know where the wolves were?" Bright Sun Flower said.

She stood next to a not so sure Makes Baskets, who had turned halfway toward the way out of the canyon. She turned her gaze to where her daughter watched. A golden fox, across the canyon wall from the wolves, pulled her four pups out of their den one by one, and took them to higher ground.

"Mother," Makes Baskets said, "do you see the mother fox?"

Stones started to fall from the wall of the canyon where Fox barked and pulled her young ones up to higher ground.

Bright Sun Flower's eyes widened. The other signs that day now made sense. "Boy, will Moon Face let us climb up to her den?"

No sooner had she gotten the words out of her mouth than Moon Face ran down and grabbed one of the pups and ran back up to the den. Quickly, she returned to get another pup and ran back up again. White Paws ran down and tried to pull up Feather Floating In Water, who had a tight grip on the smallest Pup.

"White Paws, what is wrong? Grandmother, what is happening?"

"Climb, boy, climb! Daughter, get ahead of me and pull me up."

***

A thunderous surge of water roared down the canyon as a desperate Makes Baskets reached toward her mother. She tried to drag the older woman to safety while the hungry water ate at the banks, consuming debris like a starved animal.

She used half-burred stones for advantage, but they kept uprooting, sucked away by the strength of the water's accelerating speed. One hand protected her unborn daughter, and she fought to keep her mother above the fury of the rushing water with her other hand. Bright Sun Flower panicked at her daughter's terrified gasps of breath, and Makes Baskets' legs started to give away.

She started to lose her grip on her mother, who was up to her waist in the angry current. Within seconds, Bright Sun Flower was submerged and her body leaned into the fingers of the pulling water, her legs flaying, trying to find a foothold that was not there. She held her daughter's hand and fought to hold onto a shrub at the waterline, but the shrub let go of the softened ground. The strength of the demanding waters was not one her mother could fight. She began to surrender to the water's force, as it slapped her face and she gulped it in.

Makes Baskets slipped and wet rocks and started to lose her grip on her mother. The loud crash against the canyon walls drowned out her screams. She too felt the dangerous pull of the muddy water. She reached out for a small tree above the water, but it uprooted and washed away in the torrent.

Teeth grabbed the back of her dress and hands pulled at her as she held onto her mother's slipping hand. Panic rose as her grip weakened.

She felt the furious kick of her unborn child. The pain caught her by surprise and she gasped. The water became alive to Makes Baskets. It tried to claim her and the innocent child, who had yet to see the outside world. She fought hard, screaming and praying for help. She was not going to lose her mother or the daughter who—she swore—cried inside her.

She struggled to tighten her grip on her mother's hand. Her legs cramped and she stretched them in hopes of relieving the pain, but the action made her slip more. Two hearts now beat in rapid unison inside her. Fear made it impossible to swallow. Her throat tightened.

Feather's scream brought another concern to her dwindling strength.

Please Creator, my son, my only son! Save him. He is but a boy. She felt for him, felt his foot, and pushed upward, but slipped. *Will any of us live? Will I ever see Bear Tracks again? I love you, my man.*

Her heartbeat thumped so loud in her chest, the churning water was far away in her mind.

White Paws teeth ripped into her dress and continued to pull even as he too was slipping into the water. She heard her own scream drowned out in the rush of the water as its depths pulled at them.

Her thoughts began to follow a bright light. The fear diminished. A vision showed her daughter, who held a baby, with another child standing beside her.

'Go back child. You have much to do, Makes Baskets. You are part of the future of your band'.

A push sent her back to her body.

She choked on water and heard her son. "Mother, don't lose Grandmother! White Paws, pull!"

She barely heard Feather scream above the thrashing water, but it brought her back fully from the light. Power she never knew took over her mind. Makes Baskets surged forth with Energy her body had never known.

Again, a voice commanded. *'Use your mind to make you stronger. You will succeed.'*

With a surge of strength from deep inside, she grabbed onto another small tree, and this time it held fast. She drew on that Power, and hauled her mother above the gyrating water.

***

Feather pulled at his mother, and the pup slipped from his grasp. He panicked and tried to reach with his other hand. He slid down the mud and pushed with his legs. Moon Face crawled her way to the yelping pup. Feather reached out and caught her tail just as she turned to climb back to the den, pup in her mouth. The pull made the wolf dig her back legs into the thick mud, aiding both wolf and boy. He worked his legs around a boulder that held him firm.

White Paws still had his teeth in Makes Basket's dress behind her neck, and she still held his grandmother's hand. Feather used all his strength to pull the women up higher. His small body was barely a match to the water that pulled at his mother.

"I am here, boy. Pull. You can do it." He had no time to think whose voice commanded him. He just obeyed and pulled even harder.

Bright Sun Flower grabbed onto an outcropping on the ledge, and pulled herself up as the water surged past. The pair continued to pull her up and into the den, where they all gasped in fear and exhaustion.

Everyone lay back breathing hard. The Energy in the den felt different to Feather. He looked over at his exhausted mother. Her eyes had a blue spark. She rubbed her belly and spoke words only her baby could hear.

Bright Sun Flower fought to roll over on her side, choked out dirty water, and took deep breaths into her rasping lungs. "I should have paid attention to the signs. The buzzing creatures in the lodge meant a cold night, so I paid no heed, but when the blackbirds were silent in the trees and there were no winged ones on the flowers, I knew better."

Feather's voice, hoarse from yelling, carried a high pitch. "Grandmother, it was not your fault. I wanted to bring you here, to surprise you. I wanted to show you that Moon Face and I made friends, and she let me play with her pups ever since their eyes opened and she... she...."

Feather Floating In Water broke down and sobbed his guilt into his hands. White Paws trotted over and licked his tear-wet face.

"No, no, little one, do not blame yourself. How could you know?" His mother grabbed him tightly and rocked him against her swollen belly. His Wolf Brother tried to continue licking his face by pushing himself in-between the pair. "And you, White Paws, thank you for not letting go of my dress!" She reached out to him and he crawled over to her and licked her face too.

***

For the first time, Makes Baskets felt Energy swirling within her being. *Such lightness, peace – is this how Power feels? I saw a light so bright that it had no color. I was floating or flying with no body to hold me –*

Bright Sun Flower chuckled. "We are all fine and safe. And we got to meet your wolves!" She sounded excited and laughed as if nothing dangerous had happened.

The wolf made his way to Bright Sun Flower. "White Paws, I do not need my face licked also! I guess I know now — the Spirits made this happen. We are safe in the wolves' den, and this was in its own way a Sacred Happening. Moon Face may have never let two strange humans near her pups otherwise. Now look at us. We have pups crawling all over us, and she is just watching, her tail swishing on the ground."

"Well, Mother," Makes Baskets said, "the Spirits certainly do have a sense of humor. I, for one, would rather they had found another way."

She raised her head, furrowed her brows at her mother, and squared her chin. She placed her hand on her belly, refusing to let the others know she hurt. She was far enough along to give birth, but would her daughter live?

The baby kicked hard enough to remind her mother that she was still there. The cave was just dark enough to hide Makes Baskets' clenched jaw and squeezed eyes.

Please, Creator, Great Mystery, save my baby. She has not lived outside my belly, and she deserves a chance at life. Please make the pain go away.

Her mother's voice called to her, soothing her.

Makes Baskets turned her head and saw Bright Sun Flower sitting up, staring into her eyes. She gave her mother a weak smile.

***

Bright Sun Flower gave thanks for the warmth of Father Sun on her soaked body. They had survived something terrible. Her eyes widened when she saw the blue glow in her daughter's eyes.

Oh, my... we will need to speak. Right now, I need to distract her and Feather. "Look what I still have—the robe and the food. It stayed tied during the entire adventure. We should rest and eat while the water goes back into the main river. We are safe and will be warm with the robe, even if it is wet, and our bellies will be full. We will sleep the night with your wolves."

She turned and watched the mother wolf. "Look at Moon Face. She nurses her pups and does not worry that we are here. How, I do not understand, but Grandson, you have a very, very special gift. You have Wolf Power, and I know we are safe. Tomorrow brings a new day, as always, and we will climb down and go home."

She recognized her daughter's pain, but knew she tried to hide it.

A distraction.... We need something to focus on. An ancient turtle shell lay half-buried in front of her. *A gift from Creator.*

She looked at her slumped-over daughter and decided to tell the story. She took the robe and spread it out over the edge of the cave, so it would dry some before Father Sun took the warmth away when he slipped below the land.

"Boy, this is a good time to tell you about the birthmark you have on your back. I know it faded some over the past winters, but there is always a reason for such things. Turtle is the very reason we even exist."

She settled down as best as possible on the hard ground. Her daughter crawled to her and snuggled like a small child, one hand over her belly. Feather snuggled with White Paws, quite content to stay that way.

"Turtle," she began, "lived in the big salty waters that covered our Mother before she was born. No land existed anywhere. Many birds tired of flying and of never having a place to rest. Several birds went to Eagle, the leader of the Bird Peoples, and told him they were tired and feared drowning in all the water.

"Eagle thought about this. His wings were large and he spent much of his time floating on air currents, so he did not tire. After many pleas by small birds, he understood what to do, but needed someone to dive deep enough to bring up mud from the bottom of the vast, deep waters.

"No birds—not even Eagle—could do this. Turtle happened by and asked what all the worry was about on such a fine day. Eagle landed on her large shell so he could speak to her better. 'Turtle, we need someone who is a good swimmer, someone who can stay under water for a long time, to go to the bottom of the sea and bring up mud. Too many small birds tire and have no place to rest.'

"Turtle spoke, 'Ah, I see the problem. I will do this for all of you.' She swam down and brought up mud on the back of her shell. 'Here it will stay and grow. Soon there will be enough land for all the birds.'

"And she was true to her sacrifice. Turtle is a very Sacred being. She still holds up our Mother to this day, and now many different beings have a good life."

Her grandson crawled on all fours to Moon Face, talking softly as he curled up with the wolf and her pups. "Thank you for finally telling me the story. Turtle saved many animals. Makes me think about why I have her on my back, about my dreams." White Paws went to lie next to him.

"Looks like only you and I, Daughter, will need the robe."

The setting sun shone orange in the small canyon, and the water, already calm, receded.

***

Makes Baskets felt her daughter move and relax. The pain was less. She and her unborn child were safe.

The two women ate as birds sang in the fading light. They curled up together and covered themselves with the partly dried robe.

What could possibly happen next? Makes Baskets took a deep breath and closed her eyes.

Chapter 18

Feather Floating In Water jerked up and looked around before remembering he was in the den, with the wolves and his mother and grandmother.

The dream had become more demanding each time. He had heard the trapped people shouting and running.

A chill ran up his spine even though he was warm, snuggled in with White Paws, Moon Face and the pups. The pups squirmed and grunted as they nursed. Soon they would leave the den and learn to hunt.

White Paws stirred and Feather saw his amber eyes despite the darkness. "Did you have a dream too?" he whispered. "Did you hear that woman's voice tell me to pull harder? She sounded as if she had gravel down her throat, as if she was very old—older than Grandmother."

***

Bright Sun Flower pretended to sleep so she could listen in. Just enough moonlight peeked in to make Feather visible.

She reached out with her mind and searched for the boy's father, who must still have been on his Vision Quest. His Energy told her he was in a battle of his own. She would not pry. It was far too personal. Hawk Soaring had gone with him, and waited far enough away to leave Bear Tracks alone, but close enough in case something happened while he waited for the Holy Man to come back from his vision.

She brought her mind back to the den, still damp, but warm under the robe she shared with her snoring daughter.

"White Paws, what do I do?" Feather whispered.

She wanted to ask about his dream, but did not want to wake her daughter. Unsure what all of his dreams were about, she hoped he would reveal more to her; he was confused on his own.

"I saw you," he said, "with White Moon and the Pups in my dream. The pups were full-grown and with other wolves that I did not know. You were trying to protect me, maybe the people in the band too. Some of those people I did not know. What does it all mean? I wish you could talk to me. Each dream shows just bits of things... things I cannot put together. Somehow, I think my dreams mean more than just protecting our own band. I see myself as Turtle now, saving so many Peoples."

Feather snuggled deeper into the wolf. "I see strange people in my dreams, but they are not always the same ones. Some have lighter skin. I see very big waters, but cannot see over them. Some dreams only show people like us. Our people walk away from the canyons, some of us ride on strange creatures, like big dogs, but they have hair hanging off their necks, and tails that look like human hair. What are they? These strange people and their animals scare me. Why would we leave our home?"

He shifted and sat up to hug his attentive Brother, clearly feeling safe when close to the big wolf. His hands slipped away from White Paws and he curled back up with Moon Face.

White Paws lay back down and leaned against the sleeping boy.

Bright Sun Flower wanted to jump up, grab him and hold him, but he settled in and slept. He still did this with the ease of a child.

The elder woman lay back down and tried to drift back to sleep. Father Sun would wake in a short span of time. Soon enough the boy's dream visions would connect with hers and the Holy Man's.

The Holy Man. He may already know.

***

"Mother, daylight has come." Makes Baskets woke to the sound of birds, and climbed out from the robe to see what awaited them. What she saw gave her cause for alarm. She climbed back to her mother in the den. "We must find a way out of here. The canyon floor is so full of mud we will sink to our knees!"

Feather sat up. "Do not worry, Mother, I know another way out. But I am not sure you and Grandmother can climb it. I can go back to camp and get help." He crawled over to the entrance of the den to see the mud. "That mud would cover me to my nose! When will I be taller, Mother? Will I be taller by the time the leaves fall from the trees again? What if I stay small? What will happen then? Does this mean I will not grow to be a man? I have to become a man, or I will not have the woman the Spirits showed me in my dream. Mother, what if I—"

"Woman? What woman did you dream of, son of mine who is only ten winters old? Who is this woman? Son, wha—"

"Mother, I *am* ten winters! You must remember I am gaining in age and... and wisdom!" His squared chin rose as he looked over both women's heads.

He crawled over her and to the den's entrance.

"Let him be." Bright Sun Flower reached out for her arm, and brushed off a dried piece of dirt. "He is just a boy, and children sometimes dream of words they hear from other people. Sometimes a story sticks in their minds. You worry yourself silly."

Her mother reached up to her shoulder and brushed her tangled hair away from her face. "Even if the dream proves true, you will never, ever lose your son. You do not dream like he does, but in time you will understand better what he sees in his dreams."

***

Bright Sun Flower scooted to the edge of the den, out to the ledge, and hung her legs over the drop-off. The deep mud would not allow them to make their way back. The mother fox barked from the ledge above her, and she silently thanked the fox for the warning, which she should have noted sooner in all the omens that had come her way.

She turned back and climbed over to her daughter. "I asked your man to take him for a time into the canyons, to give Feather a chance to talk to him, to open up his mind to him, if he will. Perhaps Feather just needs to be a boy a while longer. And you, my daughter, you need to rest. As soon as we get back, I am going to make you a special tea, and *you will* lie down and rest for a few days until your daughter settles down. Do not give me that withered fruit-face you say is my expression! You will do as I say and not risk your unborn child. Do not think I did not see you holding your belly."

"Yes, Mother, you saw me, but I am fine — just tired."

The boy climbed up the canyon's edge to a small path once used by animals of the past. He did this with ease, just like White Paws, who followed behind him.

"Wait, Feather," she called out to him. "I do not wish to share this with the others of our camp. I am a respected elder who should have seen the signs."

She sat and hung her head in shame. *If only this had not happened. I am expected to know better.*

Feather climbed back down and crawled over to her side. "Grandmother, do you not see why you did not heed the signs? You said it was a Sacred Happening. If you had, we would have never come here, and we would not have slept with White Paws and his family. Look at Moon Face. I bet you did not even know she was but a breath away from you."

She turned and the mother wolf really had slept next to where she lay that night. She absent-mindedly reached out and rubbed the fur on her back.

"She has accepted us as part of her pack," he said. "She could have bitten us if she had wanted, but look — she even allows her pups to wander without worry. Here, take the littlest girl and hold her. I have not named her yet. You name her."

Bright Sun Flower looked wide-eyed at the prospect of holding the pup of a wild wolf. Feather pushed the littlest one into her lap. Moon Face looked on as she would if her own sister were caring for one of the pups.

"My, what a sweet little girl. Just look at you, so precious and gentle." She watched as Moon Face climbed out of the den to relieve herself, walking past her without acting worried that another creature held one of her pups. "What a beauty you are. You have so much brown and white in you, and unlike White Paws and your mother, light orange-browns also."

She held the pup up to her face and got a wet nose for it. "You like the way I taste? Your colors remind me of the time in which all leaves change and the land lights up with the season's colors. You are so beautiful to look at, with orange eyes that shine with...." She smiled and nodded. "That is what I will call you. Bright Beauty."

She put Bright Beauty down so she could go back to the other pups, but the bark of the fox again alerted her. Momma Fox sat outside her new den with her mate at her side. Already, they had made a new home, content to be living in a canyon with wolves who would not tolerate them so near their den, unless they had their own agreement.

"How can this be? Why do the wolves allow them to share such close quarters? I wonder much about the happenings in these canyons. They seem to be a Sacred place, as if all who live within them and beside them as we do are blessed. I would like to better understand this."

The human grandmother still had many things to learn herself. "Feather, I think your mother and I will follow you up to the top. The wolves need to hunt. They stayed last night for you, Grandson. Now they must be very hungry. We must all leave so they can leave too. Makes Baskets, you really do look tired. Perhaps you need to stay and I will bring help."

She wanted to ask her daughter if she had had any dreams. The blue glow in her eyes still sparkled.

"Mother, if I had known you were going to snore so loud all night, I would have slept out on the edge of the rim." She looked at her mother with a stern stare.

"Daughter, I do not snore. You heard your own self. I lay there thinking we had a big bear in here with us." She gave her daughter the same stern look back.

"Ha! I sleep so quietly, I never wake my man *or* my son."

"Um... Mother... you do wake Father and me both some nights. Grandmother, you and Grandfather snore so loud, I have heard others in the camp talking about how glad they are to have you as part of the band, because you both scare away Bear."

Makes Baskets grabbed her belly and laughed hard enough to worry White Paws. He scooted over to her, looked into her face, and cocked his head and whined. "Feather," she gasped, "who told you this?"

"Yes, Grandson, *who* told you this? I would like to thank them for their words."

Feather Floating In Water must have been uncertain about the look on his grandmother's face. "We... uh... should try to climb to the top of the rim so White Paws and Moon Face can go hunt." He scurried out of the den.

Makes Baskets was right behind him, until Bright Sun Flower groaned with the strain of getting up.

"Oh, Mother," she huffed, "give me your hand. Leave the robe. We can get it another time. I am certain we will be back."

Bright Sun Flower mumbled something about not coming back, if they were going to have to listen to some mysterious snoring that she did not do. She reached out, grateful for the help despite being a bit grumpy.

The boy scurried up and stood at the top, waiting for the still arguing women. Her daughter dragged her by the hand. Neither had stopped quibbling long enough to realize they stood on top of the rim, until....

Feather shouted at them. "Stop it! You are acting like children fighting about silly things that do not matter." The boy stood in front of them with his hands on hips. "I do not want to hear this anymore. I want both of you to say you are sorry. Now!"

Both women were so shocked at the boy's admonishment that they just stared at him.

"Well, I guess we can settle this later," he said, "but you two need to be nice to each other."

He shook his finger at them, then turned and walked along the rim, mumbling to himself about adult behavior being so hard to understand.

**

"My son is how old?" Makes Baskets joked with her mother, who snickered, which meant she was about to tell her something about her own childhood she probably did not want to hear. That same look had started many embarrassing stories in the past, and she was in no mood for one now.

She quickly changed the subject. "Mother, the camp most likely is awake, and I am sure they will wonder why we are not up yet. When they see us coming in and see your stained clothing from the water, what shall we say?"

"What happened was meant to happen," Bright Sun Flower said. "We must share this story with the band, no matter if I shame myself. There is no reason to hide from it. This was a Sacred Happening that all should hear—even the flood. Everything that happened affects us all. We just need to make sure everyone understands. They must leave White Paw's family be, until Moon Face is willing to follow that boy of yours into camp."

They approached the camp, now becoming active. Her mother continued. "I have a feeling your man is on his way back. This is the fifth morning. We all have things to speak about."

Makes Baskets stopped, clutched her belly and stared at her home. The flap lay partway open, with the bottom raised to allow a cool breeze to pass through. Her mother's lodge still looked shut up. She stood between both lodges, confused about what to do. Her mother's arm guided her away from the lodge she wanted to go into, and led her toward her mother's lodge.

While she had floated in the bright light, she had learned much. First, she *did* have the gift to dream. Spider had shown her one while they slept in the den, which she kept to herself. Spider had shown her a disheveled web, which meant that changes would come no matter how much her mind rebelled. They revolved around her son and a stranger yet to come. And Sparrow Hawk came to her.

Change. Change. It was only a silly dream. She half smiled, trying to reassure herself.

Feather had already made himself scarce. They started a fire to dry their clothing, while others looked on and whispered. She changed into dry clothes. Her mother urged her to lie down and rest, and she did not resist.

She glanced around her parent's lodge, her home, where everything was in its right place, and where nothing ever changed. Her unborn daughter was safe. She knew it had to be so.

Home, where everything is in its right place, where nothing ever changes.

She could not quite convince herself of this anymore.

Chapter 19

Hawk Soaring stood outside the Holy Man's lodge. He reached out and ran his hands across his grandson's face, memorizing what he felt. He bent over and took in the rich smell of his hair. A small tear made its way down the old man's face. "I love you, Feather Floating In Water. Go inside, your father needs to talk to you."

Feather ducked through the flap as Hawk soaring watched him, a small ambivalence in his heart. He longed for what was, but was also proud for what would be.

Feather turned back to speak to him. "Grandfather, my heart spills over when I think of you. You took the place of my first father until my mother took another mate. You taught me much, even if you think you did not.

"You must go to see Grandmother and Mother. They have a story you must hear. An exciting story about a flood and Moon Face's puppies and.... Did you know Grandmother snores louder than Mother does? All three of us learned something and one of us needs a new dress. I mean one of them needs a new dress, not me. I do not wear dresses." He gave his grandfather a big grin.

Hawk Soaring smiled back. "You silly one! I must go see what exciting news your grandmother has to share."

He turned and walked toward his lodge.

***

Feather Floating In Water shared the old man's mix of sadness and pride, but had no idea why. He turned to go into the lodge, but glanced back, and watched his grandfather take the path into the canyon instead of going home.

His grandfather needed time to wander in his own mind, to join with Hawk and soar above the canyons. Feather understood this by the emotions Hawk Soaring expressed — sad, but content.

Feather breathed in the smells of cooking fires, and watched the silhouettes. A peacefulness washed over him, made him wonder how any of their lives could possibly change.

He turned and went into the lodge to be with his father.

***

Bear Tracks sat in the semi-dark lodge, bottom flaps open next to a dying fire. Children screamed as they raced past his lodge and the echo of barking dogs followed behind. Sister Wind teased at his feet while making her way through the obstacles on the floor.

He picked up a twig and stirred the embers. More than his own Vision Quest had happened, and he needed to share part of what he saw with the boy. Peace washed over him for the first time since he had joined with Makes Baskets. He laid against a rolled-up robe, breathed in deep the scent of home— Sacred herbs that hung above him, the herbs Baskets cooked with, the smell the lodge held naturally.

He stretched his arms above him, content to be in a familiar place, relishing the sounds of camp activity. "Sit, son. I wish to speak with you."

He motioned to Feather with his hand, and took another deep breath. "In my vision, I saw what happened in the canyon, but I was helpless to prevent it. It had already begun. All I could do was call out to you and your mother. I feared if I left my Vision Quest, I might find worse. I do know it was a Sacred Happening—not all of them are gentle. Your mother is forever changed, and your sister will be born soon. She will be safe, and will have a Power of her own that one day will appear—when the Spirits see the need for it."

He reached out and squeezed his son, but the boy's squirming caused him to let go. "I was so scared for all of you. I begged The Great Mystery to take me instead. Somehow I knew it was all part of my own Vision Quest."

He put his arm over Feather's shoulder and just stared into his son's eyes, seeing the blue glow. His own eyes reddened—a mixture of pride, joy and sadness—as he thought of this young one's future.

I feel so much for this boy, yet not a boy. At least for a short while I can relax. I thought I needed to teach him, but another comes our way. I am merely to be there to help him understand. How can I tell the band there will be no gathering this time?

"What is your new name, Father?" The boy interrupted his thoughts. "I know it changed. In the wolves den last night, in one of my dreams, I saw you wearing black feathers, not Bear's skin. I saw Bear's tracks leaving, but not coming back. I saw you change Power beings. Bear is no longer part of your name." Feather sat straight and stared into his face.

"Yes, my name changed. Bear spoke briefly to me about why he was moving away. He told me that like your grandmother and grandfather, I too needed the guidance of a winged one—a winged one that I can share the sky with, where I will be able to see things Bear cannot show me.

"Raven flew over to where I sat on the ledge, while my mind followed where the Spirits led me in my vision. He cocked his head at me, and asked if I would honor him by wearing his feathers made into a cape that will rest upon my shoulders. He said it would take time to make this cape because I cannot cause harm to one from his band. I must find the feathers, one by one."

He pulled out four blue-black feathers from a pouch. "Raven's gift. They are two pairs of wing feathers that match, two for each side.

"Raven told me much, and then allowed me to share his body. We flew over the lands, and I saw you and your mother trying to pull your grandmother from the hungry flood. I watched as White Paws helped you pull your mother to safety. It was then I called out to you."

He stared into the mystery of his son's eyes. "You have your mother's determination and Wolf's Power. I also saw your mother change. She went into a bright light where life can end or begin.

"Son, you must never share our words with anyone. They are for us alone. I say this because you are a future Holy Man of our people." He added Sacred Sage to the embers and, with Eagle's feather, brought the smoke up over his face first, down his body, then his son's, sweeping the smoke over his entire body, front to back, head to toe. "Always remember to use Sage to wash away the outside world, and it will clean your Soul."

He smiled. "My name is now Flying Raven Who Dreams."

He watched the boy through the smoke that rose from the dying fire. Feather sat taller, his expressionless reaction more adult than that of a boy.

"Yes, I saw you too in my vision. I think you know you are to spread your words to save all the Peoples who will listen, not just our Peoples. You may understand only part of all that is to come, but you will find out more soon. This I promise you, my son."

Calling him Son felt good. He would never have a son by blood—the Vision Quest showed him this—but he did have one by heart.

He stretched his arms over his head and took a deep breath. "My grandmother was there, in my vision, and told me what she said to you—about using her name for your first daughter. I know much time will pass before this happens, but I would like to hear her name again very much."

He nodded his head. "Yes, I would like that." He held his hands in front of his face and turned them as if looking for something. "I still feel Raven in me, and thought I might still have claws." He chuckled softly.

"Son, you will meet your future mate among the ones who come to follow you." He pushed the stray hairs away from Feather's face and leaned closer to the boy. "She and her people come soon, very soon."

His son's face broke into a surprised expression, which convinced him he should speak of other things his vision told him he could share.

"Wolves will be at your side always. They will not cross over as you think. None of us will."

He reached over and took the boy-man's hand into his, pulled it to his chest and pressed it tightly. His son would be a man while still in a boy's body. When he let go, he knew he let go of a man's Soul.

"Father," his son said, "I know some of what you speak, but what do you mean we will not cross over as I think?"

Feather looked deep into his eyes, as if the answer would pop out of them, but Flying Raven Who Dreams shook his head, indicating he would speak no more on it.

"I know, I know... in time I will understand." His son reached out and hugged him. "I love you."

"And I you, Son of my heart." The Holy Man vibrated from the Energy they shared.

Feather let him go and picked up a stick to play with the fire, and stirred it several times before looking up again. "You have made my dreams a little clearer. Our future is not in the canyons." It was not a question.

He stared into the Holy Man's face. Small lines formed along his mouth and forehead, something for which he was much too young.

"Many changes come our way, Son. Do not fear them. Fear or not, they come."

The two crawled out into the warm sun and stood in front of their lodge. Their presence demanded attention. All stopped what they were doing and stood. Children stopped, stood still. Women stopped scraping hides, and men who sat talking became silent.

Bright Sun Flower already stood outside with her daughter, trying to get Makes Baskets to drink tea that would soothe her cramping. The baby moved and kicked more than she should have.

Makes Baskets watched as her mate and son came forward into the center of the camp. Pride beamed from her face as she rubbed her belly. Life was about to change for more than one man and a young boy.

"I am now Flying Raven Who Dreams." The Holy Man stood tall, chin raised. He pushed his son forward. "Before you stands your future Holy Man who will take a new name very soon."

Wolves answered, howling in the canyons that echoed through the camp. Flying Raven Who Dreams began a song, and the entire band picked it up. They made two circles; each took the hand next to them and wove back and forth, while several men danced to the beat in an inner circle. To the side, two men beat on a drum the sound of a heartbeat, the beat of the Peoples and of all living beings.

Flying Raven Who Dreams broke free, strode over to where his woman sat, and took her hand. "Wait here."

He went inside to grab a humpbacked robe and his carry-all pack. He returned, took Makes Baskets by her hand, and led her into the canyons.

***

Eagles responded to each other while they danced in the sky. Bright Sun Flower stepped out to give her knees a rest. Propping them up, she rubbed them with the healing, yellow daisy flower salve to ease the pain.

She sat next to the Counsel Lodge and watched as Grandmother Spider completed her web in a crease in the lodge's front hide. A rainbow shone through the intricate webbing, the shape of a perfect circle. Above, Eagle called again.

Time moved forward, and Eagle reminded Bright Sun Flower to move forward with it. Eagle called again. She knew she must answer.

She reached for the water bladder, grabbed up the robe she sat on, left the celebrating group, and walked into the canyon. Time passed so quickly at her age, and too much of it had passed since she had last sought Eagle. To stay connected to one's Spirit Guide was as much a part of life as eating, a very necessary link to both the Mother and Creator.

She limped up the path and clung to the red-orange stones, the path she used long ago that led to an outcropping where Eagle would see her. She spread her robe but did not sit. Instead, she raised her arms and called out to Eagle, and sang a soft song. The fringe on her dress waved as if dancing itself.

There she danced and forgot her pain, forgot she was an elder. She sang and twirled, becoming young again. She inhaled deeply the very breath of life itself. How long had she sung? What did it matter? She felt well, alive and free.

She stopped, and pulled out a seashell she kept hidden inside a pouch made into her robe. A clump of Sage lay nestled in the curve of the shell. Using her fire sticks to awaken the Sage, a small curling cloud of smoke filled her nose with the aroma.

'Well, about time, Human. I watched as you followed us in the sky, and wondered when you would seek me out.'

The voice made her jerk up in surprise. She had not finished preparing her mind yet, and the Sage barely had a chance to burn. "Forgive me, Great One. Life does pass quickly, and I am shamed I use this as my excuse. Please have pity on me, Sister. My mind is on you always, but human children and grandchildren take much time. I know I have not sought you out since my grandson's birth. I have you to thank for the dream that saved his life."

She looked away and wrung her hands. "I worried I might be here for days before you answered."

Eagle stretched out her wing and pecked at an itch underneath her feather, then looked up at her mate soaring above. 'We both have watched you. You know that you and I share a combined Spirit, and I would watch over you even if you never came to me, dear Human child. I understand why you needed to watch over the Human boy. Still, you must not neglect yourself as you have done. He has his own Spirit Guides who care for him, more than I can speak to you about.'

'And yes, perhaps I should have made you wait.' Eagle turned away from the worried woman, looked across the valley's turquoise sky, and watched movement far from the Human's ability to see. 'Do not be so long in seeking me out, or next time I will make you wait. I deserve respect.'

Bright Sun Flower bowed her head. "Please, Eagle, please, I need your guidance and I responded to your call. I know you also have a message for me." She stood and waited for Eagle to answer.

Eagle's mate called and she responded. Bright Sun Flower worried Eagle might fly to him and leave her standing, head bowed.

'Worry not, Human Sister. I know what you seek. I can only answer for you, not the boy. His path is marked. You have done well teaching him and Creator blesses you for this.

'Raise your head and look at me. There, you see, I will not peck your head off. Listen well to me, woman of the people. You need to take back your Power. You will need it for the days that come. Let your mind go — I want to take you somewhere.'

The elder woman closed her eyes and breathed deep the Energy of Eagle. She felt herself lift out of her body and go into Eagle. They soared into the sky and Human and Eagle became one. *So long since we flew. I have forgotten the freedom, my Sister Eagle.*

Miles disappeared beneath them, and they flew past a band of people who slowly made their way toward the camp.

'*Power leads them to your band. One called Blue Night Sky will change your grandson forever. Let her be. Time shifts. She will guide him places you cannot.*'

In what seemed but a flash in time, they flew over a group of mixed Peoples, some strange to look at—hairy faces, shiny things on their heads. Some rode big dogs while others pushed bedraggled people before them. Some fell and were rudely jerked up and pushed forward, with the hairy-faced ones laughing. Many wore packs, bent over with the weight crushing down on them. Dogs ran freely with no packs.

Bright Sun Flower knew they did this to mock the people. "Eagle, what is this? The beings in our dreams—my grandson's and my own—what do these monster creatures want?" She nearly lost her connection with Eagle from the shock.

Eagle shook herself to remind the woman she could not fly without her. '*What you see comes to your people. There is some time before they find their way to you. Use this time wisely. Make much meat and dig rooted food. Prepare many hides. You will leave part of your lodges behind. You must. The poles will be burdensome. The day you hear my mate and me call out four times is the day you must pack and leave....*'

Bright Sun Flower found herself alone within her body again. The Sage had burned, and a cold breeze blew over her perch on the outcropping. She felt another's presence and turned.

"Now I know for sure, Grandmother. Father's dreams, Grandfather's dreams and yours are all the same—the same as mine. You were with Eagle as she flew over the camp. I came up here and thought I might not find you, that maybe you left with Eagle. I guess you did, but not with your body. Did Eagle tell you anything you can tell me?"

He stared at her. "You still wear Eagle's wings, and your eyes sparkle with a hint of blue." He put the robe over her shoulders.

She needed time—time to come back completely on her own.

He turned to leave and nearly ran over his grandfather, who had tears in his eyes. "Come, Grandson, let her be. We must allow her the time she needs. Too long has it been since she sought her Spirit Guide. She will be all right."

He put his arms around the boy's shoulders and gently guided him back to camp.

She would speak of what had happened when she must.

Chapter 20

Her breath was shallow; only the ribs beneath her worn clothes showed movement as she stood at the edge of the camp. The elder shivered, worried how the others would react to her. The band that remained hidden depended on her.

Blue Night Sky willed herself to accept whatever fate would belong to her. She had warned the others, "Remain hidden. Run if need be. Run."

They had been on the run for so long, time held no meaning. Her dream vision guided her here, and she would walk no more. Too long since her last full meal, too long since she slept in a warm place, she faltered and fell, her white hair unrestrained covering her face. She stretched out and tried to push herself up, to regain her show of strength, but it failed her. Her arms gave way and the elder closed her eyes, tears trailing down her face.

I have failed.

***

Walks Far had just come from fishing. He dropped his basket, spilling fish out onto the grass, when he saw her. He fell to his knees beside her, scooped up her crumpled form, and cradled her in his arms. Her long hair tumbled backward, tangled with clumps of dirt.

She stared into his deep-set eyes — her own widened in fear.

"I... I am of the Red Bear Clan, very far away," she said. "I am called Blue Night Sky. I come seeking Shin... Shining Light."

"I know your Peoples, Great Elder, and I know of you. You are a Holy Woman. Once a trader's son, I passed by your Peoples a few times. Being the youngest, I had to stay in our camp with the trade goods, away from everyone, so you may have never seen me."

He picked her up and carried her the rest of the way into camp. "Do not be fearful. You are safe, among friends, Grandmother, but what is this shining light?"

He did not wait for an answer. He spotted Running River scraping a hide and called out to her. "Bring water and food paste. I carry a Great Elder of the Red Bear Clan in my arms. She is very weak!"

Running River dropped her hide scraping tool and ran for a water bladder, and some fresh cooked paste made for elders who had no teeth. She motioned to Walks Far to put her down and lean her against a tree, where someone had left a padded seat leaning against it.

She knelt down beside the elder woman and offered her first water, then food. "Grandmother, who are you? Where is your family? Do you understand my words?"

She helped her to take the food and watched as she chewed it. It was a pounded meal of pine nuts, berries and meat, perfect for growing babies and elders with few teeth.

Shaky hands patted both Walks Far's and Running River's arms. "I understand you. Thank you, Grandchildren, for helping this old, worn out woman. I am grateful for such kindness. I was not certain if I would be welcome, but I had to try."

Blue Night Sky reached and ran her hands over Running River's cheeks. "I seek Shining Light. I am the Holy Woman of our band, the Red Bear Clan."

Everyone stopped what they were doing and ran to see the woman Walks Far had carried into camp.

"All of you look so worried. I am okay now... safe. I have walked for so long. Many, many times have I watched Grandmother Sun sleep."

Running River cocked her head. "Grandmother Sun? Who are the Red Bear Peoples, Great Elder?"

Bright Sun Flower and Hawk Soaring also went to their knees beside her. The woman had many winters over them. "Come," Bright Sun Flower waved. "Bring her to our lodge. Her body is wasted and needs care. Running River, bring more food, and someone heat water."

"Please, let me take her." Running River took a robe she had just finished making and wrapped it around her. "Walks Far, please ask your woman to bring clothing for the Holy Woman. She is close to the same size, and I know Many Clouds will not mind. My heart aches to see you in such condition."

She pointed to the flap of her lodge. "Feather, help us. Open the flap and hold it back. Sees Like Eagle has gone hunting with several others. I am alone, and the girls are in the canyons with other children."

Walks Far again gently lifted the woman. "You are lighter than a newborn fawn, Great Elder."

He saw a great passage of time on her face. He carried her past the young boy who held open the flap, but the Great Elder reached out and grabbed the young one's arm before the man could carry her inside.

"You," she whispered, "you are here. I dreamed I was to come here. I saw your face little one. As bright as a shining light. You... you guided me here. I found you...."

Exhausted, she went limp in Walks Far's arms.

"Grandmother?" The boy looked up to see Bright Sun Flower looking down with the same puzzled face. "Shining light? What did she mean?"

The elder woman lay on soft robes. Her footwear, long worn out, had plant fibers for bottoms, and ragged strips of tied leather kept them on.

The boy knelt next to the Great Elder. "She feels... familiar."

***

Bright Sun Flower stared into the woman's half-closed eyes. "Feather, I know what you are feeling. I feel the same kinship you feel." She put her arms around him and whispered, "This Great Elder is more than human. She holds great secrets only Spirits know."

I know who she is! I look into the eyes of the person Eagle spoke of and showed me. Her body shook with a knowing.

Walks Far's woman carried clothes and brushed past the boy and grandmother, who both stood staring at each other in bewilderment. She carried the new clothes for the Great Elder, a finely quilled dress with White Paws' face on it. The wolf gripped a tan and brown snake in his mouth. The beautiful design took up the entire top half.

"Go outside, little one," Many Clouds said, "and pull the flap down as you leave. We women must attend to her now." Her smile gentle, she offered the boy a basket of freshly cooked fish for him and his parents. "Walks Far, you must go attend our son, I left him sleeping."

Walks Far nodded and left.

"Go, Grandson," Bright Sun Flower said. "Take the fish to our lodge, then find White Paws and take Grandfather for a walk. He needs one now and so do you."

The flap dropped shut, leaving both boy and Grandfather outside with the rest of the band.

***

The Great Elder reached out toward the flap. "The boy is why I am here. We walked for many, many sunrises, near four cycles of Sister Moon." She shuddered as they undressed her rags, and sighed when warm water washed over her exposed skin, even as the air chilled her emaciated body. "Thank you, all of you, for your kindness."

The warmth of the soft elk dress made her eyes tear. "So long since I have felt the comfort of such soft, clean clothes." She waved her hand in the air. "My people... are hiding. I told them to stay put and let this old woman come to the camp first. Better than to risk the young. I told them to wait for a welcome. They are just across the river and will show themselves if you call my name. Please welcome them.

"Where is the boy? I did really see him, did I not? My Shining Light?"

"Yes, Great One, he is my grandson. I sent him to go walk with his grandfather. He is not far away."

"Then you are the one who saved his life when he was born. I know you, Bright Sun Flower. I ask that you take your Power back, Holy Woman. You never lost it—you put it away. It has come back to you now, and time grows short. We need strength to be on our side." Her eyes drifted closed.

"You must rest, then. I will bring him to you, and have someone call to your people." Bright Sun Flower got up and left the other women to care for the Great Elder.

"I am Running River, the niece of the boy's grandfather. You would do me a great honor to eat more of the food I cooked only a short time ago."

Blue Night Sky felt the love around her, one Running River appeared not to understand — warm, inviting love and... so much love. The young woman held back tears that were not from sorrow, but from the Energy of the Great Elder.

Blue Night Sky was accustomed to such reactions. She patted the young woman's hand. "You are special, Running River. Do not doubt that. I promise this to you — your future will be filled with joy." She reached up and ran her shaky hand through the woman's hair. "So soft, like the features on your face, young one. Never loose that gentleness about you. It no longer matters you were not the boy your father wanted. You are a woman who will one day bear an important child. Be proud you were born a woman."

Running River blushed and smiled. Her eyes brightened as Blue Night Sky touched her face.

The Great Elder patted her cheek. "Being strong also means of the heart. You showed it to everyone when you asked the others to let you care for me. Please see to my granddaughter and her little one. I do need to rest."

Running River beamed with pride. When she went to the lodge flap to go outside and find Blue Night Sky's family, she still glowed.

Blue Night Sky took in a deep sigh and closed her eyes.

***

Hawk Soaring gazed down into his grandson's face.

"White Paws is with Moon Face and the pups," Feather said. "They are teaching them to hunt. Why did that woman call me a shining light? She acted as if she knew me, as if... as if she appeared here... for me."

The boy's mind slipped into another place as he wandered the opposite way Hawk Soaring tried to lead him. He climbed up the winding path to the top the ridge, and began talking to himself.

Hawk Soaring could not make out the words, and he knew his company would be an intrusion. Besides, Running River brought back faraway thoughts of her mother, his younger sister. He was out hunting days away when she crossed over, victim to a fever. He had so few memories of her.

The shadow of Hawk's wings showed themselves on the ground in front of him. "Brother Hawk, why do you call now?"

He knew he must answer. He grabbed a bladder, filled it with water, and wandered down a quiet path to where he had stored away Sage the last time he and Hawk had communicated.

Hawk Soaring froze in place. *Sometimes I have flashes in my dreams of strange things I do not understand. Just a few nights before this, I dreamed of a bright white flash in the sky, a shining light.*

Hawk merely wanted to remind him of what he already knew.

He turned back toward the camp, where the Peoples were still buzzing about their new visitor.

Upon hearing approaching footsteps, he called to his woman. "Feather is wandering in his mind. I know he looks for answers. Hawk communicated with me to let the boy be, so I came back into camp. I knew you would be coming soon, so I waited for you."

He pointed up to the top ridge where the boy sat. "There sits our little man."

He turned to Bright Sun Flower, his forever woman, and spoke with a soft voice. "I too had a dream. All I saw was but a flash across the dark sky, flying toward the land where the cold comes from. Then I awoke."

He sighed, nodded and stared past her. "A shining light. Our grandson is that light, is he not?"

He turned and looked for answers in Bright Sun Flower's face. He, an old man, a warrior, sought comfort and took her hand into his. He did not care if anyone saw his open affection.

Without speaking, they walked toward the river to be alone.

She squeezed his hand tightly. "Flying Raven told me he and Makes Baskets will be gone for a short while. He must care for her. The flood was hard on both mother and unborn child.

"Soon, old man, you will have another grandchild to tease and play with. We both must let *this* grandchild, our Feather Floating In Water, go to his future. Our future is there also."

He waited to hear her speak more as they came to the edge of the water. Seldom did she remain silent; this silence worried him. She surely felt the approaching shift of time, as did he.

"Woman," he said, "why do you speak so few words? This is not like you."

She closed her eyes in concentration. "The Great Elder is the one who comes to guide our little grandson into manhood. With her comes what is left of her people. Eagle showed me this when she called me to seek her out.

"I can still feel myself soaring high above on the currents." She reached for his face. "I could never be happier than I am when I lie with you at night, but something about the total freedom of the sky.... I know you understand, Man Who Soars With Hawk. Someday we will fly away together."

She let out a long, deep sigh. "I know you have the Power of dreams the boy and I have, more than just the one you told me. As our grandson says, I can see it in your eyes."

She looked deep into his eyes, as if seeing them for the first time. "Perhaps, I have never looked as deep into your Soul as I do now. You and I are old, but the one who came into our camp this day is much older, a great Holy Woman, greater than even Flying Raven. I had hoped our little one would be grown, not an almost-eleven-winters-old boy."

She looked at the ground by her feet and swished the dirt back and forth. "Perhaps we have a few more winters, but I think this is but an old woman's wish. This Great Elder signals the change of many things. Our future and the future of entire bands of other Peoples will change now. I just am not sure how."

Hawk Soaring pulled her hand down as he sat. "Sit with me, Flower of my heart. The grass is soft. It is time we talked of unsaid things."

He needed to hold her, to speak of things Hawk had shared with him many seasons ago, before Feather was born.

Chapter 21

Feather watched the pups play hunt. White Paws and Moon Face played with them and, at the same time, taught them how to find hidden mice. The pups were now almost as big as their parents.

The season was changing, as had the urgency of his dreams.

His mind dwelled on both his dreams and the elder woman who came into their camp, one Feather knew well in his Soul. Uncertainty drove him to pack food and come up here to stay, if just for a while. He seldom talked to himself, but he wanted to hear his own words. Perhaps the Spirits might be listening too.

"I remember the flash of pure white light that surrounded White Paws and me in my vision the last time I sat here." He threw clumps of dirt at the canyon wall and watched them shatter into little pieces.

Above him, clouds captured Father Sun. Below his perch, the familiar azure river flowed, its banks lined by a mixture of trees and shrubs in shades of green, yellow and orange. The canyon's Eagles followed the air currents while just below, three smaller ones mimicked them. The red-orange colors of the canyon's stone wall mingled with splashes of white, making the sky appear a deeper turquoise.

Born here, he knew no other blends of colors, but in his mind, he saw an endless grassy land thick with thundering humpbacks, and beyond them trees unlike any in this land. He no longer wondered where it could be.

He knew.

"The ancients danced through me and a light entered my body but did not leave. I knew then that my mind grew faster than my body. Grandmother called it Energy a long time ago, and I did not understand. Now I do."

He hugged himself and rocked back and forth. The Energy, the feel of it, still made him tingle. Its vibrations filled him with every step he took now, a constant reminder that he had changed when the floodwaters had tried to claim him, his mother and grandmother.

"But what am I? Am I turning into a Spirit?"

The sound of his voice carried on Sister Wind, but no reply reached his ears. The time to move out of the safety of the canyons had become more than just a mysterious thought, whispered at in his dreams — it was a reality.

"I must convince my people to leave, but who listens to a boy? If I was born to be something different now, how can I, a... a *person* who enters soon into his eleventh winter, convince those who are older and wiser that I know of future dangers that come our way?"

He sat taller, squeezing his eyebrows together. "I will *make* myself heard. I will go to camp if I must, stand in the middle, and make everyone listen!"

He thought of the Great Elder who had come into camp. She was the way, the one to ask for help.

"These creatures on the backs of Deer are two separate beings. One being forces the other to do its bidding. The Great Elder who called me "Shining Light" is the one I must speak to."

He shivered at the thought of speaking to a stranger, yet not a stranger. *Footsteps.*

"I know the sound of your footsteps, Father."

***

Flying Raven Who Dreams sat on the ledge next to his son, and put an arm across his shoulders. "Feather Floating In Water, Shining Light—whoever you are—I will no longer call you little one or boy. I knew I was to guide you the day White Paws came to our camp, but I had no idea you would surpass even me."

This young one would one day take his place. It frightened him to think some people would not look up to him as they had for so long, yet he also held pride in his heart for his son.

"Have faith in yourself to know what to do, and it will happen. Be strong in mind and Spirit. This shining light will guide you all the days you live. Someday your body will catch up. For now, the people will have to see you as you are. Know you do not walk this part of your path alone."

He squeezed his son's shoulder and looked out over the valley.

"Another wishes to see you now." He hugged Feather and let him go. "She is a Holy Woman whose band—what is left of her band—came in across the water when Running River called to them. One at a time they waded across, and Running River showed no shame when she hugged each one and welcomed them. I have never seen that woman glow as she did two sunrises ago. Her words were soft, inviting."

He pondered how to describe the creatures that were with Blue Night Sky's people. "They... they have some kind of big dogs with them, big enough that they carried their children across the water. They are gentle, not wild, and do the people's bidding."

Flying Raven gazed into his Feather's eyes. *Where are you, my son?*

He continued. "As weak as Blue Night Sky was, she demanded they stay put until she found out if this was Shining Light's band."

Feather lowered his chin and stared at the lodge where the Great Elder rested.

Flying Raven tossed pebbles down the rim's face and watched as they disappeared. "You are now a big brother."

He smiled and let out a sigh, and tossed more pebbles down the canyon face. Sister Wind tossed his long, shiny blue-black hair, which the stars had dusted, across his face. He reached out, pulled it into a twist, and tossed it to the same side Wind insisted it go.

"The baby came early but is healthy and strong. Your mother wanted to stay a while longer just to be alone with her." He chuckled. "She actually told your new sister about the night in the wolves' den."

He laughed as he said, "Her name is Soft Breeze. She came just before the stars faded. Your mother said a soft breeze in a dream caressed her face and woke her. It was then she realized it was her birthing time. Imagine, your mother now dreams."

He watched his son's furrowed brow move up and down. "Son, are you listening?"

"Soft Breeze. That is a beautiful name, Father. I am honored to be her big brother." He turned to his father. "I have never seen you smile as you do now, or heard you laugh like that. I hope to see you laugh more often. It makes me feel safe somehow—like, if you do not worry, everything will be fine. Will everything be fine, Father? Is life going to stay as it is now? Can I be a boy, as Grandmother wants me to be?"

The Holy Man took his son's hand. They both looked down at the camp. Everyone appeared still, sitting around. Even the children sat quietly. "Nothing will ever be the same. Things change each day, and they always will. Life is like that. Each time we greet Father Sun, everything starts new. Even if we think everything was as before, it never is."

He thought for a brief time and spoke the words his heart held. "Life is a challenge, one we accept or do not. If we choose to close our eyes to what appears before them, the Spirits will see we are not worthy. They will move away and find another whose eyes are open, deep and clear."

He stared into the magic, the mystery, his son's eyes held. "Like you, my now growing Holy Man. Spirits chose well. They chose one whose body and mind are connected. Our bodies may sometimes act as if they are separate from our mind, but one cannot live without the other. Even if they are separate, they are connected in a way that... they can communicate, speak to each other."

His son leaned against him and laid his head on his chest. "Shining Light? Father, am I Shining Light? How can that be when no dream gave this name to me?"

They both gazed over the open rocky land, where White Paws and Moon Face chased their pups. Bright Beauty was far out ahead with something dangling in her mouth.

Flying Raven chuckled. "The one your grandmother named Bright Beauty will dominate her brothers. She was the smallest in the group, but she has proven her worth, just like another I know."

He took his son's face in his hands, his eyes misty. "I knew this day would come, just not so soon. You are so young to go on a Vision Quest, but I think you must. We will prepare your mind over the next few moons. I will help you find a place, unless you have one."

"Father, what happens in a Vision Quest?"

Flying Raven drew air deep into his lungs. "This journey that you will take is one only you can go on. I will be somewhere nearby, but I will not come to you. What you see, what you do, is a personal matter. Since I am the Holy Man, you will speak to me afterwa—" He had to think about that. "Perhaps it will be the Great Elder you speak to."

He never thought it would be another his son may seek. He felt a sharp pain when he swallowed. *My son. He is my son.*

***

Feather returned to throwing dirt clumps. "Grandfather and others tell me I may carry many names in my life. The Great Elder woman has named me Shining Light, and I will honor it until a new name comes my way in my Vision Quest."

He sat taller and felt excited, but his heart roared a fast drumbeat. "I... I guess... should I go see her now? Will you come with me?"

His voice pleaded that he not go alone, but in his heart he knew he must. "Please tell Mother that no matter what happens in the days to come, I will still be her little boy."

Without another glance at his father, he stood, turned and headed to camp, toward the lodge where a special woman lay. She would shape his destiny, help him create one for the Peoples that he would give rise to.

Slow steps down the worn path took him where he did not want to go. The chill in the canyon air made him feel alive. Sister Wind howled her song while she swirled around his body, giving him the courage to walk faster.

***

Bright Sun Flower stood before Running River's lodge and motioned her grandson to her, the smell of Sacred Sage wafting about her. She re-lit the Sage and ran it over his body, careful to have him raise even his feet so she could cleanse there also, all the while singing a blessing song.

"This woman who wishes to see you," she said, "has watched over you in her visions since you were born. She has spent her life praying for you, sending us both dreams, and apparently that grandfather of yours who chose to remain silent. Perhaps he had hoped many seasons would pass, as I did, before the Spirits would call upon you. I now understand she wanted us to guide you upon your path."

She put her head down. "I failed you. I wanted you to be a little boy longer."

He tugged at her sleeve to make her look at him. "You did not fail me. You taught me much and guided me to learn things on my own, without once pushing me the way you wanted me to go. If I am to be Shining Light, you are to be the star that light comes from."

He hugged her as small tears escaped and trickled down his face.

She held him against her without getting on her knees. He was not a little boy anymore. Soon, it would be she who would ask *his* advice.

Strange, there really is a soft light around him.

She gently pushed him from her and took his hand. "Come, we will go listen to Blue Night Sky together."

Inside the lodge, Blue Night Sky rested against soft hides that covered the raised platform, which allowed her to sit. Color had returned to her face, and her smile showed her thanks. A glow around her face shone a rich blue unlike any ever seen in the waking world to Bright Sun Flower. Her hair, whiter than snow and now clean, sparkled as tiny blue sparks swirled around and in it.

Both Grandmother and Grandson gazed into her dark eyes that lent a deep, mystical blue hue.

"Do not stare. It is impolite," the Great Elder said. "Sit and share my drink. The women of your band must have thought I could drink this entire pot by myself. Bright Sun Flower, go tell your man to make sure my people are fed. I wish to be alone with your grandson."

She waved her off. "And, child, do come back after some time passes. I wish to speak to you and your grandson together."

Bright Sun Flower nodded and turned.

The boy stared with wide eyes. He had never heard his grandmother called a child before.

She ignored his chuckling as she left.

***

"Do not chuckle, Shining Light, I am much older than your grandmother. Many winters older." She stared at the quilled basket in front of her, followed the zigzag pattern down the basket, took in a long breath, and began her story.

"I watched as your mother gave birth to you, young one. Your grandmother worried as she felt you shift the wrong way days before your birth, but said nothing. Instead, she went into the canyons and prayed. Her Spirit Guide, Eagle, flew and landed in my dream. Yes, child, stop raising your eyebrows at me. I know one does not speak of Spirit Guides freely, but I am a Holy Woman and know much. Just as you, Shining Light, will know much in time."

She cocked her head at the boy as she filled her small pot with the hot liquid. The young one looked down at the robe he sat on.

She tried simple conversation to get him to look up. "The warmth feels so good on my hands. I never thought to feel such comfort again, Shining Light."

She paused, smiled and said, "I give you this name—Shining Light."

Still he looks away. I feel sadness, not fear.

"Look at me, boy."

Chapter 22

Feather... err... Shining Light looked into Blue Night Sky's bright eyes. His eyelids grew heavy and he closed them, felt her Energy drift into his own, become part of him, then move out and flow away.

His mind followed their mingled Energy to a time when his grandmother prayed. His mother was giving birth to him head first, instead of backwards as Bright Sun Flower had worried. Next, his first father fought a great battle and lost. His father's Spirit rose, blending into the Energy around him, and sparks of many colors swirled and joined, then separated. They formed into a funnel and flew above him.

He looked up as they burst open and rained back down on him, on everything. The land, bright with many colors, called to him.

A band of unknown Peoples appeared, dancing, swaying in a circle around him, around everything. They were so ancient. He knew this deep inside his Soul, and at first, he backed away from them, but the muzzle of Wolf pushed him forward. The ancients wore animal hides woven together. One wore a white hide with the head of a White humpback. He wondered at the words and wished he could understand them, so familiar, yet.... One reached out to him with a yellow turtle rattle and offered it to him. His hand reached out, took the rattle.

A woman's voice called to him. "Feather, come back." Gentle hands lay on his shoulders. "Follow my voice. I am here. Grab hold of the sound and let it bring you to me, back to where your body is."

He awoke in Bright Sun Flower's arms, as she rested on a robe next to Blue Night Sky. He struggled to sit up.

"Shhh...." She rocked him gently. "You are safe. Relax and look around. Everything is okay."

Bright light returned to the lodge and shocked his eyes nearly closed. He jerked up, eyes now wide.

"Grandmother, where did you come from? Blue Night Sky showed me my birth and the battle where my first father—" He looked over at the Great Elder, who smiled as if nothing was out of the realm of normal. "How did you do that? Where was I? Did I really see what I saw? What—"

He looked up at his grandmother and smiled. "You called me Feather."

She laughed and squeezed him to her body. "My grandson is back. Blue Night Sky just showed you something special. Someday soon, you will be able to do that on your own. Your mind will take you places your body cannot follow."

She rocked and cooed to him as she would a baby. Their minds touched. Before them, in a misty haze, stood a tall man with hair dark as black obsidian that fell below his elbows. His clothes were decorated with unusual colored shell beads of blues, purples and silvers. They mixed with elk teeth and shone and from his tunic.

"Salt water beads," a voice whispered.

Who? They both realized that Blue Night Sky had shown them *their* future. But Salt beads? What were these?

The Great Elder talked on, everything normal to her. "Are my people settled in? We are not so many. You will find room for us. It will not be long before this entire band moves on. Yes, girl, you heard me. I know your dreams have already told you this, Bright Sun Flower."

She looked at him. "My granddaughter's daughter is anxious to meet you, Shining Light. She has waited a long time."

Bright Sun Flower reached out and brushed her fingers along the Holy Woman's arm. "Great Elder, I do not mean to be so bold. Forgive my outburst, but please tell me how you came to be here?"

"Child, what matters is that I am here." She raised the pot of herbs and inhaled the aroma, took a sip and gazed calmly at his grandmother before her. "I followed the stars that led me to your Fish Peoples camp. Just as my dreams told me to do."

She bowed her head. "Most of my people did not survive the attack from the others, the hairy-faced ones. They came in the night and... all of a sudden screams rang out everywhere."

Her arms trembled, spilling some of her drink. She took a shaky breath and began again. "Our men and women warriors ran out, prepared to do battle. It was dark and no one knew which way to turn. A few people tried to get fires going but were unsuccessful. All we could do was scatter into the trees and hide in the caves near our camp."

Her gaze again followed the basket's quillwork. She reached over, grabbed hold of Shining Light's arm, and squeezed so hard he winced. "No sounds came from the camp when light came. Several people were too frightened to come out, so they huddled in the cave's darkness as others of our people made their way through shrubs and grasses. The smell of fire and... and—"

Running River, apparently no longer content to sit outside with others who had gathered to listen through the open flaps, crawled in and over Shining light to reach the Great Elder. She held Blue Night Sky in her arms and cried. "Sweet Mother! I am so sorry, grandmother of the people. You are safe now. Safe."

Blue Night Sky patted her arms. "Perhaps not as safe as you think. We believe they come this way." She pushed herself up away from Running River and patted her hand. "We worried that those who did not survive had Spirits who wandered the land, so we had to stay for them, dance and sing until they went to the stars. We prayed and sang to the Great One for many days before starting our journey. We had the luck to have with us some of the attacker's big dogs. We put our children on their backs and came in search of Shining Light's camp."

She turned and looked into his eyes. "We heard them called mus-tang by one who spoke some of our words. He told us to go hide and not come out until these people-creatures left."

She took in several more slow sips of the brew before continuing. "Shining Light, please fill my pot with more drink." She patted his hand and went on with her story.

"The man who saved us, Del-ane, as he called himself, took one of our women as a mate before his own kind came. The women found him injured and hiding under the brush — moons before the attack. So amazed by his hairy face, they brought him back to us. He tried to use his words and ours to explain how his own people had abandoned him when they saw he might not live. He did not speak our language very well, and had no way of telling us of the danger coming our way until he had time to learn more of our words."

She stared off, no doubt seeing in her mind the day unfold once more. Her eyes watered as she spoke. "When he had been with us most part of a season, he tried to make us understand that we needed to leave, but we wondered why. We stayed."

She looked away and wiped tears on the soft elk skin sleeve of her dress. "We believe we lost him in the battle, as he chose to stay behind when we ran. We do know he went into their camp and took some of the big dogs, and turned loose some of the captives when they came after us. Del-ane ran back to us and with broken words — told us to ride on the big dogs' backs."

The Great Elder's words slowed. She picked up her words again, but looked down at her pot of herbs. "He pointed to himself and said, 'No all bad men.' He went on to tell us many of his own men left their people, took mates and joined with some of the bands they encountered. He turned and ran after another hairy-faced one, to do battle. The ones who push forward are those we must be wary of."

She took a pouch from around her neck, and pulled out a shiny yellow pockmarked rock much smaller than her palm. "Del-ane gave this to us and asked if we had ever seen one before. None of us had. He warned that his people sought this rock. It made his kind crazy. They would do anything to get more."

She handed the rock and pouch to Shining Light. "Keep it to show others, to warn those you will encounter. I am so tired, I must rest."

Exhausted, she let go of the pot of herbs.

Bright Sun Flower caught the pot before it could burn the Great Elder. She stared at her with much respect. "I moan over my bad knees, and this very old one drug herself for moons to get here. This is a great woman, indeed, far more so than any human I have ever encountered. Why did they not put her on a drag?"

Blue Night Sky opened her eyes. "Child, I had to push myself to show the wounded that they too could make it. *They* did not give up because *I* would not. Understand?"

She sighed and closed her eyes. "Now let this old, worn-out woman rest. Tell my story to your Holy Man, so he can tell others of your band who are not outside this lodge listening."

She waved them both away and nestled down in Running River's arms.

Running River leaned back, covered them both with a thin robe, closed her tear-filled eyes, and did not stir.

***

Bright Sun Flower pushed her grandson outside and they walked away, as did others who had come to listen. Most whispered and went into their lodges.

"Come with me," she said. "Blue Night Sky needs to rest. We will come back—"

"Big dogs? More little dogs? Why did she give me this rock and say to warn the people I would encounter? Where am I going, Grandmother?"

Her grandson scratched his confused head. He could not contain himself, even though he knew he spoke disrespectfully by interrupting another person. "In my dreams, I saw big deer creatures with some kind of beings on top of them. These must be the big dogs. Where do they come from? Only Running River and Sees Like Eagle have any little dogs, and those came from Walking Stick. I know many bands have them, but.... Grandmother, why did we never have little dogs?"

She stopped walking and grinned. "Still so many words spill out of your mouth. Where do you find them all?"

She sat on a log placed in front of a tree for that purpose, and patted it for him to sit. "I think it is because we seldom traveled as far as other bands, and little dogs need food as we do. They would have needed the food we ate. Our band trades for much of the foods we eat because we seldom leave the canyons."

Growls and snarls rose from behind the lodge, and they jumped up and ran around to find White Paws standing over a much smaller blue-grey spotted dog. Behind him stood Moon Face, who paced nervously above her wolf pups as they made friends with the other dogs.

People stood around, unsure of what to do. White Paws, they knew, could hurt or kill the smaller dog.

Out of the gathered people, a young girl whose clothing was in the same tattered condition as Blue Night Sky's ran forward. Her strong voice commanded attention in spite of her small frame. "Blue Waters, come here! You are not to cause trouble. That wolf will tear you to shreds."

She pulled him back by the nape of his neck, and looked shyly at the boy who now stood in front of White Paws. "You are Shining Light?"

Her smile made him uncertain what his name was anymore. He grabbed White Paws, called to Moon Face and the pups, and rushed off into the canyons.

Behind him laughter, both familiar and not, echoed his hasty withdrawal.

***

"Rising Moon, I do not think it was your dog who scared that boy. I think it was you!" Morning Star was having too much fun to comfort her sad daughter.

Rising Moon looked up at her laughing mother. "I know you have wanted to meet him ever since my grandmother dreamed of him the same night you did, but perhaps he likes wolves better than girls?"

An annoyed girl came to stand before the pair. She shook with anger at their jest, contorting her face in defiance. "I am Chases Butterflies and Feather is my cousin, and he likes girls! I know he does because, well, because he likes me."

Chases Butterflies glared at Morning Star. Her small round chin disappeared under a quivering bottom lip. Her brows furrowed and half hid her round eyes.

A woman slipped out of the lodge and made her way around to where Chases Butterflies stood with her little fists clenched. The woman reached out and comforted the pouting girl, hugging her and patting her back. "We all know Feather likes girls, Daughter. We need to feed our new band members some of the fish you helped with."

She took Chases Butterflies by the hand, and gently took Rising Moon with her other one, and smiled at Morning Star.

Rising Moon pulled away and snuck behind her mother.

"I am Running River, and you are welcome to come and eat, if you do not mind three little girls."

Her mother glanced at Running River's belly.

"Yes, a fourth will come in about five moons. I have a husband who needs to go hunting *much* more than he does. Where is your man? Do you have more children?"

Running River stopped her questions when Morning Star put her head down.

"I am sorry to pry. Come, eat and rest. There will be much time for talk later."

Morning Star looked at Running River with pinched brows. "You will have four children? This is indeed a rich band. We try to only have two or three children."

Running River blushed. "I will explain it to you inside." Her smile broadened.

Rising Moon still watched where the confused boy had disappeared. "Mother," she whispered, "she called him Feather. Is he not Shining Light?"

Morning Star bunched up her shoulders. "I think he is, but before that, he had another name. We are all a bit confused, Daughter. Come with me. I can smell the wonderful scent of cooked food everywhere my nose turns. We were the last to find our way to this camp, thanks to having to go hunt down your dog. I know you are as hungry as I am."

Rising Moon reluctantly took her mother's hand and walked with her to Running River's lodge, where Blue Night Sky rested. She tripped over the lodge's bottom flap while still watching where the boy had gone.

Both mothers laughed.

"My daughter has eyes for that boy," her mother said, "and they are still but babies."

Rising Moon refocused her attention on her mother. "I am going to be thirteen winters soon! I am no baby!"

She could feel herself blushing, and stomped outside, this time careful where she placed her feet. She stood but for a short span of time before realizing she had nowhere to go.

She turned around and stomped back into the lodge with her arms folded in frustration. "Baby! I will bear my own baby when I am seventeen winters old! Your own grandmother told me this, and she would know. Blue Night Sky knows everything!"

Chapter 23

Blue Night Sky hobbled with her walking stick across the mix of yellow, purple and white flowers poking through the cinnamon and green grasses of the canyon. She pretended it was easy to keep up with the young one on their daily walk. Her new clothes fit her well now that food filled her belly, instead of hunger. The yellow and blue quillwork on her dress danced around her tiny waist in small circles, the yellow inside the blue.

The elder did her best to teach the young one in only small portions, but her time to teach neared its end. "Shining Light, we must sit where we can talk. I have spent a full cycle of seasons with the Fish People, and you are a winter older and ready to learn more than the simple things I have taught you. Shall we sit over by the stream? Now that your wolf and the dogs have gotten used to each other, we need to let them wander together. You and Rising Moon try too hard to keep them separated."

They watched White Paws and Blue Waters, Rising Moon's dog, sniff under plants and big boulders. Neither the wolf nor the dog cared they were different. Moon Face had gotten used to her puppies playing with the dog pups, and no fights broke out.

"My old bones sometimes choose not to listen to me when I ask things of them—steady my stick for me." Still a proud spitfire in her own mind, she was not about to ask him to help her sit.

"Great Elder...."

"Please, call me Blue Night Sky. You have my permission, Shining Light." She chuckled at the quiet boy knowing that to remain quiet was a feat for one whose mouth always churned with words.

"Now steady my stick, boy." Her shaky hand reach for the ground as her knees bent forward.

***

He did not attempt to help her sit—to offer the greatest respect possible to her was important.

Blue Night Sky reached for his hand after she sat, and held his warm one in her cold one. "Sit here next to me," she said, "where the grass softens the ground. Close your eyes and relax, get comfortable. I wish to take you on a journey. For this journey, you need only to remain still."

She sat sideways, legs tucked and used her arms for support as she closed her eyes and took in a deep breath.

Shining Light fidgeted. *Be still? I cannot go somewhere and not move! I do not even know my own name now. I should have stuck with Feather Floating In Water. At least I would have known who I was.*

'You know who you are, boy, and yes, you can go somewhere and not move. Now breathe deep the scent of nothingness.'

She is in my head! How did she do that? Nothingness?

'Be silent, boy, and close your eyes. I know you peek. Both eyes. Now... again... breathe. This time let every thought leave as you exhale. Again, breathe in nothing... and now breathe out nothing. Breathe....'

Before them, in this place of nothing, a beautiful young woman stood with dark hair that fell about her knees. Tiny blue lights surrounded her, moved around and through her. A shining light of the purest white engulfed her.

'Boy, I have much to teach you and little time. Listen with all your being. This is the place of no sound, of nothingness, where everything exists. This is the center of the Circle, the end of the beginning, and the beginning of all that there is. There is no time. There is no need of it. This place just is. It is all that we are or will ever be... as long as the center stays whole. Ask questions if you must. I will respond. Always feel you can do so with me.'

Why, Great Elder, is there no need of time here?

'Time is what our bodies use. We are born, grow and age. Here we are beyond the needs of the body. Our Spirits continue, and they do not need time. Spirits are forever. I have much to say, much for you to absorb. Do not expect to understand all of it now.'

Both drifted in the misty fog for some time. He tried to understand, but she remained silent.

Please, Blue Night Sky, tell me more. I can actually feel your vibrations as you shift your weight onto your other hip.

'Shows me, boy, that we are one. Many things can make cracks in the Circle — anger, hatred, greed, lust, and those who think only they matter and have no respect for other beings. The land's destruction is coming from a future generation who will not understand what they do because no one ever taught them. Learn all you can, so when the time readies itself, you can teach all you know."

Neither the sound of the river nor the peep of a bird broke the silence. No color existed anywhere, yet all the colors blended into one bright clear light.

'You see only me, and the shining light around me, because I will it so. The blue sparks are of our Spirit. We are the blue sparks. Here is safety. Protect the safety of the Circle. It is important. It is the very means of our existence.'

White Paws, Moon Face and their pups.... What about —

'Do not worry for your wolf, for he and all his kind — four-legged, winged, many-legged, and no-legged — are with us. They are within the Circle. The plants, waters, stones, Sister Wind — they too are with us but apart from us. We all make up the whole. We all make up the whole.'

Shining Light's body tingled even though his mind traveled. Energy surged through him and he felt it as it flowed through Blue Night Sky, connecting them to one another. He inhaled the emotion and relaxed further.

'We are not separate from other beings. What is done to one also affects the others. If you disrespect one, you cause grief for all. The balance will be upset for every being. Remember this well, Shining Light.'

She paused and he tried to absorb all she had spoken.

'Most people have nearly half their lives to learn what I try to make your mind take in within such a short time. I myself learned from a Holy Man over many seasons. He did not teach me with words, but rather allowed me to discover most things on my own.'

He inhaled deeply of this knowledge. He understood and was grateful for what she was trying to do.

'Our Spirits create the colors of the rainbow. Always there will be a rainbow. That is why your grandfather's father followed the river. The rainbow showed him he was going the right way. You, Shining Light, must follow the rainbow within you. Your White Paws will help you.

'His sons and daughters will be with you on this side, even if their parents are on the other side. Both sides work together to create the whole, to guide, supervise, advise – but only if you are listening. Some who are coming to this land will not listen. No one ever taught them how, and their hearts and minds only accept what they can see in front of them.

'They will be the danger you must watch for, but do not think all are bad. You may find some are good and will try hard to become part of who we are. I must make you understand this. Never assume the ones who come will all be enemies. Of course, first and foremost, protect your People – always, Shining Light.'

Great Elder, who are these people of who you speak? Where do they come from?

'A long time will pass, Shining Light, before these Peoples cross a great mass of water, water so big that no one can see across it. On our Mother lives a great many Peoples. More kinds live on her than you can comprehend. Some day they will all come here, just as the ones we now must run from. Many will desire what we have, and try to take it for their own.

'Listen well to me, for I shall be returning with you but a few more times. Our Mother's ground shakes deep inside, and many, many changes come. You must be ready to do your part. Your visions are of what is to come, what must come. You must take all the people who will follow. You will know when you must leave – do not second-guess yourself. You must always follow your first instinct.

'I have brought you to the center of the Circle this time, and I will help you if you need me, but next time you must try to find your own way here. And you will. Do not ever doubt yourself. Doubt is your enemy. Doubt will lead you down a dead path. If you find yourself at the end of this dead path, reach out for guidance offered from the Spirits. You are not alone in here. Creator – the Great One, the Great Mystery – is here. All living is here. The Spirits will help.'

'I know you hear my thoughts, my regrets. Learn from them. The center of the Circle is within you, and the center is everywhere. It is within each of us, every living being. We are the Circle. By asking the High Power – Creator – for help, you will find an inner peace, and from that you will be able to spread peace to all that you encounter, even the enemy, be it the enemy within yourself or the one you confront in battle.

'There is more than one kind of battle, boy. As you grow and learn, you will know the difference, and you will learn how to deal with each one differently.

'There is no death here. Believe in all that the High Power has made, and most of all, believe in your self. Confidence will give you Power and make you strong. Many Spirits are here with us. Turtle Dove is here. If you ever question what to do, seek the silence, and the Spirits will answer. The answer you seek is already within you, but sometimes asking will help. One more thing....'

The Great Elder's chuckle vibrated the Energy.

'Rising Moon will be your woman. Turtle Dove confirmed what I already knew... and Chases Butterflies will have a special place at your side no woman has ever had.'

"Woman! Rising Moon? Where is Turtle Dove? What do you mean Chases Butterflies will have a special place no woman has ever had? She is just a little girl!" He turned around and felt dizzy. "Wha...! Blue Night Sky, where are you? Hey, what happened?"

He stood up and knew he was alone. He walked back to the camp.

How to explain this one? I cannot explain when I have no answer.

***

Blue Night Sky sat with Running River and Rising Moon, chatting away as if the old Holy Woman had never left. Her dark eyes shone a deep, mysterious blue when she turned and calmly looked at Shining Light.

How did she get back? A tingle surged through his body as several tiny blue lights danced around him.

'I was never with you, Shining Light, yet I am still there, next to the stream.'

Her sparks of Energy mingled with his. A few wisps of blue followed his movements. He began to understand, and grinned at the Great Elder. For a brief flash in time, they were one. He laughed loudly as White Paws and Blue Waters chased after each other, followed by a mix of other wolves and dogs.

Chapter 24

Running River's two daughters dashed through the camp dragging their little sister with them. In Running River's arms rested her son.

She turned to Makes Baskets and Flying Raven, who played with Soft Breeze. "He has grown strong with my milk, and now bits of chewed food make him smile. How fast he has grown! I am thankful for this precious gift, to offer my man a son at last." She snuggled her baby.

"I know rarely does more than one woman occupy a lodge in our band, but Morning Star and I cared much for each other, so I asked Sees Like Eagle to take Morning Star as his second companion." She laughed. "I could tell he knew I was not asking. He shrugged his shoulders and smiled at the decision I made for him. He is a good man."

She lifted up her son as her daughters tried to claim her lap. "Girls! My lap is not so big that all of you can sit on it! You baby brother needs my attention now. I promise we will all play together once your father has returned from hunting."

The girls raced off with the other children and laughed. Since Blue Night Sky had talked to her the day they had brought her into the camp, Running River had changed. She smiled more, loved life, and her whole being had brightened. Still, she liked to tease.

"Rising Moon's wide-eyed expression, when Sees Like Eagle told her she was now part of the family, made me choke with laughter. The girl made sure we understood she was going to live with Blue Night Sky."

She held Makes Baskets attention. "Rising Moon did not want to become Shining Light's cousin, which she would be if she moved in with us. She hugged her mother, who smiled and showed no tears when she left our lodge. She is past her fourteenth winter and should soon have her first moon time—should have had one by now, actually—and the band will welcome a new woman."

She smiled sweetly at a glaring Makes Baskets. "Oh, silly cousin, you know I joke. It will be a very long time before your now twelve-winters-old son takes a woman. I wonder if she will wait for him?"

"Cousin of mine, my son has much time yet as you say." Makes Baskets' voice became a whisper. "I do wish it was so far away that none of us could even envision it."

"Baskets, time has a way of moving forward and leaving behind those who do not keep up with it. You cannot hold him forever in your arms, only in your heart." She smiled and gently tapped her shoulder. "I need to go get some swamp plant fluff to change my son."

She got up, but glanced back as her cousin smiled at her then stuck out her tongue.

***

Shining Light meandered through the canyons with White Paws and Sandstone. His thoughts fluttered everywhere. The day promised warmth even if Father Sun hung low these days, so the pair wandered next to the river.

"Grandmother still speaks my child name of Feather, and I know she does not do this out of disrespect, but out of love.

"My father has taught me the Holy ways: how to honor gift, sing, and pray for guidance every time Father Sun wakes the camp. He spent much time alone with me in our lodge, and I learned who I was, who I would become, and everything that time would bring my way."

He ran his hands down White Paws' head and back, remembering when he had to kneel down to touch the wolf's back. He stopped to pick the last of the yellow flowers he would make into the healing salve for his grandmother, and placed them in a pack slung over his shoulders.

"White Paws, mother taught me about the plants—the ones for healing, the ones to eat, and most important, the way to make them into the healers they were meant to be."

The trio climbed up to his favorite outcropping, followed by Moon Face's nearly grown second litter. He laughed as Bright Beauty pushed them back down into the canyon. In her role as second mother, she tried to get them to stop playing and running down the stream.

That brings back memories. I remember running down that very stream and racing back into Grandmother's arms! Such happy days. How did I grow so fast?

Sandstone, the female big dog who had chosen to stay at his side, played with White Paws. The big dog would flick her tail, turn back and race past him in a blur of yellow color.

White Paws returned to his side, and he petted him again. "The big dogs make hunting and gathering firewood easier—once the animals learned the drags behind them would not attack!" He let go a loud chuckle. "We older ones must move them daily to graze, but no one minds. We are all grateful for them."

White Paws dashed off to play his games again.

Shining Light had come up to be alone and pray to the Spirits, to Creator for guidance. He took one last look at the wolves, and Sandstone racing to catch up with White Paws, and then stood arms raised.

He knew things were about to change.

***

Blue Night Sky and Bright Sun Flower had talked much about the right time to tell every one of their impending changes, and this time had arrived. They would mention the lack of food as a start.

They sat together and enjoyed the last of the humpback meat Bright Sun Flower had reheated from the sunrise meal. The Great Elder played with the knots that age had placed on her finger joints.

She loved this little canyon hideaway and the gentleness of the land. She breathed in a deep sigh and let her sadness go with it. "We must gather the people, child." She patted Bright Sun Flower's knee. "My dreams warn me so often that I do not dream of anything else. Your grandson and I have talked, and I know you have talked to both him and his father. We must not put it off any longer. We must leave before the snows."

Bright Sun Flower stretched her back, twisting it. "I know, I feel it also. My grandson finally spoke to me of a grey dust that invades his dreams. He said that when the dust cleared, the land turned darker than the dust. As hard as he tried, he found no life when he walked the dream land — not even sound." She stared off.

Blue Night Sky knew she wandered in her mind, and waited for her to continue.

"Feather took so long to tell me. The time of his vision of the ancient ones, who walked off the ridge, was the first time he opened up to me. He said they danced off the ridge pointing toward where we were to go. He knew then his childhood had faded." Bright Sun Flower bowed her head. "I am sure you remember the vision I had that showed me who the ancient ones are. I am not sure he is ready to hear that yet. I apologize, Blue Night Sky. I still call him Feather."

Blue Night Sky shifted her weight from one hip to the other. She refocused the talk back to where she needed it to be. "This is the best time of year for my old bones to soak up the warm sun. I know this cold season is going to be mild, and the ones we need to avoid will take advantage of the warmer weather. The Peoples must do the same."

She leaned her head toward Bright Sun Flower as Shining Light stood up on the canyon's ledge. He stood, arms raised in prayer. "I know what it is like to lose a young one before they are grown. Look at Rising Moon."

The two Elders reached out their withered hands and touched. They smiled.

"Pass the word among the people to meet in the Counsel Lodge after the evening meal, Grandmother of Shining Light. Your grandson may already know more than he tells us. I need time to myself to gather my thoughts."

Blue Night Sky leaned her walking stick forward and pushed herself up. The small shells tinkled on her dress fringe. "I thank you for the dress you spent much time on for me. The yellow flowers that wrap around my waist remind me of the beauty in life."

She headed to her lodge, and tied the flap shut.

***

Bright Sun Flower's knees hurt her less since Blue Night Sky had prayed over them, and the herbal salve mixed by her grandson gave her more freedom of movement than in years past.

She walked toward her lodge when the cry of Eagles captured her attention. The pair soared high overhead, while their young sat on a ledge, watching. Four times, they called. She waited to see if their young would take flight, but they perched themselves on the ledge.

Time... time. The whisper in her mind wasn't one she wanted to hear.

Chapter 25

Flying Raven Who Dreams smiled. Shining Light's big dog companion, Sandstone, named after the swirling yellow-white colors that lay in separate layers from the red-orange of the canyons, shoved her muzzle into his son's face. She had a white mane with yellow streaks, a white face and pale brown eyes. Just like all the other big dogs, light brown stripes ran part way up her legs. She followed Shining Light just as his wolves did. He took responsibility for keeping her fed. Sandstone's young one, mostly brown, now wandered more often with the main group of his kind. Most of the big dogs had colors in browns, some mixed with white, grey and charcoal.

Shining Light had mastered the riding skill. He raced through the camp on Sandstone's back with one arm raised, whooping and calling out to his mother.

Makes Baskets' hands rushed to her face and she squealed when he passed her. She poked her smiling husband in the ribs with a sharp elbow. "My son rides a big dog? Why did you not tell me of this? What if he falls?"

He shrugged. "I, for one, am proud of our son. He shows he is unafraid, and that will take him farther in life than one who cringes, as some did when Long Arrow asked if they wanted to learn." He shot her a sideways glance while watching his son race past the camp again. "I ride and you never worry for me."

He turned to her and grinned at her scowl. "Would you rather I crawl through grass that is not tall enough to hide me while I hunt a snorting humpback? Since Long Arrow taught the braver of our people to ride, we no longer worry. We ride up to them, instead. No dangerous crawling on the ground, and we do not have to run away without getting meat."

He crossed his arms, satisfied he had won the discussion.

Blue Night Sky stood at her side before Makes Baskets had time to scold her man some more. "I wish to speak to you, and I bring Long Arrow with me."

She motioned the man forward and continued. "I know some did not trust him when he arrived in camp alone. He did bring four more big dogs, one with a young one that walked by her side. He followed the trail my people had left, and found the Fish People. When I told others that he worried that the trail led right to our camp, not many listened. The band, unaccustomed to conflict or danger, save the skirmish eight winters past, thought he only boasted of possible danger to elevate himself. This is wrong. I, Blue Night Sky, defend him."

She again motioned for him to step forward even further.

Flying Raven waited for Blue Night Sky to sit. He welcomed Long Arrow with a nod. He and the man had spent time together fishing in the evenings, talking well into the darkness as old friends might. He was glad he had taken the time to know Long Arrow, to learn about him, to listen to him.

"Great Elder," he said, "if you seek my son, he just rode a big dog through the camp."

She glared at Long Arrow, who did not notice, or ignored it, as he looked elsewhere about the camp.

Blue Night Sky took her time, leaning on her walking stick as she knelt down. She no longer looked like darkness stalked her.

They marveled at the blue sparks that danced in the Holy Woman's hair.

Makes Baskets suddenly looked away. "Forgive my stare, please. Let me get you some nice hot herbs to drink." As Makes Baskets stood, she turned back and faced the man who had taught her son the skill of riding. "And you too, Long Arrow. I offer drink and food to you also."

She pulled fish from her steaming basket and placed them on woven square mats she had weaved for that purpose. With a smile, she offered the food to the pair, along with flattened bread made from the roots of the Swamp Plant.

"Thank you for such kindness, Makes Baskets." Long Arrow examined the mat. "Very useful plant." He wasted no time eating the fish prepared with tasteful herbs. "I come from a land where these plants and the herbs you use are scarce. My own people lived in a dryer land. We flourished there well enough... until the strange ones came."

He looked down for a short span, as if uncomfortable, then cleared his throat and continued. "I know you use every part of the swamp plant. I would like to know about that one."

He seemed to want small talk before telling her what they must. He leaned over past Makes Baskets to see him, but Flying Raven Who Dreams remained silent.

"Oh, yes." Makes Baskets settled on the ground next to the fire, in between her man and Long Arrow. She raised a leaf not yet used. "The life-giving plant we call swamp grass. Every part of the plant is useful. We gather the roots in the early part of the year, and eat them raw or roasted. The inside part, which grows as corn, is peeled back and the inside is boiled. The leaves are good for weaving mats, and the brown tops, when ripe, pop open. We use them to fill a thin leather tie on our babies, to keep their bottoms protected, and so the mother has a way of keeping the babies from... um... going on themselves."

She took another drink from her pot. "We make poultices from the split and bruised roots, which we use for cuts and wounds, bruises, even the stings from the winged ones who seek out the flowers. The dried stalks make our arrows, and we carry the fluff for fire starters when we travel. We must be careful to avoid a poisonous plant with leaves that look like it. It has a purple flower when in bloom, so we try to pick them out."

Long Arrow licked his fingers. "You have a gift with the herbs. I would not know the poison plant of which you speak. Perhaps, when you see one, you will show me?'

Makes Baskets sat taller. "Of course, I would be honored to do so."

Blue Night Sky sat on the other side of Long Arrow. She leaned forward to see Makes Baskets. "We will have much use for them when we travel to a new land soon. Food becomes scarce here, too scarce for a band this size." She held up a hand as Makes Baskets prepared to respond. "Be still, granddaughter, it is Long Arrow and I who must talk."

Hawk Soaring and Shining Light came to stand behind the Great Elder. Without looking behind her, Blue Night Sky motioned them to sit.

Flying Raven rubbed his mate's shoulder, then took her hand.

"Raven, what—"

"Your man," Blue Night Sky continued, "along with Hawk Soaring, Sees Like Eagle, the trader's two sons and Long Arrow, will each take a big dog and go to the nearby bands, to warn them of a very dangerous enemy that comes their way. They will leave just before Grandmother, or as you say, Father Sun, wakes."

Long Arrow played with his two twisted fingers. He grinned and explained. "While escaping with the big dogs, one animal spooked. The big dog pulled back and my fingers caught in the leather lead and broke." He shook his head continued. "Makes Baskets, your son... he will lead us with his Guides and dream visions to a new place. We all must leave the canyons if we are to keep our freedom and escape these enemy monsters."

Blue Night Sky said, "It will be all right." She leaned over and patted Makes Baskets' knee, nodded, and continued. "They seek the shiny yellow stone, the one I gave your son to show around. Not finding it, the enemy keeps coming, and they take down whole Peoples as they move. Some of our people become captives of theirs, while others...." Her head dropped forward.

Long Arrow put his hands on the back of the Great Elder's shoulders and squeezed them. "There will be time to speak of this in the Counsel Lodge. This day we must speak of gathering the minds of all the elders of each band. Shining Light will need backing. Our combined Peoples, who in moons past became one because of the generosity of the Fish Peoples, must act as one People."

He waved his arms around and pointed out several people. "Look how many wear quilled headbands as the Red Bear People do. Some Fish People even braid their hair with the same tiny shells. We *are* one People. When Shining Light stands to speak, Blue Night Sky and Bright Sun Flower, two of the most powerful people of our combined band, will stand with him. I said what I wanted to say."

***

"Great Elder." Makes Baskets looked up at her son, who came to sit next to her. She refused to let her eyes water, or to show any weakness. "Why my baby?"

She spoke so softly, her voice barely carried. Flying Raven scooted over and gave their son room to sit beside his mother.

"Mother, I am not a baby." His words were soft. "I am nearly a man now."

Shining Light tried to comfort her with a gentle smile. "I hunt, I ride Sandstone, and Father even taught me how to make my own arrow shafts and fit the arrowheads so they fly true. You see me as a twelve-winters-old child, but I am a man inside. The boy only remains outside."

Makes Baskets stared his way and gave him a quick smile, but she picked up a stick and stirred the fire.

Everyone glanced up when Chases Butterflies approached the group, grinning. She plopped behind Shining Light and wrapped her arms around her cousin, squeezing his chest, imitating Long Arrow's outward display of affection. "And, my cousin, sometimes that boy still comes out because he is meant to. It is all right to be your age. I may be two winters younger than you, but as I told my mother once, I will walk at your side, maybe to sometimes remind you that you are still young enough to be a boy."

She reached around and twisted his nose.

His face twisted with it. "Butterflies, I am trying to listen to the adults." He puffed out his chest. "After all, this is an important matter."

He turned, pushed her hand away and tried to ignore her.

Chases Butterflies did not appear to agree, and pulled on his nose again.

"Hey!"

Chases Butterflies jumped up and ran across the camp.

Makes Baskets motioned with her head for her son to go, after watching him fidget.

***

Bent on revenge, Shining Light jumped up and sprinted after her. Sandstone trotted behind him. They chased each other into the canyon, laughing. White Paws appeared from where he hid with Moon Face under the shade of the small shrubs and raced ahead of them both.

Shining Light, barely able to keep up with the agile girl, reached for and grabbed her. He leaned back on the wall and breathed hard, and spoke slow words so she would not know she had bested him. "You will be beautiful when you become a woman, Butterflies. You have the eyes of Doe and your nose is straight and long, not big, but... but." He turned away. "Anyway, you will have many who will want you."

Her face turned red as a ripe raspberry. She grinned and twirled the fringe on her footwear, which she seemed to find very interesting.

Still looking down, she said, "I know one who finds you most handsome now, cousin. She tells me your round eyes melt into your lips. What does she mean?"

"Who?"

"You know who. Rising Moon. When we walk together, you are all she has words for—the pucker of your lips, your strong chin. She asks if you always let your hair fly free and... and how nice your long legs look when you run and—"

"Enough silly talk!" He turned to scold his cousin, but his eyes caught sight of something new.

A small line of blue sparkles danced along the off-white swirls in the red-orange color of the canyon wall. His mind followed the brilliant blue color, and he felt himself lift from his body.

'Boy, go seek the silence now. Take White Paws with you. He has something to tell you.'

"Please stop, Butterflies. Blue Night Sky is inside my head again. I need to go off by myself for a while." He spun and called, "White Paws, come on."

He turned back to his dejected cousin. "Go above in the canyon, along the path closest to the camp, where you see me go every morning to pray. Yes, I know you have followed me many times."

He raised his eyebrows and crossed his arms, but still grinned. The small fringe on his light brown tunic swished, causing the tiny shell beads to tinkle.

"Go up the path to the small spot where the tree hangs over the ledge. Watch from above, but say nothing. You may not see and hear anything, but go ahead." He reached out his hand and touched her shoulder. "My faithful cousin, the one who stands beside me, defends me, I love you."

He saw his cousin's confusion, and knew curiosity got the best of her. He smiled, turned and trotted off with White Paws.

Chapter 26

Shining Light sat on a small grassy spot in the narrow alcove with the wolf. White Paws reached up and tapped gently at his face. Faint blue and pale red sparks danced around both White Paws and Shining Light. He gazed deeper to see them better.

I wonder still why I do not need to fast and pray to experience such Sacred Happenings. I am truly blessed.

White Paws raised his muzzle, closed his eyes and let out a soft howl. The air stilled.

Shining Light rubbed the rising hairs on his arms, closed his eyes, quieted his mind, and....

He found himself inside the wolf. He became White Paws. The wolf howled once more. They howled together. Never before had he not felt skin; now, fur rose on his neck and back.

'Great Mystery, I come to you as your four-legged child. It is Shining Light's Energy that gives him the desire to explore with his body. Yet his mind is also full of Power – unharnessed. He is like a pup to me, so much to learn in such a short time. Like any pup, if he does not learn, he will be of no help to the growth and safety of his own Human pack.

Shining Light absorbed Wolf's Energy and went deeper.

'I reach him through his inner knowing, through his center of being – through my own center – and there we connect. He feels me, and we speak our emotions as he would words to another Human, only we are at a deeper level – the level of the Spirit, the center of the Circle of All Living.'

Shining Light tingled. White Paw's voice echoed through his head and startled him.

'We become... one. One being with one mind, no body to hinder our feelings. Freedom of the mind is the only true freedom.

Strange, how Humans cling to the body when it is but an illusion. The boy is learning this lesson well, as he becomes the Song of Life to which he dances. When he dances with his Human pack, Shining Light moves to his own heartbeat. Others must use the sound of the drum to feel what he hears in all of nature. Cricket's song, Wind's flow, Water's race and Fire's rage – all are within his Soul.'

Shining Light breathed in the wolf's voice and smelled his breath, tasted the air. His tongue tingled.

'The Soul is everything that is, that will ever be. I have taught him there is no difference. I ask, Great Mystery, for you to guide my words as I once again connect to the Spirit World.'

In that short span of time, the young human's entire being, his entire world—what he perceived as his world—turned to fog.

'*Human Brother, you are now within my being. For the first time, you see me not through the eyes of a boy, but through the heart of a growing boy-man. The blue waves of color you see are yours. Our Souls have mingled. The red is my Spirit color, which I now share with you. No, Brother, do not speak. Listen instead. You must face the Humans of your People—and the ones to come. They prepare now for the gathering, which will be unlike any other. I do not say this will be easy, but it must happen.*

'*You will speak in front of many Humans much older than you. In your mind, you are older than they are—in many, many ways, you are. The Ancients of your own kind have danced within you, whispered in your dreams in a tongue so old, only you truly understand them. All you need to do is listen... listen with your heart, not your ears. My own Grandfather Wolf was there by my side, as your kind, the ancients, danced. He whispered to me that the time was short. You must leave and go the way of your ancestors. Go before the first flakes of snow.*

At the thought of so much cold, Shining Light shivered. The fur was no more. He was skin once again.

'*Before you do, have the ones who can carve leave their marks, and tell the story of this band and how they came to be here, and place Father Sun shining down at the end, where an arrow will point toward the direction the band goes. And, Shining Light, do not think you are so special, your Power might be taken from you to show you are not.* '

The fog lifted. White Paws licked Shining Light's face and trotted away toward his mate and their new growing pups, to teach them to hunt.

The boy-man sat stunned. "Never has White Paws spoken to my mind in words! It was always just a knowing before, one we shared many times. I have been honored by the Spirits, by Creator—I am deeply humbled. I feel so... so different. I even heard him say he had to leave and teach his pups to hunt. I feel as if everything White Paws shared with me is now part of me. I understand. How is this possible?"

Chases Butterflies plopped at his side. "Who do you speak to? Me? I am not sure what I saw from the overlook up on the ledge, but I swear White Paws was talking to you. Was he? He was, huh? I saw how you looked at him and how he never looked away. Who is my Spirit Guide? Do I have one?"

He turned and faced her, still feeling the Energy from the Spirit World. "We all have Spirit Guides. Some have more than one. It is not yet time for you to find yours."

"Well, do you know who mine is?" She rubbed her arms. "Well, do you?" She poked him in the side and squirmed when he poked her back. She reached for his hair, but he folded his hand over her playful one.

"Only you, my cousin, will know for sure when the time comes. Be patient. Some people wait for part of their lives to pass before they find out if their Spirit Guide walks, or flies, or even crawls, next to them. Others find out very young."

"Like you. You speak as an adult now, not the boy I knew."

"Like me. I cannot tell you why I have changed so much, except that I must lead the people away from here." He put his hand over his mouth, fearing he had spoken words he should not have.

Chases Butterflies put her arms around his shoulders. "I already know, my cousin. Seasons ago, when I was only six winters, I told my mother I would walk beside you." She stammered. "Not... not as... as your woman, of course, but as... as your helper. I am not sure what all of this means, I... just know it. I may never take a mate, as you will."

"How do you know I will take a mate, Butterflies?"

She stood and put her own hand to her mouth. "Not going to tell you." She dashed off toward camp.

Why does everyone know about my taking a mate? I did not know until Blue Night Sky told me, yet even Rising Moon knew I was to be her man. She knew before her band came into camp. Now, my cousin knows her role in our future while I still guess.

"Am I the right one?" He shook his head and crossed his arms, hugging himself, and turned to the sound of a new visitor.

Bright Sun Flower entered the alcove and sat next to him. "Yes, Grandson, you are. I have known since you were born that you would take the place of your grandfather's father. I just did not know it would be while you were still my little Feather."

"How is it that you know what is in my head? Do you have some special Power?"

"A very special Power—the Power of listening. I heard what Chases Butterflies told you while standing outside leaning against the canyon wall." She chuckled, sat next to him and squeezed him to her body.

A breeze teased at her hair, sending it into his face. He wrinkled his nose and brushed it away with annoyance. His mood changed, seeing so many people now moving on the band's lands. He pulled away.

"Grandmother, I only know we are to go toward where the cold wind blows." He decided he really did want to be cuddled, and reached for the comfort of her arms.

She pulled him close, rocked him lovingly, and whispered, "Yes, I know, and it will not be easy on the elders. That is why I took every humpback hide given to me. I made many into robes, with the hair still on them for extra warmth, and hid them in a cave in the canyons. That way I did not have to say why I made so many. Most probably forgot that I asked for them."

Behind her, Sandstone managed to poke her head inside the alcove. She nuzzled Bright Sun Flower. She chuckled and reached out to rub the big dog's nose.

"I learned to ride, and so did your grandfather—unknown to me. Your grandfather is a sneaky one." She shook her head and sucked in her bottom lip. "Why I, a woman of Power, cannot feel him when he does these things!"

Sandstone pushed at her when she stopped rubbing her muzzle. "Soon her young one must learn to carry packs and a robe or two. All of the younger ones must. He does not follow his mother anymore, so he must be weaned. We have much to learn about these creatures."

"He already knows how—all the young ones do." Long Arrow appeared before them. He bent over, hands on his knees to catch his breath. "I do not know how your people can climb and wander all over these canyons and still breathe! All I did was climb a small hill to see where Chases Butterflies said you two were. She said she just about ran over another sneaky woman who hid outside this small hidden curve. Yes, I too am sneaky. We all are sneaky this day. I learned how so I would not be a victim to those who now come our way. About a moon ago, Hawk Soaring, Flying Raven and I took the younger big dogs into the canyons. We learned how best to get them to accept weight on their backs. I could not teach what I had yet to learn. We started with a light robe, and then moved to a heavy humpback's robe until they stood still. After that, we added another heavy robe. This took a while, but we stayed calm and the big dogs did too. And, um... Hawk Soaring was the lightest so we—"

"Now I understand why my man had a deep purple-green bruise on his backside! Sneaky old—"

"Man," interrupted Hawk Soaring. He stood behind Long Arrow and grinned. "Yes, my sweet, caring woman. Sneaky must be in the air this day."

"You *are* a sneak." Bright Sun Flower crawled out, stood, put one hand on her right hip, and wagged the other hand at both men.

Shining Light stood. "Um, this canyon spot is getting too crowded. I think I will go to camp." He felt a pull on his tunic and turned. "Grandmother, why is your face all squished up? Ha-ha-ho, you look older than Blue Night Sky! Oops, I am sure that was not what I meant to say. You are as beautiful as the sun flower you are named after."

Beads of sweat rolled down his forehead. "I love you, Grandmother, I really do. Please do not look at me with a withered fruit face. I am but your little grandson." He made himself small to remind her.

She started to laugh so hard, both men acted as if they were finished with the conversation. Shining Light thought they might be wrong about that.

His grandmother turned back to face the other men as he slipped from her grasp and dashed for the camp. He giggled as Sandstone trotted off in another direction, head and tail high. White Paws came from another branch of the canyon and scampered after him.

He ran so fast that all he heard was his grandmother's scolding voice, and his grandfather trying to defend himself. He glanced back to see if anyone followed, and heard a yell just as he hit something hard with the back of his head.

Rising Moon stood and held her bloodied nose. He reached for the bottom of his tunic, but a soft hand held his coarser one down.

"I have some swamp plant fluff." Rising Moon's words were muffled by her hand. "I was taking it to Running Moon for her baby. I will use that." She winced at the pain as she tried to stop the bleeding. "Why did you nearly knock me down? Did you think the eyes in the back of your head would see for you?"

He had never been this close to her. She was good to look at—oval face, round dark eyes, and a short, pretty nose.

Her lips are full and round and....

He ran for the river, White Paws in tow, leaving her trying to stanch the blood flow.

***

In spite of what had just happened, she grinned. "He has such strong arms. I would love to have them around me."

Morning Star came up from behind. "I see my daughter has finally touched her future man. Is he all you dreamed of?"

Running River, who carried her bare-bottomed baby, smiled and joined in the teasing.

Rising Moon handed Running River the fluff, while she held the piece to her nose. She then ran inside Blue Night Sky's lodge, and closed the flap to drown out the laughter of the two women.

Inside, she growled to herself and paced with tight fists. "Why does he run as if I am going to eat him? All I want to do is talk. Just talk. I want to get to know him better. How do I do this?"

She spun around to the sound of a cough.

"What did you say, girl? Were you talking to me?" Blue Night Sky grinned up at the pacing, tight-fisted girl. "Because if you were, I would say something like, allow time to take its course. You are young yet, and soon, very soon, you will not be so young, and you will wish you were young again, as does this old woman who sits because her legs do not allow her to wander much anymore." She put down the tunic she mended for Long Arrow.

"I am sorry if I disturbed you," Rising Moon said. "I thought I was alone. I just want to make him hold still so we can talk like everyone else. He sees me and runs off with that... that wolf of his! Am I not nice to look at? Do I have a big blob for a nose and tiny squished eyes? Am I ugly?" Tears fell from her face and she quickly turned away.

"No, no, girl, you are as beautiful as your mother. You look as she did when she was twelve winters old."

"I am fourteen winters old," reminded Rising Moon. "Soon I will be a woman." She bowed her head. "I have no father to accept gifts from my future man."

"Girl, as soon as you came to live with us, Long Arrow became your... well, he is the man of this lodge, and Shining Light must go through him to ask for you."

"Has there ever been a time when a woman just went up to a man and said, 'I take you?'"

"Ahh...." The Great Elder laughed. "Yes indeed, girl, I was in love with my man, and he ran like Shining light. I cornered him at a gathering many, many seasons ago." She closed her eyes and smiled. "He was of a band four days' walk from ours, and I had only seen him twice before, but now he was seventeen winters and I, fifteen winters, still had no man. I wanted him."

Blue Night Sky shook her fist with vigor at a surprised Rising Moon. Her eyes sparkled like nothing she had ever seen.

Rising Moon stood still and listened to her story, not wanting to lose the moment. Her mother's grandmother seldom spoke of her past.

"I followed him very early one day to where he was about to bathe. He took off his tunic and... and... he was *so* good to look at—rippling muscles, wild, free hair, which had the blue shine of Raven, running down his back. His name was One Who Sings. He told me that I could speak his name after he went to the stars, so I do. His wondrous voice was a gift from Creator. When he sang and played his flute, many women swore it was for them. I did not care. I wanted him. I could have waited for him to be naked, but then I would have shamed him, so instead, I popped out from behind the bush and *told him* of my desire. He just stood there, not saying a word, until I shamelessly walked up to him and ran my fingers down his chest. I felt him shake and I pressed against him, and I told him that he was mine."

She started to drift off into the past. "Do not give up, girl."

Rising Moon watched as Blue Night Sky drifted away again. *No wonder she never took another mate. I never will either.*

Chapter 27

Blue Night Sky watched as Shining Light stood in the middle of the Counsel Lodge, in front of all the elders of the gathered bands, as well as the Fish Peoples. Only about half the other bands came even after the men rode up on the strange big dogs and told their story. He licked his lips and swallowed hard. White Paws stood at his side and raised his paw to push at his waist. All eyes were on him. His lips moved; she knew he pleaded with the Spirits.

Blue Night Sky coughed so all could hear, raised her hand and pointed to the motionless figure. "Listen to Shining Light as you would any adult. You see not a boy, but a man living inside a boy's body." The Great Elder pushed downward with her hands, but her legs were too shaky to maneuver. "Oh, sweet Mother! I must ask for help to stand."

Running River and Morning Star stood to lift her. They helped her to the center so she could stand next to a paralyzed Shining Light and his Wolf Brother.

She caught Makes Baskets from the corner of her eye trying to wiggle out of her spot, but Bright Sun Flower held her down. "Allow her the dignity to stand with your son. She has much to say. We must be strong and not interfere with what is happening. Let your son gather himself so he can speak his mind as any man would." She let go of her daughter's dress and looked at her grandson, then nodded at Blue Night Sky.

The mother of a great man in the making obeyed, sat still, and raised her tight chin. She squeezed her daughter, Soft Breeze, for comfort.

Blue Night Sky stood silent and took in all the staring faces. Tiny blue sparks bounced between her and Shining Light. She knew some could see, while others had no idea they were there.

She cleared her throat and motioned to several of her old band. "This camp, and all the ones who will come with us, must move within a moon's time."

The whispers she had expected echoed within the Counsel Lodge. She raised her arm and waved her hand. The anticipated silence did not come. She raised her voice to gain attention. "I know all here have heard rumors and pretended they were just that. We are too many to stay. Already our young people must go for several days at a time in search of food, leaving the camp unguarded."

She raised her voice as the people's words grew louder. "Hear me, grandsons and granddaughters, strangers come who will not care that you were here first. They will laugh as they knock you down, run over your children, and take your lives, as they did with my people."

She put her head down and her hair fell forward. She waited for the boy-man to speak.

***

Shining Light took in a deep breath and stood as tall as his height would allow. He wanted to run with White Paws into the canyons, to go with his grandfather and skip stones, find pine needles with his mother, or listen to his grandmother's stories. Instead, here he stood in front of the entire band.

His voice quivered. "I... I... Sh... Shining Light, know the Great Elder's words to be true."

Children, quieted by their mothers, sat still and men stopped whispering among themselves. He took in a ragged breath and dug his hand into White Paw's fur. The wolf stared up at him and nudged his arm. The two shared their Energies, gave him the comfort he needed to continue talking.

"I dreamed this many times since I was very young, as did my grandmother and my father, Flying Raven Who Dreams. Also..." he shot his silent grandmother a sideways glance, "...my grandfather, who chose to remain silent for his own reasons.

"If he were here, he would stand with us and tell you. He left with others to try to make the other bands listen. Each one took a different path to bands that will either believe and come back with them, or not believe and risk staying where they are. Too many who did come before our men's return left after hearing Blue Night Sky's words, thinking it impossible that such a thing could ever happen. I say this: those who do not follow us will not get another chance."

His throat bobbed as he swallowed hard again. "I know some others will not follow. Their destiny lies elsewhere. My dreams show me what we must do. It is up to each band to decide." He looked squarely at his grandmother and nodded her way.

All eyes turned toward her. She stood. "My grandson speaks words that are all true. Since he was only six winters old, I would hear him cry out in his dreams — dreams that I too dreamed — the very ones my man's father also lived with in his mind. Had he survived, we would have moved farther than these canyons. He felt we were safe here until the one born with his name, Feather Floating In Water, could take his place."

She pointed to him. "My grandson is that person. He is neither boy nor man, but a Holy Person in his own right. I have said my words." She sat again, but taller. Anyone looking could see the pride in her expression.

***

More whispers filled the Counsel Lodge. Several stood to speak, but Blue Night Sky regained her composure and silenced them with a wave of her hand. She leaned on Shining Light for support, reached out and held his hand. "My people, all of my Peoples, hear me! When we make decisions, we first consider the good of the people. If every person in the band thinks this way, then we will always make strong decisions. I stand with the boy who is also a man. I am the eldest person here. I have seen much in my many seasons. I pass into my eighty-first winter soon. Not many are blessed with such a long life as mine."

Her voice started to falter. "If you choose to stay, I fear you will age no more. After we met Del-ane, the hairy-faced one, he tried to explain that not all who were coming were bad—only some were as deadly as those we encountered.

"I will speak of some the horrors my people saw. None of the survivors who now sit with you in this lodge have to sit here and listen."

She waited for those people to leave. No one else stirred. Her eyes grew glassy, and Shining Light understood she was allowing herself to envision the attack before continuing.

"This is not a good thing, what happened to us. We were sleeping except for a few hunters who were gone before Grandmother Sun would wake us—I will always call her Grandmother even if you say Grandfather. I mean to offend no one." She gathered herself and looked at the seated people. "The hairy-faced ones came through our camp as Grandmother Sun woke. They screamed such strange things. They did not sound like words to us—no one had ever heard such noise."

She rubbed her eyes, and for those who could see, they went dark blue. "They rode the big dogs and carried long shiny sticks in one hand while using the other to control where the creatures they rode went. Some of the shiny sticks made a loud noise and every time we heard this noise, someone fell... never to get up again. Others had long knives."

Her breath became as ragged as it had moons ago when she first came to the Fish People's band. "We ran out of our lodges made of grass—not like yours—but made out of long grasses. The hairy-faced ones threw fire sticks on the tops and fire came to life. My granddaughter and her daughter, who I live—lived with, grabbed me after the two of them tore a way out through the back of our fast burning home."

She looked for her granddaughter, and saw Morning Star with her arms wrapped around a tearful, shaking Rising Moon. "Several others followed behind us out of the backs of their homes, but the smoke blinded our escape. All we could do... run... away... from the screams."

Her legs shook and she had begun to falter.

Shining Light reached for her. He himself shook from listening to her story, too much like his dream vision.

Running River jumped up. "Great Elder, do not speak of it any longer. It is far too—"

"I must make your people—our people—understand the danger we are in." Blue Night Sky allowed Running River to hold onto her, but refused to sit.

"Many of our Peoples, the Red Bear Peoples, are no more. So many... now gone. We left our name with those who went to the stars."

Her face scrunched up and showed many age lines. "Before you stands a weak old woman, the last Elder of her people, an old Holy Woman who did not see in her dreams our destruction. We cannot ever know why our dreams only show some things unless... unless some things were meant to happen."

She spread out her hands, then clutched them into fists. "No one wanted to believe such a thing could happen, but it did. I am sure I have told this story to many of you already. Did you listen? Did you make meat for the journey we must go on? Or did you think as my people thought—that it was not possible?

"We will encounter others, Peoples who do not know our tongue."

The Great Elder took in a deep breath of the smoky air and coughed. "Someone has put in too many green branches." She waved her arms in front of her face.

Two men near the entrance opened the flap to let in fresh air.

"Thank you, grandsons. The smoke is hard to breathe for one so old." She smiled at them.

"I have asked those who left camp this day to seek out Walking Stick, or other traders who may know these People's words. We will pass through land others claimed long ago, and we do not need to worry about disagreements.

"Some of these Peoples live in large bands called villages, and some are wanderers of the land, while even more are small bands like our own. Many of you have no idea what is beyond these canyons. I do. There are more kinds of Peoples than there are grains of sand. When traders speak of this, most think they boast, but I was once a trader."

She watched as people's jaws went slack. It was rare for a woman to be a trader. "Yes, I, a woman. You do not know about me as you may think.

"Some Peoples live in the outcroppings of caves, and others live in what look like big rocks, made from our Mother's land mixed with water and grasses. Some are not friendly even to traders. I carry a scar on my back from a knife because I thought every band would invite me. I learned to travel only among certain Peoples. We will try to travel through their lands as we journey to the safe place of Shining Light's dreams."

She paused and looked around the lodge. "Leave we must. We will send men and women ahead to keep their eyes open for bad signs. I have said my words."

She motioned to Running River to help her go back and sit.

She then went within herself and looked into empty air.

***

Shining Light gained confidence. "Blue Night Sky's words are all true. She speaks of what is coming our way, not what might, *but what is coming*. I dreamed of the ones she calls the hairy-faced ones. They are dangerous and will take the lives of any who... who are standing in their way. They seek the yellow rock I have shown to many of you. There is nothing like it in our canyons. One of my dreams came to me again and again. People screamed, ran and hid. I know now these People once called Red Bear are the Peoples who sit among us."

He looked down at Blue Night Sky, but she did not respond.

"The place I have seen in my dream visions — I only have seen tall grasses, and trees I cannot describe, but we must know that the Spirits will guide us, if we have faith in ourselves and prove we are worthy."

Words came to him, flowed from him as if he himself were but the carrier. "The Circle changes. Like a spiral it moves, ever shifting due to all that affects it. It changes now, and we must move with it. I will go to seek out the Spirits, in a Vision Quest, when my father returns. I have said my words with a straight tongue."

He made his way from the Counsel Lodge, White Paws behind him.

He could feel all eyes were on him.

His grandmother raised her eyebrows as he passed. He had surprised even her with the words he spoke.

Chapter 28

Bent willow branches made the skeleton of the Sweat Lodge. Robes wrapped around the outside created an airtight half-rounded basket shape, and rocks went around the bottom edge to assure no light could get inside.

Flying Raven stood and waited for his son by the entrance. "I have a story to tell. Sit beside me."

They both sat on a robe outside the Sweat Lodge.

Flying Raven handed a pipe to Shining Light. "Hold it with the red stone bowl upward as we speak."

Shining light sat beside him as he began. "A long time ago, a Peoples passed on this Sacred pipe to those who made their way through the land of many dark green pine trees, far from here, toward the land of winters far colder than our own. Those people also wandered the grasslands in search of the great humpbacks. They came across our Peoples as they made their journey from the grasslands to the canyons.

"Our people heard this story is very old, and perhaps the ones who passed it to us had it passed to them. They explained it was for special times and called it the 'Pipe of Truth.' Only good honest people could smoke the herbs in the bowl. To smoke it and then not honor the words spoken would surely doom the person."

He paused and stared at the pipe for a moment. "There are stories of people who smoked in a Sacred manner, and they only spoke with a true tongue. But some lied. It is said the Spirits took them away after they forgot what they had done, when they thought nothing would ever happen to them. This shows no one ever really gets away with bad things.

"The wandering Peoples presented the soon to be named Fish People with a beautiful carved pipe made from a red stone. We pass on a pipe when we met good people too. We must trade for the red stone because it comes from a very faraway place that is Sacred. All land has its own Sacredness, as does every being, but some places are very special, like where the red stone comes from." He used his fingers to trace the colors painted on the wooden part.

"The wooden pipe, painted in yellow, white, black and red, had decorations of hand-carved beads dangling from the leather ties, which kept Eagle feathers in place. These colors belonged to the Peoples who passed it to us. We left their colors on the stem. It was long before my time that this pipe came to be among us."

He looked up as Eagles called to each other, and watched as they vanished into clouds.

"They spoke of a woman who turned into a white calf of the humped ones — very Sacred. She taught the first Peoples to carry the pipe, and the Sacred ways of the pipe. One man did not honor the white humpback calf woman in a good way, and she turned him to bones.

"The pipe teaches us about the joy of life, how to cherish and love others, and to hear the voices of nature and Creator, who speak clearly from inside of our selves. You must look with your eyes open, all your senses open. Until you can be in your own mind and hear Sister Wind, feel the waters flowing in and on the Mother, and know all the songs of Nature, you will remain lonely deep inside."

Shining Light nodded and absorbed his words, never moving. A deep blue glow graced his son's dark eyes.

Flying Raven continued. "Never smoke this pipe with impure thoughts, or for personal gain. Smoke it for the greater good, for harmony, balance and wholeness. My grandfather passed this pipe to me. Only special people have the right to carry one. Perhaps, Son, you will earn that right someday. There is much to learn. Always hold the bowl in your right hand, the female; the stem in your left hand, the male. In time, I will teach you what was taught to me, and someday you will carry the scared bundle you see that hangs in our lodge, in the place of honor."

Shining Light held the pipe gently, bowl in his right hand, and turned it on all sides. "We are blessed to have met these Peoples." He handed the pipe back.

Flying Raven added herbs, lit the pipe, drew smoke into his mouth, and let it go to the four directions with each pull on the pipe. Each direction had its own prayer. He then raised it to Creator and lowered it to the Mother. He handed the pipe to his son, who repeated the ritual. They stood and approached the Sweat Lodge.

"Come crawl in on this side of the Sweat Lodge, the way the sun follows the seasons. There are stones placed in a hole in the center, instead of along the edges as we do in our lodges. The fire your grandfather made just before we arrived has cleansed them. These rocks are not from the river, even though I use that water. They would explode, so remember never to use that kind. They are very hot. I will pour the water upon them and sprinkle Sacred plants on the stones while we pray, sing and prepare our minds, our Souls, even our bodies. This lodge is the womb of the Mother. Treat it with respect, as you would your own body. As you enter, speak the words, 'All my relatives enter with me.' This means our animal brothers and sisters, our ancestors, all of life."

With a thin hide wrapped around their waists, they entered. Flying Raven entered first, then Shining Light. Hawk Soaring crawled in next and several other men joined.

Once inside, the Holy Man closed the flap. They dropped their robes and seated themselves cross-legged inside the completely dark Sweat Lodge.

***

The searing heat burned Shining Light's nostrils, and he held the hide up to his face. The heat made his body tingle. He dropped the hide to breathe in the hot steam that came from the watered stones. The smell of the herbs permeated the small half-round lodge. His body felt the hot steam throughout. Everywhere he tried to look in the darkness, tiny flashes of red, orange and yellow sparked in circles around the lodge, around the men. The sparks consumed their bodies.

He stared into the sparks and felt the Energy of all living. He was the sparks, and they were he, as was everyone in the lodge—everyone and everything that had lived, did live, and would live. He held up an arm in the darkness and saw the outline of it made up of the sparks. He finally understood he was Sacred. Every being was Sacred, be it a tree, a stone, animal, human, Sister Wind, Father Sun, the Mother.... All were one Sacredness connected through the Web of Life.

He joined in the singing, and when his turn came to speak, he asked Creator to give the Peoples safety and protect them on their journey. He smoked the pipe that someone passed to him, and then passed it to his father.

The Sweat Lodge was not just for one's own self, but also for every being. With each pass of singing, four times the flap opened to allow clean, cool air inside as everyone prayed and sang. Four, the Sacred number representing the four directions, was honored in this way. After everyone had spoken, and sang four times, one by one they left through the side opposite the one they had entered.

Everyone dove into the cold river and jumped out, their bodies cleansed, their minds ready for what may come.

Shining Light stood with his father by the river. Water droplets raced to the ground from their bodies. The Holy Man nodded at him.

He knew he would now go up into the canyon and return a man.

"Make a circle of stone to sit in," his father said. "Allow the stones to choose you—you will know which ones. Take only water, Sage, the pipe your grandfather will give to you, and the thin robe you now carry.

"I have instructed you what to do, what to expect. This is your personal time. It could take just two days or four days before you have a vision—if you are meant to. Some do not succeed the first time."

He faced Shining Light and put his hands on his shoulders. "I do not think you will need to worry about that. I will be near, but will not interfere in what happens. Go now and return a man."

Flying Raven looked deep into his eyes, placed his hands upon his shoulders and squeezed them, then turned and left.

Chapter 29

Shining Light knew where he wanted to go; when he was a little boy, his grandfather had shown him where his first father went for his own Vision Quest.

The circle of stones remained where his first father had placed them. Grass had grown over the stones and covered most. He picked up each stone and held it to his heart. Some he took out of the circle and replaced with others, but many of the stones he left alone. He spread the herbs that his father had given him to offer to the four directions, tossed some up toward Creator, and sprinkled more on the ground to honor the Mother. He spread his robe out, laid his water bladder to the side, and lit the Sage he had placed inside a clay pot his father had traded from Walking Stick. The late-blooming flowers teased his nose with fragrances.

Somewhere Eagle called, Wolf howled, and human voices—chanting in a strange tongue—whispered through Sister Wind.

His grandfather had carved a small wooden pipe, and even fashioned the red stone into a hollow bowl that fit the wood part perfectly. The wooden handle, laden with carvings of feathers, stretched the length of his forearm. Small handmade beads dangled from leather straps, creating a song of their own.

Shining Light put herbs in the pipe and lit it, then said a small prayer to the four directions, and above to Creator and below to the Mother. He smoked and prayed again, and placed the pipe where Father Sun would see it when he woke. His father had told him not to leave the circle, not to fear anything he saw—sing loudly if he felt fear, stomp his feet hard when he danced, if he felt a pull that might take him away from his chosen spot.

His grandfather walked up only after he made his Sacred place. Hawk Soaring sat with him and held an obsidian knife blade, the handle a notched deer's antler that, with the help of wrapped sinew, held firm the sharp blade. His arm shook as he held it up to him.

"Grandfather, do me the honor—take the small pieces of my flesh to show Creator I am ready and willing to give of myself for the people, for Creator, the Great Mystery." Shining Light nodded, looked forward and started to sing his own prayer song.

Soon his eyes looked into another world.

Hawk Soaring then held the knife, sang a prayer and took thirty small pieces of flesh from the arms held out before him, the number Flying Raven said the Spirits asked of Shining Light. The flesh, freely given, gave to Creator the only true gift one could offer—part of the self. The knife pierced the seeker's skin, taking just enough to allow bleeding.

Shining Light drifted deep as his grandfather sang. He sung his own prayer song, and did not flinch, did not feel the cuts. Instead, he followed the sparks of Energy as they became brighter with every cut.

His grandfather, now finished, said nothing. He would cut his own arms to offer his strength, but would leave Shining Light to Creator's will.

Deep inside the other world, Shining Light stood with bleeding arms raised in prayer. Only the Spirits were with him now. He felt their soft caresses, fleeting as Sister Wind.

The young boy danced and sang in place until his legs no longer held him. Darkness crept in as Father Sun made his way down below the spot Shining Light had chosen. He watched in his mind as colors of peaches and yellow faded into obsidian darkness.

***

White Paws lay flat in the grass. He watched as his Human Brother stood with head high in prayer. His Brother would not sleep, no matter how much trickery the Spirits might use to make him feel he could to do so. The wolf would not allow it.

In the distance, his family called to each other while hunting. He would not hunt until the Vision Quest had ended.

White Paws sent Energy to Shining Light; it now swirled around the boy and mingled with yet another's Energy. Wolf knew the Great Elder watched too. They felt each other and allowed their Energies to intertwine into a web around the praying figure.

***

Shining Light's mouth dropped. *What do I see?* He knew he would never be alone, but what he saw made him wonder who was with him. Blue and red swirls danced in the darkness and formed a Wolf-Human before him. The face of a woman rose as she stood up on the hind legs of a wolf. Her long flowing dark hair mingled with the thick, grey-white hairs of Wolf. Her human arms reached outward, turning into paws as she howled then faded into a swirling mist.

"Blue Night Sky, are you here? White Paws?"

The echo of thunder his only answer, he looked up and found a clear sky.

When did Father Sun wake? The heat bore down on him. His legs shook from dancing most of the day. He bent down and scooped up the water, took a drink and tossed it aside. His throat now moistened, he prayed in a stronger singing voice.

He continued dancing as Father Sun left him in darkness again. Arms swayed above feet that kept in time with his heartbeat, until Cricket woke and chirred a new beat for him to dance to. Music filled the night—Wolf howls, night birds, and Sister Wind's whispers through trees all added to the song within Shining Light. The campfires in the sky appeared to send their own sparkling music, giving him the strength to dance even more.

He smiled. Here was Power. The comfort of the cool night caressed his body, allowed his mind freedom.

***

Once again, Shining Light reached for a drink of water as Father Sun woke, but he could not find the water bladder.

Father Sun must have taken it. Why would he do that? Does he not know I thirst? Tired... I am so tired. What if nothing happens? I stand here, thirsty and no water. Tired... so tired and my throat hurts from singing and praying.

He stood on weak legs, raised his arms again, and tried to swallow. He repeated the same prayer, and cried for a vision. His legs collapsed and they folded beneath him. He bowed a weary head, one his neck no longer wanted to hold up.

If only I could sleep....

Father Sun again left him in darkness. Before him sat the water bladder, right where he had tossed it. He reached out and grabbed it, worrying it might not be real.

How is it that I can see it? It is so dark. Not even the Mother's sister, the moon, gives brightness to the night.

He looked up and searched for the campfires in the sky, but found none. He raised the water bladder to drink, and his cracked lips burned when the cool water touched them.

Three harsh swallows later, a voice said, 'Take no more. You will waste it upon the ground as your body refuses it'.

He dropped the precious liquid.

"Who is there?" He spun around. "Father? Grandfather?"

Only Sister Wind responded, chilling him in the darkness. He wrapped his robe around himself.

Cold... why am I so cold?

He shivered and his teeth chattered. From somewhere deep inside the darkness, drums echoed.

Drums? Chanting? I watched Father Sun go to sleep, yet I see as if he had never gone to do so.

An image formed before him—a circle of the ancient ones dressed in animal skins, dancing around him. He let his robe drop in the rising warmth. One of the dancers came to stand before him, and took off a head-covering made from a humpback's horns and hair. The body glowed, and then turned into snow that fell in front of Shining Light.

A noise made him turn. Another ancient one stood before him. His long animal skin fell to the ground. The lines on his face were as canyons, so deep.

"You know me. Your blood flows in your body because of me. Come." The elder put out his hand. *"Do not just stand there, take my hand."*

He reached for the hand, but it faded.

A tiny mouse jumped out of the darkness onto his shoulder, and rested next to his ear. '*You think I have nothing to offer? I feel the Mother, I feel her quake, and I feel her dance. I am quick in my decisions. My life would be very short if I did not feel with my body. My knowing, the ability to delve deeper in search of answers — these gifts I give to you. In return I ask that you always leave me seeds by your lodge, so I know I am not forgotten and my gifts to you are not wasted.*' The tiny mouse jumped into the air and was gone.

A growl split the night as White Bear stepped up. '*You think I have a temper? It is strength, Power, courage. I use it to protect my own. Never abuse this gift or it will betray you. Remember where I winter — in a cave of my own making. In this cave is silence. When your mind is in need of healing, seek the silence and filter out the noise that clutters your mind. I give you special gifts — the gifts of healing and of patience. Honor me by seeking my cave, and always leave Sage for me.*' White Bear stepped backwards into a land covered in snow, and became the snow. Tall trees faded with him.

Blue and red swirled within Shining Light — around him, through him — and a grey wolf sat before him. '*I am the grandfather of the one you call White Paws. He is your Spirit Guide who chose a body to be near you always.*'

Howls echoed from every direction. Everywhere Shining Light looked were wolves of grey, red, white, brown and black. '*We are your protectors, your Guides. To you we give an inner knowing, like Mouse, yet unlike his. You will be able to know if you can trust another with your inner eyes — your Human skin will tingle, the short fur on your arms will rise if danger is near. You honor us by walking with White Paws. Never go far without him.*

'*You have been given many gifts, little Human. More than many. But know you are not infallible. You will have the same weaknesses as any Human. Do not think you are so special that no harm will ever befall you. As soon as you think this, all of your gifts will fall away and you will be naked as any newborn. You must always remember to honor us as we have asked. Power that is given can also be taken away... just as quickly.*

'*The gift I offer you is Wolf, your Guide to ask questions of, to stand with you. I give you my courage, my determination to see things through. I am a teacher and others listen to me, as they now will you... Holy Man. Never take of my body anything you don't ask for first. You must be willing to die for me. Will you die to protect me, little Human? Will you die for your pack? Wolf and Human?*'

The red and blue colors intensified. '*You are the Shining Light of your people. We are also your people.*' This vision did not fade.

Shining Light reached out and felt fur. "Of course, Brother, I will die for you."

Before him stood White Paws, who reached up and licked the dried blood from his arms. Shining Light fell to his knees and cried hard tears into his fur.

"My Brother Wolf, my life I give to you." Father Sun warmed his cold body and he stood smiling. "Did Father Sun ever go to sleep, White Paws? Was it ever dark?"

White Paws wriggled his body in response.

Chapter 30

Shining Light hiked back down the canyon and into a quiet camp. He wondered if he had gained a new name, repeating to himself what he had heard in his Vision Quest. "You are the Shining Light of your people. We are also your people."

A chant all around him echoed the words. *'You are the Shining Light of the Peoples.'* The last of the swirling colors of his Vision faded.

He was a man now, not a boy. He breathed deep the air of a man, stood as a man, took his first steps as a man. He strode into the camp, a man.

A howl in the distance took White Paws in another direction. He trotted off into the canyon and out of sight.

Shining Light turned and watched him go. As much as he wanted to follow, he knew it was not the right time. People stopped and watched the new man stride with purpose toward his father's lodge. Girls giggled and whispered behind their hands.

I am a man.... He tested the words in his mind. *I am a man. I am a man.*

Shining Light entered the lodge where he would speak of his Vision Quest. The fire burnt low and the aroma of herbs filled his nose. The soft shake of a rattle and light drumming touched his ears, and the taste of fish wafting on the breeze greeted his senses. He sat on his old childbed and waited. His new bed would not be next to his mother, but on the man's side, next to his father.

Where are the sounds of the rattle and drums coming from? Am I still in the canyons, and only thought White Paws and me had walked down? Soon I will live in a lodge of my own. I hope it will not be far from my parents. What do I wish for? We must move or no one will have a home. Where is everyone? Am I not to speak to my father of my Vision? I wonder why the bottom of the lodge is closed and not open to fresh air? My mind wanders. Be still, silly.

He squirmed and chewed his nails.

Sunlight blinded his eyes as the flap of the lodge opened. Before him stood the Great Elder, Blue Night Sky. She came in, added a small branch to the fire, and sat opposite him. From the darkest part of the lodge came Hawk Soaring, who gently shook a rattle while he chanted.

He had expected to see his father.

Who is drumming? Do I really hear drums? The new man sat still, waiting for someone to speak.

His grandfather handed him a warm cooked fish. "Eat. You must wonder where your father is. He was beside you for your whole vision and never once left your side. He now goes to pray for the new Holy Man, the one he and Blue

Night Sky will guide, teach, and learn from as well. Speak now, Grandson who is a man. Tell of your vision so we may hear and help you to understand."

Sister Wind picked up speed outside, and the air that whistled through the open flap of the lodge felt crisp, new.

The new man told all. To his surprise, Blue Night Sky and his grandfather looked at each other with furrowed brows. Shining Light stilled himself, slowed his breathing, wondered why neither spoke. The fire in the lodge turned into dark embers, flickering upward, fighting to live. He tossed a few small pieces of wood chips on the fire. They caught and the hot ash became a small blaze once more.

No longer could he hold his words in. "Why does the air in here feel tight? Were my visions bad? Must I go back?"

Blue and red sparks drifted through the lodge toward him. He breathed them in as anyone might a sweet smell.

Blue Night Sky shifted her weight and took a deep breath. "No one has ever had so many guides come to them and actually speak in the way yours have done. Even my Spirit Guide speaks to me through feelings, not words. Are you certain you *heard* words, not felt them? I do not doubt you, neither does your grandfather, but this is unusual. I believe you may be stronger than any one born in my time."

She reached for her necklace. "My grandmother and grandfather, well known for their carvings among my people, carved me several animals from stone. When I would dream of one more than a few times, one of them would carve another for me to wear. I treasured them and thought I would never give one away."

She untied the knot that prevented them from falling, and handed one to Shining Light. "My grandfather told me White Bear lives in a land where snow keeps the ground hidden, except for a short span. I have only seen this in my dreams. Wear this always, Shining Light. Bear will remind you when you need to be alone. White Bear has special healing Powers, my young Holy Man."

Shining Light watched her eyes turn deep blue as she gifted him this most special carving. He ran his fingers over the White Bear. Sky beads pressed into tiny holes made up the eyes. He turned the carving over and over.

"The stone feels cold." He smiled and looked into Blue Night Sky's deep eyes. They pulled him in and held his gaze.

"I see much Power in your eyes, Shining Light. As you grow, you will become a strong Holy Man. White Bear is a powerful Guardian, a Healer, and he is strength in the face of trouble, hardship or suffering. I remember a story about this when I was very young."

"Bear...." Shining Light rubbed the raised bumps on his arms. "My father... why does Bear no longer follow him, but now offers me the honor?"

Hawk Soaring cleared his throat. "He has Raven for reasons he did not wish to share. He just said Raven gave him the ability to see what he had not before. Bear has not left your father. Bear still walks by his side as protector."

His grandfather raised his left hand. "I am here as your blood relation, the eldest of your family. Do not widen your eyes so much, silly one, or they will fall out. Yes, I am a *few* winters older than your grandmother."

His widened smile reminded Shining Light of another day, when he had worried his grandfather might laugh hard enough to split his belly open, and he himself had laughed. "I remember another time, Grandfather, by the river."

Old, experienced eyes met his young, curious ones.

"Silly one." Hawk Soaring's grin showed his few teeth. "Listen well to me. Mouse is important too. Remember his words and you will stay safe. Many depend on Mouse to survive, in more ways than just as food. Mouse pays great attention to details, takes time before jumping from cover. Remember this. Think before you do anything that may involve danger."

He stared into Shining Light's eyes until the new man nodded.

"You know more about Wolf than any of us, Grandson. Perhaps you will be the one to teach us." He rubbed his head. "I will not be doing that anymore." His voice lowered with his head.

He brought his eyes back to his grandson's. "Your grandmother awaits you in our lodge, to offer you special gifts only she can offer. These are stories of her People's long ago past, the ones in your dream visions. She herself did not know until she went to find out why she heard drumming and rattles echoing in the canyons."

Hawk Soaring squeezed his arm and pulled him closer. "You come from a powerful people your grandmother knew nothing about. Much time has passed, and the stories were not told, becoming as the passing wind. They are the future, and must never be tossed away again. Everything comes full circle in its own way, Grandson. The seasons—rain makes plants, which animals eat—like the story your grandmother told you when you were a boy. I am a bit saddened by a past never to be known again." He smiled, but his eyes watered.

Blue Night Sky leaned toward him and chuckled. "Silly old man! Circles! Circles! In its own way."

Chapter 31

Shining Light sat on the ridge above the canyon, his hands busy with fidgety fingers as groups of people formed and moved apart below. Many bands had flittered in and had celebrations, traded and found mates, as they would have at any gathering, but then most packed up and left. Not many were willing to give up the life of plenty they already had and take a chance on uncertainty.

Who could promise this new place really existed?

Since his Vision Quest, more people had listened to him in the Counsel Lodge, but some of the newer ones settling in were not convinced. He repeated the same story he told the first time with Blue Night Sky. Two bands picked up and left right after.

He felt he had failed. His mood wore on his companions.

Chases Butterflies sat with White Paws on one side of him. Rising Moon sat on other side next to Moon Face, the smaller dog Blue Waters sleeping on her lap. The wolves' second litter, now grown, stayed near their pack, but wandered the top of the canyon chasing unlucky prey.

His cousin had invited Rising Moon to follow her to the top, and he knew she had excitedly accepted.

Sandstone had made her way up behind Rising Moon. The big dog still refused to follow the rest of her own kind. She pushed her muzzle against Shining Light's back until he reached over and rubbed the animal's leg. Sandstone pushed her muzzle at his head. He needed to take her for a ride. She relished her runs on open ground, but would not go without him.

"I wonder why the big dogs stay around and do not run away as other animals do? Sandstone, you will knock me down into camp. Quit pushing!" He laughed for the first time in days, as the big dog nibbled his hair. "Your Energy is comforting, calm, playful, and your mouth and nose are so soft, softer than anything I have ever touched."

He laughed again as he watched all the wolves. "Soon I will have my own band—nine wolves, a big dog too stubborn to follow her own kind, and...." He turned to look at his newest companions. "And two girls who need to go help their mothers as the other bands settle in the short grasslands."

I am not sure I even sound like me anymore. I do not want to grow up so fast. He longed for what he knew had faded.

Chases Butterflies lowered herself and shoved her shoulder into his side. "Cousin, how many times do I have to tell you? I said I would be beside you!"

She mumbled more to herself than to Shining Light. "Even if I am only going on ten winters, I still am old enough to think for myself. My mother knows this." She pouted and made him look at her. "Besides, she is too busy chasing after my two sisters and my brother to go help the people who settle in."

Shining Light cocked his head at her. "Then why don't you go help her care for your—"

"Because you need company." The girl took one of his hands. "I might be just a girl to you, but I have feelings, you know, and I care about you. You know that too!" She crossed her arms and looked away, kicking at the edge of the overhang they sat on.

"Aww, cousin... Butterflies, you know I love you." He wrapped an arm around her and gave her shoulders a shake, then playfully pushed her away.

White Paws moaned at being forced to move and lay in front of them.

Shining Light turned and stared at a quiet Rising Moon, who looked ahead and said nothing. He knew she was unsure of herself, but that she wanted to be near him. It was up to him to make the first move.

Chases Butterflies nudged her cousin with her elbow and motioned for him to speak to the silent girl. Annoyed, he turned Butterflies' way to show her his withered fruit face, but her expression made him think that maybe Rising Moon's face was not as mean to look at as his cousin's puckered sour face.

"Um, Rising Moon?" He turned to face her, uncertain what to say.

She still looked ahead at the bands who were trying to fit in somewhere.

His hand shook when he reached across and touched her shoulder. "Please look at me."

She turned and smiled back and reached over to squeeze his hand. Both laughed as Chases Butterflies grunted.

"We are all right now?" Rising Moon asked. "Me and you?"

Her bright smile made his heart pick up speed. "I am sorry for the way I act."

He wanted to run away, run with his wolves and act like the boy he longed to be. "Everyone says I am more than a boy, but I only go into my thirteenth winter. I am a boy! I have boy fears, I look like a boy, and yet...."

His future mate turned to face him. "I am but a girl, I look like a girl, and yet... yet I have deep feelings for you. I know we have some time before either of us take mates. Do not let anyone push you into being a man until you are ready, Shining Light."

She hand-signed behind Chases Butterflies back that she was now a woman. She put her fingers to her mouth telling him to show no emotion.

Still, his body jerked, his eyes wide. For the first time, he really looked at her, not just her face, but also every part of her—inside and out. He felt her Energy swirl with his own, and he knew she was Blue Night Sky's future replacement. "I wonder why I never saw you as I do now. You are... more than a girl."

He squeezed her hand and continued to stare deep into her being. Bumps grew on his arms and his neck hairs rose. Several tiny blue sparks circled her. "I feel you inside me. I feel—"

Chases Butterflies coughed.

They both turned Butterflies' way and laughed.

***

Over the next few days, many arguments erupted. More than one hand waved his way as new people dismissed him. He held tight to his Wolf Brother's neck fur and stood away from everyone. His grandmother and Blue Night Sky defended him, but he grew tired of adults treating him as a little boy.

He longed for the days his grandfather took him out to the place where he first met White Paws. He walked out of the Counsel Lodge and knew eyes followed. Emotions of every person passed through him, confusing him, stressing him, his frustration mounting as he stomped toward the canyons.

"Grandson!" Hawk Soaring stood in the canyon entrance and motioned him to follow.

"Grandfather, you must have been in my mind."

He ran to catch up to his grandfather. White Paws trotted to catch up.

The elder shook his head and smiled. "There are so many bands, I cannot count all the Peoples, but they came on their own, knowing they would follow a boy... I mean a young man." Their eyes met. "I see only my grandson."

Shining Light took the hand of his grandfather. "Thank you for calling me boy. My heart tells me I am a man, but my body shows me otherwise. I know I will grow up and everything, but I am not tall as you are, and I need to be taller before people will take me seriously. What if—"

His grandfather squeezed him and laughed. "Now you sound like my little Feather. Glad you are in there somewhere, boy."

He rubbed the top of his grandson's head and Shining Light relaxed. "Some bands only laughed and refused to follow, and when we rode up to them, they backed away in fear of the big dogs."

He stopped walking, bowed his head, and dropped to his knees in front of him. "Grandson, you will always be our little boy. Your grandmother, your mother, your father and I know your heart, your true emotions. Tonight all will sing and pray within their own bands. Each person's own mind will lead them and, when Father Sun wakes us, we will know how many have slipped away and how many will follow.

"Today, you and I—and your wolf—will go sit on that grass where that boy sprinkled me with dust, and maybe go to the stream and drink up a fish, eh?"

He took his grandfather's outstretched hand and allowed him to lead him to the place they had both grown to treasure.

Chapter 32

"I will be fine, Rising Moon." Blue Night Sky scooped up her small robe and slung it over her shoulder. "Stay here and help others make dried meat, and learn how to pound the swamp plant root so it can be used dry. This is personal. Bear calls to me, and has for days."

She waved Rising Moon away, her usual response when she needed to make a point, and wandered into the canyons, away from the playing children.

***

She cleansed herself and prayed for many days, but with no luck. Just as she decided to return to her lodge, a paw brushed the back of her neck.

"So now you come. This old woman is weak after days of thirst and hunger. At least the Fish People take water. I prepare to walk home, and you decide to call me back. We are nearly ready to leave, Bear. I thought you had decided to let me walk alone, without you at my side."

She grumbled a bit, but knew the Spirits had their reasons. She walked back to the narrow canyon that few ever visited. She knew Shining Light would see to it that no one bothered her. She had not asked him to come, but she felt his Energy nearby.

She crawled into the small cave and took out the stone-carved Red Bear her father had made when she was just a baby. He had known, before she was even born, that Bear would follow her.

She re-lit the Sage she had left behind and allowed it to smoke before blowing the small fire out. Bear had a way of ensuring that one was worthy, and might not show the first, or even the second, time called. Bear required patience.

"Bear, you are a good and caring Guide. In my youth, you taught me to remain calm and not allow my temper to take my mouth. Now, in the late season of my life, you teach me still. I go deep within to reach answers others cannot find. I thank your cousin, White Bear, for guiding Shining Light. He has the strength of Bear, but not yet the quietness!"

She chuckled and settled down against the canyon wall so she could stretch her legs.

'You are the strong one, Woman of The Night Sky.' Bear Cub sat next to her on her haunches. 'Your words aided the boy. Only then did they look at the young one in the Counsel Lodge. Your words gave him courage. Shining Light will one day be a great Holy Man, but even in your eyes, he still wears the skin of a young one. Like you at that age, he holds Power. You, Holy Woman, must understand something.'

A She Bear appeared in the cub's place. '*Our time is not so near. You think we are old. We are not. Shining Light will need you for many moons to come. He has not yet mastered the way into the Center of the Circle. Few ever do. And some of the Peoples will still need you, Human She Bear, to remind them that they – and any newcomers – are one band with one common goal.*'

An old She Bear stretched her arms forward and let out a growl. '*Forward is the way, Spirit Woman. The many Spirits who surround you, and swirl about your being, are there to remind you that age is but a word. Hear me, woman, and listen well – become one with your mind, and your body will follow. I am here to remind you that we Elders carry the wisdom. We are not so old. You are stronger than you think.*'

She Bear's paw reached out and brushed both her legs.

The elder Holy Woman rubbed her limbs, surprised they no longer pained her as much. She smiled; Bear had given her Power to continue.

She grabbed her stick, gave it a toss, and stood to test her legs. She would return to the camp taller than when she had left.

***

Shining Light and a pack of wolves sat above the Great Holy Woman and watched as she tossed her stick. "Power... I will never see such a strong person – man or woman – as Blue Night Sky. I can only hope to have even part of her Power. Did you see, White Paws? Moon Face? I felt Bear all around as she grew stronger. I wonder –"

Sandstone shoved her muzzle in his back. "Hey, how did you get up here? You never tried this before. You have walked nearly straight up, silly one!"

Her nicker joined with a new arrival's laughter.

"Never doubt a female's ability to surprise a man, Shining Light!" Rising Moon stood beside the big dog. "I held onto her tail and she pulled me up" She sat a few feet from him and shyly looked away. "I have a gift, which my mother calls 'Animal Speaking.' That was almost my name. Deer, Raccoon and Hawk each appeared the moment I was born, but my mother insisted I be named after the rising moon she saw."

"Who wanted to call you Animal Speaking? Bet I know." Shining Light's face deepened in color when he looked her way. "I watched one day as you called to some birds in a tree, and they landed on your arms."

"So now you spy?" She shot him a sideways glance, but her grin told him she held no anger in her words.

"Well, um, no... I... I...."

She laughed and pushed at this shoulder. "I do not bite. I may growl sometimes. Blue Night Sky says a Bear Spirit follows me, along with Fox who teaches one how to fade in plain sight and escape pain."

She wore a dress, decorated in elk teeth and sky beads on the top half, and a matching headband quilled in white and turquoise-blue. He admired them and smiled.

"Ah, so you can smile! I see you with a frown most days. It is good to see your mouth turn the other way for a change."

She handed him her headband, and when he did not respond, she put it on his head. "Now you have something from me to wear always, to remind you I am first a friend. We will see, as the seasons turn over, what we will be."

She got up to leave, but turned back. "You must come down from your perch and help pack, friend of mine."

She then made her way back down the rocky path with Sandstone.

He knew he sat on his "perch" for the last time. Both saddened and excited, he stood and looked one last time across the open valley, and locked the image in his mind. Orange-red canyons jutted up around him. Pine trees mixed with other trees and shrubs. Clouds appeared to stay still in the turquoise sky where two Eagles soared on the currents. Down below, the winding river they would follow reflected Father Sun's light. On both sides of the river, plants dressed in colors of the season's changing beauty. Late white and yellow asters dominated the land.

I wish I could paint as well as others that I have watched. I would paint this on a hide and carry it to our new home. Down below, several bands moved away from the main group. *They will go their own way, to their own destiny, as Blue Night Sky called it.*

***

Father Sun rose over an already busy camp. As Flying Raven had expected, several bands had picked up during the dark and vanished. Flying Raven Who Dreams looked in the direction they had gone, and his first thought was to jump on his big dog and go after them. But he knew they would not come back.

To their own future, they go. They will remain, join forces, and prepare to do battle or try to make friends with the newcomers. I envy them some, for I feel the urge to stay. I must not do so. The Peoples who stay will need their Holy Peoples to help make a new beginning. And the ones who leave need me... and my son.

He whistled and his big dog, Flies As Wind, trotted over and stood still as he put the woven grass rope around his neck and up over twitching ears. He twisted it behind the animal's head, wrapped it around the muzzle, and tossed the two ropes from either side of his neck onto his back. The pair had bonded well, and Flying Raven could whisper words of comfort that made the animal respond — the only human who could make that claim. The man felt Power surge through the four-legged as he swung on easily.

Long Arrow was right to choose him for me. I feel so free on his back. I could chase Wind and catch her. Now to give Sandstone back to my son.

He smiled as he envisioned the look on his son's face. He rode over to where Long Arrow held the rope to a dun-colored animal. Larger and stronger, he would be better fit to pull the drag.

Shining Light's wide eyes and smile told him his son understood. Hawk Soaring took the new big dog and with no words spoken, Shining Light hopped onto Sandstone.

"You, my son, are the true leader here. I will follow you."

"Father, we go beside one another, two men—one a Holy Man, and the other a *budding* Holy Man who learns the ways from his father."

Flying Raven sat tall, chin raised, and rode beside his son as they led the bands out of the canyons and along the river. He remembered the speech Running River had strongly expressed to his son, and chuckled. Her daughter would never be far from his son, even when Chases Butterflies became a woman.

Chases Butterflies rode her dun-colored, frisky Bouncing Dog next to Shining Light. Her mother had told her not to ride the freshly broken big dog, but her daughter's pouting lips, and her speech about Running River never allowing her to do anything, made the nervous mother go talk to Shining Light. He had to promise on his very life to keep both big dogs tied together. She made sure he understood "together" meant a short rope connecting both animals by their heads.

Bright Sun Flower carried her granddaughter, Soft Breeze, in her arms as she rode on the drag.

He chuckled as White Paws stayed with his kind, but close enough to Shining Light to see him. *So, the wolves really do follow. I had wondered what would happen.*

***

Blue Night Sky refused to ride. Her step now more sure-footed, she walked beside Long Arrow, turning to watch many take last looks back. Most held tears in their eyes, though some showed no emotion.

To leave the only home they have ever known, and knowing they are never to return, makes many adult hearts heavy. Children chase each other and laugh, free of burdens—too young to feel the loss, they are excited to see such commotion. She sighed and turned back. *The rest of the bands fall into place behind us, and to the surprise of many, Walking Stick came with his women and children. He and I will prove to be invaluable with our skills at hand-signing.*

She turned forward with a light step. *We follow the river's course as it rolls out of the canyons and spills onto the grasslands, leading us onward—toward a new life, a new beginning.*

Chapter 33

Flying Raven thought it a better idea for them to keep moving, instead of trying to talk to people who stayed half-hidden. The Peoples they saw dressed differently and shouted strange words as they passed. After an arrow whizzed by him, he raced back and forth on Flies As Wind to warn his gathered bands to move farther away and deeper into the grasslands. He had Flies As Wind rear upwards several times to scare off the ones who shot the arrow. The strange ones melted into the grass.

He spoke to Shining Light, who still, even a moon later, led Chases Butterflies' big dog. "The first moon has inspired much exploring by everyone, and I see parents chase down children who run without worry. Most of the Peoples we encountered stayed their distance after they saw the strange big dogs. Still I worry what lies ahead."

"Father, what lies ahead will be as it may." His son turned and curled his lips inward. "My dreams did not tell me anything more than to go this way. Do not worry. The Spirits have plans for us."

Shining Light now spoke no differently than any other man might. He nodded and turned his head forward, inwardly smiling. *My son grows with every rising of Father Sun.*

He squeezed Flies As Wind's sides and the big dog responded, leaving his son behind. He needed to make sure that Elders who walked did so because they wanted to. Everyone looked after them, but he wanted to assure himself all was well.

***

Shining Light felt more confidence as his people made one fire to sing and dance around each night. Each sang for guidance as they journeyed deeper into unknown lands. All eyes turned toward him to lead the songs and dances. Now, he felt honor when they asked him to retell of his dreams.

Some asked if he knew what he was doing; leading so many adults to a place he himself had never seen. But those who had started out with him did not once try to turn back. They believed in him, though he still chased after other children and made jokes to make them laugh when they heard noises in the dark.

Sentries stood guard and occasionally, out of the darkness, someone using hand-signs came to join, saying they had heard of this great Shining Light. Though surprised to see this Great One was a boy, they stayed.

"Father," whispered Shining Light one night while they sat and watched others dance, "we started out as seven different bands two moons ago, and now we are more than I can count. More join every day. How is it that they know of us?"

"I have no answer, Son. None who joins us speaks our language, but Walking Stick and Blue Night Sky tell me the People's own Holy People speak of their strange dreams of a Shining Light. Many followed across the lands because they dreamed of him leading Peoples to safety, protecting them from a deadly future. Some laughed, but others felt the truth. We now have several more Holy Peoples, and even if we cannot speak the same words, we feel the same things."

Flying Raven looked toward Makes Baskets, who laughed with Bright Sun Flower as they played with Soft Breeze.

"Soon my daughter will run with the other children. She already takes small steps from mother to grandmother." His father turned to face him. "Son, I had a dream I must share. Before the snows come, another People will join us."

"I know. The ones we try to avoid. Several are on our path but I have no fear of them. What I do feel is *their* fear." He looked down at his uneaten food, and picked at it for a moment before looking into his father's eyes. "I know you will reject what I have to say, but you must listen to me. I do not wish to cause you or Mother any worry, but I must leave the safety of the bands and go with Blue Night Sky to these ones who follow."

Flying Raven did not react as Shining Light thought he would. He did not widen his eyes, nor did he open his mouth to object. He continued to look at his son with no emotion.

"I... I thought you would react differently and tell me no, Father. You look at me as you would any man who chooses to speak of his decision. Did you know what I was going to say?" He stared into the Holy Man's watery eyes. "Father, please speak to me."

"I cannot make the choices for another man. Before me, I see a man who has made his choice, and I will stand by it. Your mother will not be convinced and will worry herself into a terrible fray. For her, I ask that you allow me, your grandfather, Long Arrow, and Sees Like Eagle, to go along with more experienced warriors from the other bands.

"Each of us has our own experiences you may need. Sees Like Eagle, because I know his daughter will follow, Long Arrow knows some of their words, and your grandfather can fly with Hawk to see if danger lurks behind these... these others. And the warriors will offer protection. I will tell Walking Stick we need him here in case he needs to communicate with others who may come into camp. I already know Blue Night Sky will follow you no matter what. How I will tell your mother —"

"I already did. She cried and begged me not to go, and said I must not go without your consent. I wish I knew how to surround her in comfort."

He did not possess all the gifts he wished for — no one did. Not even the Great One of all the Peoples, Blue Night Sky, enjoyed special privileges.

***

Bright Sun Flower stood by her campfire as Shining Light trotted past on Sandstone, and the group prepared to leave.

Chases Butterflies ran up to Shining Light, out of breath. "You did not think you would leave without me, did you? I will not be left behind!" Her anger turned to tears and, in her frustration, she pushed the middle of her cousin's chest as he tried to get down from Sandstone and hug her. "I am not a baby! I told you I would be at your side even if I must run to keep up with Sandstone and the wolves!"

Morning Star grabbed hold of Running River's arm. "Our man is with them. He will watch out for his daughter. I feel this is her mission also. Let her go, sister of my heart."

Running River relaxed in Morning Star's grasp. "I... I just have a mother's worry."

Rising Moon dashed past the mothers on a small horse to catch up with the leaving group. She wore a pack with provisions.

"Daughter!" Morning Star cried out.

"So now your daughter goes also. She has Blue Night Sky and Long Arrow to protect her." Running River turned and grinned at the distraught mother.

Bright Sun Flower now needed to have her say. "I do not want anyone to go, but does anyone listen to this old woman? Does her own man? *No!* Why should anyone listen to me? I am just an aging Holy Woman who knows nothing and has no connection to the Spirit world!"

She turned to walk away, but changed her mind, spun back and crossed her arms. "When, Morning Star, are you going to announce your unborn child?"

"I meant to, but so many other things—"

"Unborn child?" Running River looked at her belly. "I was so busy worrying about where we were going that I never saw your belly swelling. Why, dear sister of my heart, have you not at least told me? I thought we shared everything."

Running River tried to look stern, but her dancing eyes betrayed her frown's intention. She hugged Morning Star, pushed her back and shook a finger at her.

Bright Sun Flower strolled away, humming a song as she went to gather wood. The band would go no farther this day. She turned to watch her man and grandson ride away.

Hawk Soaring and she had taken their robes to get away from everyone when Father Sun went to sleep, before the camp had even settled into their night meal. She smiled at the memory.

She said a prayer for all who left, but shed no tears. What good would it have done? Many men remained to watch over the camp and hunt. She should be happy.

Her grandson looked back at her, and they both smiled and waved. *That boy will always know my heart, and I his.*

Chapter 34

Hawk Soaring felt the pull and could not deny it, for to ignore one's Spirit Guide—no matter the weather, no matter the time, no matter the reason—risked offending the Guide, who may choose not to appear when called upon in the future. The elder man had refused food for the past three days to prepare his body to welcome Hawk, and now the call was too strong not to answer.

The rest of their group camped under what cover the mostly bare trees offered, and unpacked robes and food. Father Sun had begun his descent, showing the sparse landscape's dying yellows and reds on near leafless plants, as the land grew dark.

Down below, the Great Elder moved about.

All he could do was stay and wait for Hawk.

***

Blue Night Sky unpacked pemmican, along with dried fish and humpback meat, and settled down on her robe. The riding had been hard on her. The stiffness of her body showed this to the others, but she refused to complain.

She stretched her legs and arms, smiled, and offered Long Arrow some of her food. Rising Moon had packed enough for several other people, so she did not need to spread around the third night's meal.

Smart girl. She shows her worth to everyone, especially to a certain young man who peeks her way every chance he gets. They will make fine mates one day.

As tired as I am, I can feel someone watches. I must not panic everyone. I am so tired, my mind might be making things up. Still—

***

As the fire blazed in the darkness, the wolves set out to hunt. The dogs that followed stayed to beg for food. Flying Raven sat next to Shining Light and poked him in his ribs. "The wolves hunt in silence, but the two girls chatter so much, surely every mouse and rabbit ran into hiding. Their hunting may be in vain this night."

Even though his laughter was soft, both girls had heard him.

"Perhaps we will allow the men to cook their own food this night." Rising moon spoke without looking at anyone.

No one dared offend a Holy Man, but she meant for him to hear her loud voice. She did not care. Her bottom pained her from bouncing on the small horse and her shoulders ached from the pack she wore heavy with food. She had had the sense to pack provisions: dried fish, plant roots, pemmican, and even swamp plant root pounded into flour — all of which the men thought were too burdensome. They preferred to hunt, but in three days, they had found only two rabbits and a few ground birds that had no interest in running or flying away.

"I agree, Rising Moon. They can hunt while we eat the food you still have," Chases Butterflies added. "I think they are being mean! Just because we have things to say... I mean, we only talk about important things, right? So why —"

Flying Raven knew the girl did not like teasing. She started to walk away, but remembered she was not in camp and stopped, but she would not turn around.

Sees Like Eagle went over and knelt down before his daughter, trying to comfort the strong-willed girl. "Little one, they only jest. Do not be offended. We are all a bit nervous about being away from the rest of the people. We need to relax, and to eat the wonderful food the thoughtful Rising Moon brought."

Sees Like Eagle looked up as if to thank Rising Moon, but she stood stiff with fear, pointing into the darkness.

***

Hawk Soaring sat on his robe, singing and praying for Hawk to come. The half moon lit the lands below, casting shadows on the near leafless shrubs that formed a dark barrier around the people below. The small fire where his grandson and the others waited stood out but as a spark.

A deep chill raced across his body, one that had nothing to do with the cold night air. Invisible wings brushed his face.

Hawk had sent him a warning.

Too high to see movement in the camp, he abandoned his outcrop and made his way down the hill. He had brought no bow, and had only his knife in his leather waist wrapping.

Silent as a falling leaf, he crept closer to the campfire. His heart drummed so loud in his chest, he slowed down for fear his racing heart would force him to make a mistake. He could make out something shiny in the clearing, and the sound of voices — some he recognized, some not.

Chases Butterflies stood up to a creature with a shiny head, shaking her finger at it as she scolded it in harsh words. She stood in defiance with her other hand on her small hip. Her father tried to grab hold of his fiery daughter from behind, but she leaned forward as he struggled to hold her back. She leaned on her toes and continued to scold the shiny-headed being.

Hawk Soaring crawled closer. The creature laughed and... and took off its head! It knelt down before the girl and offered its hand. *Hand?* Hawk Soaring now stood to see the creature's head. *Human!*

He stood up from the bushes and held out his knife as he entered the camp. The strange one jumped up and stepped back in surprise, raising his empty hands. His words sounded like gurgling to Hawk Soaring. The stranger tried to disappear into the darkness, but Long Arrow stood directly behind him and prevented his escape. The stranger smiled and put out his hands to show they were empty, and without taking his eyes off Sees Like Eagle in front of him, he pulled his long knife from its sheath and let it drop.

No one had expected a woman of the people to jump out and push the strange one to the ground. She did so and spoke with her hands, to explain that this one was not their enemy. Her clothing, a tunic decorated with elk's teeth, reached below her knees. She wore men's leggings instead of a dress or skirt. Her disheveled hair reached her shoulders. The woman, clearly panicked, stared at Blue Night Sky. Her fast-moving hands begged the Great Elder to understand.

Blue Night Sky smiled and stood, showing the woman that her hands were also empty. "Hawk Soaring, put down your knife. Now! Do not disobey me. We must show we mean no harm. I thank you for showing up just as you did. You surprised the strange one and made him take notice that we were not helpless."

Hawk Soaring put away his knife, but kept an eye on Blue Night Sky as she moved forward cautiously. He knew she was alert for any movement from the strange one who sat on the ground, and seeing the other men of his people move forward, he relaxed.

She signed with the woman, nodded her head, and motioned for the pair to sit by the fire and warm themselves. "The woman comes from a place far toward the rising of Father Sun. Her people are called Likes To Fight. The woman's people captured some of the strange ones who slept unguarded—a serious mistake. Her people saw their hairy faces, thought them to be sent by the Spirits, and allowed them and their big dogs to join the Likes To Fight band.

"Her people are not peaceful and like to raid other bands, and the big dogs made it easier. Some of the hairy-faced ones, tired of fighting, wanted peace. When the rest were on a raid, the remaining left on foot, and several women followed them. Now they hide from the women's People. For the past nine sunrises, no one has sought them. They worried when they saw our fire, and were ready to fight."

She pointed to Chases Butterflies. "That little smart mouth of hers saved us. They were going to attack, and worry afterwards who we were." She pointed to the hairy-faced man and chuckled. "He stopped short when she wagged her finger at him and yelled strange words. He did not need to know what they meant to understand her bravery!"

"They?" Hawk Soaring looked past the two and saw nothing but darkness. "Where are they and how many?" He reached for his sheathed knife.

***

Shining Light stepped forward. "Grandfather, no." He spoke calmly and hoped his gentle voice would help to keep everyone relaxed. "Do not ready yourself for a fight. I have seen in my dreams these strange ones coming, just as Father did. Let us do what we came here for—welcome them, offer the food

Running Moon was smart enough to pack. We can hunt on the way back to the camp. You know they run and seek safety. We came not knowing what we would find, but look at these people. They seek only peace, as we do."

Shining Light stood his ground, not willing to back down. He motioned to the hairy-faced man's woman, and pointed to Blue Night Sky. "Please tell her to have her man call the others in."

The pair looked at Shining Light, then to Blue Night Sky, who explained who he was as best she could. They grinned at the young one.

"Sweet Mother! Shining Light, they know who you are. A dreamer comes with them. One of the woman's people saw you in his dreams many seasons ago, when you were born, and his Spirit Guide told him to seek you out." She shook her head and laughed. "Why did I think only I was privileged to know of your birth?" She signed and instructed the woman to tell the others to come in.

The small group stood in awe as many came out of the brush. Ten hairy-faced ones took off their shiny head coverings and dropped them, along with spears and knives, to the ground, and showed their hands were empty. Women came next; all dressed similar to the first one. A few carried babies on their backs.

The new Peoples smiled at Shining Light and sat next to the fire. More wood added to the flames made it easier to see how many new people gathered. No longer did anyone call them the strange ones. Laughter filled the night as everyone tried to communicate.

Rising Moon and Chases Butterflies sat next to Shining light as the food made its way around the circle. Babies nursed in comfort, and the newcomers eyed the one called Shining Light. Their dreamer started a song and his people clapped in time. Everyone, even those who did not understand the words, swayed back and forth, and peaceful Energy filled the night.

Shining Light reached for Rising Moon's hand without worry of taboo. Blue sparks passed between the young couple. Several wolves howled in the distance.

Chapter 35

Fog filled Shining Light's mind. Screams, loud thunder and crying children jerked him awake, and he yelled out. He sat up so fast, several people around him jumped up guarded, ready to fight. He looked at the people standing around and nudged his already wide-awake father.

He yelled to Blue Night Sky, not knowing where she slept. "Dream, I had a dream. Great Elder, please explain to the new Peoples before we all end up in battle!"

She spoke to no one in particular. "Fire... get the fire started, and be quick about it!"

Flying Raven Who Dreams scooped up a handful of long yellow grass and started the fire.

Wolves snarled and Shining Light yelled for White Paws and Moon Face. He wrapped an arm around each wolf. Out of the darkness, seven more wolves appeared and formed a circle around him. He reached for the only weapon he could find, a large branchless log nearly his own size.

Be strong! I must stand still and show no fear! "These Wolves are my... my Spirit Guides who choose to live in bodies. They will cause you no harm." The strength in his voice boomed with courage.

White Paws brushed against him, stood on his hind legs, and used a paw to pull at his raised arm. Shining Light responded and let go the log. It fell and rolled past them.

With the fire now bright, the new people stared in shock at the wildness of a half-crazed boy and the wolves who pressed tight against him.

***

Blue Night Sky raised her hands and spread them wide. She explained with fast motions that there was nothing to fear. To prove her point she walked to where White Paws stood with Shining Light, dug her hands deep into his fur, and sat in front of him. She motioned him to lie next to her. White Paws lowered himself while his amber eyes warily watched the strange humans, who in turn stared back.

"He only watches all of you. Not ever seeing you before had made him wary, nothing else." She let go of the wolf's fur, stood, and motioned to Shining Light to step forward with her toward the new people. His wolves followed.

A small child of the new people broke away from her mother, giggled and ran to White Paws. The wolf rolled over and allowed the little one to jump in the middle of his thick-furred belly. He licked her face, rolled over, and nudged the child with his nose while his tail waved his friendliness. The parents stopped short of pulling their child away. Instead, they sat and ran their hands across the wolf's head and shoulders, allowing their daughter to play. Two other small children started to toddle over, but fast mothers grabbed them.

"You see for yourselves this wolf will cause no harm. None of them will." She rubbed the child's head and looked up at her parents. "All is well."

From across the camp, Long Arrow coughed and moved toward the bright fire. He waved his arms, and his voice carried as he made his way to stand next to her and Shining Light. "Now that we are all awake and have met the wolves, perhaps...." His laughter nervous, he tried to wave the new people over to the warm fire. "We need to talk."

He hand-signed and spoke the few words he knew of the hairy-faced ones. "Father Sun wakes soon. Everyone did get some sleep." He looked over at White Paws and grinned. "Thank you, Wolf. I had wondered how to start this, and you gave me a good idea... um... if everyone will agree."

He waited for Blue Night Sky to respond. She stood up and nodded for him to continue.

He rubbed his eyes and motioned to one of the hairy-faced men to step forward. "This man, who goes by his new name, Smiles A Lot, or Many Smiles, has told me as best he could with what I know of his words—and his hand-signs—that many of his people are less than a day's ride toward Father Sun. They have captives."

Long Arrow swallowed hard and turned to ask, "Are my words right, Blue Night Sky? He says the captives' skin color is the same as ours, and they dress in leather and.... Sweet Mother! Blue Night Sky, help me, I can only understand that he wants help to get his women's sister away from them."

He urged them forward with a wave of his hand. One woman came forward and clung to her man. She signed her name, Brown Bird Woman.

Blue Night Sky caught his arm. "Long Arrow, do not touch her. We have no idea what her man would do if you did." She motioned them both forward and started signing. "Brown Bird Woman is—was—a captive of the Likes To Fight people, who helped to raid her people with the hairy-faced ones nearly a cycle of seasons ago. How she became the woman of one, I do not know, but they split up the captives and she ended up separated from them after their brother was... was...."

She looked at Shining Light and the two girls. *I cannot speak of his cruel end. I will not in front of them.*

She motioned them to sit by the fire. "This man took her and both her sisters as his mates, and one of her sisters was then taken away from him, given as a gift to another hairy face before he understood. He tired to stop it, but one of his own kind shot him. The wound took much time to heal. Soon as he was able to travel, they prepared to leave. I think he says... others followed to escape. They thought the Likes To Fight people might take their mates away also."

She turned to Long Arrow with a cocked head. "I only guess at all their hand-signs, as some I do not remember seeing before."

This time she turned to Shining Light. "They do want to know why you woke screaming. They now worry that they could lose their women and have to fight us."

***

Shining Light shook his head, sat near the fire with White Paws and the parents of the young girl, who now played with the wolf. "Tell them I had a bad dream, a dream of maybe their people we are to rescue. I... I feel this is possible because I saw the hairy-faced ones forcing many people and children before them. Please tell them I am going to go somewhere I can be alone to seek guidance."

He grabbed his robe, left the group, and made his way into the shrubs Hawk Soaring had come through a while before.

He turned and called back. "Father, please make everyone stay until I return."

With that, he vanished into the shrubs, leaving behind his water bladder. Every wolf followed behind him.

Terrified children still screamed in his mind. *I feel, somehow, Blue Night Sky holds both fear and excitement inside her. She knows, or feels, things I cannot.*

***

For what felt like days to Shining Light, Father Sun stayed above the horizon. *How many times, Father Sun, have you awakened me? Is this the third time, or have I not slept? Did you ever leave me in darkness?*

Shining Light's body begged for water. His eyes ached. *Something in the distance, but what is it? My nose burns and my mouth is dry, yet I do not thirst.*

He felt Energy grab his mind, and turned toward the pull of the unknown. *Unknown land. Where am I?*

Bear's growl rose above him, and he looked up to see a small cave. He stepped to it, but had to get on his knees to reach inside. Something slashed his hand and he pulled it back. Warm, bright red blood ran like a small river through the creases in his hand.

The cave entrance was too small for any bear to enter. He blindly reached in again, not knowing what to expect. His hand once again fell on a sharp object. He pulled it out into the light.

Bear? The head is too small for....

Energy swirled around his hand and the skull.

A bone that is not a bone, but a stone that was once a bone. So old. When did you live, my brother?

He placed the ancient bear skull at the entrance of the small cave. *Forever, my brother, you have guarded this cave, perhaps just for me.*

He wiped his bloody hand on his robe, and dragged it in behind him while trying to guess which way the cave might become larger.

Tiny pairs of eyes scurried past him, save one pair—those eyes jumped onto his shoulder. Mouse nibbled at his lobe. *'So, Human, you seek what you cannot see? I see clearly what your eyes do not. Close your eyes. They are useless. No one can truly see with his eyes. What good do they do in this cave?'*

Shining Light breathed deep the musty air, and closed his eyes. "Mouse, Great Mystery, please have pity on this child and show him what weak human eyes cannot see."

He managed to sit, and took out his fire sticks to make a small fire on top of the Sage, in the little bowl he now carried with him. Once fire caught, he blew it out, allowing the Sage smoke to rise above him.

Wait, how did I light it? There is no light in here, yet I see.

A scent of snow filled his nostrils and he wrapped his robe tighter. *I still have the gift of my Spirits simply making themselves known. I am special, as Grandmother told me. What makes me think I am special? Shame on me for being so bold. I am no more special than a stone, than a tree, than... than....*

Wolf's Paw touched his cheek. *'Shining Light, we are all special. We are all children of Creator, but no one is more special than the other.'*

Grandfather Wolf's amber eyes captivated him, took him into a place full off colors that danced, twirled and wrapped themselves around both human and Wolf. It held them both like a sticky Spider's web.

In the distance several songs, each belonging to a single wolf, intertwined and became a combined song—yet no song at all, but a color. The shock of thunder dropped Shining Light to his knees.

Was I not already sitting? I cannot remember. I... I feel... so strange, so loose.

Colors shot out of his body. Blues—so many blue colors spun into the web and joined colors for which he had no name.

'Human man who hides in the body of a boy, I, Wolf, one who can see distances you cannot, swirls before you, dances through you, becomes you. Look far away, past the swirling colors. See before you a future you cannot change for everyone. I say this: listen to me, and you can help the Humans who follow you now, and those who will soon follow your way. Your dreams are not only of one lifetime. Your destiny lies beyond those who call you Shining Light. No, do not shut out what you do not understand. Look... look... see it.'

But I do not wish to see it. Why must I? What are these strange things on such big waters? Who are these... these pale beings that are inside these big floating logs? Please, I do not understand! I came seeking answers how to save my Peoples, not see more things I do not understand. Please, show me what I need to know.

'You already know what to do. Look beyond yourself. I, White Bear, will heal your hand, but you must save this generation, lead them to safety so they will be able to heal the minds of the generation yet to be born. This generation will not be born of the Peoples you lead, but of those born outside the safety. Take them to the place where they shall live forever in peace. Know, Shining Light, this peace for you is only for a while....'

Shining Light sat up in the cold grass. "What? Where is the cave?"

He looked down at his hand still covered in blood. He wiped it on the grass before him and stared at his uninjured hand.

"No wound? Where is the cut? What has happened? Wait... what does this mean that the peace for me is only for a while?"

***

Blue Night Sky sat so close to him, yet he could not see her. She gathered her things up and slipped away. *The future, my boy, belongs to the strong....*

Chapter 36

Flying Raven Who Dreams had not waited for his son to return, knowing Blue Night Sky watched over him. He had asked Hawk Soaring to lead the people forward.

After wading through the waist-deep river, he lay flat in the long grass and watched.

Several women went for water, accompanied by only a single guard. A straggling girl limped, and the guard ignored her. Flying Raven decided she would be the one to grab. Her frayed footwear shuffled, and he knew by her body language that she would soon give up.

He took every caution to make sure the guard would not see him. When he crept toward the girl, he wondered if the guard had even heard the water splash behind him when two ducks landed, as he did not turn to see what made the splash.

He staggers as if he is half-asleep, his eyes narrow, and he speaks to himself. I doubt he even watches the women, let alone looks for danger.

The girl appeared to mean nothing to the guard. Flying Raven hoped she would understand him. Long Arrow had said, '*Pick a person who wears your style of clothing. Their words are the same as both mine and yours.*'

How can I be sure their words are the same as mine? What if I take the wrong person and she screams in panic? So many captives are dressed in strange clothes. Several of the women wear clothing I have never seen before, brightly colored and not of leather. Where are the men?

The girl's rasping breath drew near, and he reached out and grabbed her. He placed his hand over her mouth and pulled her back. To his surprise, she gave little resistance. Her body felt thin. He feared crushing her ribs, and released part of his hold.

"Do not panic, girl, I will not harm you. I am a Holy Man." He looked down into her blood-shot eyes; her will had faded long ago.

She searched his face, and a flicker of recognition appeared when she saw how he dressed. She went limp, and Flying Raven loosened his hold. She wrapped her arms around him and softly sobbed.

"Thank you. I gave up hope after I knew I was the only one in my family left alive." She let go and sobbed into her small, dirty hands. "I am fifteen winters, a woman. I am called Wandering Wind."

Her pleading eyes stared into his. "Are you here to take me away? Please? No one will even notice. I have to fight their dogs for scraps. I... I promise to be a good woman for you. I will bear you many children. The enemy monsters laugh. Twice I ran into the trees and no one came after me. They knew I had nowhere to go."

Tears fell from weary eyes and she shook her head. "They did not care." She hugged her rescuer again as tears dripped from her chin. "I am Wandering Wind. I know we are not of the same People, but does it matter? Our words are close to the same. I know because I have seen your clothing at a gathering when I was eleven winters old. I will be no trouble and will listen to you, do as you ask."

She curled up into his chest.

"Wandering Wind, I have one mate and two children and do not want another...."

Her grip tightened. "Please take me as your woman. Do not leave me here to die."

"Listen, girl... err... woman. Listen to me. I am here to rescue all the captives. You will help me." He hugged her, caressed her hair as he would a child, and let her cry herself calm.

They watched as the group of women and the guard made their back into camp. Several women stopped to rest before moving on. One woman turned their way, staring right at the place Flying Raven and Wandering Wind hid, then turned back and pretended to be interested in the guard, perhaps to distract him. The burden of a branch across her shoulders, which held four containers of water, began to slip. She slid the weight off and rubbed her neck, still looking at the guard, who just laughed at her.

Wandering Wind clenched her fists, but still lay curled in Flying Raven's lap. "Her name is Mourning Dove, a favorite of the human monster who leads these... these... evil ones."

"Wandering Wind, what I have to tell you will give you the ability to save all your People, and the ones who are not of your People but captives just the same. I know you do not want to go back, but you must." He tried to smile and comfort her, his eyes gentle. "Go. Speak to the woman who saw us. Tell her of the plans I will now tell you. Soon, you will all be free, and we will ride away. The big dogs—"

"Big dogs? What are big dogs? Oh!" Her eyes brightened. "I understand. *Mus-tang*. We all have picked up some bits of the enemy monster's words. Oh no, you must know—"

He tried to calm her words. He knew she was excited to have someone care about her, but he had to gain her attention. He squeezed her shoulders and spoke in a soft tone. "Girl, stop talking! First listen to my plans."

"But... but I must tell you something." She looked back and watched as the guard shoved the last woman forward. "Another band of their kind follows. They parted five sunrises ago and took no captives. If I understand, they will join back up soon. That is why you found us here. We wait for them."

The Holy Man's eyebrows rose at the news. "We must act fast. Listen, and speak no more."

Flying Raven told Wandering Wind what she needed to know, and helped her slip back in amongst the women. No one noticed that she did not have a branch over her shoulder with water containers.

The Fish People had to act faster than planned. Flying Raven shuddered. That meant no going back to the main camp for more help. It would be them on the run then. Could they fight them? What he had learned about their weapons assured him of the answer — no.

We will have to sneak in during the darkest part of night. Would this be a good idea? Some say Souls cannot find their way home in the dark. Others say Creator would always find them if they lost the battle.

He decided to trust Creator to find his Soul if something happened.

My woman, my children — Creator, please guide them if I do not return. And... and help Baskets find another mate. She cannot live her life without a man.

His thoughts turned to his son. *Shining Light is only a boy in my heart, though I will never tell him that. I will make him understand that someone needs to stay and watch out for the women and children. Yes, this will make him proud, to be in charge of things and wait for us to return. If we return.*

Flying Raven looked up when he heard rustling in the tree next to him. Father Sun glistened on the wings of a black-blue bird. The bird hopped down the branches and stopped just short of him. Their eyes locked, and a surge of strength passed from Raven into him. Two wing feathers dropped as the bird cawed and flew over the enemy's camp.

The raven landed on top of a structure made of a strange covering, and cawed again. Three of his kind joined him. A man pushed a flap aside and stepped out at the same time the four birds flew over him and dumped their waste on his head. He yelled and stomped backwards, his hands full of the gift the ravens left him.

Flying Raven came close to bursting into laughter, but stilled himself. Several of the captives did it for him. Even the beatings they received did not still their laughter. He whispered his thanks. He knew now which one led the enemy.

He picked up the two feathers and crept backward into the grass.

Chapter 37

Mourning Dove watched Wandering Wind make her way back into the camp, and hid where she knew the poor little one would find her.

I hope our lives are about to change. The man who grabbed you and pulled you into the thickets – I wonder who he was. His clothing was of the people. Has someone finally come to rescue us?

She had worked hard not to smile while struggling past the pair with her heavy load of water. Her beauty had made her a favorite of these human monsters, and she did not share their desires. At night, despite her best efforts to hide, one always found her, as if he had his own magic. She longed to escape, to return to her People... or any kind Peoples.

She watched from behind some acorn shrubs as Wandering Wind walked with a happier step. She kept her head bent down and dropped some twigs next to the main fire. She then shuffled her way toward Mourning Dove, a bone bell she wore at her waist jingling as she moved.

The girl's voice quivered as she whispered into the bushes, "Mourning Dove, may I sit with you?"

"Come, sit. I saw what happened and knew you would seek me out. Here, I brought some food for you."

Wandering Wind crept forward, grabbed the dried meat and tore it to shreds with her teeth. "Thank you, I have not eaten this day."

She swallowed the meat and Mourning Dove gave her water from a clay cup.

"I know our words are not the same, but over time we have learned to speak to each other." The girl swallowed hard to get the food down. "I have good news for us all!"

Mourning Dove looked around her, and silenced the girl with a finger across her own mouth. "Speak soft words, girl. Too many may hear what they are not meant to."

The girl told her of the Holy Man's plans. "Soon we will be free! Soon we—"

Mourning Dove held a hand up and tried to calm her down. "Let me pass the word around. Go find a knife, and be ready to cut the mus-tangs free of their leg ropes. Tell only children and the older ones you know who will not act foolishly to help you. Have each one find a knife that no one will notice. The Spirits must have planned this, for there will be only a sliver of Moon this night."

She glanced upward to see how much daylight they had left. "Tell the children to make their way toward the mus-tangs after darkness takes the land,

and gather their ropes up. Only then, cut their legs loose. If they nicker to each other, rub their noses to calm them, and lead them to the waters. Get them across before you try to ride them, those of you who will.

"No one has allowed us to ride the animals, so we must imitate what we have seen. Do not come back. It may draw attention. Let the others do what they are expected to do." She held the girl's shoulders and faced her. "Some people may not make it. Let the older adults take care of them. Just do your task and do not look back. And, girl, take off your worn footwear. It makes noise. I heard you coming long before your bell. Tell others to bare their feet as well, if they must."

"But, Mourning Dove, what about that human monster who seeks you out every night?"

She stared ahead. "It will be the last night he ever seeks me out." She turned back to Wandering Wind. *Poor girl. Your hair is so matted, and you are painfully thin.* "Do not worry for me. Worry for yourself. Now go! I must reach as many of the women as I can so they can pass the word."

She prayed to Creator for strength, and asked her Guardian, Fox, to help her be cunning and invisible. She also said a prayer for the rescuers, that they would remain safe.

Mourning Dove tied her dark, shoulder-length hair back and slipped through the shrubs. She stood behind the lodge of the man who sought her out every night, and slit the back while he still ranted about the bird mess in his hair to everyone outside. She waited until he stomped off to the stream to clean up, and stepped inside.

She took his fire stick and his long knife, and tossed them out the slit.

Fox, guide my steps. Keep me quiet and invisible.

She slid out and placed stones across the bottom so no light would show through to expose the slit. She scurried to the next lodge and put her ear up to the strange cloth.

No sound. I must hurry. With so many lodges, surely someone is sleeping in one of them.

Chapter 38

Hawk Soaring stood with arms up to the sky. He was frustrated after fasting and waiting two nights, his body still weak from the first time. Worry weighed on his thoughts.

"Hawk, I cry out to you. Hear me. I need guidance. I have fasted for days and have had only water. Please show me what I need to know. We are not a people of battle. So many years have passed in our peaceful canyons. Now we travel to an unknown place with so many joining us. We are asked to fight to save a Peoples who may not have a future if we do not."

His skin prickled. He bowed his head as waves of soft Energy caressed him. "Hawk, I feel shame. You were waiting to find me worthy. Two days is not so long to wait."

Hawk spoke to him in a calm voice. '*Your destiny, child. You are here because you are meant to be here. You are not responsible for everyone. Each has their own future, their own choices to make. Worry not for the others or for yourself either. When you have returned to the camp with the freed ones of your kind, look to the sky, and be prepared to move fast.*'

A single red-tailed feather floated onto his lap. "Hawk, I worry for my grandson." He lit his pipe and blew smoke upward. "Creator, he is my only grandson. I know of his plans. Great Mystery, Grandfather of us all, please take *me*, if you wish, but to not allow harm to come to him."

He held up the feather and allowed the breeze—Sister Wind, Creator's Breath—to bless it.

He unwound the small piece of hide he carried with him when he ventured off alone. It held items of special meaning to him, things to remind him of past gifts given to him when his mind troubled him. He placed the feather in the pouch, retied the flap, and laid it on the ground.

Absentmindedly, his hand reached for the Medicine Pouch around his neck. A very long time ago, he had placed tiny shards of a broken Hawk egg among many other tiny treasures. On his first Vision Quest, he had found them sitting next to him when his mind returned to his body. Hawk had been with him ever since.

He rolled up his robe, and wandered back to the camp with a peaceful heart.

***

Flying Raven rode up on Flies As Wind. Now he knew what to call him: Mus-tang. He jumped off and let the near-white animal join the rest. Man and mus-tang had bonded, and a simple whistle would bring Flies As Wind right back to him.

He motioned for people he could not see to come his way. The camp rested in a small valley with trees and low shrubs, where it was easy to stay hidden in the dense underbrush even without leaves.

People, once invisible, now showed their selves. A few of the women started a small fire and placed several robes around it for people to sit on. Rising Moon and Chases Butterflies passed out jerked meat and fresh fire-roasted rabbit.

Shining Light and several others returned to camp with even more food — ground birds and rabbits, enough to feed the people. They handed them off to others to prepare.

Flying Raven sat cross-legged next to Blue Night Sky, who would sign words for him. He looked up and smiled as his son came to sit as his side. "So, my son has returned from his time on the hill. I am glad to see you."

He turned to face the others now gathered. "I spoke to a young girl who had the mouth of our own Shining Light." He needed to start the conversation with lightness, and he knew his son would take no offense. "She called herself Wandering Wind, and her mouth deserved that name well."

He took a piece of the hot rabbit and tore at it with his teeth, then told the story, leaving nothing out. He grinned and finished his story by telling of how the ravens had pointed out the leader.

Many laughed and relaxed. Everyone felt comfortable enough not to worry about anyone in the camp.

He maintained his air of confidence and continued to speak. "By tonight, when Father Sun goes to sleep, we must act. I know many who decided to help us in this, must decide if they wish to continue. There are many more of the enemy than we expected — three for every one of us. This is why you must try to go and speak to your own Spirit Guides."

He waited as everyone looked at each other. Some shook their heads; time was too short.

"We all know only a small sliver of Sister Moon will show. It will be our chance." He swallowed hard as he thought of Makes Baskets. It would be up to his son to care for her and Soft Breeze.

Shining Light, a boy soon passing into his thirteenth winter — only his thirteenth winter — grows into manhood before me so fast.

He shook his mind clear, and wrapped the edge of his Raven cape about his shoulders to have Raven's Energy near him.

Once again, several shifted and looked at each other. He knew by their body language that he needed to offer an alternative to them.

"If your beliefs tell you not to do this, you can help in other ways. We will need more food. Hunters can help this way. Others can make footwear, sizes for children to adult. What I saw tells me many would be grateful."

Several of the worried faces relaxed.

"When we move out with the rescued people, some may be injured. We must give our... our mus-tangs — this is what they call the big dogs — to them and run while leading the animals. We will not have time to make ropes. Instead, cut strips of leather so we can lead the new mus-tangs." He spread his arms wide. "Use your own judgment, but try to make the ropes three full arms long."

He sighed and stared over the group of people who were not his people, yet were. "I ask this of you. I do not tell any of you what to do. For those who follow me to the enemy camp, more of these—"

He was unsure of what to call them now that their group had these people among them. "These we now call enemy, bad men, are but a short span away. We must act fast this night. We must make sure to take every mus-tang, every water container, foot covering, and anything they might use as weapons, so they cannot come after us."

The hairy-faced man that Chases Butterflies had confronted stood. He pounded on his chest. "We go... go help." He turned to Blue Night Sky and nodded.

"Flying Raven, you can count on him—his men, and women who have no children—to help. Allow them to lead. You will be safer that way." She nodded back to the hairy-faced one. "His name is Tall Smiling Man... or Warrior. I can tell you to trust him, for he will not betray you."

Blue Night Sky sat down. Flying Raven could tell her mind was elsewhere, but did not have time to ask what bothered her. She would tell him if something was wrong.

He turned his attention back to the gathered Peoples. "Wandering Wind will find the woman who watched us and make plans with her. The women, their captives, will try to get the hairy faces to drink a red drink that makes them stagger and sleep, which I hear is not hard. They like the feeling."

In Flying Raven's mind, he imagined Mourning Dove and the other women passing out the red drink. They would feign interest in the hairy-faced ones, and no man would turn their advances away.

Shining Light spoke up. "Father, we must try to find a way to avoid battle. If we take lives, it may forever haunt our memories. I know we must rescue these people—do what we must to rescue these people from their captors—but...." He lowered his head.

Flying Raven stood. "The Fish People are a peaceful people who have always found a way to avoid battle. In my lifetime, there has been but one. Living in the canyons has given us a peaceful life. I understand my son's words. I too do not wish to speak to our children of killing. Not all Peoples listen to words of peace. They strike out in anger, revenge, and for many, it comes from what life taught them. I, myself, will avoid killing if I can. I cannot speak for those who are here and will go with us. Nor do I know what the people we go to save will do." I have spoken my words."

He turned and walked into the shadows, Shining Light following.

"Father, what I said... did I... did I speak the wrong words"? His son reached out and stopped him from going any further. "It is not part of my dream vision."

"What dream vision?"

"In all my dreams and visions — not once have I seen us killing."

"Perhaps your dreams, your visions, do not show any killing because there will be none, or it will not be us who kill. I will defend myself and do what I must only."

He turned and continued his walk, motioning Shining Light to follow. He explained to his son that he was to stay and protect the Peoples here, and the boy's... *man's*... disappointment grew in his eyes.

"Son, I need someone with your... your Power, to help Blue Night Sky if something goes wrong. You must be ready to take the women who are not warriors, and their children, as fast as you can away from here to our main camp. To do this is a great honor." The Holy Man stood tall and pushed his shoulders out. "You will be the only one who can do this. The others are children and too young."

He knew he had spoken the right words when Shining Light's shoulders also pulled back.

***

Shining Light stared deep into the Holy Man's eyes. He knew it was to keep him out of the fighting, but he needed to accept this to make his father feel he would be safe.

He never thought he would have to betray him. "I will do my best to deserve this honor."

Flying Raven grabbed both his shoulders and squeezed them. "Good, this is what I needed to hear, to know I have a man for a son."

The words stung Shining Light's heart. He and Blue Night Sky had already made plans, and he dare not go back on his words with the Great Elder.

Shining Light waited until his father left with the warriors, then left with White Paws. Only a few knew Chases Butterflies and he had plans.

His frustration mounted. *Do I have the Power Blue Night Sky claims I have?*

He wandered off to be alone, to try to connect with his grandmother. Much time passed before he could. He needed to know if he was wrong in his decision, and to tell her of his plans. Several small boulders gave him the privacy he sought away from any eyes that might turn his way. With a deep breath, he sat on the cold, yellowed grass and stilled himself. His mind floated above, away from his body — searching, feeling, waiting.

Finally, he felt a connection. He watched Bright Sun Flower as in a dream. He felt what she felt....

He felt her body tingle, and she stopped to listen, to wait for the vibrations to find her. *'What is wrong?'*

She got up without wincing from her knees. Worry took her mind away from the usual pain as she spoke to Makes Baskets. "I must go finish gathering wood while you get the food ready to cook, Daughter."

Shining Light floated above her—saw her every move, heard her thoughts.

She made her way into the wooded area and found a group of large stones beside a stand of small, leafless trees and shrubs, which hid one side of the stones. He felt her breathing slow.

Both of them floated, connected with the blue sparks, and found each other.

'So, my Shining Light has found his way into the center of the Circle. Why are we here? And why so late? I had to fumble through unknown ground.'

Shining Light's voice vibrated with the waves of the Energy. *Grandmother, I found you. I have tried for most of the day to do this. Blue Night Sky is already gone and I must tell you something. I am about to dishonor myself in Father's eyes. He asked me to stay with the women and children, to get them ready to run if need be. I cannot. Stop! I am loosing you. Come back, I need you. Grandmother, where are you? Grandmother, come back!*

Shining Light found himself sitting alone... so alone, and for the first time in his short life fear washed over him. He slumped and paid no heed to the flash of Mouse in his mind.

White Paws whined and licked his face.

***

Chases Butterflies walked up behind him, her footsteps soft upon the hard frosted ground. "They may still call me a little girl, a child, but cousin, I felt you try to connect with your grandmother. Can a child do that?" She wrapped her arms around her shaking body. "I don't think I like the feeling. I felt like my feet had no ground beneath them. I am here because somehow I knew I needed to be. Rising Moon is waiting back at camp for you to tell us what to do."

For the first time in her life, she wore a sheathed knife. Fine sinew stitching snugly held it to the outside of her long knee-high footwear. All but a small part of the antler that held the obsidian blade told of its hiding place.

Shining Light looked away. "I would never tell anyone else this but... Butterflies, I am scared."

"I know. I am scared too. I do not even know who my Spirit Guide is. What if something goes wrong and... and there is no one to take me to the stars? How will I find the right campfire?"

"There will always be someone to take you. Never doubt that. When I was in the center of the Circle with Blue Night Sky, I knew many Spirits both human and animal. Plants and stones surrounded me too. All living beings were there. We do not die and be no more. We live on."

He looked at the knife on her boot, pulled it out, and felt the sharp obsidian blade. "We, all the adults and able children, carry weapons, but do we know how to protect ourselves with them? I know we played many games with wooden knives, but these are sharp enough to cause real harm if used against us."

He turned and faced her, his face stern. "You and Rising Moon are to take the Peoples back if our warriors do not return. Our people are a peaceful, gentle people. To say warrior leaves a sour taste in my mouth. Just stay on the one you call Bouncing Dog and be ready."

Chases Butterflies squeezed her face tight, and clenched her jaw. "I... I am going with *you*, cousin, not the others."

She stepped closer to him, her body shaking. "Rising Moon will lead the people back to the main camp if she must, but I am going with you!" She stamped her foot on the ground. "If you try to leave without me, I will follow. I will follow you, cousin, so get used to me being at your side. Who knows, I may save your life."

She turned and trotted toward the camp to tell Rising Moon that she must lead the Peoples, if need be.

Chapter 39

Flying Raven followed behind the ones he once called enemy, the hairy-faced ones. They led the group toward a place that held the destiny of many. *Too cold for crickets. So much silence.*

The sliver of Sister Moon offered the only light by which the slow-moving people could see to follow each other. Enough snow had fallen to deafen the sounds of hooves that otherwise would have crunched leaves. Everyone wore heavy robes with fur on the inside, and they covered their animal's backs with robes as well. Clouds of fog came from the mouths of each person and animal.

He tried to catch up to the many thoughts that raced through his mind. *I wonder if the enemy sleeps on the ground or in their lodges. It is cold — too cold for them to sleep outside, unless the drink has made their minds crazy. If all went well, the men do sleep full of the red drink, and about now, the children stir. If the hairy-faced ones fell into the deep sleep, as Wandering Wind said they would, will any of the women take advantage and use knives to silence them?*

Flies As Wind snorted and raised his head. The mus-tang tasted the air, stomped his front hooves and snorted again, trotting sideways.

He smells the females of his kind. This is something I had not thought of. He will want to go to them.

He pulled back on the braided leather wrapped around the muzzle, and reached forward to touch his companion's shoulders, one hand on either side, and closed his eyes. He sought a way to find the mus-tang's center. Both animal and man became still. Blue and violet-red swirls swam around each other, danced within one another, then blended into one deep bluish-violet hue.

Big dog, mus-tang, Flies As Wind, do not fear me, I am the one who rides on your back. Already we are as one, and now we mingle our Spirits as one.

In response, the mus-tang's breathing slowed, and he stood still and nickered softly.

In a whirlwind of Energy, they met each other's minds — their Souls.

We are two beings who see each other, know each other, and become one another. We must work together as one. I will always honor you by allowing you to have as many females as you desire. I know you can smell them. They will be yours and you will have many sons and daughters. I ask in return that you will do my bidding, and allow me to guide you where we are to go.

Flying Raven felt the cold and knew the connection had ended. He jumped down so he could face the big dog. The mus-tang brushed his head against the Holy Man's and breathed in his breath. In return, the man breathed in the mus-tang's breath. They connected again. Man and four legged were now, and would always be, encircled in each other's Energy.

He jumped back on as Raven called above him. He followed the sound and saw several more birds calling to each other in the trees ahead.

In darkness, Raven still guides me.

He squeezed Flies As Wind's sides, and they moved toward the trees. He twisted back to see if anyone had strayed away. Every one of the people who started out with him remained. They waited in the dull light for him to motion them forward. Many saw enough of what had transpired between man and animal, and they knew it was a Sacred Happening.

The group moved their mus-tangs forward in unison.

***

Shining Light and Chases Butterflies rode beside each other in silence. Both stared ahead, lost in their own thoughts. Each of them carried a bundle tied tightly on their backs. They made their way up and over the top of a rocky hill. The greys and browns of the large boulders, and the tall blond grasses along with leafless brown shrubs, helped them to blend in. Shining Light had smeared wood ash on Sandstone to cover her blond color, and the browns of Chases Butterflies' animal blended in naturally.

White Paws stayed behind the mus-tangs with his pack, not because he worried that a hoof might hit him, but rather to sniff the air and keep an eye on his mate and grown pups. Shining Light twisted back just in time to see the wolf nuzzle his mate before the pack vanished into the darkness.

He gazed down at the rocky edge and worried the big dogs might lose their footing. The sliver of Sister Moon moved in and out of layered clouds.

His mind fragmented. *I wonder where the rest of Sister Moon goes. I wish I had been able to contact Grandmother. Did Grandfather go with my father? Gentle Rising Moon has truly found her way into my heart. Will she be able to handle so much on her own? I know Blue Night Sky travels in her own mind. There is a soft cover of comfort over me from her, like a well-tanned deer hide. She gives me confidence, but still I am alone. I have Butterflies, but I will not risk her. Is this the first snow? Am I now fourteen winters old?*

The light snow drifted past and swirled about as it pleased. He wrapped his robe tighter. The layers of clothing they wore were thanks to Butterflies' smart thinking.

Several small fires below caught them both unaware.

Chases Butterflies whispered, "Maybe they needed the light to see what they do. Shining Light, I trust Blue Night Sky. She said we would be safe and I believe her."

She grabbed hold of her single braid of hair and twisted it with her free hand. The other hand squeezed the rope that guided Bouncing Dog.

Shining Light led them past the camp. They disappeared over the ridge and faded into the shadows.

Spirits, please watch over my People. Soon, danger will be all around them while they seek to save others. Butterflies and I must do what we planned with Blue Night Sky.

Mouse appeared on his shoulder. '*Heed me, Brother. See with your mind, or your eyes will deceive you. Only in your mind can you clear the sight your brain shows you. Let your senses be your guide.*'

White Bear floated before him. '*Silence, Human. Go within the silence. Become the quiet and allow it to be your mind's guide.*'

He had to tell her now. She would be angry with him, but he would not risk her life. He had to think of something to say, something to make her feel important. He rode on for a while longer. He had to say the right words, words to make her proud and feel honored... as his father had tried to use on him.

He played with Sandstone's guide rope. "I am glad you came along, cousin. Without you, the lives of many might be lost. You will be my guiding light this night, as I do what I must."

He twisted around on Sandstone's back, trying to see the expression on Butterflies' face. She moaned, and he knew he had better explain.

"I... I remember you trying to scare your younger sisters with the very good owl sounds that you made, one cold night, when you were still a little girl. My grandmother and your mother had to talk with every single person and tell them it was you, and not a bad omen as a night hooting owl can mean!"

Perhaps a whispered laugh was not as impressive as he thought it might be. She said nothing.

Girls. Women. Why did Creator make them so mysterious? I am beginning to understand why my father takes long walks.

"I need you this night to help me. Without you I might not make it back." He thought about what he said and realized he could be right. He jumped from Sandstone and took the pack off his back. "First, I need you to help me smear myself with the wood ash. I brought some bear fat with me to make my hair stand up too. I have the humpback horns Blue Night Sky gave me to wear on my head, but I will need you to help me tie them up there."

He reached up and caught her hand. She sat on Bouncing Dog, not moving.

"Butterflies, this is the most important thing of all. I need you to use your owl call if you see something go wrong. From up here, even in the near dark, you will be able to see more than I can. I will be counting on you to make the owl call, but only once. I do not need everyone to become afraid — no more than they will be when they see me."

Her hand reached down and squeezed his. "Thank you for saying I was not a little girl anymore. I know I am, but hearing you say it makes me feel I can do anything. Of course I will watch over you."

She jumped off her big dog and took Bouncing Dog to a shrub, and tied the rope on a branch.

Shining Light turned his robe inside out so the humpback's hair was on the outside, and Chases Butterflies smeared the bear fat in his hair to make it look like spikes.

She choked on her laughter, trying to be quiet. "If I did not know who you were, I would think an evil Spirit had come to take me away!"

The horns were another matter; the fat made them slip. They turned upside down, pointed backward, resting on top his ears. Chases Butterflies had to take two of the spikes in his hair and tie them back behind his head, to raise the horns up so he could hear. His hair was not long enough, so she took out her knife, cut a strip from the bottom of her tunic, and used that.

Shining Light swayed backward. The weight made him lose his footing, and he swung his arms wildly to upright himself.

She swallowed her laughter again and stepped back to look at her evil Spirit cousin. "You look like a monster the Elders tell stories of to keep us from wandering away from camp in the darkness! I hope we have covered all your skin with the ash. I cannot tell that well because it is so dark. Good thing you have Sandstone to ride, or your horns would force you to lean backward with your arms way out in front of you!"

This time she laughed out loud, and put her hands over her mouth, looking horrified.

They both stood motionless. Nothing.

Shining Light whispered, "They must all be silly on that red drink. I wonder if they have guards posted." The hair on his neck rose like cactus spikes at the thought. "Now we wait for our warriors to show up. I need to get closer so I can be ready when they do appear. Everything will be mixed up and everyone will be running different directions, so I must be ready."

The last part he repeated for himself. He reached to hug his cousin, but pulled back. "Guess I better not risk undoing your fine work."

He smiled, imagining how his white teeth must look on his black-grey face in the sparse light. He didn't have to imagine hard, if Butterflies' face was any indication.

He took Sandstone to a large boulder, climbed it as best as he could, and slid onto his all black-ashed mus-tang. He put the Ram's horn, which Blue Night Sky had given him to blow on, into the carry all pouch slung over his right shoulder. The horn's sound would draw attention to him—possibly stop everyone from fighting. He reached up, felt his hair and grinned.

He remembered White Paws veering off. *What are they are up to on their own?*

A howl responded off in the distance.

Chapter 40

Mourning Dove wiped the knife on the hairy-faced one's body. He had done as he pleased with her for far too long. Never again would he force her to do his bidding.

She stepped out and listened for movement in the quiet camp. The nicker of the mus-tangs alarmed her. She held her breath. Shuffling feet and the low rumble of objects scraping the ground made the loudest noise. She dared not move.

Why do I not hear the snoring of the hairy-faced ones?

Wandering Wind bravely crept up and slipped into the lodge with Mourning Dove. The girl stared down at the unmoving figure facedown on the floor. "The hairy faces sleep," she whispered. "The children and elders are moving the mus-tangs now. The rest of us took weapons. We slid them into the water where it deepened enough to sink them."

Wandering Wind gasped at the sight of blood on Mourning Dove's clothing. "Wh—when Flying Raven and... and his warriors come across the waters, they will find most of the hairy faces tied up. But some did what the red drink did not do. They took the hairy face's own knives and... and...."

She looked down at the blood on her own tunic, and shook her head. "The only ones we need to worry about are the guards in the rocks, and the ones who have yet to return from hunting. I know some of the women went to the guards, but they did not come back yet."

She twisted her hands, her eyes large as full moons. "Do you think they are safe?"

Mourning Dove pushed her toward the lodge's entrance. "Girl, if you worry for others you cannot see, you may come to harm yourself. Go now with the others and the mus-tangs. I am going to start cutting our men loose, and explain to the women who remain to silence the hairy-faced ones that might have escaped the fate of their companions."

Is my revenge wrong? She shook her head. *I did what I had to do!*

Will our rescuers know our men from the enemy in this battle? We have done more than expected of us. There are less than half of our captors left. If the guards up in the rocks are still aware, they may have their thunder sticks with them.

***

Flying Raven stopped Flies As Wind before seeing the water. He breathed in the smoke that tainted the air, heard the water trickle past him, and tried to remember where he had crossed the first time. It was shallower there.

Sounds of running hooves rumbled their way, but no human voices or clanking of long knives met his ears.

"People...." He spoke above a whisper. "I hear the mus-tangs, but they may be without riders. Do not move. The fog from the river covers us as much as it covers those who come our way."

Mus-tangs raced through the warriors and did not stop, save one. "Flying Raven? Holy Man, it is Wandering Wind. Do... do not harm me pl—please! I cannot see you. Are you there, Flying Raven?" Her voice rose again and carried her panic.

"Wandering Wind, I am here. Follow my voice." He used his night bird call to stop his people from advancing.

"All the children and women I could find are not far away. Most feared riding the mus-tangs. They wade across the water's low spot. Only ten of us are riding. The rest wait by the waters for me to call them, so they can ride the mus-tangs out front to protect the others. I must tell you, the woman I went to, Mourning Dove, has done more than get the hairy faces to drink. Many will never move again, but there are those who still hunt. They may return, and guards surround the camp. I do not know how many there are. Some of the women went to them with the red drink... and—"

Flying Raven rode toward the sound of her voice. "Slow down your mouth so I may hear your words better, and speak in quiet words." He reached out to still her prancing animal. "Where is the rope to guide him with?" He held onto neck hair.

"I... just jumped on and put a rope around his neck. I did not know any other way. I knew the Spirits would guide me. My faith is strong, Holy Man."

"Of this, I have no doubt, young woman. I should have given you more respect. Your wits are quick and your mind sharp. Call the others so we will not trample them."

Soft cooing sounds carried through the fog. Chirps came back in response. "They come. Many carry with them what they could hold above the water. Some have children. Others have things the hairy faces use to hunt with that we call thunder sticks. Some have long knives, and leather things they slipped on the mus-tangs to make them go where they wanted them to go. I have this."

She pulled out four short, shiny knives twice the length of her hand. "They do not break as ours do."

She handed him the knives as sounds of frightened children and women approached.

"Care for your Peoples, Wandering Wind. Get them far away as fast as you can. Keep a straight line by using the brightest campfire in the sky."

He pointed to one that shone much brighter than any other, and wondered if it could be the Peoples' Counsel fire. "Use your birdcalls as you go. That way my people will know you are not the enemy."

He used his own call to tell his people to move forward.

***

In the commotion, Wandering Wind had forgotten to tell Flying Raven about Mourning Dove cutting their men loose.

Now it was too late. The fog swallowed them and they floated into nothingness.

She dared not call out, and there was no way to know the direction they had vanished.

"Mus-tang, big dog, turn around," she whispered. "Please turn around!"

She tried to twist herself around on the animal's back, but the big dog moved forward after the rest of his kind.

***

Shining Light tried to see his Father and the warriors who followed. Nothing.

Whispers surrounded him, but not human ones.

Listen with your inner knowing, small one who is a man....

Feel what surrounds you....

Become part of everything. Allow everything to become part of you....

When he centered himself, Sandstone stopped. With his mind, he interred the silence. No sounds, not even his own breathing, entered his mind. His body took over the functions it needed, while Shining Light's Spirit rose above everything.

The young people scurried, grabbed big dogs, took shiny long knives and tossed them in the river. Children led the animals into the shallow waters. Many refused to ride and, after leading the big dogs across, hid behind shrubs in the tall grass. They used bird calls to contact each other, to let others know they were safe.

One woman stood out. Her body appeared as part Fox, part woman. She looked up right at him! Their eyes locked and she smiled.

The Fox Woman crept across the ground unseen by the hairy faces. He gasped when she used a knife on several of them. She moved forward to stop one from harming a child. The hairy face had not seen her, yet he stood before her when she stilled him forever.

Shining Light pulled back into his body and shivered. His grandmother once told him people who had Fox medicine could hide in plain sight.

He allowed Sandstone to make her way to the edge of the rocky hillside, where they both would wait. Shining Light could see little. All he could do was wait and worry. He worried his father's plans might not have been the ones he watched from above the camp.

He shook his head. *Too much is mixed up. Where are my people?*

***

Cold water splashed on Flying Raven's leggings as the others followed behind him. He urged Flies As Wind up the dark, rocky bank. Twice the mus-tang stumbled on loose rocks, forcing the animal behind him to stumble also. The mus-tangs twisted around and riders fell into the water, adding to the fear. The animals reared up and swam toward the water's edge. Hands reached out toward them, but pulled back nothing.

Now, most on foot, the people splashed through the chilly water gasping for air.

Even with all the commotion, no one came out to fight. Flying Raven maneuvered up the bank and peered through the shrubs at the water's edge. Small fires showed men who made no move. The camp, deathly still, unnerved him.

Too silent. Where are the captives? Not all could have made it over the waters.

Raven's caw in the trees just above him alerted his already tense nerves. A feather fell, landing on Flying Raven's hand.

Danger! Raven warns, but of what? My body tingles — even my feet.

Flies As Wind appeared beside the chilled man. He started to jump on, and to warn his warriors to back up into the shrubs, but a scream sounded and a man raised his weapon.

He pulled the man away from the mus-tang, protecting Flies As Wind, and something sharp sliced into his shoulder. He pushed the man away, ready to strike a defending blow.

Chapter 41

Shadows of the firelight hid faces; clothing and dust from around the campfires further blinded everyone. So much noise, confusion and fear filled the air.

The freed captive men that the women had cut loose retrieved weapons from beneath the water. Arms rose in mid air and they held long knives ready to slice into any stranger—they had no idea their rescuers were the ones they prepared to fight. The taste of it frightened the few still controlled mus-tangs; they reared, twirled around and fought to be free. Some snapped their leather holds and ran into the center of camp before finding their way toward the river.

Beside the campfires, those of the real enemy who still lived sat in a drunken confusion that showed on their faces. The enemy begun to back away into shadowed trees as other hairy-faced men came forward to do battle. Dogs tied to trees behind the enemy snapped and bit them. They stumbled forward to avoid the dogs and felt the long knives rush through them.

***

Shining Light heard the screaming and tried to connect to Sandstone in the brief time they had. He closed his eyes and held onto her neck hair.

Feel me, sister. We are about to save lives, but we must act together, as one. Do not fear, Sandstone. I am with you... in your mind... on your body. We are connected. Feel me.

He squeezed his legs on her sides and urged her forward. His own legs shook, as his mind held terror never known to him before this night.

Brave, I must show no fear and be the one who causes fear, not be the one in fear!

"Now, Sandstone, we have little time. My people are in danger!" Shining Light urged her forward down the hill, ignoring the jolts his body felt with each rock Sandstone's hooves stumbled over.

Shining Light reached for the ram's horn and blew it several times. Sandstone kept moving under his urging; though her body stiffened, she did not balk, did not fight to turn and run the opposite way—the way he knew she wanted to go.

He let the horn drop, screamed, waved his arms and raced through the camp on a snorting, charging Sandstone.

White Paws and his pack spilled around both sides of animal and rider. Wolves circled the pair, snarling. The dark grey creature screamed as horns bobbed on either side of its head. The evil one rode an ash-smeared creature that reared high and spun in circles. The commotion Shining Light created with the help of Sandstone stopped what was about to become a bloody battle.

In terror, the captives who were ready to strike dropped to their knees and covered their heads.

White Paws neared the cowering men with bared teeth, sending more terror into their hearts, especially when the other wolves followed White Paws into the light.

Shining Light relaxed and breathed deep, now that it was over. His animal Brothers and Sisters indeed had executed their own plan.

How is this so? Will I ever understand?

The wolves stood with their back hair, clearly seen in the fire's light, raised high, causing more terror on the faces of those who dared to look up. Shining Light jumped off Sandstone and ran his dark ash-smeared hands through each wolf's fur. The jump from his animal had caused the wobbly horns to slip from his head, and they now rocked under his ears. The dark demon raised his head.

A voice that did not match the horrible looking creature spoke. "These are my companions. They are here because I am here."

***

Mourning Dove grinned. She knew this evil one and his wolves.

An owl screeched as another figure came out of the darkness, its dark hair spiked. The little creature jumped off its dun-colored mus-tang and ran in circles, ranting.

The Fox woman now came out of dense bare shrubs. She called to their men who refused to uncover their heads. She knew these creatures were not right, especially when the horns started to fall from the first one's head. This silly looking one yelled in words she had heard once before. She had seen this one before, in their shared vision.

A man, one of the few who stayed on their animals, encouraged his mus-tang into movement. "Grandson, what in all the Spirits' names are *you* doing here? Did not your father say to stay with the camp?"

He jumped down, used his tunic to wipe the boy's face, and stared in disbelief. "You will need to tell all of us how this came to be once we are with our own on the other side of the river."

The little screaming one who had been running in circles stopped, and with great speed ripped off the robe that hid her identity, and cried out to the young man to save her. "It is me, Shining Light, not an evil one!" She took her garment and wiped a clear streak across her face. "See? It is me, cousin, I came to help you!"

Her chest heaved and the whites of her eyes looked much larger surrounded by wood ash.

Women added wood to the small fires and the camp glowed. Everyone stopped and stared at the scene before them. Some laughed, some stood in fear, while others still kept their heads lowered to the ground.

Mourning Dove assessed the situation. She turned at the sound of a man pushing aside shrubs, his shoulder and leg red with blood.

"I believe my son, whom I remember giving a great honor to stay behind and protect the women, now stands next to a yellow, ash-smeared mus-tang." He held his bleeding shoulder. "Thank you, son of mine who thought as a man would have. You saved many lives in this confused camp. The hairy-faced ones who came back with us, along with our own warriors, nearly fell prey to those we meant to rescue."

Mourning Dove shouted at the men who still cowered in fear. With great caution, they raised their heads and stared at the strange beings with human voices, and saw the evil ones were humans, and not very large ones at that. Each man, with embarrassed looks, went and stood in the center of the camp with her and the other women.

She stared down at the hairy faces. Only a few still breathed.

Flying Raven whooped loudly in honor of his son and embraced the young man. Joyous shouts echoed on both sides of what would have been a bloody battle. He finished wiping his son's face with the tunic and a grinning Shining Light appeared before the shocked men, who now wore even more embarrassment on their faces.

"My man!" Mourning Dove ran to one of the hairy-faced ones who had come with the rescue party. Tears flooded from her eyes, mixed with cries of joy. "Tall Smiling Warrior, I missed your hairy face!"

Behind him stood two women smiling, waiting for the crying woman to see them. She squealed her joy and reached out to them. "Sisters, we are now one again!"

She hugged both women, whose tears mingled on their faces in the light of the fires. Tall Smiling Warrior tried to wrap his arms around all three, his own tears mingled with theirs.

Flying Raven let go a low laugh. "I guess we came to rescue a people who did not need us."

A man approached Flying Raven with his head hung low, and held a knife out to him.

The Holy Man of the Fish People reached for the man's face with his good arm, and raised it. As best as he could with one arm and hand, he made the sign for peace, smiled and gave the man back his knife. "Me, you, are not enemies."

Mourning Dove let go her embrace of her sisters and Tall Smiling Warrior. She made her way through the crowd of people and stood between the two men who had almost battled. "A long time past—I was but a child at the gathering—I remember the way Fish People dressed. Some found our gathering on their way back to their own people."

She reached out and gently touched Flying Raven's blood-soaked shoulder. "I do not speak all of your words."

She shrugged her shoulders and tightened her expression. "Soon you will be fine. You made the sign of peace with our healer. His dreams helped us live through this... this bad torture. His dreams said a boy would come and save us. We did not believe him, and thought maybe he made up this story to keep us hoping."

She lowered her head for a moment, and looked back at Flying Raven. "He said that among you, a Holy Man also comes, a man of Raven. Our people find many feathers that Raven leaves behind. When we are away from here, this place of death, we will give you the feathers. Our healer says there is enough to make a... robe?... cape?... of them. His vision showed him this."

Her Peoples' own Holy Man reached under his tattered shirt and pulled out a leather pouch, which the man had carefully folded flat. He handed it to the man he had nearly killed.

Flying Raven unfolded the pouch and stared in wonder. The man had protected many of Raven's feathers from harm. He squatted and spread them out in a display greater than both his arms could stretch across.

Mourning Dove motioned for the crazy-looking humans dressed as evil ones. Both came forward, but stood out of her reach, the wolves beside them. "You both do well and... wolves? I see they do not hurt people."

She cocked her head and stared deeply into the young man's eyes. "Blue. I see blue in your eyes. You are... are... Shi— Shining Light. You are the one our healer dreamed of so many nights. I see a Holy Man who wears the skin of a boy. If not for you, we would not be safe, or alive. We know the hairy faces were going to end our lives. With no more use for us...." She shrugged her shoulders. "We would be no more. They did not find the yellow stone. Many of the enemy tire and want to turn back. One or two more suns, and our blood would have been on the ground."

She pointed to men the women killed before the battle. "Not theirs. Ours."

She turned and faced the small girl. "Who is this that had such braveness to scare big men?"

The girl grinned up at her through a soot-filled face. "I am Chases Butterflies, and I—"

Another man walked up and hugged her against him. She looked at the blood trickling down his leg. "Father, you are hurt!" Tears filled her eyes and made paths down her smeared face.

The man squeezed her tighter. "Daughter, my Chases Butterflies, you must not cry. I will be fine. I am proud you, and so will our people when I tell them of the brave girl who, on her big dog—mus-tang—came down the hill to save her cousin and her people. This will be a story told at campfires for many winters."

He scooped her up, and rubbed her soot-filled face on his battle-sweat one. He turned toward Mourning Dove, smiled and nodded. "I am Sees Like Eagle."

Shining Light stood by his mus-tang and cleared his throat, and Mourning Dove understood. All shared in the pride, but they must move fast as Sister Wind to avoid the hairy faces who would return soon. Nothing would stop them once they saw their own people lying in blood.

The young Holy Man raised his hands. "We must leave this place now, in the dark. We must not stop. I can feel Energy swirling around me that is not of the Peoples."

Flickering shadows of flames shooting up through the smoke gave his face the appearance of Bear.

He continued. "Gather what we may be able to use. We must make fast for the other side of the waters to find the children and women in the mist."

His confidence truly did belong to a man, not to a boy.

An owl hooted in the distance. Another answered.

They all made haste to gather what they could.

***

Mothers who had left before the fight, before knowing what would happen, held onto their children's hands while roped mus-tangs followed. Hushed tones of small children mingled with birdcalls the women used to keep track of one another. No one knew where to go, just to leave and keep going as Mourning Dove had told them.

Away from the water, the fog lifted, allowing the mothers to stop and place small children on the backs of the animals. They could now see if anyone followed, and the women could search for the camp Wandering Wind had told them to find.

Several turned at the sound of a pair of owls, and some mus-tangs broke loose and vanished into the darkness.

Chapter 42

Long Arrow helped Blue Night Sky from her mus-tang.

Blue Night Sky pointed to several places along the ground. "I ask that you start fires along a line starting here. Too many come our way to stop them in time. If we cannot call out to the girl who speaks our tongue, we may not be able to save anyone. Grandmother Sun will not wake for some time yet, so we must use a few small fires that we can put out right away."

She raised her arms up to the darkened sky to pray, and pulled her mind away from her thoughts of fear, focusing only on her own voice. No longer did she feel anything, save Sister Wind who carried her voice to the Great One Above.

"Hear me, Great Mystery. Many of your children need your help this night. Guide them toward us so they will find safety, not death."

She prayed loudly, hoping not only the Great One would hear her, but also the people who wandered in the darkness. Calling out was a risk she had to take.

A familiar voice called out from the darkness. "Blue Night Sky, is that you I hear? Where are you? I am now called Wandering Wind, but before, when I was in our band, I was Running Fast Girl."

A girl emerged into the fire's light. "Aunt!"

She jumped to the ground and ran screaming into Blue Night Sky's arms, crying loud enough to spook the mus-tang she rode. He reared and turned sideways. The other two animals carrying children stopped.

"Child, I thought you lost in the fire!" Blue Night Sky hugged her, pulled her back and stared at her. "Oh my, little one, I can only try to understand what you have been through."

They hugged and allowed their tears to mingle.

Blue Night Sky pulled away. "Call to the Peoples so they know it is safe."

Wandering Wind wiped tears from her wet smiling face. "Oh no! The children! I am silly to have done what I did."

She ran over to the pair of mus-tangs, helped the children down, and brought them to Blue Night Sky. The children wore cast off pieces of clothing and most had bare feet. "They are from many Peoples."

The children stepped up shyly, holding onto one another. One small boy grinned and ran forward to embrace her.

Blue Night Sky recognized him as one of her own people and hugged him. "I cannot lift you, little one. This woman is too weak."

He turned his head upward. "That is okay. I am a big boy now. I am happy to see more of the Red Bear people, that is all." He hugged her again and would not let go. "I, Talks In Sleep, now follow you." He smiled broadly up at her with two of his front missing teeth. "See, Great Elder, I lose my baby teeth."

Wandering Wind glanced about. "Why are you here?"

The small fires burned brightly now. Wandering Wind glanced to where the land ended and put her hand to her mouth. "Sweet Mother! We would have... had—"

Blue Night Sky hugged the girl to her, and held tighter the boy who refused to let go. "It was not your time, nor anyone else's of the Peoples. Use the words you know and speak to all who follow. Tell them the land ends here, that we must go another way. Have them follow the line of small fires. When the fires end, stop and listen for a girl called Rising Moon. She will lead you into a camp where people wait with food and footwear."

She pointed to Long Arrow, who came forward.

Wandering Wind grinned when she saw the handsome man.

"I am Long Arrow, one who was also captured by these cruel ones I will not call human." He raised his head, pulled back his long hair, and took off a bone choker to show the scar around his neck. "Until I found freedom, I wore a rope around my neck that was attached to other men." He put his choker back in place. "I will go out in front and lead the way. I will spark small fires, and ask that you be last in line and put them out. Can you do that for me?"

"Yes, Long Arrow. Um, do you have a mate? I am fifteen winters, almost sixteen, and have no mate. I will be a good—"

"Young woman!" Long Arrow took in a deep breath. "We must be on our way, but I would like to speak further to you about this. I am without a mate and am twenty-two winters old. There will be plenty of time to speak of such matters. Listen well to me. Do not come any closer to the edge. Tell the others to stay back and follow my night birdcall. The sliver of light in the sky is not enough to see by, but we must not light torches. We do not know who might see them, and now that people are finding their way to us, we must put out the fires as we go. I ask again, will you do this?"

"I... of course. You can depend on me. I am a woman, not a child, and I listen well."

Blue Night Sky reached for Wandering Wind and caught her thin arm. "Girl... I mean young woman, how many Red Bear people are mixed in with the others?"

"Many, Aunt... many of our people survived."

Chapter 43

Bright Sun Flower was the first to look up from her cooking. Her man had told her—through Eagle—they were coming back with hairy-faced men and their women, as well as the ones they went looking for, but she had not expected so many!

The big dogs they had ridden out with carried packs, and one carried a smiling Blue Night Sky with a baby in each arm, while a young boy led her mus-tang.

How many come? While they were gone, more Peoples filtered into our camp. Creator, please let this new place have much unclaimed land and many animals! How can we feed so many? Already, both men and women hunt. Hah! My Feather and his wolves walk in front, and Rising Moon is next to him. Dreams unfold this day! He leads the Peoples as our dreams said he would. He walks with pride and smiles and—

"Is that his hand I see reaching for hers?"

Bright Sun Flower, startled her from her thoughts, turned to her daughter.

Makes Baskets said, "My baby reaches for the hand of a girl who is older than him? Mother, you must talk to your grandson. He listens to you about such matters. He is too young to—"

"Daughter, hush!" She pointed at the people entering camp. "Do you not see they follow behind *him*, not the others? Even Hawk Soaring and Flying Raven give him the lead. You have a baby boy no longer. You have Soft Breeze as your baby and Shining Light as your son. Well, I just called him Shining Light, not Feather!"

She shook her head and chuckled. "Go tell the others to gather much wood and start cooking. We will have a feast tonight, and there will be many stories told, and much to sing about."

Men with hairy faces held far back in the rear of the group. Their women, who dressed differently from any of the Peoples that Bright Sun Flower had ever seen, also stayed back.

A bit frightened by their appearance, she hesitated, but then scolded herself. *All Peoples are welcome.*

With open hands, she smiled and walked toward the unusual mix of people.

***

Shining Light let go of Rising Moon's hand and ran toward his grandmother.

"I have so much to tell both of you! Blue Night Sky found many of her people she thought lost! And we have more different Peoples with us, and hairy-faced ones who are not enemies... and... and you should have seen Butterflies! And the big dogs? They are called mus-tangs. We had a battle that was not a battle and—"

"Son, there will be much time to talk. Save your air!" Makes Baskets bent over and squeezed his ribs tight enough to stop his words.

"Mother... can... not... breathe! Father comes. Go... to... him!"

She laughed and ran to her man.

Shining Light took in a deep breath, allowing his dizzy head to change back to normal.

He turned as the new people cautiously followed his father and grandfather into the large camp. One of the women broke free from the group of new people, and ran to a woman who dropped the wood she carried, and in turn raced to greet her. Many more people broke free and ran into waiting arms.

"They find relatives and friends. I am so happy for them!" Bright Sun Flower laughed as she reached for her grandson, who stepped back. "Do you not wish to have to fight to breathe again? Tell us all about your adventure, my Shining Light. Father Sun soon sleeps, and we have gathered much wood for this day because your grandfather kept in touch with me through my dreams—"

"He did?" Shining Light turned his grandfather's way and watched his friends greet him. "He never told me of this. How did he do that?"

Bright Sun Flower managed to get her arms around him and give him a squeeze. "There is much about being a couple you do not know yet. Not everyone can enter another's dreams. There must be a deep connection. I woke thinking he was actually there next to me. And, Grandson, I am proud that you were able to connect with me."

She brushed his hair from his face. "You must tell me everything that happened. I am sorry we lost contact. It was not you." She laughed. "I sat on a sharp stick!"

Her smile broadened as Hawk Soaring approached her.

Shining Light stepped back so as not to get in the way. He felt as full of joy as his grandmother obviously did. He could feel it as they squeezed together in one powerful hug.

He raised his eyebrows as he saw a young man reflected in his grandfather's eyes.

***

Flying Raven jumped off his mus-tang and turned him loose, and watched as Flies As Wind kicked up his heals and ran toward his own kind.

He then sped toward Makes Baskets. No worries this day about showing affection, he reached out and hugged her. He turned her around, pulled Soft Breeze from her sleeping basket, and raised her up into the air. "I am so happy to be back! My daughter and woman both look so beautiful! Our son has a story to tell and I know all of us who have come in this day are hungry. We did not expect to bring so many people back with us, but we hunted all the way back and have much meat.

"Also, woman of my heart, Blue Night Sky made our son and Morning Star's daughter promised mates. Since Long Arrow is the man of her lodge, she said Shining Light must speak to him when the time comes." He laughed at her expression. "Baskets, if your eyes get any bigger, they will pop out of your face! I did say *promised mates*."

He could not help himself. He was so happy the journey had come to a safe ending that he had to tease his wide-eyed woman. He pulled her arm and tried to get her to sit. "You do know they love each other?" He was not sure she heard his words. "Woman, did your ears hear me? Your face is red."

She pulled away from his grasp. "I can imagine it is red, man of mine who allowed his son to... to get so close to that girl!"

She crossed her arms, and her fringed sleeves smacked him in the face. She nodded toward Shining Light and Rising Moon, standing in a grove of mostly dried berries and eating them as they talked.

She turned to Flying Raven with a faint smile. "I accept this, as I must. But perhaps with our daughter, we will have a say?"

He gently reached out for her shoulders and stared into her obsidian eyes. "Promise to not smack me in the face anymore?"

Her laughter filled the air. "Perhaps... perhaps not." She stared back, her lips parting in a smile.

"We will learn together as Soft Breeze grows." He gave her shoulders a soft shake. "Do not worry, woman, we have many, many seasons before our daughter even looks at a boy."

With those words, Soft Breeze wobbled over to a baby boy and handed him her grass doll. Both parents called to her at once, and burst out in more laughter as she plopped next to him giggling.

He said, "Do you think we need to speak to his mother about promised mates now, before another boy shows up?"

"Flying Raven Who Dreams needs another smacking!"

She raised her hand and he playfully reached for it. "Woman, I am hungry, and wish for some of your very good cooking." He rubbed his nose against hers. "Tonight, our son will tell his incredible story. And Butterflies has her own to share. This night starts another generation's beginning.

"Also, our son had a dream, but would not speak of it until we were all together." He put his fingers up to his woman's lips. "Before you ask, I do not know of what he dreamed. All I know is what Blue Night Sky told me. He dreamed of the place that we are to go, to our new home. And that is all he told the Great Elder."

He gazed around the camp and nodded toward his daughter. "She will have many men to choose from when she grows up—so many little ones! All these people and still more come. I am anxious to know myself where this place is, and how it can hold so many people.

"You know, we may need to have a giveaway for them once we settle into our new home. We must test the plants we encounter for new quill dyes, so you can make many baskets to give all the new people. I have heard Morning Star paints things people describe to her, without even seeing them. You know, we—"

"Slow down, anxious Raven Man who thinks he sees our daughter's future in other babies. *I* must make many baskets? My man will need to find all these quills for me to dye, and all the plants that Morning Star will need to use for colors."

They walked toward where Makes Baskets and Bright Sun Flower had chosen to camp. She bent and reached for a hide bundle hidden under sleeping robes. "I have worked on this since before we left, Holy Man. I was going to give it to you when we reached this new land our son leads us to, but you should have it now."

She pulled out an off-white, elk hide-fringed shirt decorated with several colors of paint, blue quills, sky beads and elk teeth. On the top, toward the middle, a very good likeness of a painted White Paws and Moon Face sat next to each other. The bottom fringe softly tinkled with small seashells.

She smiled. "This is befitting the head Holy Person of the Wolf Peoples."

Flying Raven stepped back in surprise. "Such a handsome gift! Wolf People?" He could not take his eyes off the shirt.

She twisted around and pulled a smaller version of a similar shirt. "Our son's eyes will pop out of his head when he finds out Rising Moon made this one for him, while we sat around the fire with my mother and her family. I quilled while Rising Moon and her mother painted them. They are both skilled."

She pointed out the painted red canyon behind the two heads of White Paws and Moon Face. "Look closely and you will see the wall our Fish Peoples painted, which point the way we had gone moons ago."

"My eyes pop out of my own head! To have such a gift is more than an honor. I am so... so.... Words do not come to me." He laughed. "I do wonder what our son will say at such a beautiful gift."

He took off his old shirt, gently pulled the shoulder ties loose on the new one, and slipped the tunic over his head. "Nothing has ever fit so well as—"

"So you say nothing I ever made before fit?"

He thought he had spoken kind words, but now feared he would have to eat them for his meal.

She smiled playfully. "You look good in the *expertly* made tunic. You are lucky to have such a woman."

"Yes, my woman, I am lucky."

"I must tell you that while you were gone, Mother had a dream—"

"Why, I wonder, do so many of us have these dreams? Most bands have one, maybe two people who are special enough to have this great gift. Yet the Fish Peoples—"

"Hush, I still talk."

"Baskets, do not interrupt me, I am—"

"You are the one who interrupted me—"

"Woman, I am a Holy Man, as you said. I have the right—"

"You do not—"

"Ah, but I do—"

"Will you allow me to finish my story? Then you can be the Holy Man again!"

He crossed his arms and stood grinning, but silent.

"*As* I was telling you, Eagle told her to gather the other Holy Peoples who have joined us and tell them a new band meant a new name. As she spoke, I pulled out this shirt and showed everyone. I told the story of how White Paws and Moon Face came to be part of our band. I passed it around for everyone to look at closer, and the peoples spoke in agreement. Each group of Elders—of each band—stood up and declared themselves Wolf People before everyone. All nodded in agreement.

"And...." She glared at him as his mouth opened to speak. "Since there are so many Holy People, another meeting must be called when we reach this new place. A decision must be made of how to split the land so as not to overburden the gifts it may have. Those who came in while you were gone wish to hear more of this place from my baby... err... son.... *Our* son. I must remind myself he is now promised to another."

Her glare at an approaching Blue Night Sky met with a smile from the Great Elder.

***

Makes Baskets released the weight of her jealousy so it could fly away. She knew she stood in the presence of the greatest of all Holy People. Blue Night Sky had taught her son much more than anyone else could have ever done.

The Holy Woman said, "I hear the mother of Shining Light helped to name our combined Peoples. I am proud of you granddaughter of the Peoples. My great respect for your mother prevents me from giving you a new name. She told me why she gave you your name, so I will not call you another, but know that in my heart, I think of you as Wolf Band Storyteller Woman.

"You thought you had no purpose in life but to give birth to the one—an even greater Holy person than the two you see before you. You are now the Storyteller many bands will seek out. The story you will tell to every generation yet to be born will be of your son and his wolves—a story no child will ever forget!

"Not only that, Wolf Band Storyteller Woman, your baskets have traveled farther than you. Those who followed us have several of them that they traded for from an even more distant band. They call them canyon baskets."

Her eyes sparkled as she spoke. "Now they will need another name—Wolf Baskets!"

She patted Makes Baskets on the arm and walked past her to greet other people.

Chapter 44

Once again, Shining Light stood with his hands at his side, in the center of his people — the Wolf People. Blue Night Sky stood next to him, and a playful yellow mus-tang pushed her head into the woman's side. Father Sun graced them this day with his warmth, and Sister Wind stilled herself as if to listen to the young Holy Man. He glanced up at the lazy clouds and noticed one had taken on the shape of Wolf.

He had dreamed the night before they returned to the main camp, and he needed to share that dream. Only Blue Night Sky and Rising Moon knew of its message.

He turned toward Running River. "What is this I feel? Something is different about my mother's cousin."

Words spilled out of the side of her mouth. "Ha! So *now* you feel *other* people's bodies." She looked forward and smiled. "She carries a sacred child. Do not jerk your head to stare at me. In time, you will know more. Keep your face forward, young Holy Man."

Shining Light did his best not to look at Running River, motioning toward Long Arrow to stand with Tall Smiling Warrior, to show his support for the hairy-faced ones.

Various interpreters came forward. They would have to first receive their own translation, and then turn to their people and hand-sign the words.

"Do not be surprised that so many come to hear your words, young Holy Man," Blue Night Sky spoke in low tones to him with a sideways glance. "Many believe in you, in your dreams. This is your future — to know things others do not. Do not resist. Do not shiver so. Allow the Power to flow through you. Breathe it in and accept it as part of you. Feel as I close my eyes — take in a deep breath as I do, and turn it loose to go where it may."

Blue sparks flew from her and into him. The thrill of a thousand butterfly wings fluttered through him. His body quivered with the new sensation. He no longer feared being at the center of his and other people's lives.

I... feel... whole. I feel I am part of the Energy of all living, and the Energy is... everything.

His breathing now slow and steady, he reached out to not just the humans, but to every living being. "I, Shining Light, have a dream I wish to share. This dream is for all of us. Our future unfolds this day."

He stared at the people before him, some faces familiar, some not. His grandparents stood with others of his band. A familiar Energy emerged on his right side, as Chases Butterflies stood by him, just as she had promised. That seemed like another lifetime to him. She pet White Paws, who stood next to him. Moon Face stood in front. The rest of the pack lay around him, stretched out, watching. His father held his mother's hand, directly across from their son in the circle of people who surrounded him, and smiled with recognition and acceptance.

Shining Light was no longer just a young man who had turned fourteen winters with the first snow. He was a Holy Man.

He spoke slowly enough for the interpreters to convey his words. "The night before we left to come back here, I knew I needed to go off with my Brother Wolf, and sleep away from the Peoples. Blue Night Sky was close by if I needed her."

He turned and grinned at her. The Great One's Energy was part of him now; he knew where she was all the time, even if they could not see each other.

"I found a small outcropping to sleep on, and White Paws settled beside me. Soon the whole pack joined us—the pack of our band, once called the Fish People." He grinned inwardly. "I do not remember falling asleep. I am not sure I did."

He stopped and listened for chatter. There was none.

"I faced Bear. He said nothing, but led us to a mountaintop where Eagle waited. He told me to sit. Soon many animals arrived—some I knew, and many I did not. Each animal spoke, one at a time, of this beautiful place with large trees and many waterfalls, where plants grow so thick, only animal trails are without growth. It does not get as cold there as it did in the canyons where the Fish Peoples lived. An animal I had never seen before told me this."

He shifted his feet and turned around in a circle to stare at every person. "Another said rainbows lived in the waterfalls. A white Deer, who had two white Fawns, told me the trees grow so tall, one would get a cramp in their neck before they would see the tops."

A collective gasp spread through the circle as their interpreters spoke and signed to them. None spoke out in disbelief; they only whispered among themselves, awestruck.

"I know that much of what the animals said seems impossible, so I will only speak of some of it. We will discover the rest together.

"One thing each animal spoke of was the dangers those who stayed behind will face. Many will not survive. This land we walk upon, which we call the Mother, is far larger than we will ever see. Many, many different kinds of people will come here, not just the hairy-faced ones."

Stunned murmurs and widened eyes of many people turned to stared at each other, and back at Shining Light. All eyes turned to the hairy-faced ones, many of whom hung their heads.

"Those among us are our friends. Do not ever think of them any other way. As Blue Night Sky said, not all are bad. But come they will, good and bad alike. Our Peoples, and ones we will never meet, will fall under weapons unknown to us. There are more strangers coming than there are campfires in the sky."

He looked up to the soft, blue sky, and became still, his thoughts drifting to those who chose to stay behind. His cousin poked him to continue. They would have to fight for land they had no chance of keeping, and their little ones would never know the teachings of their Elders. They would know of the many tears that would fall upon the Mother.

He sighed and decided not to speak of this. Instead, he smiled as best he could, and continued.

"We are not far away. Another Peoples have lived there for many, many cycles of seasons. They know we come. Their Holy Man stood before me after the animals faded, and I was back on the outcropping with the wolves. He stood in a mist, which he said was not of the Spirit World, but of the Forest of Trees. That is the name of our new home. I know everyone speaks of us as the Wolf People, but we will have two names. One we will share with those already there—Tall Tree People. Our band, the Wolf People, will join the Nation of Tall Tree People."

He let this filter into people's minds. He needed to explain what his father had told him about no one crossing over, as their ancestors had.

'No, Shining Light, speak none of this.' Mouse sat on his shoulder.

The young Holy Man turned to look at this people. No one could see the mouse.

"You will understand more soon."

How do I tell them these other Peoples are generations old?

'Shining Light, allow them to find this out on their own. Fear could make some turn away from the gifts of this land. Future... future... they are the future.'

Mouse started ahead, and White Bear approached them. *'Some things, my young Holy Man, are not to be told.'*

White Bear vanished, and Mouse with him.

White Paws stood up and tapped his shoulder. *'Human Brother, follow me and my pack. There is something you must now be part of, you and your cousin. This is a place of wonder, mystery, and so much more. Come.'*

He focused again on the people. "We are hungry and tired. We must rest. I will follow White Paws and his family. I need to be alone."

Chases Butterflies grabbed his arm. "I will go with you, even if I have to tie us together, cousin."

"I too will go." Rising Moon jumped up and joined them so quickly, that Sister Wind could not have been there faster.

***

"Stop, you three." Blue Night Sky clapped her hands to silence the whispering that had started the moment Shining Light stopped speaking. "I, Blue Night Sky, now speak."

She motioned for Rising Moon to stand beside her. "I give this new woman the name Animal Speaks Woman. She has the gift of calling animals, and I will now take the next few days to guide her on this path. Her calling will be different than any animal speaker has ever had. This new place will be much different than the place we are all used to."

Blue Night Sky grabbed Chases Butterflies before the girl knew what had happened. "I give Chases Butterflies a new name also."

Running River tried to jump up and run for her daughter, but Sees Like Eagle took her arm. All heard him say his words. "No, woman, this is your daughter's destiny. You will be proud of her. I also know about the new one you carry in your belly."

Running River stopped, but instead of glaring at her man, she grinned with pride and sat back down.

Blue Night Sky nodded to Sees Like Eagle, and twirled Chases Butterflies around to face part of the circle of people, and spoke so all could hear. "She is now Gentle Wisdom, Shining Light's advisor. She is wise, for she carries the blood of many before her who were council leaders. Her father's people forgot long ago about these advisors. None of the Fish Peoples knew, because he was born to the People With No Respect—the story that Bright Sun Flower told even before my Peoples joined with hers. Gentle Wisdom has not blossomed into a woman yet, but this has nothing to do with her knowledge."

Several people stood to speak, but Blue Night Sky waved them down.

"You see, children, I see the future of many combined Peoples. Were we all born as adults? I think not. The future is in our children, where it has always been. Every generation passes, and the next generation leads in turn. Never forget this. Every child born carries the future of the whole, of the Circle of Life. These children, be they friend or enemy, remain our future, and in that future we will find either sadness or joy. I have no more words to say."

She turned to Animal Speaks Woman. "Gather your things, girl. We will walk alone for the next few days."

Animal Speaks Woman's eyes drifted toward Shining Light.

"No, do not look at him. You two will be together for a very long time, but for the next few sunrises, you belong to me. I wish to teach you what you already know."

The newly named woman went to gather her packed belongings, while stealing glances at Shining Light.

Running River sat tall and straight as her daughter walked away with her cousin into the forest, but her tears fell anyway.

Morning Star cried softly, leaving Sees Like Eagle looking very confused. He turned to Blue Night Sky and shrugged his shoulders.

Blue Night Sky smiled and made the sign for 'Let go. Let it be.'

***

Hawk Soaring sat grinning. He held his own secret, one others would find out about as they approached the new land.

He looked down at his darkening braids and grinned even wider.

When he was a boy, he had dreamed of a place called Forest Of Trees, where rainbows danced down waterfalls and splashed onto lush plants. At the time, he had thought it a child's dream, and said nothing to anyone.

Not even to his father.

Chapter 45

The beginning of change....

"Where do we walk to, cousin?"

"I, Chases Bu— err... Gentle Wisdom, am following White Paws while you follow me."

He turned to look back for Rising Moon... or Animal Speaks Woman... or whatever her name was now.

Gentle Wisdom grinned at his uneasiness. "You will see your woman again, so stop worrying, cousin. The two of you are joined in mind, and will someday join in body also."

Shining Light's head spun around so fast his neck hurt. "Shame on you, Gentle Wisdom Girl! That is a secret for couples to know about!"

"My name...is *Gentle Wisdom*! And I am not a little girl!" She crossed her arms and looked ahead.

Shining Light grinned, satisfied.

"I... I must always find a way to sound less like a girl, but I am a girl! I am only twelve winters old. How am I supposed to sound like a... advisor? What is that, anyway? What am I to do?"

She looked to him for answers. "I have questions too. Butter— er... Gentle Wisdom, I think this is your time to let things be. Allow the Spirits to guide you. Perhaps you know more than you think." He laughed. "You stood up to that hairy-faced one, Tall Smiling Warrior, when he walked into our camp. He stepped back so surprised that a... a soon-to-be-grown woman had such great courage!"

She walked taller and looked ahead, chin up. She repeated his words. "A soon-to-be-grown-woman. And I am!"

***

White Paws led them to a well-used animal trail. A mist formed, becoming denser the farther they went. In the distance, drumming and singing echoed off the large boulders the trail followed. White Paws stopped and howled. Several howls answered him, and he continued forward.

Gentle Wisdom held tight to Shining Light's arm.

They entered an opening where singers danced in a circle to the beat of the drum—the beat of all living, the Mother's heartbeat. The people wore animal skins, and behind the people, animals followed in their own circle. The ancient voices rose as one, and the sound of many creatures joined.

Shining Light twirled around to the sound of pawing at the ground, a sound Sandstone used to gain attention.

Sandstone stepped up to him, her eyes level with his. *'So, my young Human, I now give you my Energy to join with your own. My Energy is Power, loyalty to the one who treats me as an equal. My life and yours will be interconnected, as will the young one I now carry. You have proven your worth by your actions. You are a true Shining Light, a leader of more than Humans. Someday, you will save many beings from being no more.'* She turned and walked into the trees.

A tiny mouse scurried in front of Shining Light, looked up and scurried on past.

White Paws walked forward, and Moon Face joined him with the rest of their pack. The wolves looked back at the two humans.

Gentle Wisdom said, "Shining Light, did I just hear Sandstone? Na, my mind is crazy." She shook her head as if to clear it, and scooped his hand into hers.

Energy sparked through the air — bright, warm colors.

Shining Light stepped forward with his cousin, who still held his arm. Blue sparks joined with the warm colors and floated everywhere — through the dancers, through the wolves, and into the young couple.

The words to the song no longer sounded ancient. The words were clear.

> *'We honor all living.*
> *We honor all.*
> *We are the Circle, the Circle of Life.*
> *Through the Great Circle, all are brought together.*
> *All are connected. All are connected in the Circle of Life.*
> *We are One.'*

Shining Light closed his eyes and swayed to the music. Gentle Wisdom sang the song she had never heard as if she had always known it — as though she had known since she was born that everything connected through the Circle of Life.

***

Five sunrises later, they returned changed. Blue sparks danced around them and reached out to the others. The people, wolves, dogs and mus-tangs all sparkled blue. Sandstone glanced up and raised her lips, exposing teeth, and then continued to graze.

"Shining Light, why does everyone look so different? Where are the Elders?"

"They are there, cousin. Look with your heart and you will see them."

Blue Night Sky stood behind them with Animal Speaks Woman. "Young ones, it is time to lead the people."

Shining Light turned and stopped, stunned by what he saw. Blue Night Sky still looked as she had the day they started this journey.

"Did I not tell you once, it is impolite to stare?" She grinned and continued. "I am not going with you. My time has come to... to a different beginning. I miss my man, and I am going to go be with him. If I go with you and all the people, I will not see him again.

"You lead the Peoples of many to a safe place, where no harm shall befall them, no matter how much time passes. I will be there, little one — in your dreams, in your visions. You need only seek me out and I will come. Surely, you know there is no such thing as death by now. Did not the ancients you sang and danced with prove this to you?"

"Yes, Great Elder, they did."

He stared long into her eyes before she turned and walked a different path away from them.

"To her own future, she walks. To our own, we also go."

All the gathered Peoples were ready to follow.

Shining Light took the hand of Animal Speaks Woman on his right, then of Gentle Wisdom on his left, and walked on to their future.

---THE BEGINNING---

About the Author

Ruby has been a wanderer, and has seen most of the USA. She's the mother of an amazing son, and the wife of a patient husband who indulges her need for animals. She was also the first woman journeyman newspaper pressman in Colorado.

She spent years rescuing animals and learning from them. They taught her that life does not have to be so hard, if you go with the flow and not against it. Forgive today, because tomorrow may not come.

Her life revolves around writing and her family, which includes, of course, her animals. Two car accidents in the mid-nineties changed her life. She resented it at first, until she understood she had simply been put on another path. It was not an easy one, but she accepted it, and while it continues to be a challenge, she now learns with each step she takes.

She writes because she is compelled to pass on knowledge.

Find out more about Ruby at www.RubyStandingDeer.com, or online at Twitter (@R_StandingDeer) and Facebook (R Standing Deer).

Also by Ruby Standing Deer

Special Preview of Spirals
(the sequel to Circles)

Chapter 1

Falling Rainbow's ceremony, a joyous celebration, turned sour when Night Hunter came to her parent's lodge with three mustangs as an offering for her. Elk Dreaming, her father, refused. Night Hunter could do nothing but walk away and promise to return with his last mustang, the prized male. He gave her father an angry glare as he left.

Falling Rainbow knew her father did not want his only daughter to go to a man whose face was etched in anger; he'd told her so days before when the man entered their camp. He'd told Night Hunter that his daughter was worth more than mustangs.

She hoped her father would come up with an impossible request for another gift.

She backed away into the darkness of their lodge and curled into her mother's arms. Her mother held her, cooing and rocking her as she had done since Falling Rainbow was a child.

Tears fell from both women, and the new woman pulled away. "Mother, I will never be Night Hunter's woman. I will leave the band first. Night Hunter is four winters older and I hold no desire in my heart for him. I do not understand why he wants me as his mate. I heard him speaking to his brother about Power. I do not understand."

"I know, Daughter, more that you think I do. But you must also know a man changes with the right woman, and four winters is not so much. Your father is eight winters older than I am. You must not judge a man by his age."

Her mother reached behind her for a pack. "Here. You will find food, a knife, and an extra humpback robe to keep you warm. I knew you would want to go into the canyons, after you ducked into one of the lodges of your friends when he showed up with his brother. Night Hunter will leave soon. I know your father will tell him you have other men who ask for you, and that he must allow each one to speak to him. It is not a lie, Daughter, not really. I have watched young men follow you with their eyes. Come back after maybe two sunrises. I smell snow even this late in the season, so you must walk with care. You can take one of your father's mustangs."

Her mother reached out and ran her hands over Falling Rainbow's face as if memorizing it. "Be safe. If the snow starts to fall, you turn around and come home, you understand?"

She nodded and hugged her mother. Taking a mustang would mean hoof prints to follow. She intended to walk where she would leave few footprints, but did not want her mother to worry, so she said nothing.

She slipped out under the lodge's edging, and disappeared into the coming darkness.

***

Falling Rainbow did not know which way to go. After two days of walking, the snow, a light fluff at sunrise, had turned into a fierce, howling blizzard. Sleeping on the ground with her robes would leave her shivering too much.

I should have listened to Mother about the mustang! The snow whisked around in deep circles, and her steps became more labored. Soon darkness would take the land.

Of all nights, this had to be the one when Sister Moon chooses to hide. I am sure he waits for me still, and I have no more food! Shelter now became more important than finding the paintings in the canyons.

Many times, she had searched for the paintings. Her parents knew, but no longer worried. The hairy faces had long ago stopped coming this way to hunt for the yellow stone. This is why her people had settled here this last time. The band moved to the new campsite four moons ago, just after the leaves fell, to escape the raids on their old camp.

Why do they steal our women when they have their own? And why my closest friend? Had I not gone home when I did, I would have been captured along with her.

She shook the memory from her mind and tightened her light ceremony robe, and the humpback one with the hair on the inside, around herself. She kept her arms inside, her fingers clinging to the outside edges. Neither robe did much to cover her ice-crusted hair.

"Why do these things happen?" She stared up searching for blue sky, but found only thick, grey clouds.

Are the Spirits angry with me? Do they wish me to be Night Hunter's woman? No, they sent me the dream vision! A vision of the paintings, so they must have plans for me that I do not yet understand.

"I am freezing! Why do you torment me?" she yelled, raising her fist to the darkening clouds, but quickly put her hands over her mouth and let her robes fall.

Angry Spirits might make the storm worse. She just needed shelter, but had no idea where to go. Father Sun had already lowered, and she could not see that well.

She scooped up both her ceremony robe and the one her mother had made her, and flung them back over herself. Beautiful tinkling shells and quillwork across the bottom of the ceremonial elk hide did little to keep the new woman of fourteen winters warm. Every turn she took looked the same. With so much blowing snow, she could barely keep her eyes open. Her teeth hurt from chattering, and her fingers ached, burning from the cold. She blew into cupped hands, her breath barely warm, and touched her round face, but her numbed cold skin felt little. She shoved her hands back inside and pulled what robe she could over her head.

I am lost! Lost! How can this be? Many times, I have followed these canyons on one-day rides or two-day walks. Stupid! Why did you walk? Where was your mind?

And where was your mind when you let Night Hunter take you that night, moons ago? You were lucky a baby was not made. Did he use some kind of trick to draw me to him? Why did he take me knowing I was not yet a woman? Why did I allow him to dishonor me? Teardrops froze in little balls on her cold face. *No other man will want me now.*

Three moons ago, she heard his flute music as it floated past her lodge, soft on the cold night air. Her mother had told her every woman knew the sound of her future man's voice in the music. Not knowing who called, she followed the sound. Quiet footsteps led her to him. She could not see who it was, but went to him even though she should not have until her ceremony had passed. Hypnotized by the beautiful sound, she faced Night Hunter unafraid. The flute stopped, then their eyes met and he lowered her to the ground. It was wrong, very wrong. Even the cold and snow-covered ground did not stop her from lying with him, encased in the warm humpback robe.

Another blast of cold brought her back, reminding her she had yet to find safety, and that she did not have the warmth of another person. She started to drift in her mind, thoughts jumbled. Her body shivered uncontrollably, and her feet ached from the freezing water that had found its way through the sinew used to make her footwear. She rounded another curve in the canyon. Orange-red colors plastered in icy-white greeted her. Her eyes combed for caves, indents in the stone, even a curve that would get her out of the wind.

Nothing! There is no shelter anywhere!

She arched her neck toward the now nearly invisible clouds and cried out. "Creator, help me please. I am young and afraid. I am not brave. I fear loosing my life in such a way. Who would sing my Soul to the campfires in the sky? I would be lost in-between this land and the Spirit's land. Please, Great Mystery, help me to help myself. I know I am weak. I am sorry. I wish I was braver."

She pushed away her snow-covered hair that escaped from the robe, but it whipped around, slapping her face. *Stupid! I smelled snow! Why did I not take my winter footwear?* Her ceremonial footwear soaked up even more of the icy water. She'd hurried, and the air was warm when she'd left. Still, even after her parents had taught her about sudden cold, she had not listened. She had acted as a child, and now must pay for her haste. *Would a woman act this way?*

Cold and exposure started to claim her. Numb feet no longer ached. She could no longer feel the tips of her fingers. *Sleepy.... If I could just rest.*

Thunder rolled and lightning sparked in pink above her. Thunder snow. The old ones said it meant Nature herself was confused, and the cold season was always much worse. At every turn, she found only white ice that clung to jutting edges of stone — no shelter anywhere. She pushed on, head bent against the blasts of cold pelting her face. Ice concealed the uneven ground, and the tip of a hidden stone tripped her. Frozen ground rose up to meet her. She lost her grip on the robes, and gasped when the icy water splashed up her dress. With numb hands, she pushed herself into a sitting position, and laughed.

I finally feel warm. Am I seeing the last place of my life? I should have stayed and accepted Night Hunter's offer. He was not so bad to look at when he did not wrinkle his face in anger. He did smile at me the first time we saw each other. I did not see anger then.

Instead, I lay here freezing. So sleepy.... If I could rest but for a short span.

"No!"

She reached out for the pack her mother had given her, hoping she had missed extra clothing. She clung to the rocky face of the canyon wall, pulled herself up and reached her arm behind herself to pull the pack off her back. The canyon's snow crusted wall gave in and some hand-like thing pulled her through.

Her own hands touched fur, and she screamed.

What's Next?

Watch for the release of *Stones*, the third installment in this historical exploration of the Native American Indian culture by Ruby Standing Deer, due in late 2013.

Find some more of Ruby's work in *Evolution: Vol. 1 (A Short Story Collection)*. This anthology, edited by Lane Diamond and D.T. Conklin of Evolved Publishing, boasts 10 Stories by 10 Authors, including Ruby's gripping tale, *Courage through Fear*. The anthology is available as an eBook or softcover.

Recommended Reading from Evolved Publishing:

CHILDREN'S PICTURE BOOKS
THE BIRD BRAIN BOOKS by Emlyn Chand:
Honey the Hero
Davey the Detective
Poppy the Proud
Tommy Goes Trick-or-Treating
Courtney Saves Christmas
Vicky Finds a Valentine
I'd Rather Be Riding My Bike by Eric Pinder
Valentina and the Haunted Mansion by Majanka Verstraete

HISTORICAL FICTION
Circles by Ruby Standing Deer
Spirals by Ruby Standing Deer
Stones by Ruby Standing Deer

LITERARY FICTION
Torn Together by Emlyn Chand
Hannah's Voice by Robb Grindstaff
Jellicle Girl by Stevie Mikayne
Weight of Earth by Stevie Mikayne

LOWER GRADE
THE THREE LOST KIDS – SPECIAL EDITION ILLUSTRATED
by Kimberly Kinrade:
Lexie World
Bella World
Maddie World
THE THREE LOST KIDS – CHAPTER BOOKS by Kimberly Kinrade:
The Death of the Sugar Fairy
The Christmas Curse
Cupid's Capture

MEMOIR
And Then It Rained: Lessons for Life by Megan Morrison

MYSTERY
Hot Sinatra by Axel Howerton

ROMANCE / EROTICA
Skinny-Dipping at Dawn by Darby Davenport
Walk Away with Me by Darby Davenport
Her Twisted Pleasures by Amelia James
His Twisted Lesson by Amelia James
Secret Storm by Amelia James
Tell Me You Want Me by Amelia James
The Devil Made Me Do It by Amelia James
Their Twisted Love by Amelia James

SCI-FI / FANTASY
Eulogy by D.T. Conklin

SHORT STORY ANTHOLOGIES
FROM THE EDITORS AT EVOLVED PUBLISHING:
  Evolution: Vol. 1 (A Short Story Collection)
  Evolution: Vol. 2 (A Short Story Collection)
  Pathways (A Young Adult Anthology)
All Tolkien No Action: Swords, Sorcery & Sci-Fi by Eric Pinder

SUSPENSE / THRILLER
Forgive Me, Alex by Lane Diamond
The Devil's Bane by Lane Diamond

YOUNG ADULT
Dead Embers by T.G. Ayer
Dead Radiance by T.G. Ayer
Farsighted by Emlyn Chand
Open Heart by Emlyn Chand
Pitch by Emlyn Chand
The Silver Sphere by Michael Dadich
Ring Binder by Ranee Dillon
Forbidden Mind by Kimberly Kinrade
Forbidden Fire by Kimberly Kinrade
Forbidden Life by Kimberly Kinrade
Forbidden Trilogy (Special Omnibus Edition) by Kimberly Kinrade
Desert Flower by Angela Scott
Desert Rice by Angela Scott
Survivor Roundup by Angela Scott
Wanted: Dead or Undead by Angela Scott

CPSIA information can be obtained
at www.ICGtesting.com
Printed in the USA
BVHW040531130320
574961BV00003B/89